God, He Hurt

The panic, the fear, all weighing him down. He quickened his step, but the exertion was ill-considered; he stumbled, neglecting to observe a fallen branch in his way. The dizziness was more acute; everything he tried to focus on danced and gyrated or floated out of his visual field.

And then he registered in the back of his throat a sudden nauseating sweetness that replaced the metallic taste that had been there before. Blood.

Then it was as if someone had punched him hard in the solar plexus. His whole body was convulsing, he was leaking, he was throwing up. Blood rushed into his hands. He saw nothing but a blur of trees, foliage, and lake. An instant later he pitched forward and the world went black.

★　★　★　★　★

THE DYING

THE DYING

LESLIE HORVITZ

POPULAR LIBRARY

An Imprint of Warner Books, Inc.

A Warner Communications Company

POPULAR LIBRARY EDITION

Popular Library® and the fanciful P design are registered
trademarks of Warner Books, Inc.

Cover illustration by Tom Hallman

Popular Library books are published by
Warner Books, Inc.
666 Fifth Avenue
New York, N.Y. 10103

 A Warner Communications Company

Printed in the United States of America

First Printing: September, 1987

10 9 8 7 6 5 4 3 2 1

The author gratefully wishes to acknowledge
the help of Dr. William Haseltine of
the Sidney Farber Cancer Institute.

"Some say that it descended upon the human race through the influence of heavenly bodies, others that it was a punishment signifying God's righteous anger at our iniquitous way of life."

—Giovanni Boccacio

"Historians of medicine have suggested . . . that every pathogenic agent has its own history, which runs parallel to that of its victims and that the evolution of disease largely depends on change, and sometimes mutations, in the agents themselves."

—Ferdinand Braudel, *The Structures of Everyday Life*

"the plague makes us cruel, as doggs, one and another."

—Samuel Pepys

"E dure questo pistolenza fino a—"
(And during this pestilence there came to an end—)

—Giovanni Villani
(Cut off in mid-sentence by death—of the plague.)

BOOK ONE
Specimens

"...they bore in their bones so virulent a disease that anyone who spoke to them was seized with a mortal illness."
—Michael of Piazza

"In the 19th Century man lost his fear of God and acquired a fear of microbes."
—Anonymous

"There are pestilences and there are victims, and it's up to us, so far as possible, not to join forces with the pestilences."
—Albert Camus, *The Plague*

THE RAGING COLD....

Darkness was flooding the sky, turning it black as ink except in the west where a thin amber ribbon of light clung to the horizon. Night was bringing with it a rising wind, a wind out of Russia, blowing mercilessly across the Bering Strait. The cold was, if anything, more biting than usual, and endless.

The trapper was familiar with the sounds the wind could make, how the snow-clad slopes might suddenly groan with the intimation of an avalanche or mimic voices and cries, producing a doleful chorus in its passage through the barren and craggy landscape. There were wolves out there, and other creatures he'd only heard about but never laid eyes on; sometimes he was able to distinguish their voices from the voices the wind conjured out of nothing, but often he couldn't tell the difference.

Mostly what he heard was the sound of his own foot-steps against the icy crust snow and the restless breathing of his dogs as they headed into the wind. Turning his eyes back on the way he'd come he saw that his trail was being obliterated by a dusting of snow blown by the infernal Russian wind.

He was about seventy miles north of Fairbanks now. But he didn't pay much attention to towns and landmarks the way other people did. He relied instead on the location of his traps to define the terrain for himself. It wasn't other human beings he identified with but his prey. He'd gotten to know them intimately, as one should always know an enemy: how they migrated and fed and mated. He did not feel alive anywhere. But here in this white world, alone with his prey, he felt less dead.

The mountains he maintained in sight radiated a faint bluish light which was the only thing left of the sun in this part of the world. The mountains had names in atlases, but those names didn't mean a damn thing to him. Long ago he decided to give the mountains the names that he believed suited them best.

Straight ahead, maybe twenty-five miles distant, was the mountain he called Ghost. To the east, much closer, was the mountain he called Miriam after the woman he'd loved, and then abandoned over forty years ago so that he could come here and seek his fortune. The mountain behind him, due east, he'd named Unborn.

The wind had a bad feel to it this evening; a storm was coming with it. He would have to find shelter. But that did not present a problem. There were all sorts of caves and hollows to take refuge in for those who knew where to look for them. There was a cave he'd used in the past at the foot of Miriam. Another five miles of trudging through this wil-derness would bring him to it. As he set out in the direction of Mount Miriam the wind was at his back, but as he drew closer, it chose to play with him, coming around from the other side and blasting him in the face.

Throughout the night he was awakened again and again by all the cold that his sleeping bag couldn't keep out. The sound of the attacking wind filled his ears. The falling snow, just beyond the entrance to the cave, came with a light all its own, disclosing in the gloom of his shelter the sleeping forms of his dogs.

By morning the wind had died, and the trapper awoke finally to sun. Ice crystals glistened in the mantle of virgin snow with blinding intensity. To protect his eyes the trapper carried with him polarized lenses; they had the capacity to endow the landscape with a shimmering beige light that could have come out of a dream.

The snow hadn't fallen evenly. In places it lay in awesome drifts, sculpted by the wind into shapes that reminded the trapper of Miriam's plump round body, which of all the bodies he'd held close was the only one he really remembered.

And then there were those places where the wind had swept away the snow, almost as if it were in the business of carving paths out of the wilderness to guide solitary seekers like himself. All that was left behind, where the snow used to be, was ice, sheer ice.

It was the dogs that noticed it first, their eyes picking it out from all the whiteness that surrounded it. They strained against the trapper, barking furiously, refusing to move.

Whipping off his glasses, he observed something pink and ill-defined embedded in the ice. On closer inspection he saw with horror that it was a hand, mostly pink but also black where the frostbite had done its work.

The body the hand was attached to revealed itself once the trapper cleared away enough snow to see. Embalmed by the ice, a man of about forty years of age was gaping up at him as though through a thick window, his eyes open and fixed in an expression of surprise and agitation. His face was weathered and scarred, like a map with a great many gulleys running across it; his beard was coarse and peppered with gray. One ear was half gone. At first the trapper suspected that frostbite had gotten to it as well, but then he saw that there was blood congealed around it. To the trapper's experienced eye it looked like the man had been shot.

Whoever he was he hadn't been dressed for the arctic rigors of this climate—that much was certain. All he had on was a plaid shirt and woolen trousers, and no shoes. His feet, predictably, were in worse shape than his hands.

This man had been on the run, the trapper decided. He could think of no other explanation for why he'd ended up in this desolate place. Maybe he'd survived a gun fight long enough to escape into these parts, only to succumb to the cold. There was no telling how long he'd been buried here.

But the trapper reasoned that the police might still be looking for him. The town nearest Mount Miriam was Samothrace, though that was still a good forty miles away. Even so the trapper was sure that Samothrace's mayor, Jim Jillian, would be interested in having a look at this poor bastard. The trapper liked Jillian as much as he liked any human being; the man had done him favors, given him credit when he'd needed it and generally overlooked violations of any trapping laws he'd committed. So he figured that the least he could do was bring the dead man back.

There were times during the next several hours when the trapper regretted his decision. For the frozen corpse didn't seem to want to be released from his icy tomb. What's more, the corpse turned out to be encased in a thicker layer of ice than the trapper had originally thought. The trapper grew exhausted hammering away at the ice with his ax hour after hour until enough of it gave way for him to free the body.

The man, he guessed, must have weighed close to two hundred pounds alive. But now, frozen solid, he weighed three or four times that. It was all the trapper could do to pull him out of the hole and drag him over to a spot where the sun could begin to thaw him out.

At the same time the trapper was doing what he could to restrain his dogs; they seemed to think that he'd just found a new source of sustenance for them. There would have been nothing left of the corpse if the trapper had let them have their way.

At last the body was thawed enough so that the trapper felt he could manage it. The afternoon was wearing on and if he hoped to reach Samothrace before night he had to set out soon. The body was wet from the thawing and was so slippery that he could barely keep a hold of it. Just as he was lifting the body onto the sled, a noise came from somewhere down inside the stomach. And then the corpse seemed to explode, shooting a thick, brackish juice from its mouth and into the trapper's face, simultaneously releasing a stench that caused the dogs to recoil.

It was all that the dead man had to give by way of a last will and testament.

ONE

Without warning it turned black. Lightman had never seen anything like it. It was a blackness altogether different from the blackness of storm clouds he'd flown through previously, although he reasoned that a storm cloud was what it was; no other explanation suggested itself. But this blackness was denser and more enveloping. Had he just now awakened he would have thought it the middle of the night, but a night without a moon, without stars.

And then they were out of it, back into the morning sun. There was no one to turn to in the cabin to ask what they'd just been going through since he was the only passenger.

They began to descend, banking toward a snow-draped peak, then dropping further among the mountains, headed for what might have been the most desolate looking airstrip in existence. The plane's descent was wobbly, the small six-seater being buffeted about by devious wind currents as it got closer to the ground.

Lightman was used to flying. He'd flown in craft as frail as this one before, but that didn't mean he had to like it. His stomach lurched, he held on, breathed deep, then didn't breathe at all—not until the wheels, with a great clanking and screech of rubber, touched down.

It was a bumpy ride down the length of the runway to an undistinguished, gray squat building whose aluminum siding shimmered in the sun. The fierce wind whipped the American and Alaskan flags savagely about at the tops of their respective poles.

As soon as Lightman had his feet planted on solid ground he saw the man he presumed was McKay. He was burly and bearded, two attributes that must come in handy in a climate this inhospitable. He was standing by a Land Rover, with its motor running, motioning for Lightman to join him. One glove removed, he extended his hand. "Welcome to Alaska, Doctor Lightman," he said.

A single, winter-scarred road led from the airport in the direction of Samothrace and, eventually, Fairbanks.

"This your first time in Alaska?" McKay asked once they were on their way.

"That's right. Somehow I always pictured my first trip here would begin with Juneau or Anchorage, though."

"We don't get many tourists out this way, that's for sure. A few hunters in season, a few climbers, that's it. I myself seldom get into these parts."

"Just when you're on assignment?"

McKay nodded. He was working out of the State Department of Health in Juneau. "I fly my own plane— makes life simpler. You?"

"What? Fly my own plane? Sorry to say I don't."

"You should learn. The important thing is to stay calm and collected—and make sure you're high enough off the ground. Your engine cuts out, you've got five thousand or more feet to work with, you have time to deal with it. The worst thing is overconfidence. You run out of space, you run out of time, you're fucked."

"My eyes."

"What about your eyes?"

"Myopia. Glasses don't compensate enough."

"Too bad." He paused, considering Lightman's disability for a moment. "Still, I imagine you get around a lot."

"All over the world."

"For the National Institute?"

The National Institutes of Health was sponsoring this assignment, but he had in his time done work for the Centers for Disease Control and the World Health Organization as well as various universities with money to burn on research.

"For anybody who'll buy me a ticket," was how he answered McKay.

Lightman took out of his coat pocket the letter he'd received from the National Institutes in Bethesda outlining what was known about the case he'd traveled all this way to investigate. He wanted to check the facts he'd been given with the facts as McKay understood them to see how—and if—they lined up.

"Tell me about this cadaver, and this man," he glanced down at the letter for the name, "Emil Brown. . . ."

"Browning, it's Emil Browning."

Lightman made the correction. "Emil Browning then. He found a cadaver while he was out trapping, is that right?"

McKay nodded. "About thirty miles south of here as the crow flies. There was a storm the night before he made his discovery. He took shelter in a cave. Next morning he walks out and sees this cadaver lying under a sheet of ice. He brought it to the police in Samothrace. That was only natural. He thought he'd found the body of a fugitive who'd gotten lost in the wilderness and died of exposure."

"The body was lying out there for several years according to the information I have."

"Eighty to be precise."

"Eighty?" It didn't say that anywhere in his letter.

"Guy's name was Joe Taylor. He'd escaped from jail and was on the run."

"What was he in jail for?"

"Murder. Shot three fellows in a dispute over a land stake. Shot two dead and left the third wishing he was."

"How was the identification made?" Lightman asked.

"First off, his clothes weren't what you'd order from L.L. Bean. They belonged to another age. Then, I don't know how to explain this, there was something about his face that didn't look like it was contemporary. It looked like an old photograph, you understand?"

"You saw the body?"

"Of course. I wasn't present at the examination, but I got a good look at it. He was a big man, you wouldn't have wanted to mess with him."

"Was the pathologist from around here?"

McKay laughed. "A pathologist in Samothrace? You crazy? No, he came in from Fairbanks. More business for him in Fairbanks."

"And he was the one who determined that the cause of death wasn't exposure?"

"That's right. When we get into town I'll show you his report."

"He back in Fairbanks?"

McKay shook his head. "No, he's dead." He gave Lightman a doubtful look. "Doesn't it say so in that letter?"

"No, it just states that three people died and that a viral agent is suspected. Who were the other two?"

"One was the trapper, Emil Browning. The other was a fellow by the name of Vinny Russell—the cop who first examined the body. He was all that Samothrace had by way of a police force. A real pity."

Lightman raised his eyes toward the road. They had it all to themselves; there were no other cars or trucks to be seen. It was as if there was nothing out there where they were headed.

"And when did these deaths occur exactly?"

"First week in December. Browning first, then the other two. Browning died here in Samothrace. Russell was taken to a hospital in Fairbanks and died there."

"And the pathologist?"

"Burt Lyon? Oh, he died in Fairbanks too."

Lightman asked if postmortems had been conducted on the three deceased.

"Not that I know of. The families refused permission. Remember now, we got around to this after it had already happened, there was no chance for the state to intervene. We wouldn't have had any way of knowing that there was a suspected outbreak until a Fairbanks physician, Lloyd Baker, let us know. He'd treated Lyon for pneumonia. But Lyon didn't respond. He went fast. At the end his blood turned black."

Lightman shot him an astonished look.

"Air hunger, oxygen starvation. I've never seen anything like it myself, I thought maybe you would have."

Lightman did not reply.

Samothrace appeared after the road took a sharp turn, skirting the side of a mountain. The town was nothing much to look at, not from a distance and not from close up, either. Anywhere else, in the Lower Forty-eight, you'd say that the town belonged to the mid-1950's. Eisenhower era was written all over it. The buildings, houses and commercial establishments alike were practically all prefabricated. There was no hint of an architect's hand at work in these ugly structures, only an impatient contractor's. Although some of the owners had made an effort to paint their homes a more acceptable shade of pastel, the dominant color scheme was still a revolting lime and pink, quintessential fifties' colors. About the only thing of any charm that

Lightman could see were the wooden sidewalks which creaked loudly anytime somebody set foot on them.

They pulled up in front of a building with a sign proclaiming it Luisa's General Store & Cafe.

"Thought you could do with lunch before we went to work," said McKay.

Luisa's was crammed full of goods, some of which appeared to have been collecting dust for years. In back of the store there was a scattering of tables, each with its own candle melted into old Coca-Cola bottles.

Luisa in person was just what Lightman imagined, breezy in manner and abundant in body, with untamable blond hair and forty years at least of bad weather and unruly times etched on her reddened face.

"Is this the guy you were telling me about, McKay?" she wanted to know.

"You're looking at one of the top virologists in the world, Luisa."

She frowned. "Virile? That sounds okay in my book. You'll get lots of competition around here, though. Every guy who passes through thinks he's virile."

"No, no, Luisa, you got it wrong," McKay said. "He's a specialist in viral diseases."

"Oh," she said, fixing her gaze on Lightman, "so you're going to tell us what was it that got poor Vinny?"

"I'm going to try."

"Anybody can do it, he can," McKay said.

Luisa still hadn't taken her eyes off Lightman. "Just how old are you?"

"Luisa!"

Obviously in the short time McKay had been in Samothrace he'd struck up something of a friendship with the woman.

"That's all right, Howard. I'm forty-two. Forty-three in June."

Luisa seemed to be thinking this over. Then she said, "You could do with some fattening up." She pinched his arm. "Why, you're all skin and bones, good God in heaven! You married?"

"Not anymore."

"Well, I can't see why. This morning I saw old Jim Jillian with one hell of a good-looking broad. Don't know where she came from. She's not a local. Our homegrown stock couldn't hold a candle to the likes of her. A bit stuck-up though."

"Jim Jillian's the mayor here," Howard put in.

"What I'm saying is that if Jim can do that well for himself there's no reason on God's earth you can't find a girl to haul up to the altar. We'll just have to see what we can do about putting things right." Cupping her hands to her mouth she shouted toward the front of the store to somebody out of view. "Ernie, fix up a number three special for our guest! And a tuna melt for McKay." To Lightman she said, "This'll fatten you up, you'll see."

Lightman decided it would be better not to ask what the number three special was. He didn't even ask after it was set down in front of him.

Over coffee they reviewed what they had.

Following the discovery of Joe Taylor's body three people had died after experiencing symptoms that suggested an influenza type syndrome. Each case, as reported by the attending physician, was marked by severe headache, a nonproductive cough, marked prostration, substernal pain, persistent fever and pneumonia caused by a secondary bacterial infection.

While Browning was getting on in years (at various points he claimed to be sixty-five, sixty-seven and seventy-two), and consequently might be more susceptible to the flu, both the pathologist Lyon and the police officer Russell were in their thirties and in apparent good health. Why they should have died and so quickly after being admitted for treatment was the most alarming aspect of the case. Of the three, only Russell's blood had turned black from oxygen starvation.

Having made the initial epidemiological surveys, McKay had come to the conclusion that there was only one factor that the three had in common: they had all come into contact with the body of Joe Taylor.

"As I said, there's no chance of getting an autopsy on either Russell or Lyon."

"What about Browning? Did his family deny permission too?"

"He had no family. The fellow was all alone in the world. However..."

"However what?"

"He's beyond our reach as well. He was cremated by order of the mayor, who was afraid of infection. We were lucky he didn't do the same with Taylor, but my guess is he was confused about how to dispose of the corpse of a man who's been wanted by the police since 1918. It's funny, you should see the wanted poster we dug out. Looks just like him."

Although the loss of the three victims was discouraging, Lightman was certain that the hospital in Fairbanks would have preserved specimens of blood and tissue from them that harbored the virus—if it was a virus.

But McKay had already checked. "You're not going to like this."

"Don't tell me the specimens are gone."

"Let's just say they're not immediately available. Our department's still trying to find out what happened to them. But I have to tell you it doesn't look promising."

Lightman was getting annoyed. "Didn't they send specimens off to Atlanta too?"

Atlanta was the headquarters of the Centers for Disease Control.

"No, just to London," McKay said. "At the present time the only hard evidence available to us is Joe Taylor."

"And where is Mr. Taylor at the moment?"

"Not far from here. Of course, nothing in Samothrace is far from anything else in Samothrace."

"Well, shall we then?"

McKay stayed seated. "We can't do a damn thing until tomorrow morning, I'm afraid. Taylor's being kept in the back of the dispensary. Only fellow who can open it up for us is Jim Jillian."

"The mayor?"

"That's right. Nothing happens in this town without his okay."

"And he's the one who authorized Browning's cremation?"

"That's right. We were called in by the people in Fairbanks, not the people here. Luisa's all right. The rest of them though." He made a face.

"There's nothing we can do about getting in?"

"Absolutely nothing. I talked to Jillian this morning before you arrived and explained the situation. 'Rules are rules' is what he said. Anyway, he's gone for the rest of the day. You'll just have to be patient until tomorrow at eight when he opens up."

It turned out that the only lodging to be had was in a house painted violet in front and blue on the other three sides that was owned by a cousin of Luisa's who spent most of the year in the Lower Forty-eight. Luisa collected the money. McKay had a room downstairs and Lightman was given one above him that looked over the street, allowing him a view of the dispensary a block away.

There was nothing much else to do but read and watch television. The news was on when Lightman wandered into the parlor. McKay had already settled into an armchair and was loudly sucking on his pipe in an attempt to fire the tobacco. On the screen tanks were advancing through a desert landscape. Clouds of black smoke hung on the distant horizon.

"Middle East," said McKay.

Lightman sat down next to him with a shot of unblended scotch, one that was sufficiently strong to fortify himself against the tidings of violence, disturbance and sudden death that he was sure would soon follow.

"They at war yet?" Lightman asked.

"This? No, just border fighting, skirmishes."

Nonetheless, it looked like war to him.

Next came a volcano eruption. Long dormant, Mauna Kea was now spurting out smoke and lava over the island of Hawaii. Thick black clouds of dust and particles from the volcano were being carried westward by the wind currents. Some of them were reaching the coastline of the Northwest U.S. and parts of Alaska.

Seeing this, Lightman recalled the black cloud his plane had flown through earlier in the day. He was sure that it must have been from the volcano.

McKay didn't seem surprised. "It happened years ago. I don't remember whether it was Mauna Kea or not. Might have been another volcano on the Hawaiian islands. But you can see what it did to some of the beaches. You walk along them and you'll find only black sand. It was strange how it worked, leaving certain beaches just the way they were, blackening the others. I hear that some of those beaches that escaped last time are being hit now. Not that it matters except for the color. Still, it's strange, all that debris from Mauna Kea coming this way."

It was, Lightman thought, like a sign.

TWO

During the night Lightman kept waking up, surprised as hell to find that he'd been dreaming about Stephanie—his ex-wife Stephanie. The last time they'd had any communication was two years ago. She was in San Diego at the time, pursuing research on amyloid proteins, trying to discover what they were doing in the brains of victims of Alzheimer's Disease. She'd been involved in the same research when Lightman was married to her. She used to suspect that any success he had was at her expense, although she allowed how foolish the notion was. Life didn't have to be a zero-sum game but she couldn't get it into her head that it might be otherwise.

As time had passed, Stephanie became just as consumed by her proteins as Lightman was by his, specifically, hemagglutinin and neuraminidase, both of which were common to all flu viruses. It got so that they rarely spent time together and more rarely still had anything to say to each other. Eventually they had turned into strangers.

But why was he dreaming about Stephanie now? And the dream was a disturbingly erotic one, tinged with longing that in waking life he did not feel at all. He certainly didn't want her back; they had nothing to say to each other. But perhaps some subconscious part of him had a different opinion.

In his dream she appeared as she had when he'd first met her, pretty and overly serious, her skin too pale from all those years studying in flourescent-lit carrels, her hair in braids, not so much indifferent to fashion as wholly unaware of it. Bare to the waist, she was standing over him, her image reflected in the bedroom mirror, a family heirloom she'd taken with her when she left. There was a sensual pink light in the room and it fell over her skin, lending it a faintly rosy hue. She was saying something to him, but he either couldn't remember her words or else never comprehended them in the first place. He began to reach out to her, but she stepped back, receding according to the custom of all mirages.

And then he'd awakened.

He put the lamp on over his bed, thinking it foolish to try to go back to sleep. He resented sleep's intrusion on his life. There was simply too much to read, to write, to think about, and in the daylight hours it was practically impossible to find a quiet moment to do any of that. It was at such times, on the road, in the middle of the night, that he could set his mind to work uninterrupted.

Although his principal research—what he was given National Institutes of Health grants for and what he was hauled in front of cameras on news programs for—focused on unlocking the secrets of three types of hemagglutinins and two types of neuraminidases, his insomniac hours were spent on something else altogether.

Ever since he could remember, even before he decided to become a researcher, he was drawn to history—specifically the history of diseases. He didn't view disease, in all its myriad manifestations, as an aberration, a sideshow in the conduct of human affairs, but rather as an active agent, a profound influence on the course of civilization. The English language, for instance, might never have attained such importance for the millions of people it had were it not for the Black Plague. Through much of the Middle Ages, until the plague struck, it was Latin that enjoyed a major role in education, a role fostered by the church. But by making off with so many monks the plague in effect broke the hold over language that the church had enjoyed until then, allowing the English to speak their own vernacular tongue.

His interest these days focused on the Americans in the age of Columbus. What intrigued him in particular was a thesis expressed by anthropologist Dr. Arles Hrdlicka. He believed that before Columbus, the Americas were perhaps uniquely free of disease, a conclusion adduced from the study of skeletal remains. "Whole important scourges were wholly unknown," he wrote. "There was no rachitis; there was no tuberculosis. There was no pathologic microcephaly, no hydrocephaly. There was no plague, cholera, typhus, smallpox or measles. Cancer was rare, and even fractures were infrequent. . . . Notwithstanding some claims to the contrary, there is yet not a single instance of thoroughly authenticated pre–Columbian syphilis. . . ."

It sounded to him like the Americas in those years were the closest man might ever have come to a Garden of Eden. The white man had more to answer for than the murder and enslavement of untold thousands of Indians. Having looted and pillaged, he took back gold to Europe and left in its stead disease. Every galleon, every tall ship carried Pandora's Box to the New World.

Recently Lightman had developed a thesis that the decimation of Caribbean Indians, following Columbus' arrival, wasn't due to smallpox, though that was a widespread view. Rather Lightman was inclined to think a flu virus was responsible, one similar to the strains of flu that periodically swept through the contemporary world. He was preparing a paper on this question to be delivered at an international conference on epidemics that coming March in Hong Kong. How he would find the time to do the needed research and put the work into a coherent whole wasn't something he'd quite figured out yet.

It was difficult for him to concentrate. Thoughts of Joe Taylor kept returning to his mind, distracting him. He got out of bed, stepped over to the window and gazed at the town of Samothrace. Apart from a few lonely streetlamps it lay in darkness. His eyes sought out the dispensary which was really only a glorified Quonset hut. As he watched it, a light came on. The front door opened and two men appeared. Briefly silhouetted, they stood together, presumably conversing with each other. One was short and wearing a cap; the other, maybe six inches taller, had on a fur hat with mufflers over the ears and sported a beard. Then the light went out and the two were enfolded in darkness. He could hear the sound of car doors slamming and two engines protesting the cold before they finally turned over. And then, for several minutes, there was nothing else to listen to but the two cars riding on the icy road—in opposite directions—out of town.

Why the dispensary was open in the middle of the night, after Lightman had been told it was open only in the mornings, was something to find out from McKay.

In the morning, over breakfast, Lightman described to McKay what he'd seen. "Are you certain you were looking at the right building?" McKay asked.

"I'm positive."

"Well, we can ask Jim about it when we see him. I called him and he says to come over as soon as we're ready."

Jim Jillian didn't seem pleased to see them when they showed up in front of the Quonset hut half an hour later. He was a stub of a man, compact, with ruddy skin and silver hair, about seventy.

He stared at Lightman without curiosity. McKay he treated perfunctorily.

"You want to see Joe Taylor, is that it? Haven't you seen him enough?"

It was as if Joe, since his arrival, had become a member of the community, maybe not a desirable member, but a member all the same, who people referred to like a boyhood chum who'd gone wrong.

"Dr. Lightman hasn't had the pleasure yet," McKay said. "And we'd like to take any specimens Dr. Lyon collected in the postmortem."

"You have authorization?"

Lightman said that he had and produced the letter from the National Institutes. "It's possible that the specimens, maybe the cadaver itself, are hot. We need to take every precaution. The sooner we can remove the specimens for testing the better off we'll all be."

Jillian barely glanced at the letter. "You know what I think you fellows ought to do?"

"What's that?" McKay countered, flushing with irritation. "Are you going to show us the cadaver or not?"

Ignoring him, Jillian continued, "What you bureaucrats

ought to do is get your act together. First I get somebody from Juneau, then I get somebody from Washington—"

"Bethesda," Lightman corrected him.

"Then I get somebody from WHO."

"From WHO?"

"That's right, last night, Dr. Marsh. George Marsh. Said he was with the World Influenza Centre in London. He showed me some papers, I signed what I had to, he took the specimens and was on his way. Didn't say much." He was on edge, apparently unwilling to go into detail.

"Damn," Lightman said. "I don't understand. Somebody fucked up somewhere."

"What did I tell you? You better get your act together next time. I don't like being woken up in the middle of the night. I tell people that but they never listen."

"Didn't I ask you not to do anything with those specimens until Dr. Lightman got a chance to look at them?" McKay was seething. "Just because some doctor says he's from the World Health Organization is no reason to give him everything he asks for. You should've called me first. You don't have the authority."

It was the wrong thing to say. Jillian bristled. "Like hell I don't! Where do you get off saying that shit, McKay? Remember who's mayor here."

"All right, wait a minute, calm down everyone," Lightman said. "What's done is done. If the specimens are in the hands of the Influenza Centre it shouldn't be any trouble getting hold of them. It's just a matter of a couple of phone calls. I'm in touch with London on a regular basis anyway." To Jillian he said, "But if you don't mind, I would like to see the body."

"You still want to see Joe?" Jillian looked incredulous. "Well okay, you want to see him, follow me."

They proceeded down an unheated corridor, passing a succession of doors. They then entered a room that Lightman guessed to be Jillian's office. Pictures of him were all over the wall; the people he'd had them taken with were easily identified, most of them politicians who must have passed through Samothrace in search of votes. Clearly Jillian had his own little cult personality.

He sat down at his desk but pointedly failed to invite his visitors to take a seat. "So you want to see Joe, do you?" Jillian said, reaching down behind his desk. "Well, here he is."

They were looking at a black sealed jar.

"What is this, a damn joke?" McKay asked even though it was obvious what it was.

"Dr. Marsh insisted for safety's sake that we incinerate him. Or maybe you'd prefer I use the word cremate. It's just that what I use is an incinerator so I think of it as incineration." He eyed the jar. "No disrespect intended." He then thrust the jar toward Lightman. "Here, go on, take him. It's what you came all the way up here for, isn't it?"

THREE

Lightman had been back from his abortive excursion to the wastes of Alaska less than three weeks when he received two surprises, neither especially welcome, in the mail.

Sometimes mail had to be rerouted in order to reach him. He was a man of many addresses but no fixed location. While he maintained an office at the National Institutes and another in New York City, where for a brief period he'd served as the Deputy Commissioner of Health in the late seventies, his home base was really Boston, where he was employed by the Harvard School of Public Health. Just about all the time he spent in the Boston area was at his lab—a private concern that thrived (or not) on a combination of government grants and private foundations. Anyone who wished to contact him was advised to write to him in care of the lab, never at his home in Cambridge. Save for a very few close friends, he didn't like the idea of anyone knowing where he lived. It was either a quirk or paranoia, he supposed. Maybe both.

The first piece of mail that gave him pause had come via Bethesda. On the face of it it shouldn't have had any effect on him at all. It was a program for the Hong Kong conference—a glossy publication with photographs of all those who'd been invited to present papers. Among them was Lightman.

Distantly he recalled being sent a request for a current photo. He guessed that there had been two or three similar requests, each more urgent than the last, but he'd never gotten around to obliging the organizing committee. So he naturally assumed that there wouldn't be a picture of him in the program at all.

Wrong.

Somehow they had located a photo of him from a *U.S. News and World Report* article on flu pandemics published ten years before. The sight of it jarred him.

The young man with such intense and inquisitive eyes looking up from the page at him was a half forgotten acquaintance he was in no mood to meet again. What a full head of hair, he marveled, and not a strand of gray in it either. And no wonder his eyes were so intense; they were already beginning to go on him and it was likely that the intense stare the camera had caught was due to his trying to see twelve feet in front of him.

He couldn't help it, he took the program with him into the bathroom and compared his ten-year-old picture with the man who now regarded him, rather critically, from the incriminating surface of the mirror.

Getting old in a hurry, he thought. Not enough sleep—definitely a problem. Look at the eyes, sinking little by little into hollows. Gone was his bold youthful stare. And

if he escaped the predicament of others his age, putting on
weight, growing thick in the gut, it was not because he
either ate well or exercised regularly. Or even exercised at
all unless you counted the long walks he took—on those
rare January days when weather permitted—from his
house to the lab in the mornings. No, his thinness—a thinness that women like Luisa and his grandmother abhorred,
convinced he was wasting away—was attributable mostly
to a fast acting metabolism and an alarming tendency to go
without food, to forget about it altogether as a matter of
fact. No time to eat was one problem. Wanting to do something with the time other than eat was the second.

He wished now that he'd complied with the request from
the organizing committee and sent in a more recent photo,
sparing himself the embarrassment. Though he would
know most of those who showed up for the Hong Kong
conference, having run into them dozens of times previously for similar events, there would inevitably be some
who, looking from the picture to the podium, would
wonder who the hell he was.

Returning to his office he found a second piece of correspondence that would prove even more disturbing than the
first. It was a manila envelope addressed to the lab. The
return address was K. Saunders, World Health Organization, World Influenza Centre, Mill Road, London, N.W.

He eagerly tore it open, expecting to find inside the lab
reports run at the Centre on the specimens resected from
the organs of Joe Taylor. Since his return from Alaska he'd
given the case little thought with so many other things
commanding his attention. While the three deaths in Samothrace were cause for concern, if only because of the
virulence of the infection and the rapidity with which the
men had failed, it wasn't as if it represented a major calamity. Had there been further incidences of the disease in the
area then epidemiologists from the state and federal governments would undoubtedly revitalize the investigation.
There were about a thousand outbreaks of disease in the

U.S. every year—rabies, samonella poisoning, chicken pox, rubella, Legionnaire's Disease—most of them known quantities. The flu in all its variety wasn't even a reportable illness because it was so commonplace and often misdiagnosed to begin with. So there were obvious constraints on how much of an effort could be put into a single outbreak of a flu that had claimed just three victims.

Still, he was curious. Should the tests performed in the Centre's labs reveal the presence in those specimens of a dangerous and highly infectious virus, as Lightman suspected, then it would surely bear further investigation.

There was a cover letter accompanying the test data:

Dear Dr. Lightman,

Thank you for your inquiry regarding the specimens delivered to the World Influenza Centre on 11.1.98. We have conducted all relevant bacterial and viral tests only on pure isolates. Owing to the absence of blood and serum specimens we were able to perform tests on the brain, tissue and other organ specimens provided us. We trust that you will find the data satisfactory. Please contact me if we can be of any further help.

(Signed) Kathleen Saunders
Diagnostic Services

Through such standard tests as indirect flourescent antibody and complement fixation, several viral and bacterial diseases had been ruled out as the cause of the three Alaskans' deaths. But what surprised Lightman was what the tests did reveal.

According to the Centre's researchers, the infectious agent was a Type A H1N1 virus related to earlier flus like the A/Russian/77 and A/Taiwan/86.

But how to account for the black flood, for the fatality

rate which, for this small sample, was one hundred percent? Even the researchers were caught offguard, unable to square their findings with the field report. They were forced to admit that the strain they were working with was far from lethal; most of the mice and chicks they'd tested it on had in fact survived. Yet after repeated checking they had concluded that there was no mistake: the flu virus was the same one that had been brought to them from Alaska by Dr. George Marsh.

The elusive George Marsh again.

Lightman asked his secretary Rebecca Ackerman to see if she could track him down. "Start by calling WHO headquarters in Geneva, then try their office in New York," he said.

She was tireless in her pursuit, and relentless with bureaucrats in extricating information. Yet by the end of the day she'd gotten nowhere. "WHO has no record of him. There was no George Marsh authorized to pick up any specimens in Alaska. Not in January, not any time. There are two George Marshes who are members of the AMA, but neither of them has any connection with WHO. The British Medical Association knows of only one George Marsh and he's been dead for fifteen years. As far as I can tell, Doctor, this man just doesn't exist."

FOUR

Hong Kong, a year after its return to mainland China, looked much the same to Lightman as it had six years before when he'd last been to the colony. If there was any nervousness among the inhabitants it was well hidden from the view of the tourists and businessmen who circulated through the bustling shops off Hennessy Road in search of bargains—and at night in search of B-girls, the peril of deadly diseases notwithstanding.

The Eighth Annual Conference on Pandemic Cycles was being held in the Peninsula Hotel, surely the colony's most famous and just as surely one of its most expensive establishments. But the four hundred and fifty-five guests invited to attend were part of an elite made up of scientists, businessmen and bureaucrats who rarely had to shell out a penny of their own in life as there was always some agency or corporation to pick up the tab. Money came and went, but because no one in this rarefied circle ever really considered it theirs to begin with, it had little more meaning than the currency in a game of Monopoly.

Money wasn't the reality. Reality was the sweeping view of Victoria Harbor from the seventh-floor room Lightman had lucked into. Reality was the splendid food he consumed at Gaudi's and Hugo's and the Cafe d'Amigo. Reality was signing bills and laying out gold and platinum cards for them without so much as glancing at the total. Reality was the endless procession of spectacular women who floated through the lobbies of the Kowloon hotels, imperious beauties who were seen only in places where money held people so spellbound, as it did in Hong Kong. It was a subject that fascinated his friend Geoff Hopkins.

"Do you want to know how they distribute license plates here?" Hopkins asked him over breakfast the third day of the conference.

Lightman, whose thoughts were elsewhere at the moment, said he hadn't the faintest.

"Well let me tell you." Hopkins was an enthusiastic gambler, and any time he came within a mile of a racetrack or a casino a certain madness would overtake him. You could see it in his eyes. Only after meeting him on his home turf—home was Stanford University, where he studied acute febrile respiratory diseases—did Lightman realize that he was, at heart, a sober and diligent researcher. It was just that it was impossible for him to resist the lure of high stakes once he got to a place like Hong Kong.

"I'm all ears."

"They hold a bidding for them. Because the Chinese have such an obsession about numbers, plates with lucky numbers go for the most. Eight means luck in money. A plate with 888 on it is so coveted, they tell me, that it's worth more than the car itself. Somebody willing to spend a fortune for a plate like that, you can imagine what kind of car he must own." Hopkins saw that Lightman's attention was flagging again. "Hey, are you still thinking about that damn paper? So what if Elston gave you shit. What did you expect from a schmuck like Elston?"

Elston was a virologist out of Chicago and, while Lightman couldn't say he cared for the man, Hopkins despised him and thought his research stank. But it wasn't Elston's opposition to his paper or the skepticism with which it had been received by most of the conferees that now weighed on his mind. He was convinced he was right about the identity of the plague that struck down the Caribbean Indians and he believed that someday he'd acquire the evidence necessary to prove his thesis even to the likes of Elston.

"No, it's the grant. I expect to hear today—tomorrow at the latest—what's happened with it."

"Ah hell, John, you've been through this before. We all have. You'll get the damn grant. You always do."

"This is a bit different, Geoff. We're talking a lot of money with this. A million two. I've never been in a position where everything hangs on one goddamn decision. It's frustrating as hell."

"Jesus, cool it. It'll happen, I'm telling you. You got your data, you've got your credentials. How could they not go for it?"

Maybe it was Hopkins' gambling instinct at work, the confidence, however unwarranted, that of course his number would come up on the next roll of the dice. But Lightman didn't feel it and that was what mattered; he just didn't feel it this time.

"Now that's interesting, that's what you should be paying attention to, not torturing yourself over that proposal."

Following the direction of his eyes Lightman saw, standing at the buffet table, a woman of rather remarkable beauty with reddish brown hair and a fantastic tan emphasized by her white dress. A man Lightman remembered from one of the previous day's sessions was standing beside her, deliberating whether it was the shrimp he wanted or the dumplings.

"I tell you, if I wasn't married..." His voice trailed off but his eyes remained on her.

Lightman had the sense that Hopkins didn't allow marriage to stand in the way if the temptation was really overwhelming. But he never would ask; it wasn't his business. Although they'd known each other for nearly two decades, their friendship renewed two or three times a year at conferences like this, they never strayed over certain boundaries. Hopkins had met Stephanie and liked her and awkwardly expressed his sadness to learn of their breakup, but that was as far as it went. He never pressed Lightman for the reasons, nor did he offer any himself when he divorced his second wife in favor of the woman who was to become his third. On the whole, Lightman preferred it that way; he wasn't particularly happy when friendships became too personal.

He looked up again. The woman had returned to her table but the man hadn't moved. He still seemed to be trying to decide between the shrimp and the dumplings.

Almost twelve hours later Lightman was sitting down for another meal, still torturing himself over the grant money. In a short time, by his reckoning, the foundation would be open for business in Washington. It was even possible that he'd hear the news before this dinner was over.

It was the final night of the conference, held in the Peninsula's newly renovated ballroom and marked by a Chinese dinner composed of a seemingly endless number of courses. Lightman was getting drunk. Hopkins to his right was becoming lost in a gentle haze. It was all Lightman could do to concentrate on what he was saying to Saul Broyden who was seated on the opposite side of him.

"Pardon me, are these seats available?" a woman asked.

Lightman lifted his eyes to see a woman standing over him. It took him a moment to realize that this was the same woman he'd seen that morning by the buffet table. She'd done something to her hair, tied it back to dramatize the lines of her face. He breathed deeply into the scent of her expensive perfume. Only then did he observe the man with her, the one who had been with her that morning.

"Yes, yes, they are. They are available. Please."

Her smile was his reward.

She was wearing blue now, a dress that described a great vee down her back. Her breasts revealed themselves through the thin fabric, then were lost in shadow; it depended largely on the light and in which direction she moved. She could not possibly be a researcher, Lightman decided.

The man leaned forward, toward Lightman. His features were economically compressed into his face which didn't appear to have enough room to contain them. There was a pinched look to him suggesting that he might always need to be worrying about something. His companion, however, looked serene and entirely distant from the proceedings. There was, too, Lightman noticed, a vaguely Levantine cast to her face; perhaps the darker tint of her skin was not altogether accountable to the hours she spent in the sun but was simply a part of her genetic makeup. God, he loved her perfume.

"You're Dr. Lightman," the man said as though Lightman might need reminding of his identity. "I would like to say that I very much enjoyed your talk yesterday." He had an educated English accent.

"It's kind of you to say so. I was beginning to think that my supporters were scared to show themselves."

The man stuck out his hand. "I'm Bill Wellington." Nodding toward the woman he introduced her as Diana Cleary.

"I'm pleased," she said, taking Lightman's hand in turn.

"You're not with the conference, are you?"

Wellington thought this amusing. So did Diana. "Oh, I should say not." She too had an English accent, of a kind that Lightman was a sucker for, one that he could have listened to for hours without hearing a word she was saying.

"No, Dr. Lightman, I own a fashion designing business —a very modest business believe me—in London. The factories I deal with are located here so I'm often in Hong Kong. Bill and I are friends."

Friends? What kind of friends?

"This conference happened to coincide with one of Diana's trips so we came together."

A soup course arrived. Diana inquired from the waiter what kind of soup it was.

"This is blood nest soup," the waiter replied. "It is very rare. It is made from the saliva and blood of swallows."

Wellington screwed up his face but Diana reacted differently, putting a spoonful to her lips. "It pays to try anything," she said.

Hopkins meantime was taking an interest in their exchange, drawn to Diana. He pretended, however, to direct his attention toward Wellington. "Where are you working, Dr. Wellington?"

"I'm at the Mayfair House."

"I don't believe I've heard of the Mayfair House," Hopkins said, frowning. He didn't like to be caught unawares.

"Isn't that Patrick Martindale's clinic?" Lightman asked.

"Yes, that's right," Wellington said. "His clients and laboratories are based there."

To show that he wasn't wholly ignorant Hopkins put in, "Oh yes, Martindale, I remember now. He has quite the reputation. He isn't here by any chance, is he?"

A strange look passed between Diana and Wellington, but Lightman could make nothing of it.

"No," Wellington said, "if he were here you'd know it in an instant. You wouldn't call Patrick shy exactly. But he stopped coming to affairs like this long ago. It's my impression he thinks them a waste of time."

"He may have a point," said Hopkins, anxious to insinuate himself into the conversation.

Then Diana turned to Lightman. "What was the subject of your talk yesterday?"

"I don't know whether it would interest you," he demurred.

"Try me. If it bores me I'll let you know."

"Believe me, she will," Wellington said.

So Lightman began to tell her. It might have been the drink fueling him, but more likely it was the proximity of this woman whose very presence was intoxicant enough. Soon he got carried away, going into far more detail than he'd intended. Then he caught himself, thinking that truly he must be putting her to sleep. She was only being polite by refraining from interrupting. How interested could she possibly be in the tragic fate of the 300,000 Tainos on the island of Hispaniola, after all?

But she seemed surprised that he'd suddenly stopped. "Go on, please. I find this fascinating, really I do."

Though he knew himself to be a fluent and persuasive speaker when addressing the company of his colleagues, he never felt at home in social situations like this, certainly not when they included women of Diana's quality. But he complied with her request and continued. In effect, what he had done was repeat his presentation almost verbatim, but this time with more care to explain any technical term or obscure historical reference Diana might not have known.

The others around him had moved onto other conversations, leaving Diana to him.

"Are you in London very often, Dr. Lightman?"

"Maybe once or twice a year, usually for a few days at a time."

"I was just wondering. Should you ever find yourself there in the future, please ring me up. I'd love to talk more, but the truth is I'm beat." She lowered her eyes to her watch. "It is getting on, you'll have to excuse me."

As she rose from her chair Lightman asked how he could reach her.

"Bill always knows where to find me."

He took her hand, surprised to discover how cold it was from the glass of iced mineral water she'd been drinking. Lightman realized that she'd touched nothing alcoholic all night.

As he watched her make her way out of the hall Wellington said, "That's her own creation, you know."

"What is?"

"The dress she's wearing—she designed it."

But it wasn't the dress that he'd been focusing on.

Completely stuffed, Lightman declined Hopkins' invitation to L'Aperitif, the Peninsula's bar, where a pianist was trying, not with a great deal of success, to breathe new life into "Yesterday When We Were Young." He opted instead for a postprandial stroll around Kowloon, but before he could get to the exit he became conscious of someone coming up alongside him. He looked and saw Wellington.

His smile of greeting seemed strained. "I don't mean to bother you, Dr. Lightman, but would it be possible to have a word with you?"

He sounded serious. "If it won't take long."

"I think you'll be the judge of that." He scanned the Peninsula's lobby. "Perhaps we could find someplace a little more private."

Lightman didn't appreciate his deliberately enigmatic tone.

"Could you tell me what this is in regard to?"

"Yes. It involves those specimens from Alaska you've been looking into. I believe I know what might have happened to them."

FIVE

They returned to Lightman's room, and there by a window allowing a spectacular panorama of Victoria Harbor, Wellington proceeded to tell him a strange and unsettling tale. He began dramatically enough by predicting his own death. He was very straightforward about it too, putting it directly to Lightman without exhibiting any sign of anxiety.

"What are you saying?" Lightman asked with alarm. "Are you dying?" He was afraid that the man had sought him out for medical advice.

"No, but what I'm about to tell you may lead to my death." He continued to speak with such deliberate calm that Lightman didn't know what to think. It was not in his experience for somebody to offer him dangerous confidences.

"Then maybe you ought to reconsider and save it for somebody else."

But Wellington was determined. Nothing was about to stop him from reciting his story. He was some kind of Ancient Mariner. "If you proceed with this investigation, Dr. Lightman, sooner or later you'll have to come up against Patrick Martindale. And when you do, you should know that you are running a terrific risk. Just as I am doing now. You should be aware of what you're getting into."

"I still don't see what he has to do with the missing specimens."

"Hear me out. First keep in mind that Patrick is astonishingly well connected. The patients he's treated are almost invariably wealthy and politically powerful. He's always used his practice as a means of advancing himself. What motivates him particularly is being accepted, you see. He can't bear the idea that he won't be accepted."

"That's no crime."

"No, but it makes it easier for him to commit one. He abuses his power as a matter of course. He's gotten away with murder. And I mean that literally. In the first years of his practice he had a much more active surgery. But he hardly dares go near an operating table anymore. And do you know why? Because at least two patients have died as a result of his butchery.

"Not that this taught him any humility. His friends and colleagues covered up for him of course. When he saw that he could get away with bungling operations it only encouraged him to commit other outrages. Not all of them involved murder, but they are all equally unforgivable. To build up his vaunted reputation he didn't hesitate to steal from his fellow researchers at Mayfair House. Oh, but he was clever about it. Often the victims were ignorant of what he was up to or else he flattered them into thinking that they were somehow going to benefit from his theft. He didn't call it that, naturally. Actually, he liked to call his victims his collaborators, as if they'd somehow volunteered to be cheated. I know this for a fact because I too was one of his unwitting collaborators. Yes, Dr. Lightman, he did indeed steal my work and appropriate it for himself, then passed it off in published papers as his own. If you ever get to London sometime I can show you his work and my original notes so you can compare them for yourself.

"Of course Patrick is brilliant, I don't deny that for a

moment. But he fancies himself a polymath and a Renaissance man whose genius is manifest in everything he touches. Since he rarely has the time to do the proper research and experimentation on his own, he feels constrained to steal. When he doesn't steal then it's worse—he publishes papers with such flimsy data and shoddy methodology that no self-respecting schoolboy would risk turning them in to his tutor. But he gets away with it, you see. He doesn't even have any trouble finding co-authors to go in on it with him."

"Why is that?" Though Lightman had no personal knowledge of Martindale he was still somewhat taken aback at hearing him characterized as a butcher and con man.

"How many scientists do you know who are willing to try and duplicate someone else's work in their laboratories? Of course they'd rather pursue their own. It's just as easy to assume that what's being published is correct and go on with your business." Without a pause he added, "And the women."

"Excuse me? I'm sorry, I don't think I heard you right."

"You heard me right. I said the women. The women are Patrick's real interest, not his lab. They're what drive him, they're what obsess him. He seduces his patients when they're female and their wives when they're not. It's appalling really how these women respond to him." There was heated passion to his voice when he spoke of Martindale's women as if this were his real flaw, his fatal weakness, and not the rest of it. Even the prospect of his own death hadn't gotten him so excited.

Lightman, fearing that there might not be any way of stopping him once he got going on the topic, tried to steer him back to the subject that concerned him most. Interrupting him he said, "I'm sorry, but don't you think we could talk about Dr. Martindale's affairs some other day? Right now I'm interested to find out about those specimens. You implied that you know something about what became of them."

"Yes, I do. They were delivered to Mayfair House."

"From the World Influenza Centre?"

"In spite of whatever you may have been told, they never arrived at the World Influenza Centre. They went directly to Mayfair House. Don't you understand what I'm trying to say, Dr. Lightman? Dr. Martindale stole those specimens right out from under your nose."

SIX

Lightman knew a great many things about viruses. He understood how they were constituted, with RNA nucleoprotein on the inside and a lipoprotein envelope on the out; he understood how they went to work hijacking normal cells and turning them into factories for the production of still more viral agents; he understood how viruses infected not only humans but also animals and plants and how they would lie low for long periods, hiding out as if in ambush; and he understood how it was possible in a great many instances to inactivate and destroy these viruses. But one thing he did not know was what procedure to follow when a virus was stolen.

First of all, he had only Wellington's word for it, but no proof. And Wellington himself had admitted that he was basing his conclusions on circumstantial evidence. While he'd promised to try to find out more and then let Lightman know, two weeks had gone by without any word from him. Lightman had to assume that Wellington had either come up with nothing or else had stumbled upon certain

facts at variance with his hypothesis and decided to with-
hold them.

Yet Lightman didn't discount what he said completely.
He put out feelers through friends of his with the World
Health Organization and contacts in London who might
have reason to know about Martindale's operations. Simultaneously, through these same channels, he solicited information about Wellington. No matter how well his
statements stood up there was still something about the
man that seemed unbalanced to Lightman. It could have
been the fear that he was living in that had him so on edge.
But it was also conceivable that he was delusional, suffering from paranoid fantasies.

While waiting to see whether his feelers would bear any
fruit, Lightman asked Rebecca to obtain as many papers of
Patrick Martindale's that she could lay her hands on at
Harvard's medical school library.

Of the seven papers she located (published in *Lancet*,
Annals of Medicine, and *The Journal of Infectious Diseases* among others), all but two appeared to be satisfactory. The two most recent papers, though, seemed suspect
to him even without going into the lab and attempting to
replicate the results. Both of these papers, curiously
enough, were signed by over forty co-authors, most of
whom, Lightman suspected, hadn't read the material. It
was as though by the sheer weight of numbers Martindale
hoped to make up for any lapses and mistakes he'd committed. And what about the editors and the referees? With
just a cursory reading Lightman had detected about a dozen
errors in the two papers that couldn't be obscured even by
Martindale's obviously brilliant command of the language.
Had the editors and referees also failed to read the papers?
Or were they so bowled over by Martindale's reputation
that they'd let the papers pass their inspection untouched?

Even if Martindale was guilty of violating a professional

canon of ethics, that alone could not implicate him in the theft of a lethal virus.

But the reason Lightman wasn't disposed to move faster on the case had nothing to do with Martindale or the specimens. His thoughts were almost entirely taken up by the impending decision on his grant proposal. There was little room for anything else in his mind.

It was the fifth of June and he hadn't been able to get a damn thing out of the NIH, pro or con. He was repeatedly told that his and a score of other proposals were under review and that he would have to appreciate that there was a backlog and a need on the part of the review board to make sure that the money was disbursed in "a manner consistent with the current priorities of the administration."

While Lightman had become accustomed to delays and bureaucratic excuses, he was still frustrated, especially because he had so much riding on this decision. He had a feeling that it wasn't a matter of backlogs or a need for additional experts to see whether his work stacked up against some impossibly high standard of academic achievement that was behind the delay this time. No, there seemed to be something else at work.

If he didn't sleep more than five or six hours at a stretch before he now slept barely four. And when he did sleep he experienced troublesome dreams. There were dreams of fire and dreams of Stephanie. He realized that he only dreamed about his ex-wife when things weren't going well for him.

It was also becoming more of a problem to plan ahead. What sense did it make to chart long-term projects that, for want of the necessary money, would never reach completion? Although he believed it bad luck to act as if misfortune were already at the door, he went ahead and drew up a list—a proscription list really—of the employees he'd have to let go in the event the foundation turned him down.

He hated doing this even in theory; the only people he'd ever fired were workers who proved derelict in their duties.

Rebecca, more than anyone else in his life, sensed his unease, his doom-laden preoccupation. She counseled him against giving into despair. Fresh flowers appeared on his desk every morning to buoy him up. Nuts and fruit became a regular afternoon custom; it was his secretary's way of reminding him that man does not live by fast food alone and that if he didn't pay more attention to the kind of food he ate he'd do damage to his health.

Gratified as he was by these little attentions he still was unable to relax or collect himself. He started to think that he'd brought on his trouble by investing so much in this one proposal.

But why the hell not? It was a damn good proposal, it represented significant research, and there was no reason why it shouldn't be funded.

And then the phone call came.

There were dozens of calls made every day to his office, but somehow he knew this was the one, this was the call that counted.

Rebecca buzzed him. "Doctor, it's Dr. Westbrook on the line."

Westbrook was the man named to head the review board and he'd have no reason to call other than to break the news, good or bad.

Lightman hesitated for a moment before picking up, breathing deeply, rummaging through his mind for some prayer, some Buddhist chant possibly, any words of the ages that might give him courage, but he could find none. He put the receiver to his ear and pressed a button. "Dr. Westbrook, this is John Lightman."

It didn't take long for the message to emerge. "I'm afraid, John, I don't have good news for you. You know how much I've admired the work you and your colleagues have been doing and . . ."

Lightman failed to hear what followed; he understood the message being imparted.

It was strange that, having expected the worst for so long, when it actually happened it wasn't all that bad. It felt unreal; there was a peculiar numbing sensation that he supposed was the body chemistry's natural cushion against shock.

One thing he was grateful for was that the call had come at the end of the day. Had it come at eight in the morning it would have been impossible to continue as if nothing had happened. He would have been obliged to alert everybody in the lab before word got around—as it inevitably would have—before he could announce it himself. This way he could wait for tomorrow, maybe pull himself together overnight.

He stayed at his desk, going through the motions of getting paperwork done, hardly conscious of what was happening around him. He didn't even hear the phone when it rang again, not more than an hour after Westbrook's unhappy tidings.

Rebecca signaled him. "Doctor, there's a Winston Cage on the line who would like to speak to you."

Winston Cage? Lightman couldn't recall anybody of that name, nor was he much in the mood for conversation. "Would you tell him to leave his number and I'll get back to him?"

Some seconds passed. Rebecca buzzed him a second time. "He says that it's most urgent he speak with you. He says that you will be interested in what he has to say."

Lightman was annoyed. "I don't care how urgent it is, Rebecca, take his number. I'm not accepting any more calls this evening."

But Mr. Cage wouldn't take no for an answer. Rebecca buzzed Lightman a third time to say, "I'm sorry to disturb you, Doctor, but Mr. Cage is insistent. He told me to tell

you that, if it helps, he is the personal representative of Dr.
Patrick Martindale."

Lightman decided to take the call.

"I'm Dr. Lightman, what can I do for you?" Brusque, to
the point.

"Yes, Dr. Lightman, I'm sorry to intrude on you like
this. But some disturbing news has just reached me. It's
my understanding that the NIH has rejected your grant proposal and that this may leave your laboratory sadly short of
funds. Is that true, Dr. Lightman?"

How the hell did this man—who lived on the other side
of the Atlantic—find out about the NIH decision? Who
had notified him so quickly? Lightman asked him.

"How I obtained this information isn't relevant," Cage
said. "I take it then that my facts are correct."

Lightman didn't reply.

"You may be interested in what I have to tell you, Dr.
Lightman. There may be a way out of your dilemma."

"Oh, and what would that be?" Lightman didn't like the
turn the conversation was taking but he couldn't bring
himself to hang up.

"There is a chance, perhaps just an outside chance, that
the review board could be prevailed upon to reverse its
decision and put through your proposal."

This suggestion struck Lightman as preposterous. In all
the years he'd been applying for grants he'd never once
heard of the NIH reversing itself. Rarely, a proposal rejected in one form, overhauled and revised a year later,
might be accepted, but not the exact same proposal.

"You'll excuse me, Mr. Cage, if I don't believe you."

"It can be done, Dr. Lightman. Let me assure you that if
Dr. Martindale brings his weight to bear it can be done."

There was something about the way in which he said the
words that caused Lightman to think that just possibly there
might be some truth to them.

When Lightman didn't immediately respond Cage went
on. "Listen, Dr. Lightman, you really don't have very

much to lose. All that would be required of you is a quick visit to London. You and Dr. Martindale can talk and if you can come to an agreement—"

"An agreement about what?"

"Then so much the better," he continued, deliberately ignoring Lightman's question. "Would this Monday, the eighth, be convenient? Say four o'clock at Mayfair House?"

"I don't know what my schedule is. . . ." Already, he knew, he was agreeing to meet.

"Please, Dr. Lightman, remember that Dr. Martindale has very little time available for appointments. Several weeks might have to pass, perhaps months, before he would be able to see you again. And then the opportunity to rectify the board's . . ." he was looking for the proper— and diplomatic—word, "the board's oversight might be forever lost." He barely paused to allow Lightman to answer. "So let us say definitely this coming Monday at four at Dr. Martindale's office in Mayfair House."

Lightman mumbled his acquiescence and was about to hang up when Cage hastened to add, "Oh, you are booked to arrive on Sunday—British Airways Flight 75 departing JFK Airport at 9:10 Saturday. A ticket will be waiting for you at the airline counter. And a room has been secured for you at the Grosvenor."

Before Lightman could say another word Winston Cage had terminated the connection three thousand miles away.

SEVEN

This positively was the last time, she resolved. Her dependence on the man was intolerable; it was crucial that she be able to step back and get a sense of what was really happening in her life rather than returning to him week after week.

Downstairs, adjacent to a peep show promising passersby a feast of flesh for their eyes, was the Ariadne Bookshop. Diana always wondered why Jonas Beck would establish his offices and main commercial operations right in the middle of Soho among massage parlors, striptease joints, porno bookstores and two-quid clubs kept perpetually in the dark so that their patrons could easily be forgiven for mistaking high noon for midnight.

The Ariadne Bookshop catered not to the pursuit of the flesh that went on next door but to things of the mind and spirit. From what Diana could tell, most of the bookshop's customers would have sloughed off their bodies if they could to live purely the life of the mind. Their eyes bulged and gaped. In fact, their eyes were the most prominent thing about them, their most important organ. The books they leafed through or inspected with such astonishing scrutiny ranged from exegeses about the Kabbalah to sidereal charts and the chronicles of people claiming to be mouthpieces for the dead. But of all the esoterica available there, it was the works of Jonas Beck that sold best. And that was as it should be; for this was his bookshop, this was the place from where his words of inspiration and prophesy were spread.

Although Diana had never actually laid eyes on it herself, she knew that somewhere else in the building there was a small publishing company and printing shop where additional works of Beck and his followers were turned out. Sometimes she could hear the presses running, a clamor of machinery that caused the fragile walls of the bookshop to tremble and flakes of plaster to come floating down.

Several volumes, principally *Annals of the Ariadne Society*, published in this building rested on her bookshelves at home. But it was Nicholas, her late husband, who'd purchased them, not her. She never spent money on these books herself. What need did she have of Jonas Beck on the printed page when she had access to him directly—in person?

Today, this fifth day of June, there was noticeably more movement in and around the shop, a feeling in the air that something significant was about to happen or was happening already. But the behavior of these people, these adherents of Jonas Beck, was as much of an impenetrable mystery to her as was the meaning of most of the arcana around her. And she did not care to have this mystery explained to her.

Diana began walking down an aisle that would lead her past books on channeling and reincarnation (on her right) and witchcraft and Gurdjief (on her left), headed toward an elevator at the rear. There were many other settings where a woman of her looks would be sure to turn heads. Not here. Here she was one more customer who came in from the afternoon rain.

The purpose of the elevator was not identified, and it was likely that most customers believed it was used to convey books from the stockroom, variously thought to be in the basement or on one of the upper floors.

The man running this elevator, a West Indian, knew by sight all those who were authorized to take it. The elevator had only one destination, the fourth floor, the consulting offices of Jonas Beck himself.

His offices were set in the back, overlooking an airshaft and insulated against the turbulent sounds of Soho and Picadilly Circus. There was one room where visitors, disciples of Jonas Beck, waited—alone, always alone—and another where Beck consented to see them. Customarily visitors waited an hour or more in the outer room, however long it took until the door leading to Beck's office would slide open. At no time would visiting disciples see a secretary or other disciples (the word client was anathema). Diana was certain that there must be somebody charged with the responsibility of orchestrating the comings and goings of Beck's visitors. She suspected the presence of hidden video cameras, imagined a man who never saw the sun logging people in and out, calculating the amount of time each one of them could endure waiting before his patience wore out, opening the door for him at that moment when he was most susceptible to whatever Jonas Beck had to say.

Or maybe not: maybe it was all in Diana's imagination.

The walls of Jonas Beck's office were bare. A beige curtain at the window concealed the view outside, although, of course, there was no view to speak of. In some ways the room resembled the office of therapists that Diana had consulted in the past, but it lacked the framed certificates attesting to education and honors bestowed by professional associations. Here were two couches, both well-worn and more comfortable for being so. On one Beck was sitting, as usual, one leg draped across the other, a Dunhill Blue pinched between his fingers. A mane of white hair showing no sign that a comb had passed through it any time recently was his most dominent feature. His eyes were kindly and wise now. But they could change in a flash; there could be darkness in them too. It was crazy, but Diana could have sworn that he was capable of altering the color of his irises along with his mood. The bluest eyes in the world could turn a greenish gray in a instant and what was a window into the soul would became a curtain every bit as opaque as the one hanging in the window.

From their very first encounter nearly two years before when Nicholas fell ill, she had never been able to guess his age with any reliability. In some respects it was as if he wasn't any age at all. In one book of his she'd picked up but never finished reading—*Memoirs of the Ariadne Society*—he'd declared that he'd been born in 1939. But other books cited his age differently, and so she never knew.

A private reading from Jonas Beck was a privilege, much sought after in certain circles whose numbers were expanding all the time. Individuals desperate for counsel, unwilling to endure the three month waiting list, were known to pay upwards of a thousand quid per session if he gave them priority. Diana didn't know what her readings cost; she wasn't the one who was paying for them.

Beck had a way of looking at her that right away caused her to brush aside any thought of lying to him. Unlike a conventional therapist who would coax and even, when necessary, badger his patient into revealing what was going on in his mind, Jonas didn't need to hear a word. *He knew.*

"You're on edge today," he said, "it's apparent you'd rather not be here." His voice was sonorous, authoritative, strangely disembodied; sometimes it seemed not to be coming from him at all.

She acknowledged that that was true. "I stepped off the train at Oxford Circus and was about to leave the station, but something stopped me. I just couldn't leave. When the next train came along I took it."

"You were wise to do so." He was silent for a moment, crushing his burned-out Dunhill in an ashtray. "You shouldn't worry so."

"I know I shouldn't worry. Still, it's hard."

Not a night passed anymore that she could sleep all the way through.

"Once you believe, once you have total faith, then you

will be surprised how easily the fear, the dread, will slip away."

He'd tried to impress this upon her many times before, but she sensed the kind of faith he was referring to was beyond her. How she wanted—needed—such faith, and envied those who had it.

"I could tell you things that I see right now, Diana, things that might lift your spirits if you could understand their meaning. But that is something I cannot do. I've tried to give you an idea of what you must face in these next few months. It will be an ordeal for you. There is no guarantee that you will be equal to it. You must summon the necessary courage for this challenge."

"Can you see my son, can you tell me when I'll find him?"

She hated herself for her desperation, for allowing this man the right to bare her soul, this man whom she held in such contempt—and needed so very much.

"I see him, yes, I see him. He isn't as far away as you suspect but he could be standing here, in this very room, and you would still fail to see him. And why? Why, Diana?" His voice wasn't loud, it was barely above a whisper, but it was insinuating, capable of working its way under a person's skin. "Because you've yet to keep your part of the bargain. You take one step forward and two steps back. You renounce me and at the same time you understand that without me you will remain forever in an abyss of pain and guilt and longing. Is that what you want, Diana? That endless longing?"

No, of course that was not what she wanted. She might die, she thought. She might die and wouldn't know the difference. The pain might be indistinguishable from the pain she felt now; an exchange of one prison cell for another was no exchange at all.

"Give yourself over to the Divine Will and you will be saved, and you will have your son back."

"And what would the Divine Will have me do?"

There was a sharpness in her tone, a sarcasm that she couldn't repress in time.

Beck was quiet, observing her the way he might an animal that was slowly dying from hunger. In time he would have his dinner.

After a small silence he spoke. "After today, Diana, it may no longer be possible for us to meet. Certainly not regularly as we've been doing. Perhaps not at all."

This brought her up short. "What do you mean?"

"In a few days we shall be relocating outside of London."

"Where outside of London?"

"I cannot tell you that."

Only moments before she was praying that she might never have to see Jonas Beck again. Now that her prayer seemed to be answered (and by one who could read her mind and interpret the stirrings of her heart), she was thrown into a panic. It was one thing for her to tear herself away from him, quite another for him to drop her.

"I don't understand."

"In due course you will, Diana. Things are changing very fast. Each morning when you awake you will see a world completely different from the one you knew when you went to bed. We will not be lost to each other even though we may be physically separated. Not so long as you put your trust in the Divine Will, if you place your trust in me and the church."

The church? It was the first time he'd ever mentioned the church to her, although she'd heard vaguely that he had founded a church of some kind in another part of London.

"You have the choice now between death and immortal life. If in this life on earth you wish to be reunited with your son and enjoy riches and love then you shall. But if in this life on earth you renounce the Divine Will and go your own way then I can promise you nothing but everlasting torment. Do you believe me, Diana?"

She said nothing.

"Do you believe me, Diana?"

Slowly, she nodded. Slowly, she said, "I believe you, I believe."

"Then go in peace, Diana, and live."

EIGHT

When the movie ended they were still over Ireland. Darkness was surrendering its sovereignty and the clouds became gilded with a golden pink light. Practically all activity had ceased inside the craft as weary passengers fought for a few minutes more of sleep before they were forced to participate in the indignity of customs at Heathrow.

Lightman wasn't interested in sleep. Any sleep he'd ever gotten twenty thousand feet up in the air had never been very useful. Instead he spent his remaining time before landing engaged in what he'd been doing since departing JFK five hours previously: studying the life and career of Patrick Martindale.

As hard as it was for him to believe, he could come to no other conclusion but that Martindale had somehow gotten to the review board of the National Institutes of Health, manipulating enough of its principals to turn down his grant proposal.

He supposed that it was possible that the proposal had failed on its own merits—or lack of them. But Martindale's timely offer of intervention made Lightman think that the man had played a part in the decision from the beginning. That Martindale chose to involve himself in Lightman's life at all could only be a result of Lightman's inquiry into the missing specimens. Otherwise it was too great a coincidence. Lightman was convinced that he knew why he was being called to England; it was for the purpose of being bribed, the grant money approved in exchange for his agreeing to drop the investigation. He had no doubt about that whatsoever. What he didn't know was exactly why he'd consented to go, what he hoped to get out of it. There was no way he could escape the feeling that he was painting himself into a corner.

Sliding up the shade to peer out of his window, he spotted the sun making its way above the clouds in an accelerated dawn.

He resumed his reading.

The problem in uncovering the facts about Patrick Martindale's life was that there were so few available, and of those, even fewer that seemed beyond dispute.

The accounts Rebecca had managed to locate stated that Martindale was born in November of 1942, the older son of refugees from central Europe. (This was where the first uncertainty crept in: One source gave Berlin as their former home, another Prague.) Their names were Bruno and Mary Martinberg or, according to a second biographical sketch, Saul and Flora Gwertzman.

Nowhere could Lightman find out what became of the younger sister; there was one mention of her existence, then she seemed to disappear without a trace.

If certain facts about Martindale's professional career had been adequately documented, everything about his education was nebulous. One source indicated that he graduated with a baccalaureate from King's College in 1962 at the tender age of twenty; another declared that he'd received his undergraduate degree from the University of Köln in the same year. He earned his medical degree at the University of Chicago and advanced degrees in immunology and molecular biology at the University of Warwick in Coventry. At various times he had served as Chairman of the Department of Virology at Saint Thomas' Medical School in London, headed the Wellcome Research Laboratories in Langley Court, Beckenham, Kent, briefly held tenure as Director of the Global Epidemic Intelligence Service for the CDC, and for the last fifteen years had served at the discretion of the director-general of WHO in a variety of postings: as a special consultant; as a permanent member of the Advisory Committee on Medical Research; as a member of the Executive Board; as director of the European Region of WHO based in Copenhagen.

References to Mayfair House abounded throughout everything Lightman read. Described as an experimental medical center where diseases resistant to treatment elsewhere could be fought and sometimes conquered, Mayfair House was the apotheosis of Martindale's dream, if the publicity releases Lightman had sent away for could be believed. The laboratory facilities, assembled at a cost of "in excess of sixty million pounds," and subsidized by both the government and private donations from all over the world, were said to be among the most advanced anywhere.

What was left out were the qualifications a patient would need to be admitted to Mayfair House, aside from being afflicted with a disease sufficiently intriguing to Martindale and his colleagues, and what kind of payment one could expect to make. Nor could Lightman discover any references to Martindale having personally practiced medicine. Was there anything to what Wellington had said about his having killed two patients while performing surgery? He certainly wasn't going to find out from the literature in his possession.

One pamphlet in particular caught his eye. The pamphlet included the text of a lecture given to an unidentified audience at the Max Factor Institute of Public Policy, a five-year-old think tank established at the University of North

Carolina in Chapel Hill. The lecture was entitled "The Cult of Participatory Democracy." In it Martindale described a crisis in leadership that was partly due to a more cynical and jaded electorate. Education, far from instilling any moral or spiritual values in children, was only fostering still more acquisitiveness, more obsessive materialism. Collective leadership in capitalist as well as communist states was becoming more the rule than the exception. While charismatic leaders like Hitler were clearly dangerous, the world was undoubtedly ready for leaders with moral vision, leaders who could do more than manage countries as if they were just very large and somewhat ungainly corporations. Everywhere institutions were failing their constituents; everywhere these frustrated constituents were crying out for a guide, somebody to navigate them into the next millenium. "These individuals are there," he concluded, "prepared to step in and do their part. It is regrettable but true that the world will not welcome such leaders until a crisis is upon them and the need of one and the destiny of the other coincide at last."

To Lightman it sounded like a prescription for the takeover by an authoritarian government, but perhaps he was interpreting it wrong.

"Excuse me, sir?"

He lifted his eyes to see the flight attendant. "We'll be landing in just a few minutes. Would you mind putting your seat in an upright position?"

Winston Cage was waiting for him, which wasn't what Lightman had anticipated. Lightman would have preferred not to have dealt with Cage until the next day, after he could get some rest and collect his thoughts. It occurred to him that it was Cage's intention to take him by surprise, to keep him off balance.

There was no crowd Lightman could imagine that Cage wouldn't stand out in. He was of average height and conservatively attired, but there was about him the air of a disreputable Bohemian who kept late hours among suspect company. His most distinctive feature was white eyebrows shaped like fantails. He sported an unruly mustache that lent him a faintly Oriental aspect; it too was amazingly white.

If he looked upon Lightman as the enemy there was nothing in his greeting to suggest it. Quite the contrary, he acted as though his American guest was a dear old friend who'd been away for much too long a time.

Scarcely having gotten his wits about him, Lightman found himself sitting in the back of a Mercedes, a brand new Mercedes from the smell of the upholstery, with Cage sitting next to him inquiring anxiously as to how his trip had been and apologizing profusely for the suspension of Concorde flights. "But they're still trying to find out the cause of that terrible crash a fortnight ago and until they succeed, they'll remain grounded."

Lightman assured him that he was accustomed to conventional jet aircraft and that first class was fine with him.

"Well, we'll see that you have some rest before your meeting tomorrow."

"It's still set for four?"

"Yes, I've checked with Dr. Martindale's secretary. Everything is on."

Lightman kept waiting for a hint as to what exactly he could expect to happen at this meeting, thinking he might discover how well-founded his suspicions were. But Cage mentioned nothing more about it, preferring to ramble on about the unusually hot weather London was experiencing and how it compared to Boston's.

When Cage momentarily fell silent Lightman asked him what it was that he did for Martindale.

"You could say that I'm something of a coordinator for Mayfair House. It's my job to take care of his finances and many of the business affairs he has no time for. But it goes further than that; the two of us enjoy a close friendship and so, inevitably over the years, my responsibilities have expanded to include practically anything Dr. Martindale wants me to do. But please, Dr. Lightman, I'd be interested in learning something about the operations of your own laboratory."

He seemed to mean it sincerely, conveniently ignoring the irony inherent in his words. Without the grant money there would be no operations of his laboratory to speak of. Nonetheless he thought he acquitted himself competently enough, describing the nature of the experiments he was working on and the limited success of a vaccine undergoing trial use. But he was cautious not to go into detail, saying no more than wasn't public knowledge. It was as if he were being grilled by a cop: anything he said might be used against him.

As they continued down the A-1 into London Lightman became gradually aware of how hazy it was getting. The sun, shining so brightly when he'd gotten off the plane, was now a pale shadow of itself. He'd been on this route many times before but nothing he observed through the Mercedes' windows was recognizable. Any landmarks he might have identified were blotted out; it was as if the whole world were smudged in charcoal.

"It surprises me how bad the smog is," Lightman said. "I thought things had gotten better since I was last here."

"Oh no, my good man, this isn't smog—it's smoke you're seeing. The smoke from the riots."

"The riots?"

Had Lightman not been so caught up in acquainting himself with the facts (such as they were) of Martindale's life he might have had a chance to read a newspaper. His life was so hectic lately that he hadn't kept up with the news.

Cage was surprised he hadn't heard. "It's particularly bad in the East End. The minorities, you understand. I don't know what they say over in the States, but you might not be aware of the recent tide of illegals."

Lightman had to admit that he wasn't.

"Just like you Yanks had a problem with Mexicans slipping over the border, we're beginning to experience the same phenomenon. Years ago it became apparent that we couldn't possibly afford to play host to all the Indians and Ugandans and Kenyans and Jamaicans who held a Commonwealth passport. There are limits to generosity when your own people are unemployed. But that didn't stop them. And there's evidence that certain elements are actively engaged in smuggling these people into the British Isles. It's gotten beyond the point where the authorities can cope with them. They pack into the slums and naturally they reproduce like mad. It builds up into a pressure cooker. Inevitably you have riots."

"And smoke."

"Yes, and smoke."

Lightman asked him what elements exactly he was referring to.

"No one is certain. Naturally there are many theories. I myself would hazard an opinion that the people responsible are radicals whose interest is in fomenting dissension and ultimately bringing down the government. All figures of authority are their targets. Why do you think there's such an outcry to restore the death penalty? Prison will no longer do the trick."

Lightman could tell that, if allowed to go on much longer, Cage would turn vehement. He was already red in the face, fired up with rage. Lightman tried to swerve him from the course he seemed bent on.

"But would you say that it's safe to go out at night? Just for a walk, I mean."

"Absolutely, absolutely. You mustn't think that our government will permit these upheavals to disrupt life for the rest of us. You will discover the streets of London to be as safe as they ever were."

It wasn't the thought of taking a stroll after dark that disturbed him so much; rather, the possibility that the smoke might not lift for the duration of his stay and he would leave London without really ever getting a good look at it.

As they approached Buckingham Palace Lightman observed dozens of police along the streets. London was beginning to take on the feeling of an armed camp.

Just before they arrived in front of the Grosvenor, Cage turned to Lightman and said, "There's one more thing that I am obliged to tell you."

His tone suggested that something serious was on his mind that he'd been saving the whole time they were driving in from Heathrow.

"I understand that when you were in Hong Kong last month you were introduced to a certain Bill Wellington."

"We exchanged a few words, that's all," Lightman said cautiously.

"I must warn you, Dr. Lightman, that this individual is a troublemaker. His conduct has been so unprofessional that we have felt it necessary to terminate his services. I can't tell you how many needless hours have been spent by our researchers trying to rectify the mistakes he made in his experiments. He has gotten it into his head that Dr. Martindale is some sort of monster. But the truth of the matter is altogether different, and if you don't believe me, you are free to talk with any of our researchers."

He lowered his voice as if he were fearful that the driver might overhear. "I suspect that somehow Wellington got on the subject of the women he believes Dr. Martindale has—" He was at a momentary loss for words. Or just one word actually. "That Dr. Martindale has conquered. Of course, it's so much rubbish. If you are to take this lunatic's word for it, Dr. Martindale's love affairs would rival Casanova's. Did Wellington bring this up with you, this matter of the women?"

"I don't think it would be fair of me to discuss what we talked about."

"Ah, I thought so." Lightman's demurral only served to confirm what Cage suspected. "You see, Wellington, I'm afraid, is madly—and hopelessly—in love with a woman who shall remain nameless. But the truth is that this woman and Dr. Martindale have been seeing a bit of one another."

Diana, Lightman thought. It would have to be Diana.

"The plain fact of the matter is that Wellington is jealous. Not only of this woman but of everything that Dr. Martindale has achieved: his success, his renown, his celebrity. As I'm sure you know from your own experience, when a man feels so inferior, so frustrated in his attempts to get to the top of his field, he often lashes out blindly, neglecting to consider the consequences. And so Wellington's gone about making all sorts of wild, fanciful accusations, vindictively blaming Martindale for his own failures. We kept him on as long as we could at Mayfair House. At one time, as he probably told you, the two were on good terms. Dr. Martindale on several occasions suggested that Wellington ought to seek help. There's no question in my mind that the man is suffering from severe mental illness. But of course one can't simply allow a man to spread slander and calumnies because he is deeply disturbed. When he repeatedly rebuffed us and refused to accept help we were forced to dismiss him. There are also questions of certain financial irregularities that we are currently investigating. And it is likely that Dr. Martindale's solicitor will institute a suit against him for breach of contract. If this man persists in his madness then we shall have no other recourse but to pursue legal remedies."

Recalling that Wellington had expressed fear that he might be murdered, Cage's threat to invoke the law for redress seemed comparatively mild.

Lightman didn't know who to believe. He needed to talk to Wellington—if he could get in touch with him—before he ventured a guess as to where the truth might lie.

"You will promise me that if this man tries to contact you you won't have anything to do with him?"

Without hesitating Lightman said that he'd steer as clear

of him as he could. "Besides," he added, "I have no business with Dr. Wellington."

Cage shot him a questioning look but said nothing more until they were in front of the Grosvenor and it was time to say good-bye.

"Tomorrow at three please be waiting in the lobby and my driver will come to pick you up. If there's anything you need in the meantime, feel free to ring me up at Mayfair House. They'll know how to put you in touch with me in the event I'm not there."

Lightman watched the Mercedes until it was sucked into the haze and disappeared from sight.

For generations the Grosvenor had been popular with people in transit since its back door gave way to Victoria Station. It was a particular favorite of people with departure times early in the morning who wanted to grab as much extra sleep as they possibly could. It was from Victoria that the boat train left for Calais. And in the 1920's and 30's it was from Victoria that colonials began the long, sometimes hazardous journey that would take them through Russia and China to the crown colony of Hong Kong. How many adventures were begun there, embarked upon in high spirits or in desperation, flight being the only alternative left? How many of those envisioning the fortune they would attain once they reached their destination had never arrived? Such places inspired Lightman; he had to confess that he himself harbored a fantasy of one day cutting loose and going. And it was the going that mattered, not the getting there. Wherever there was.

Wellington had given Lightman his home number and it was this that he tried as soon as he'd settled in his room.

"Who did you say this was?" Wellington asked as soon as Lightman identified himself. Lightman reminded him how they'd met.

"Oh, Dr. Lightman, what a pleasure to hear from you. Where are you calling from?"

"Here, in London, I just got in."

"Do you think you could meet me? I can't talk over the phone. I believe it might be tapped."

Perhaps, after all, there was something to what Cage had said. The man might be a paranoid schizophrenic, his madness heightened by jealousy and a desire for revenge.

"I'm sure I could arrange it."

"Good. Listen, there's a pub just across the street from the Paddington underground station called the Bull and Cross. Do you think you could meet me there in, say, forty minutes?"

Lightman wasn't certain about forty minutes, but the most he could prevail on Wellington to give him was an hour. It was as though he had so little time to spare that he was obliged to ration it out, minute by minute.

A copy of the *Mirror* was gripped in the callused hands of the man who sat next to Lightman on the train. The seminude lass on page four was an eyeful but what captured Lightman's attention more was the headline TRAM RIDE TO DEATH. Underneath it read "Six Struck Down in Orkney Isle." A picture of a tram—presumably the one on which the six fatalities had occurred—occupied whatever of the front page that the headlines didn't.

Noticing the intensity of Lightman's stare the man put down his paper and said, "You a Yank, right? I can spot 'em right off." Glancing at the headline he ventured his opinion that it was entirely natural that people would be dropping like flies. "Happens all the time, only you never hear of it. Here you have these chaps on their way to work." He opened to an inside page. "They take the tram every morning, same time, think nothing of it. Suddenly this one chap keels over. Just like that. Blimey if the chap sitting ahead of him doesn't do the same thing. Before you know it, a third chap's a gonner. Imagine. Odd thing about it was that none of them was sick before they keeled over. One minute you're feeling right as rain, the next you're dead. Would you believe it? The bloody tram takes half an hour to get where it's going and five chaps get on don't get off. The sixth's the conductor. Just when he's going about getting the bodies of his passengers off, blimey if he isn't a gonner too."

"It says all that in there?"

"You can take a look at it if you want."

The story obviously had made quite a vivid impression on the man; his account of it turned out to be fairly accurate. The only thing missing from the story was the most crucial element of all: an explanation. The *Mirror*'s unidentified "special correspondent" said that authorities on the island, which was located off the northwestern coast of Scotland, were still investigating "this bizarre and mysterious illness." Their tentative conclusion was that it was food poisoning.

But it didn't sound that way to Lightman. Food poisoning wouldn't be so insidious in its onset; the victims would have experienced nausea or cramps or severe diarrhea if it were a result of salmonella, for instance. A more virulent infectious agent might be at work, but what?

When he got off and scanned the other dailies at a kiosk by the tube station he failed to find any mention of this incident at all. The *Mirror* was full of sensational stories —about the possibility of a royal divorce, about an actress's claim to be in communication with the spirits of Rock Hudson and Andy Warhol—and it was possible that nothing like this tram ride to death had happened at all.

Lightman's reunion with Wellington at the Bull and Cross was anything but auspicious. No sooner had Lightman entered the pub than Wellington seemed to materialize out of nowhere. Rather than so much as say hello, he grabbed Lightman by the arm and steered him back onto the street. "Not safe here," he muttered. "There's another pub a couple of blocks away where we can talk without anyone seeing us."

Lightman was too tired for this cloak-and-dagger business. "Is all this really necessary?"

Wellington looked pained by the question. "Do you think I'd go to this trouble if it wasn't?"

The pub Wellington preferred might have been safer, but it was also dull. The atmosphere seemed to consist entirely of dust; it was an allergist's nightmare. No one sitting at the bar looked to be under the age of sixty.

Wellington bought them each a pint of ale and, never once inquiring as to what purpose Lightman might have had in coming to London, began to give his version of the events that led to his dismissal from Mayfair House. "They knew I was getting closer, they knew that if they didn't let me go I would prove that those specimens were lifted, that they were never received at the World Influenza Centre."

He was flushed and breathless. His appearance gave no reassurance of his sanity, either; he was disheveled and at least two days of stubble had collected on his face. "But the theft, the fraud, that's the least of it. Listen to me, I don't know what Patrick means to do, but I promise you it'll happen quickly. We have to do something."

Lightman sat stiffly, deliberating as to whether he should indulge Wellington further or excuse himself and leave.

"You see this?"

A magnetic card was cupped in the palm of his hand.

"What is it?"

"It is a card that I can use to gain access into Martindale's private laboratories."

"I thought you told me you couldn't get into them before."

"That was before. I . . . well, I pinched this card. The person it belongs to is still out of town so I'm sure they don't know it's missing yet. But it has to be used before Thursday when he'll be back. Listen, it struck me just after you called that tonight would be the absolutely perfect time to go in. I think it's a terrific stroke of luck that you're here. You'll be able to see for yourself that I've been telling you the truth." Evidently he sensed Lightman's growing doubt because he rushed on, not allowing him to get in a single word. "It won't take but a few minutes. We'll draw ten cc's of blood from the infected animals and run tests on it elsewhere, find out just what viral strain Patrick inoculated them with."

His scheme sounded crazy and Lightman wanted no part of it, and he said so.

He expected Wellington to react badly, but instead the researcher just fixed him with a steady gaze. "I don't owe you anything, do I?"

Lightman said no, not that he knew of.

"You admit that what I am saying, mad as it might seem, could turn out to be true?"

Lightman couldn't argue with that.

"You agree then that it is possible that the specimens were switched and that Patrick now has possession of them?"

"Wait a minute, Bill. Even supposing that those animals have been injected with the same virus that I was investigating in Alaska, how do you think you're going to prove it?"

"The proof is in the data. And that data has to be in that laboratory. The one I mean to get into tonight—with or without you."

There was no uncertainty in his voice. All doubt, any allowances for scenarios other than what he'd conceived were banished from his mind. Wellington, Lightman decided, wasn't over the edge, but he was perilously close to it.

"Listen to me, it is up to you what you want to do. But don't expect me to take the risk alone and then provide you with the blood samples afterwards."

"I understand your position." Lightman was keeping his voice purposefully neutral, anxious not to excite him more than he was already.

"You won't do it, will you?" Now he was sounding disappointed.

"What would have happened if I hadn't called you? You'd have gone it alone anyway, right?"

"But that's not the point, is it? You *are* here and you won't help me."

Lightman didn't like being pressed to the wall this way, but he couldn't quite let it go. A nagging sense that Wellington was onto something persisted.

Then a smile, a very unsettling smile, came to Wellington's lips. He said, "I heard."

"Excuse me?"

"I heard what happened to you with that grant money."

Christ, Lightman thought, he might as well have released the news to the press at this rate.

"You can be bloody sure it was Patrick who fucked it up for you. It wouldn't be the first time he's done something like that. That's why you're here in London, isn't it?"

No wonder he hadn't asked at the outset. Lightman let him go on without speaking.

"I assume that you were met at the airport by that old pederast Winston Cage. Don't give me that look. It's true, ask anybody. If it weren't for Patrick's protection they would have run him in long ago because of his predilection for prepubescent flesh. We all have our weaknesses, I know, but his, if you don't mind my saying, is a particularly nasty one, don't you think?"

Yes, Lightman was thinking, he should have had that nap; it would make all this much easier to take.

"What are you going to tell Patrick when you meet? That you'll do nothing to cast any aspersions on his reputation, that you're grievously sorry if you offended him in any way by pressing ahead with your inquiry as to the fate of the specimens, and would he please consider putting in a kind word with the review board about your grant, and thank you very much, it's been a pleasure?"

Actually, Lightman had no idea what he was going to

say, but he knew that if it resembled to any degree the words Wellington just uttered he'd leave London without a shred of integrity intact.

"Think of it, John, if you help me, if we do find those specimens in that laboratory, you'll have some leverage, you won't have to go on bended knees to Patrick for your money. You can bargain with the bastard. Right now what have you got?"

Lightman was silent. He was trying to think, but he knew the answer to Wellington's question already. He had nothing.

"Listen to me, make no mistake about it, Patrick and Winston are vicious, predatory people. If you don't fight back, if you don't use all the ammunition you can get ahold of, you're fucked. And that is the Lord's honest truth. Look at me. Look what they've done to me."

For a moment Lightman thought Wellington might break into tears. He did not. "So what do you say?" he asked. "Are you with me on this or not?"

NINE

The sky held an eerie lavender glow, a spectral light. It was from the fires burning in the East End she was sure. Even in Hampstead, which was miles from the districts of Wapping and Limehouse where the riots were taking place, she could hear the sirens of the police cars and ambulances building into a mournful crescendo, dying out and then starting all over again. From time to time she could make out what she believed must be explosions or the crackle of gunfire, but they might only have been her imagination.

Maybe it just sounded worse than it was. The BBC reports
and the newspaper accounts were often so confusing. What
the *Sun* called a full-scale insurrection the *Telegraph*
dubbed violent clashes while the *Times* settled for civil disorder.

At first she didn't hear the phone ringing; and then when
she did, it seemed to be coming from outside her flat like
all the other sounds this early June night—no, morning.
Twelve-ten by the digital clock.

Answering it she heard on the other end a man's harsh,
whispering voice. It took her a moment to realize it was
Patrick.

"What is it?" She had never heard him sound like this
before.

"I need you, I need to see you." This desperation was so
new to her she didn't know how to react. It had her scared.
"Listen, Diana, something tonight . . ."

"Something tonight what?"

"Happened tonight. Jesus God, it wasn't supposed to,
shouldn't have. You must believe me."

"Patrick, I don't know what you're talking about. What
are you trying to tell me?"

But he wouldn't answer her. "You have to come, please,
it is absolutely necessary that you be with me tonight."

"Where are you?"

"Home."

"Home?" Home could be any one of three or four different places.

"Kensington."

Kensington was where he lived with his wife and family;
she wasn't going there. "I can't, Patrick, I just can't." And
then she held the phone away from her so that his voice
grew more and more distant. And that gave her further
courage to hang up.

But she couldn't get the sound of his voice out of her
mind, nor ignore the vehemence of his appeal. Impossible
to let it rest there; her conscience wouldn't allow it. While

she couldn't face the thought of confronting his family to-night, there was one person she was certain who could.

Winston Cage was reading in bed, *The Lives of the Saints* perched on his lap, when the call came.

He was surprised to hear from Diana, at this late hour or at any time. Even when she was in Patrick's company they seldom communicated.

"I just heard from Patrick," she said.

This was puzzling. Why should she be ringing him up to inform him of this? It was her business.

"He sounds in a bad way, Winston. He's at his home in Kensington. I don't know what happened to him, but you've got to go to him."

"Diana, I'm sure that there's nothing that I can do."

"You must. You're his friend, he trusts you. I can't go to him."

"But why on earth not?"

"Rachael, for one."

Patrick's wife. Now that was a bit sticky. "Yes, I can understand your position. Are you certain it's as serious as all that?"

"I've never heard him worse."

Grudgingly Cage agreed to see what the matter was.

As unusual as Diana had made Martindale's appeal sound, what struck Cage most was that Patrick wanted to see her at the Kensington address.

To Cage's knowledge, Patrick owned three homes, the London residence, the country home outside Warwick and another in Switzerland. But it was seldom, if ever, that anyone was invited to his London residence. Cage, who was one of Martindale's closest associates, had been there twice. And only once had he the opportunity to meet his family, his wife, Rachael, and his two young children, Edward and Marisa. They were a perfectly presentable family, Cage had thought at the time, and he couldn't understand why Patrick was so disposed to keeping them out of the way, almost hidden, as if they constituted an embarrassment—a threat to the image he wished to leave in people's minds. It was obvious to Cage that Rachael was entirely subservient to her husband, content to live in his shadow; he could not recall anything she said the whole hour he was in her company. The children, too, appeared to be docile, desiring nothing but to please their father.

It was only later that he began to get a glimmer of why Patrick wanted his family so isolated, why he rarely referred to them in conversation.

It had to do with his women. The man's obsessive desire for them baffled Cage, who could remain for years enraptured over one beautiful youth he could never hope to win. Why did he need so many of them? Even when it was Diana whom he was in love with, the temptation of beauty available elsewhere was something he could never bring himself to resist. Aside from the need he had for beauty in his women, he also expected that their backgrounds be socially acceptable. Statuesque, blue-blooded women delighted him; they were his ornaments, his prizes.

But somehow, for appearance sake, possibly out of guilt or even a mysterious love that persisted against every effort he made to shake it, he remained married, and at rare intervals returned to the hearth to resume his customary role as pater familias. Still, there was little question that his family constituted an embarrassment, an obstacle that must be shunted out of the way lest it intrude on his work and his affairs.

Yet Cage did not think it was some affair of the heart that had Martindale so distraught tonight. The more he thought about it, the more convinced he became that it had nothing to do with Diana. He wanted her with him to comfort him. Maybe her fears were groundless and he'd sent his family away. It occurred to Cage that, if he was as desperate as Diana said, then it would be because of Wellington and Lightman. They were the ones responsible for causing him so much anguish and pain.

Of course, there could be no other explanation: Patrick was afraid that events had gotten beyond him, that together Lightman and the renegade researcher would find a way to do him great harm. Cage resolved that this must not be allowed to happen. All the work they had done in building up Mayfair House could not be destroyed at the hands of men driven by an irrational vendetta.

Half an hour later Cage was standing in front of the door to Martindale's house, two blocks from Edwardes Square. No lights that he could see were on in the house. For the first time it occurred to him that something was truly wrong. The sight of so many darkened windows disturbed him. But why should anyone be awake now? He'd known of instances where Patrick would burst into a frenzied rage, then minutes later act as though nothing had happened. It was possible that, having made his importuning call, he'd decided to go to sleep and wait until morning to deal with whatever the problem was. If no one responded to the bell, Cage thought, he would go home.

But it took him several long moments before he could bring himself even to do as much as that.

The bell was jarringly loud—or so it seemed in the silence of Kensington. But it failed to produce any response. No sound, no light flashing on in one of the upstairs windows where Patrick and his wife maintained their bedrooms.

He rang again.

Nothing.

He was about to leave when he was struck by the thought that it might be a medical emergency. He imagined Patrick lying helpless in bed, unable to get to the door.

He pressed the bell a third time. Silence.

He pushed against the door, thinking that someone might have left it open for him. But it was securely locked.

Stepping away from the house he cupped his hands and hollered up toward the second floor. A light came on, but not in the Martindale home. A woman pressed her face to the window of a neighboring house and threw him an indignant look. If he persisted in shouting, he knew, he would find himself being arrested for creating a disturbance.

He started walking alongside the house, taking a path lined with rosebushes and hedges trained by generations of gardeners. Around in back there was a second entrance used to provide access to the garden. It smelled like perfume with all the mint and jasmine that Cage realized must be planted in it.

Through the leaves of the century-old oak tree, in whose shadow the whole house stood, Cage could see the sky filling with a dull predawn light.

But that was all the light there was. The rear of the house was just as dark as the front had been.

With no bell to ring at this door Cage knocked. Expecting no response he wasn't surprised to receive none.

He saw now that the door was ajar.

Entering he called out, "Hello! Patrick? Rachael? Is anybody here?"

He thought he heard voices—a voice, anyhow. But he couldn't be certain.

After a moment's hesitation he switched on the light. A scrubbed, spanking white kitchen came into view. He ventured further. There was, he noticed, a peculiar, faintly medicinal smell he was unable to identify. Now he was sure he heard a voice, a man's voice.

"Patrick! Is that you?" he called out again.

But there was no reply.

When the light from the kitchen was no longer sufficient to find his way into the rest of the house he searched for another light switch. But in the darkness it was difficult. His hand moved along the wall without any luck.

"Some say ask, some say given," he heard—or thought he did at any rate. It was definitely not Patrick's voice, though.

Inching his way down a corridor he approached the living room. Even in the absence of much light he was beginning to orient himself. He could just about make out the front door at the end of the corridor. The ticking his ears registered would have to be coming from the antique Victorian grandfather clock.

"Some say come and be not driven. Some say seek and some say find," he heard now.

A pale orange light shone on the Persian rug as he came nearer the front door. Its source, he observed, was a table lamp with a tassled shade left burning in the living room off to his left.

"Some say find, some say leave things behind."

What caught his eye first as he stepped into the living room was the wall space over the mantel. It took him a moment to absorb the sight that greeted him.

This part of the wall was paler than the area surrounding it, and no wonder: for so long as Patrick had owned the house, the portrait of Alfonso the something, long-dead king of Spain, as rendered by the magnificent Velásquez, had hung there. And it was gone.

Now, with its removal, was revealed the wall safe, and that was gaping open like a wound, dark and hollow inside. It had been Patrick's idea of a joke: to conceal a safe with a painting worth more than all the jewelry and cash that he could ever think to store in the safe itself.

The security alarm should have gone off. The painting was wired, the safe was wired; for that matter, the very doors of the house were wired. But if the alarm had gone off there was no sign of it; the police obviously hadn't been there in response. No, it was evident that somebody, acting on inside knowledge, had foiled the system before or immediately after the break-in.

Wellington, he thought. It would have to be Wellington. He'd been inside the house in the past, he was cunning enough, and vengeful enough, to do this thing.

"Some say come back again."

The sound of the idiotic voice drew Cage's attention back. A compact disc player, blazing with as many colored lights as a Christmas tree, was what was producing the voice, he saw. He went and turned it off, unable to endure it an instant longer.

Only then did he become conscious that he wasn't alone in the room. Turning, he looked to the end of the room, by the open bay window.

Rachael was settled in the olive green armchair. Edward was seated on one side of her, on the floor, his head buried in a pop-up book while Marisa, stretched out on the couch on the other side, was studying a half-finished sketch she'd made on manila paper from a box of worn pastels.

"I'm so sorry," he sputtered, "I didn't mean to—"

Rachael was staring directly at him, her expression unwavering. Her hair was pulled back, giving her the look of Victorian women Cage had seen in daguerreotype photos, severe and indomitable and lost in some unfathomable sadness. The dress she was wearing was silk and lace; it was a dress she might have worn to her wedding.

"Rachael, it's me, Winston Cage," he said, approaching her.

There was no reaction. The children, each as formally dressed as their mother, didn't even raise their eyes.

He felt very cold although the air coming in through the open window could not completely account for it. He snapped on another lamp to see better.

Then, knowing what he would find out but needing to be sure, he reached forward and touched Rachael's hand. And then he looked hard into her eyes.

It was then that her lips started to move and he thought for a moment that his initial impression was mistaken and that she was about to speak. But that wasn't it at all. Her lips parted not to utter a word but to permit a maggot to climb out.

TEN

Lightman wasn't sure what he'd expected Mayfair House to be, although he held a vague picture in his mind of an impressive piece of Georgian or Edwardian architecture discreetly set in among a row of elegant homes with drawn curtains in every window. But the reality turned out to be very much at odds with this image. Rather than one building there were several, nine or ten it looked like, each about three stories, gathered around a manicured lawn that even now, well after midnight, was being sprayed with jets of water from sprinklers embedded in the earth. Quartered in these various buildings, according to Wellington, was the main clinic, a chronic care unit, an intensive care and cardiac unit, several laboratories, a library, a movie theater for documentaries and demonstration films, a small movie and video studio for producing those documentaries, and the auxiliary facilities required for keeping the whole enterprise running. It was meant to be Patrick Martindale's living monument.

In addition, there were guest houses located in the blocks nearby where friends of Martindale's, visiting specialists, VIP's and families of patients could be put up.

"I think that if Patrick had his way he'd make this into a city within a city, then wall it off," Wellington said.

Now there wasn't any wall, only hedgerows and a guardhouse.

Although Lightman expected trouble the guard waved Wellington right through. "We're old friends," Wellington explained. "In any case, I still have access to the library, so it isn't as if I don't have a right to be here."

Wellington drove his beat up '91 Ford Panther along a macadam that skirted the complex and ended in a vast parking lot bathed in the glare of solar lights.

They had a considerable distance to walk before they got to the building housing the lab where Wellington believed Martindale was conducting his clandestine experiments.

They approached by way of the rear of the lab. Black cylinders, all marked in white MAYHOUSE, stood like sentries against the stone wall, their purpose as mysterious to Wellington as they were to Lightman. "They used to contain some sort of gas under pressure, but I don't know what," he said.

Along the top of the building Lightman noted an intriguing configuration of pipes that reminded him of nothing so much as the internal mechanism of a church organ. A door with a glass eye was facing them.

Wellington slid his stolen card through a slot immediately beneath the eye. It snapped back a second later, causing Lightman to think that maybe it hadn't worked.

But then the door yielded to the pressure Wellington applied and they entered.

A corridor led as far as he could see to another door that, in almost every respect, resembled the one they had just come through.

The only sound they could hear, apart from the careful cadence of their own feet, was the constant drone of air being churned out by the ventilating system.

"It's down this way, off to the left."

Lightman tried to remain composed, though there was no way of fighting back the anxiety he'd been feeling since he arrived in London.

"Here," said Wellington. "This door."

He didn't seem afraid at all. But rather than reassuring him, Wellington's seeming nonchalance alarmed Lightman.

Again Wellington employed the magnetic card to gain admittance, although in this case he was obliged to pick out a sequence of five tones from a keypad set into the wall. It was some sort of code, Lightman assumed. He asked Wellington how he'd managed to obtain it in addition to the card.

"It was in the same desk drawer," Wellington shot back. Such details clearly were not on his mind now.

"Seems a bit careless to me."

Wellington ignored him, stepping into the room and flipping on the switch for the overhead light. The light didn't go on.

"That's funny." He tried it again.

From over his shoulder all Lightman could see of the lab were cages of mice and rabbits stacked against the far wall. There was a great deal of gibbering and screeching that Lightman suspected was a response to their intrusion.

"Goddamn light, what the hell's wrong with it?"

Wellington advanced farther into the lab, Lightman a few paces behind him.

"Would you shut the door, please?"

As Lightman did the darkness took over completely. They were shadows among shadows. Lightman could distinguish only eyes that shone like phosphorous and bared teeth.

It was like going into a movie theater. Gradually the eyes adjusted. Suddenly Wellington cried out, "I see them!"

And Lightman, too, saw them: six monkeys, their scrawny forms pressed up against the bars of their cages, hardly moving, maybe not even alive.

As Wellington stepped closer to their cages, he produced a syringe he'd brought along to extract the blood. Lightman stood by, straining his eyes, that were never the best in ordinary circumstances let alone in the dark, to see if there was any cabinet or desk where records of ongoing experiments might be kept. He wasn't having any luck.

Before Wellington could put his hands on the cage door it sprang open and one of the monkeys leaped out. It hurled itself against Wellington with such terrific force that it nearly toppled him over. Before Lightman could fully comprehend what was happening, the creature buried its teeth in Wellington's face, his neck, his shoulder, clinging to him ferociously, resisting every clumsy attempt Wellington was making to throw it off him.

He was reeling back, shouting, grabbing at the back of the monkey but succeeding only in pulling out great tufts of hair. Blood was racing down his face, he was shouting, screaming in agony. Lightman groped for something, anything he could find with which to dislodge the animal. The other monkeys were crying out, producing a fitful babble punctuated by shrieks that Lightman was sure must soon reach the ears of a security guard and bring him running.

His hands found nothing useful to employ against the beast, and he couldn't very well try to pull it off, not without endangering himself. It was then that his eyes fell on the syringe that had dropped out of Wellington's hand. He scooped it up.

Then he drove it into the animal's hide again and again, blindly, hoping that the pain would loosen its grip. A scream tore from its throat, but rather than letting go it dug its teeth and claws in deeper, causing Wellington to cry out. Lightman this time aimed for the neck, plunging the needle in through skin, through muscle, until it bent and broke against the bone of the spinal cord.

That was all that was needed. The monkey convulsed and slipped to the floor, the needle still embedded in its neck, dead.

There was something caught between its teeth, Lightman saw, only belatedly realizing that it was a sliver of Wellington's flesh.

His hands pressed up against his wounds to staunch the bleeding. Wellington was on his knees, retching.

"We have to get you out of here, we have to get you

help," Lightman was saying, doubtful that Wellington heard him.

Though Wellington was taller than he, he didn't weigh so much that Lightman found him an extraordinary burden. The trouble was that Wellington didn't want to move; he was too lost in pain and shock to respond. Lightman had to force him, taking hold of his arms and propelling him out the door, leaving a zigzagging trail of blood in their wake.

The corridor was as empty as before. But in the fluorescent glare Wellington looked more wretched than Lightman had imagined. There was no telling exactly where the blood was coming from, which puncture wounds the deranged simian had produced.

"Let's get you to the clinic, tell me where the clinic is," Lightman was shouting in an attempt to elicit some response from the man.

And he did—but not the response he anticipated.

"No, not the clinic! Don't take me there!"

"But we're close by, we've got to get you help."

Wellington was having none of it. "No, fuck no! Not there, get me out of here. I'll be all right, but get me away from this fucking place."

Taking Lightman unawares he pulled away, snarling, clearly having decided to make it without any aid. He kept shaking his head back and forth so that blood flew off of him, as if this might help him get more of a grip on himself. His face, Lightman now saw, was a mass of gouges and cuts. One eye was closed.

"All right, we'll get out of here."

In his condition there was no sense in arguing. The important thing was to treat the wounds and address the trauma.

Wellington began to lurch and stagger in the direction of the exit. Lightman kept abreast of him. "Where do you want to go to?"

"The car, the car," Wellington replied, spitting blood out

with his words. There was a good chunk of his lower lip missing.

"Yes, but once we get to the car, where should I take you? Where the hell's the nearest hospital?"

They reached the exit, opened the door, stepped out into the night. God, Lightman thought, if there was one thing to be grateful for it was that they hadn't—so far—been stopped by security personnel.

It seemed to take forever to reach the car. Wellington returned to his pain and wouldn't speak a word. Lightman suspected that the pain was growing worse now that the initial numbness of shock was wearing off; the nerves were coming alive again.

Lightman remembered the handkerchief he carried and handed it to Wellington. It was virtually useless, soon so saturated that he discarded it.

Feeling in his pockets to see if he might have another Lightman realized his watch—the gold pocket watch Stephanie had given him for his fortieth birthday, her final gift to him—was gone.

Maybe he'd left it back at his hotel. No, he realized, he'd taken it with him. It must have fallen out. There was no going back for it. It was lost now. This night kept getting worse, there seemed to be no redemption at all in it.

At last they were at the car. Locked.

"The keys! Give me the keys!"

Wellington looked at him in confusion.

"You can't drive, goddamnit, give me the goddamn keys!"

Now he understood. He fumbled in his pockets and found them. They were all bloody when he handed them over.

As soon as Lightman was behind the wheel and turning on the ignition he said as forcefully as he knew how, "Now which hospital are we going to? Tell me where we're going!"

Wellington muttered something Lightman didn't catch. "What was that?"

"I said I'm making a mess of the upholstery."

Lightman couldn't believe this. "Would you tell me where the hell you want me to take you or I'll leave you here to fend for yourself."

Really, he was beyond thinking of the ramifications of what had just happened. He just needed to get away from this place, and he'd do it with or without Wellington.

"Diana's, I want you to take me to Diana's."

"Diana's? You need to get to an emergency room, Bill, somebody has to look at those wounds."

"Be all right, do what I say, take me to Diana's . . . no fucking emergency room."

Lightman decided not to waste any more time arguing with the man. "You want to go to Diana's, I'll take you there, but you're making a terrible mistake, I'm warning you."

"Diana's!" Wellington repeated angrily.

"All right, but you're going to have to tell me how to get there."

ELEVEN

Winston Cage couldn't stop to reflect on the strange and macabre sight he'd just seen. His mind wouldn't absorb it. Yet he knew he had to act, and act immediately. How the deaths had occurred, why Patrick's family was dressed up as if for some bizarre formal occasion (though maybe death was as formal an occasion as any) were questions that Cage refused to contemplate—not now. But he was convinced that somehow the deaths and the theft of the Velásquez and the contents of the wall safe must all be related. And though the connection would not form coherently in his mind, he was certain that in some way Wellington must be involved. Nor would it come as a surprise to him if the American, Lightman, had something to do with this. No longer was he quite so ready to discount Patrick's dark hints that he was the victim of a conspiracy.

His thoughts now turned to money. No one took his fiduciary responsibilities more seriously than Winston Cage. It occurred to him that if Wellington was guilty of perpetrating this crime he was equally capable of looting the corporate assets of Mayfair House. All he would need to do would be to acquire the right password and code and he could break into the computer system with no more difficulty than he had Patrick's home. He needed to check the books without delay. At no point did he think of alerting the police to his discovery—not until he spoke to Patrick.

But where was Patrick?

There was little traffic at this bleak hour, but along the way Cage kept hearing sirens wailing close by. Curiously, though, he failed to see the vehicles which were making such a racket. Not that it mattered to him; his only thought was to get to Mayfair House, an objective he managed to achieve in record time.

The administrative area of Mayfair House was empty, as would be expected this early. Cage could always tell when he was alone, simply by attending to the hollow sound his footsteps made as he proceeded through the corridors toward the records room.

Once inside he seated himself before an advanced Digital console and logged himself in. In a flash the screen began to fill up with columns of figures. Money in, money out. Money denominated in pounds sterling, in U.S. dollars, in yen, deutsche marks, francs, lira and rand. To the uninitiated, these figures, together with all the names, dates, tax and invoice numbers necessary to identify each transaction would be as indecipherable as Sanskrit. But for Cage they were perfectly lucid, conveying a story with drama equal to any that Dickens or Hardy ever put to paper.

Time was needed to sort through the thousands of transactions and check the requisition forms and tax statements against the data that he had in front of him. But even a cursory glance told him that his suspicion was not unfounded: large amounts of money had been withdrawn from company accounts without the authorization of the comptroller. Certain order numbers didn't jibe or else there were duplicate charges—three centrifuges listed as purchased when only one was marked as received. Even Wellington, however cunning and devious he might be, could not have pulled off the fraud that was documented in these data. He would have been caught long ago. No, it could not be him—or not him alone.

It began to dawn on Cage that there was only one person who could have overridden the authority of the comptroller and misrepresented these withdrawals on the balance sheets—Patrick Martindale himself.

This realization horrified Cage. He didn't know what he should do, whom he should confide in. Now he was compelled to view the hideous spectacle he'd come from in an altogether new light. It might be that Wellington had nothing to do with it, that it was Patrick who'd dressed up his dead family and made a show of stealing from himself. But it didn't make sense. What Cage refused to consider altogether was the possibility that Patrick had had a hand in the deaths of Rachael and his children. That was madness beyond any he'd ever experienced. He had to take action, had to get word to the proper authorities. But who exactly were the proper authorities? He didn't want to go to the police prematurely, not without knowing what was going on. So he stayed where he was, his eyes fixed on the computer screen, his immobility accounted for by shock as much as it was by a desire to see just what magnitude of fraud was represented here.

But he was becoming rattled, making mistakes, pressing wrong keys, erasing the screen without meaning to and finding himself obliged to restore the whole system again. His hands were shaking—that was part of the problem.

No, it isn't going to work, he thought, not like this. He needed to rest, needed to collect his thoughts. It was impossible to work under such strain. He decided that he'd print out the entire body of data and take it home with him.

But he'd barely gotten the printer started when it abruptly stopped, emitting a piercing whine as it died. Naturally enough he assumed something had gone wrong with the printer, or else it wasn't reading the computer correctly. Though he knew nothing about the workings of such machinery he began tinkering with it, turning knobs and switches, resetting his program and repeatedly demanding answers from the computer as to why the printer had gone down. He was so preoccupied by the task of getting the printer back on line that he failed to appreciate the significance of the sound outside his door. Only when the door started to open did he react and then, of course, there was nothing he could do.

TWELVE

Wellington appeared to have lost consciousness somewhere during the drive to Hampstead. His head sagged against his chest and his breathing grew alarmingly rushed and shallow. Several times Lightman thought of taking him to an emergency room despite his wishes, but periodically Wellington would stir and sit bolt upright, demanding to know whether they were headed to Diana's as he'd insisted. As soon as he was satisfied that they were, he'd collapse back in his seat. Blood was getting all over the upholstery, and while Lightman couldn't see it too well he could detect by the smell how much there must be.

There seemed to be some flickering awareness in Wellington's mind, for how else could he have known when they arrived? He raised his eyes toward the building off to their right, muttering, "That's the one—third floor up. Take the lift." Then his eyes closed once more.

It was likely that Lightman had awakened Diana by ringing the bell; for several long moments there was no response. He paced impatiently back and forth on the marble floor off the vestibule, wondering what he would do with his charge should Diana fail to answer.

Then he heard her voice—or what he presumed was her voice since, through the intercom it sounded nothing like her—asking him to identify himself. There was a sharpness to her tone which Lightman took as further evidence that he'd disturbed her.

He had to repeat his name and then add that he had Wellington with him. "He's in trouble," was all the explanation he provided, afraid that if he told her the truth she might tell him to do the sensible thing and go to a hospital. Instead she said she'd be right down.

About half a minute later he heard the motors of the lift coming alive. It was only then that he became aware of an excitement gathering in his chest that had nothing to do with Wellington's plight and everything to do with seeing this woman again.

The memory Lightman had of Diana from their brief meeting scarcely coincided with the reality of the woman who stepped out of the lift. Wearing a silk robe, still cinching the sash, with her hair hanging loose along the slopes of her shoulders, and without any makeup on, she gave an entirely different impression than she had in Hong Kong.

Then he'd felt that she was out of his league, that she was one of those unobtainable fashion plates he was always spotting in magazines and on bus shelter ads for designer jeans and seductive lingerie. But while her beauty survived intact even in her obviously groggy and unkempt state, there was something more real, more accessible about her.

For an instant he wondered whether she recognized him. Then a smile played on her lips and she said, "Oh, it's you, Dr. Lightman, how curious to see you here."

"I'll explain later. I've got your friend Bill Wellington out in the car. He's in urgent need of attention."

She frowned, confused, and directed her eyes toward the car. "Is he hurt?"

"Yes, badly, I'm afraid. But he was adamant that he had to see you. There was nothing I could do to persuade him to go to a hospital."

Diana had already begun hurrying out the door and Lightman followed. "I can understand that. You see, he's gotten it into his head that if he goes to a hospital he'll never get out. It's because of Patrick, you see. He believes that there's no doctor he can trust. I may be the last person in London he feels he can talk to freely."

Before they could reach the Ford the door groaned open and Wellington lurched out, but too weak to maintain his balance, immediately toppled to the ground.

Together, Lightman and Diana hoisted him up. "My God, he's bleeding!" she said, unable to tear her eyes away from Wellington's mutilated face. "How in God's name did this happen?"

Wellington mumbled something.

"What did you say, Bill?" Diana asked.

But Lightman thought he knew. "He said that he thinks the door was deliberately left open."

Diana was completely mystified, but more concerned with getting Wellington inside than she was in discovering how he'd come to this pass.

"The door to the animal cage is what he means. We were set up is what he means," Lightman thought to add.

But Diana wasn't listening and probably wouldn't have understood what he was saying even if she had been.

Finally they got Wellington into the building. It was a shame to see blood on that beautiful marble floor but it couldn't be helped.

Even from her doorway Lightman could see that a considerable amount of money had been invested in the flat. It was the sheen of the furnishings, the way they glowed in the faint light that convinced him. It was the depth to which his feet sank in the carpet, it was the texture of the paint on the canvas of the Impressionist painting that was hanging on the wall facing him that convinced him.

"In here," Diana said, guiding him through the living room toward a room still in darkness. She turned on a lamp, revealing a bed. They got Wellington on it.

Diana went into an adjoining room. Lightman heard her dial a phone, pause and then ask for a doctor. Meanwhile he ripped open Wellington's shirt and started wiping the blood away with a damp sponge. It was astonishing to see how many gouges the monkey had taken out of his skin. Most of the wounds had been made by its claws, but the damage done by its incisors looked equally serious.

Diana returned with some pills cupped in her hand. "I don't know how effective they'll be. They're a brand of painkiller that I don't think is available in the States yet. They're not so strict about these things here, you know. I just spoke to my family doctor, he'll be over directly." She managed a smile. "Don't worry, so long as I'm here Bill will cooperate."

Wellington was slipping in and out of consciousness, alternately moaning and mumbling. But he was sufficiently alert to take the medicine Diana handed him.

It must have been a powerful painkiller indeed because suddenly the tension went out of his body and he fell asleep. From the sound of his breathing it seemed as restful as any he could have hoped for on this night.

While they waited for the physician, Dr. Rhinebeck, to come, the two had a drink—eighty-year-old brandy that Diana said she brought out only for special occasions, both good and bad. They sat across from each other at a table inlaid with a mosaic. There was a circus scene on the table, replete with gaudily adorned clowns, trapeze artists, lion tamers, jugglers, Indian elephants and contortionists. But descending into the midst of all this brightly colored chaos was a ghostly figure, his features indistinct but ominous, his presence unseen by the entertainers cavorting below. Diana caught Lightman staring at it.

"It was inspired by a Jewish legend that says when the Messiah comes it will be the clowns who'll be the first to meet him."

Legends like this appealed to Lightman.

"Where did you get ahold of a table like this?"

"I made it," she said.

"You did? I thought you were in the business of designing fashions."

"I am. But does one preclude the other? I've done lots of things in my life. Once I even used to act. I didn't do so badly at it, either. Only I didn't much care for the people you find in that line of business."

"I didn't mean to offend you." Once again he was feeling at sea with her, just as he had in Hong Kong.

"You didn't, I assure you. It takes a great deal more than that to offend me." There was no trace of self-mockery in her voice. "Now tell me again what happened at Mayfair House tonight."

Lightman had tried to explain earlier, but he realized he'd probably not been very clear.

"Oh, it wasn't you who were at fault," she said, "it's just that with a couple of brandies under my belt I think I'll better be able to get it through my head what you were trying to tell me."

Only then did it occur to Lightman that perhaps he ought not to have gone into such detail about what went on at Mayfair House. What exactly was her relationship with Martindale? Wellington obviously trusted her, but that didn't let him off the hook; it was possible that anything he said to her would find its way back to Martindale. If Martindale thought he'd willingly gone along with Wellington and broke into his lab, then there was absolutely no chance of their meeting working out tomorrow. The one thing Wellington had held out to him was the one thing that he needed and still didn't have: leverage.

But he was too exhausted, too confused by the events of the night to exercise the discretion he probably should have had with Diana. She was a good listener, an ardent listener, and God knew there weren't many of those around. Even the way she held her body, leaning in toward him with her head slightly tilted, gave him the impression that she was wholly involved in everything he had to say. He suspected that her memory might be a formidable one, possibly a dangerous one.

The arrival of Dr. Rhinebeck, a studious looking practitioner who was old enough to have delivered Diana, caused him to break off his narrative. Dr. Rhinebeck was like a throwback to an earlier era when patients liked to believe that their cure might lie within the magical bulging black bag he'd brought with him.

Apprised of the patient's condition, Dr. Rhinebeck naturally wanted to know how Wellington came to be savagely mauled by a monkey in the dead of night. "What was he doing, cleaning out the monkey house at the municipal zoo?" he asked irritably.

"No," Diana explained without explaining, "he was attacked by the monkey in a lab. He's a researcher, you see, it's his job to work with animals."

This answer seemed to satisfy the doctor. "I will have to treat him for tetanus and rabies."

Fortunately, a vaccine had been developed for rabies in

the past few years requiring only a single inoculation, sparing the patient the necessity of undergoing a torturous protocol of painful injections that took weeks to complete.

But Lightman realized that the real threat was from neither tetanus nor rabies. If the monkey had been infected, as Wellington believed it to be, then the question was whether it had transferred the infection. If Wellington had become infected, then it shouldn't be long until they found out. Wellington had just made himself, however unintentionally, into his own test subject.

By the time Dr. Rhinebeck had left it was after two and Lightman decided that he, too, should be on his way. He could barely keep his eyes open. "Is it possible for you to call a cab?" he asked Diana.

The request appeared to take her by surprise. "Would it be too much of an imposition on you if you stayed here tonight? You can have Nicholas' room. I'd rather not be here alone with Bill—in case anything should happen to him. But please don't feel obliged if you must go. I shouldn't want to do anything to upset your plans."

"No, it's fine with me, really. I wasn't looking forward to going back to my hotel at this hour."

In truth, he was gratified that she'd asked him to stay; he had the feeling that there was some kind of connection evolving between Diana and himself, and he didn't want to lose it quite so soon. In her presence he could, at least for a time, forget the troubles besetting him. Wellington's fate, even his own, didn't have half the hold on his mind that this woman did.

Nicholas' room was the only room in the flat still permeated with an unmistakably masculine feel to it. An oil portrait of the late Nicholas Cleary hung on the wall over a desk. If the painter had done any sort of competent job at all, Nicholas was a man of exquisite good looks with refined, beautifully sculpted features and eyes that were hungry for something unattainable. But there was also something otherworldly, even spectral, about the way the painter had captured him; it was almost as if some essential part of him had already escaped these earthly coils, leaving a pale husk of a body behind.

But there was a sense Lightman had that Nicholas wasn't altogether absent, even now. Lightman could imagine him walking in at any moment and demanding to know what this intruder was doing in his room. Everything—his books, his computer, his papers—looked much as they probably had on the day he'd died.

"You'll be all right in here?"

Lightman glanced up to see her standing in the doorway.

"I'll be fine."

"There's nothing else I can get you?"

Lightman assured her there was not. Then he noticed that her eyes were not on him but on the portrait.

"Do you know," she said, "that you're the first person to stay in this room since Nicholas died."

Lightman hadn't the faintest idea how he was supposed to respond to that. Maybe he wasn't supposed to.

He couldn't get to sleep. Tired as he was, it wouldn't come. Too much was going on in his mind. In the darkness there were sounds, some he could identify, some not. He could hear Wellington—faintly—letting out small cries from time to time just on the other side of the wall. He could hear Diana leaving the bathroom and padding on bare feet back to her own room. He could hear a sound resembling the hum that might come from an electric appliance.

He put on the night lamp and decided that if he was going to be awake he might as well do something useful with his time. Getting out of bed he stepped over to the bookcase in search of something promising to read. The books a man owned usually could tell a great deal about who he was. By the evidence on the shelves Nicholas had been an omnivorous reader; any collection that boasted of

Pliny the Younger, Lucretius, and Virgil along with Robert
Hughes, Aime Cesaire, Niehls Bohr, and Heidegger testi-
fied to an interest in the classicists and humanities rarely
exhibited among readers of Lightman's acquaintance. But
what struck Lightman the most were the large number of
books devoted to holistic healing and the paranormal—
ESP, out-of-body experiences, prophesy, telekinesis, and
reincarnation. They were the kind of books that a man
might draw some comfort from in the waning days of his
life.

But the books that commanded Lightman's attention
especially were a set collectively entitled the *Annals of the
Ariadne Society*. Bound in expensive leather whose pungent smell Lightman realized was what he'd picked up on
the moment he'd entered the room, they were numbered
volumes XLVI through LXIII.

Leafing through Volume XLVI was no more helpful than
an inspection of Volume LXIII in illuminating him as to
what the Ariadne Society was all about. They were composed largely of bibliographies that were themselves lists
of arcana and incunabula Lightman would have had no way
of knowing about. Obscure references abounded, and what
text there was was devoted to monthly reports going back
to 1976 chronicling the society's meetings. But there
would be little even in these reports to indicate what went
on in them. "A discussion of the experiments of A. Graph-
son, C. Smith, and C. Bright on psi activation in children
ages 9–12" was one typical entry. Certainly none of it
made for bedtime reading. He had just closed the final
volume in the series—dated two years previously—when
he realized that he'd just seen something that jarred him.
He reopened the book. What had caught his eye was right
there on the title page: COMPILED BY GEORGE MARSH.

THIRTEEN

Three days after he was married, Julian Wilks still didn't know whether or not the wedding was over. The celebration had been going on for a very long time and there seemed no end in sight. Who was paying for all of this? It was possible that he was. At any rate, he kept signing for things — hotel suites, gambling tabs, food bills, airline tickets, drinks for twelve at some place with a gorgeous view (only he couldn't remember of what) — and so he supposed that he was going to get stuck with most of it.

But then he was in love with Nancy and he would do anything to make her happy. Still, he would have liked to have known where the hell he was. It was one thing to know that he was in a hotel bar surrounded by half a dozen people who acted as if they were all good friends of his, it was quite another to be sure which hotel this was. His own or another one? And where was his bride? Looking around, he could see no sign of her. He asked the stocky fellow with the high blood pressure face next to him if he'd seen her any time recently.

"Didn't she go back to the room to take a nap?"

"Yes, of course she did. I just wanted to be sure."

The man regarded him as though he were an idiot. Idiocy had nothing to do with it. Untold quantities of Polish vodka, unblended scotch, true Kentucky bourbon, imported beer and Taittinger champagne (which Nancy liked to call Tate as if it were an old friend which, he supposed, in a way it was), were to account for his depleted and

disoriented state. Also, he couldn't remember getting any
sleep.

He knew better than to ask this man which country this
hotel was located in. It was bad enough that he'd forgotten
what had happened to Nancy.

Excusing himself, he exited the bar and found his way
into an ornately decorated lobby. He was in search of
something that would clue him in as to where he was.
Dimly he had a recollection of a ride in a limousine from
an airport, but whether that was earlier in the morning or
sometime yesterday afternoon was lost on him.

Walking outside, he breathed in the unspeakably humid
air of a summer day. He was surprised to see that the sun
was still out. He'd been expecting to find that it was the
middle of the night. The way he was feeling it should have
been the middle of the night.

When the thought occurred to him to go find his sleeping
wife he realized that he did not have any idea which room
she was in. He dug his hands into all his pockets but discovered no key. This embarrassed him. Stepping back inside the hotel, trying to ignore the disapproving gaze of the
uniformed doorman, he went up to the desk.

He found himself staring into the patrician face of the
concierge.

"What can I do for you, Signore Wilks?"

"May I have the key to my room?"

The concierge cast a glance at the rows of mailboxes in
back of him and said, "Signora Wilks has the key."

That was what he was afraid of. Now he had no alternative but to ask which room she was in. It wouldn't do to
lose one's wife only three days—if it was in fact three
days—after marrying her.

There was no visible reaction on the part of the concierge who merely directed him to Room 886.

The door wasn't open; he had to knock. That failing, he
shouted Nancy's name.

When she opened the door she gave him a long quizzical look before announcing, "You smell like a brewery."

She was a spectacular looking girl; even groggy and red-eyed, with all her makeup removed, she was an impressive sight. Not the sharpest girl in the world maybe, but a mental giant wasn't what he was searching for.

Without another word she turned on the balls of her feet and threw herself back on the bed.

Julian was tired. He was more than tired; he was in a condition that transcended exhaustion. But he wasn't sleepy.

There was a smell of stale cigarette smoke in the room and everywhere he looked cocktail glasses that hadn't been drained of their contents. The air conditioning didn't seem to be doing a great deal to dispel the decadent odors from the room and so he reasoned that maybe some good would come from opening up the window.

For the first time, standing at the window, he had a clear view of his surroundings. Rome had been his choice to begin their honeymoon. Somehow, for all the traveling he'd done in his life, he'd never quite gotten here. And as lapsed as he might be, he was still enough of a Catholic to feel that he could not go through life without ever having laid eyes on the Eternal City.

It would have been better, though, if the weather were more cooperative. Lord, it was steamy out there, he thought, impossible to take. He closed the window.

Rather than endure the stale odors in the room he thought of asking for another. It occurred to him that for a honeymoon suite this wasn't large or magnificent enough. He should call the manager and ask him to change it. That was what was lovely about having so much money, how easily you could make things go the way you wanted them to—or escape to somewhere else, somewhere better, if they didn't. He wondered if he'd regard it differently if he'd gone out and earned the money himself, but it had come to him, like out of a dream, from a trust fund. The trust fund had in turn come from Grandfather Wilks, shrewd merchandiser of grain, rubber hosiery and gizmos without which jet engines didn't function nearly so well as they should. This trust fund was a wonderful thing, but very mysterious. It worked rather like the cosmos itself, Julian thought, with a similarly infinite dimension to it. Grandfather Wilks had become something of a kook toward the end of his life, squandering fortunes, great and small, on strange right wing causes, obscure philanthropies, and semi-secret organizations. One he remembered was English and called the Ariadne Society. The reason he remembered the name was because in school he'd been fascinated by the myth of Theseus, how Ariadne with her ball of thread provided him with the means of letting him find his way out of the labyrinth. But of course he never went near Grandfather Wilks—a more intimidating figure he'd never before or after encountered—and so it wasn't as if he had the chance to question him regarding what all these foundations and societies he was putting his money into were about. He only hoped that the old man would die before there was nothing left in the trust fund for him. The old man seemed to have respected his wishes.

One day he would have to put his money to much better use than his crusty forebear. He would lay out a plan and talk it over with lawyers and accountants, solicit opinions from idealists with enough of a practical bent to be able to spend the money where it most counted. But he couldn't do it all today. No, he didn't even have the energy to call the manager about switching rooms. Tomorrow, everything could wait until tomorrow. It damn well would have to.

He lay down next to Nancy. Her nightgown was damp, and she was snoring lightly.

Stirring, she opened her eyes. "Hi," she said.

Then she threw her arms around him and slid one long bare leg between his and wrapped it around him. What a glorious way to become entangled, he thought as she went to sleep.

* * *

Julian woke before her and wished he hadn't. Nancy had rolled away from him, twisting her gown so that he could see what he wanted of her excellent ass and the dark sweet crevice between her legs.

He finally broke free of the trance that the sight her sleeping form had put him into and stood. His legs were wobbling and his head pounded. To make certain he'd be able to sustain himself through the day—whatever day this was—he had a stiff shot before setting out from the hotel.

The hotel, he observed now, was the Excelsior. An excellent hotel, perhaps the best in all of Rome. Even blind stinking drunk he didn't lack for taste. Or money. Lots of that was necessary, of course.

On the Via Vittorio Veneto, which the Excelsior fronted, he found a cab and told the driver to take him to Saint Peter's. It was an impulse, but still he felt he needed to do penance of some kind after such a dissolute spree.

The cab driver kept trying to tell him something in an interesting mixture of Italian and English, but Julian paid him no attention.

Mysteriously, the driver insisted on letting him out on a side street rather than driving into Saint Peter's Square.

He soon discovered why. In Saint Peter's Square there was now such a huge crowd assembled that it was absurd to think of driving across it. The basilica was, in any case, inaccessible; Swiss Army Guards were massed in front of it, barring entry. This must have been what the cab driver was talking about, Julian thought. No wonder he wouldn't approach closer.

All at once a cry went up from the crowd. Julian looked to see a cloud of black smoke rising above the Vatican. For a few seconds he couldn't fathom what was going on. Then it occurred to him that this was the signal that meant the College of Cardinals had failed to agree on a new pope.

But then that must mean the old pope was dead. Sometime in the last three days while he and Nancy were drinking themselves into oblivion, the pope had died and the cardinals were brought to Rome from around the world to elect a new one. It was astonishing the things one missed when one was drunk for seventy-two hours in a row.

If he was planning on doing any penance today then it would have to be done at a church less celebrated than Saint Peter's. But the urge had passed and he was content to spend the remainder of the morning sitting in a cafe perusing a copy of the *International Herald Tribune* to see what else he'd missed by going on a protracted binge. It seemed that the pope had succumbed to the flu. A younger, healthier man, the paper said, might have survived, but he was already infirm. Even a mild flu could carry him off. Like the wind.

FOURTEEN

In spite of his lack of sleep Lightman felt functional enough by morning. Diana was already up and dressed, the remains of her breakfast left on the kitchen table. She was rather severely dressed in a business suit, her hair swept back and her manner brusque. She was obviously in a hurry to be out of the house.

"How's Bill?" he asked.

"Still sleeping. I looked in on him and he seems to be resting comfortably. I've got to run out for a few hours on business. Would it be terribly inconvenient for you to stay here in case he needs something? I should be back by noon—in plenty of time for your appointment at four."

"I'm glad to wait," Lightman said. "But before you leave, I have a question."

"And what's that?"

"Last night I happened to be looking over some of your husband's books and I came across a collection called *Annals of the Ariadne Society.*"

"Oh, those. Nicholas belonged to the society, it kind of struck his fancy."

"What exactly was—or is—the Ariadne Society?"

"You'd have to ask somebody a little more knowledgeable than me, I'm afraid. Nicholas used to tell me that some of the most famous intellects in the country belonged to it at one time—Lytton Strachey, Clive Bell, John Maynard Keynes, Roger Fry, Arthur Conan Doyle. The list goes on. But there's no way of finding out who belongs to it these days—not unless you happen to know one of the members personally."

"Why? Their names are clearly spelled out in those volumes. Anyone with access to them could find out."

"The names you see there are pseudonyms that members adopted when they joined. It is a rather secret society not so much because they have anything to hide, mind you, but because there are members—scientists, businessmen and so on—who would prefer not to be associated with anything having to do with psychics and astral projection, that sort of thing. It spares them ridicule and sometimes, I imagine, the loss of business."

"Would your husband have told you who some of the members actually were?"

Diana shrugged, obviously not terribly interested in answering questions about her husband's affiliation with this curious society. "If he did, I'm sure by now I've forgotten. Women aren't permitted to be members, so I never took much of an interest in their proceedings. Does it matter?"

She'd now put on her coat and was heading for the door; this was a very different Diana, too businesslike for his liking. He was thrown a little, uncertain now whether the connection between them he'd felt the night before had in fact existed.

"Let me just try one name on you?"

She shot him an impatient look.

"George Marsh."

If the name meant anything to her at all he couldn't tell. There might have been some slight change in her expression: a quick shifting of her eyes, a pursing of her lips. But it was impossible to make anything of that.

"What about Patrick? Was he a member?"

She laughed. "No, Patrick didn't need to join any secret societies. He has enough secrets of his own. Now, if you don't mind, I really do have to get going."

And she was out the door.

Only then did Lightman become conscious of the television in the background, the insistent voice of a BBC commentator delivering the news in an accent suitable for reciting Hamlet. Global catastrophe, when filtered through such a voice and with such elegant intonation, didn't sound nearly so bad. Military buildups in the Middle East, border skirmishes on the Mongolian border, a tsunami wiping out villages along the Philippines coastline, and the slaying of radical dissidents in Mozambique were just so much filler, sure to be forgotten by lunchtime. Even accounts closer to home of rioting in the East End—five people killed, sixty-two injured—barely succeeded in catching Lightman's interest.

The report that followed, however, provoked his curiosity enough to give it his full attention.

"Authorities also report that an undetermined number of people, most of them from the riot-torn areas, have been stricken with an incapacitating flu-like virus. Ministry of Health officials advise anyone suffering from bronchial disorder or any other symptoms of the flu to seek medical attention at once."

Lightman hoped for further news about this outbreak, but that was all he was apparently going to get. As he was soon to understand, what was uppermost in the minds of Londoners these days—if the BBC service had it right—

wasn't the prospect of yet another war in the Middle East, it wasn't even the rioting and looting in the East End. No, it was the weather. The weather was behaving strangely lately, from what the BBC's meteorologist was saying, and if his predictions held true, in the days to come it would behave stranger still. Arrows and painted clouds were beginning to move across a map of the British Isles as the meteorologist spoke in increasingly dire tones. Lightman didn't know what to make of it and switched the tube off rather than suffer an explanation as to why wind currents and above normal tides were about to play such havoc with the reliably damp and mild English summertime.

At the instant the TV went dead he heard Wellington crying out from his room. It was possible that he'd been trying to get his attention for some time now, only the TV had drowned him out. Lightman hurried to his side.

Nothing had prepared Lightman for the sight of him. His face was a mess, worse now that there were so many scabs that had formed during the night. The sallowness was expected, but not the high fever or rasping sound issuing from his lungs that might be mistaken for a banknote being crisped. His face was twisted with pain and swollen. Any speech he attempted became lost in a feeble spasm of coughing. It was a bad sign, Lightman knew, when someone could barely manage to cough. When Wellington tried to lift his head up he left behind something of himself on the pillow: big tufts of his hair. Apparently the fever was raging so violently in his system that it was causing the follicles to fall out. When Lightman looked into Wellington's eyes he saw not the man but the disease itself; he was burning up just as surely as the East End of London was.

FIFTEEN

The headache, the constant loginess he felt he was quick to attribute to the strange wind that had come up and was now blowing ceaselessly, maddeningly, through the London streets. For all the nine years that Ezra Omaru had been there he could not remember such a wind. And apparently he was not alone. On the telly, the weather forecasters said that it was quite an extraordinary phenomenon, a wind like the sirroco, like the hamsin, known to Africa and Arabia, to Spain and France, but never to the British Isles. There was an explanation, of course, although it was not one that Ezra easily comprehended, having something to do with tides and volcanoes and what was called the El Niño off the coast of Peru. None of these forecasters seemed to have any idea when the wind would die down or head elsewhere.

It was a hot, baking, feverish wind, and from experience Ezra knew that it could make men crazy, cause them to do things which they would later regret. It was a wind from which no good could ever come. In Uganda, where he was born and raised, and in Kenya where he lived until migrating to England with his family, such winds were customary, malign events but at least predictable.

Dust and soot got into the cramped flat that Ezra rented and into the herb and medicine shop he owned right below it on the ground floor. There was nothing to be done about it. Shutting the windows and barring the door were ineffectual, and besides, it was so impossibly stifling that no one would think of doing such a thing. There was little money and none for a luxury like an air conditioner.

All the time the telly was going; it drove Ezra nearly as mad as the wind did. His wife, Nassa, and the children watched it constantly. Even when their attention flagged or there were household chores that needed doing, they would not think to turn the bloody thing off.

Worse was the station that Nassa insisted on watching. Expressing no interest at all in either of the two BBC channels or the independent network, she tuned to a station broadcast from a ship off the coast—no one was sure where—a pirate station the government would shut down if it could.

There was a man who appeared on this station, day and night, who said that the end of the world was near and that the signs were everywhere that this was true. Nassa listened to this man. And believed in this man. His name was Jonas Beck. Some called him apostle. Some called him savior.

Ezra wondered what had happened to her, why she needed this man Beck. Nassa was a fine woman, but gone too fat since he first spotted her on the dance floor at Hanihan's, down the block from the New Stanley, the only place he could find open past midnight in Nairobi. Such a splendid, supple dancer, he couldn't take his eyes off her. And she was so saucy, teasing him but not maliciously. He had never loved another woman before or since. He wished only that the Nassa he'd met and lost his heart to on the dance floor at Hanihan's was with him now. The woman who every month sent off two quid to Jonas Beck, with her family so desperate for money, was becoming a stranger to him. He loved her still, but he did not think that she would ever love him back the way she once had, and this caused him to dwell in a constant state of despair.

Ezra thought that he'd already seen what the end of the world was like, before he ever met Nassa, and no man—no white man surely—could make him afraid that the end

was coming. He'd seen his friends die, mowed down for
being members of the wrong tribe. He'd been stripped of
his clothes, his papers, even his family Bible, and gone
fleeing into the brush, naked and hungry, waiting for days
until he could slip over the border. And even then he
wasn't safe; in Kenya he was one of thousands of refugees,
jobless, penniless, undocumented, hoping that the UN
would come through and provide him papers that would
make him legal, give him an existence in the eyes of the
world. There was never any way to contact his family, to
know whether they were alive. That, for him, was as close
as he believed it possible to come to the end of the world.
It *was* the end of the world—the end of his world.

Until that night on the dance floor at Hanihan's. Which
was when the world began again.

But what did Nassa know about massacres, legal documents, and nights spent huddled naked in the brush? She
preferred to spend her days lazing about the house and her
evenings in the nightclubs. She urged Ezra not to have any
faith in the UN but in God. God, all the time it was God.
Nassa's God was like no other God Ezra had ever heard of
and he didn't think that he cared much for him, either. This
God controlled everything, leaving very little for anyone
else. This God of hers was always betraying people or
making their lives miserable with ceaseless rains or unend-
ing droughts. To listen to her, he'd survived the massacres
in Kampala because of God, his friends had died because
of God, the spy who'd informed on them had done so because of God, and if he ever got his papers it would be
because of God. Now they were almost destitute, with five
children, all below the age of twelve, and they were sweltering in a two-room flat in the East End of London, and
this was because of God, too.

"This man here, he is of God," Nassa would tell him any
time Jonas Beck appeared on the screen. "You see his
beautiful eyes and you know this is true."

But Ezra couldn't see it. There was nothing beautiful

about his eyes. He was an ordinary looking man with a face that glistened as if it had been scrubbed too hard. Ezra didn't trust him. Never had he been so jealous of a man. It was madness to be so jealous. After all, she wasn't sleeping with this man. But why did she insist on spending so much time sitting in front of the telly, drinking in his every word and talking about him to their children with more admiration than she ever talked about her husband? "When you grow up you be like this man of God," she would say.

How were they going to have any chance to grow up, Ezra asked her, if the end of the world was so close?

"But you don't see, Ezra, we are members of the church. And members of the church will be saved."

Her logic was unassailable. But it was no logic at all. Ezra did not know what to think. He refused to be a member of this crazy church.

And now the wind. It was a bad thing and everybody knew it. But Nassa seemed to welcome it; a look of satisfaction had settled on her face when it first began to whip through the streets. "It is a sign," she said. "This is what Mr. Beck told us would happen. Now it begins."

Ezra had been about to ask her exactly what was about to begin but decided not to; he didn't want to know.

The second morning of the wind was when the headache and the stiffness in his neck hit him. He had once been told that the wind carried positive ions and that ions of this kind caused headaches and that there was nothing to be done about it but wait it out. He went downstairs to work, but as the day wore on he felt much worse. A pain unlike any he'd ever felt before took up residence behind his eyes and his ears. The mingled aromas of the many herbs, medicinal teas and spices in his densely packed shop, which he normally found so intoxicating, now just made him nauseated. He decided to close the shop and go to bed, thinking that a few hours of sleep would help him.

But when he woke he felt worse. Not even the most potent herbal tea could take the pain away. Actually, the pain had spread, reaching into his groin; it was as if someone had set his blood on fire.

Nassa took his temperature. It was up to 104. No wonder he felt like he was on fire. She sat by his bed and sponged him down. When he managed, in spite of the pain, to open his eyes he could scarcely see her; she kept going in and out of focus like a poorly projected movie. His throat was dry and it ached horribly and there was an uncomfortable heaviness in his lungs so that whenever he breathed too deeply it was agony.

He was only forty-three years old, vigorous, rarely sick. He could not understand why this was happening to him. The winds that blew in his youth never had this effect on him.

"You want to know why you are sick and why I am well and why your children are well?" she asked him.

He didn't answer her.

"It is because you do not believe and because you do not believe you will die."

The only thing that he could imagine was that his high fever was making him hear words that had not truly been spoken. For surely Nassa would not speak this way no matter how convinced she was that Jonas Beck was the messenger of God.

He tried to speak but his voice was nothing more than a rasp, inaudible even to his own ears.

But Nassa understood what he was saying to her.

"No good. It is too late to bring a doctor here. You must suffer the scourge of God. No doctor can help you, no medicine can deliver you. It is up to God only."

Again he opened his mouth to speak, but what emerged was a racking cough. The coughing seemed not to start in his chest but deeper, in his belly. The cough was savage and his whole body shook. A salty liquid moved up the back of his throat with the coughing. But he had no idea what it was until he saw the blood on the sheets.

When he managed to bring his eyes to focus on Nassa he

saw that there was not the slightest alarm in her face. It seemed that she'd been expecting this to happen all along. Twenty-two years had passed since the night he'd danced with her at Hanihan's and he had absolutely no idea who she was. Their children were crying in the next room, but Nassa did not move from the chair by the bed. It was almost as though she were waiting for him to die, hoping that he would get it over with fast.

Now it wasn't the sickness lodged in him that he feared so much, it was his wife—his wife and the messenger of that mad God of hers. If he survived, he told himself, he would leave her. No, he thought, he would kill her. Then a new spasm of coughing obliterated all thought from his mind.

Outside, the feverish wind blew relentlessly.

SIXTEEN

Lightman didn't want to stay around long when Diana returned. He could see she was in a sour mood and besides, he had to get back to the Grosvenor and prepare himself for his appointment with Martindale in a few hours.

Before leaving he urged her to send Wellington to a hospital regardless of how vigorously he protested.

"Is he that bad?"

"He could be dying." Lightman saw no point in hiding the truth from her. One look at him and she would suspect the worst herself.

"I didn't think...I didn't imagine it was that bad." Lightman sensed that something was giving way inside her, that she was fighting to hold on. She turned her face

away from him, her shoulders tensing with the motion.
"I'll ring up Dr. Rhinebeck and see about having him admitted."

"It's possible he's been infected by the same flu that's
broken out elsewhere in the city—I heard on the news this
morning that there's been an outbreak."

"The flu? You say he's dying of the flu? I thought it was
only young children and old people who were stricken that
severely."

"He might also be suffering a more toxic reaction because he has, in effect, been inoculated by means of the
monkey's bites. If he'd been exposed by another vector—
from somebody sneezing or coughing, for instance—then
it might not be quite so bad. But this also seems to be a
different strain of flu, a more virulent strain. Tests will
need to be done to find out what it is, precisely."

Lightman suspected that these tests must have already
been done on the monkeys at Mayfair House.

As she lifted the receiver she said, "John, do you think
there was anything to what Bill said last night?"

"About what?"

"About that cage being left open on purpose? Do you
think he was right to say that somebody wanted him
killed?"

She must have been aware of who Wellington had been
referring to, but Lightman could understand her reluctance
to utter the name aloud.

"I honestly don't know. I hope not. It could as easily be
me lying there."

By this point Diana had gotten Dr. Rhinebeck on the
line. She wanted Lightman to take the phone, thinking that
he might better be able to convey the nature of the emergency, but Dr. Rhinebeck wouldn't allow her to get that
far.

Whatever the doctor was telling her, it was evident that
she didn't like it. After she'd hung up she said to Lightman, "He wants to wait another day before admitting him

to see if there's any improvement in his condition. He says that Saint Mary's hospital is being overrun by flu victims and they're having difficulty finding beds for them all. The same, he says, is true in every hospital in the city. Most of them are from the East End, but he tells me he's also seeing patients from other parts of the city and has absolutely no doubt that it will spread."

Lightman said he thought it ill-advised to delay, but added that there was a chance Wellington would show some progress over the next twenty-four hours. "If he doesn't, then we're going to have to get him admitted even if we have to set up a cart for him in the corridors."

"You're putting yourself out a great deal for both of us. It really seems to me you have enough troubles of your own."

"I don't mind at all, really I don't. As soon as my meeting's over I'll come back and check up on him."

"I can't tell you how grateful I am. If ever I can return the favor you will let me know, won't you?"

"Maybe you already have," he replied.

She was puzzled by his remark as he expected her to be, but how was he to make her understand the feeling of anticipation he had that he was about to discover something crucial here in this flat, something that might change his life? He couldn't even explain it to himself.

When Lightman left he took something of Wellington's along with him: his blood. Drawn with his permission, even his encouragement, it resided in a small vial in Lightman's coat pocket. If it harbored the virus he believed it did then it had traveled a very long way from the frozen lungs of Joe Taylor to reach Wellington by means of a lab animal. As soon as he could, Lightman intended to subject the blood to a variety of tests to see whether it corresponded to one of the several hundred viruses already typed.

Walking through the streets of Hampstead in search of a

taxi, Lightman's attention was drawn to a terrific clamor that seemed to be coming from the next corner, just on the other side of a small Anglican church. Others strolling along the street also paused and looked in that direction.

A few moments later Lightman found himself witnessing the strangest, and certainly the most revolting, parade he'd ever laid eyes on.

As many as two hundred people were marching in this parade, announcing their arrival with a paroxysm of sound —blaring horns and snare drums and cymbals clashing, all of which made for a cacophony that obliterated all melody and rhythm. As far as he could see the ranks of the marchers were about equally divided between men, women and children. The majority were young, in their twenties and thirties, and while many were black or colored, even more were white. Virtually all were bare to the waist and covered with blood.

Lightman stared, disbelieving, sure that his eyes must be deceiving him. But it was there in reality; the people around him had the same look of astonishment and disgust on their faces. The marchers were whipping themselves with metal-studded whips, and they were shrieking in pain but also in ecstasy; some of their expressions were practically beatific. They were held spellbound by some force, some transcendental power; whatever the reason, the pain wasn't reaching them. It was all Lightman could do to remove his eyes from the younger women among the throngs. Like Dionysian maenads, they'd thrown themselves into an orgiastic frenzy, and the beatings they inflicted on themselves took on an erotically charged aspect. Their bare breasts, smeared with blood, rose and fell in their excitation. One young woman Lightman spotted was carrying an infant in a Snugli and the infant's head was being spattered with blood, not from its mother but from the man who was directly ahead of them. The baby's cries went unnoticed amid all the tumult.

"Fucking flagellants," muttered a silver-haired man standing to one side of Lightman, straining to keep his short-haired terrier from lunging out at the marchers who passed by.

"Who are these people?" Lightman asked.

"I just told you, they're flagellants."

"Yes, I got that, but what do they represent? What's this all about?"

"They seem to have gotten it into their heads that this is how you do penance—you don't go to confession, you beat yourself to a bloody pulp. They say the end of the world is coming and this is how they're getting ready for it."

As the man spoke, a young man separated himself from the procession and began to pass out leaflets. He was distinguished by the T-shirt he wore with a green cross on it—no words, just the cross. Out of curiosity Lightman took a leaflet from him.

"The Church of the Redeemed Invites You to Embrace Life," it proclaimed. The silver-haired gentleman snorted when he read it. "Fucking rubbish, all of it." Looking at his growling terrier he said, "What do you think, I should let Christopher have a go at them?"

"Seeing that they don't respond to the pain they're inflicting on themselves, I can't see that Christopher would have much of an effect."

The man seemed to find some wisdom in this and continued to maintain his hold on the leash.

"Why don't the police do something to put a stop to a demonstration like this?" Lightman asked.

"Don't you see? These are the followers of that bloke Jonas Beck. And he has friends in high places. They don't dare touch him."

Unable to stomach the sight of this spectacle any more Lightman set out for the underground.

As he searched for an underground station, Lightman had a vague sensation that he was being followed. He kept glancing back but saw no one he could readily identify as a tail, yet the feeling wouldn't leave. As he walked he dipped his hand repeatedly into his pocket to make certain that the precious vial was still there.

It took him nearly an hour from the time he found the tube station until he arrived back at the Grosvenor. As much as he needed a shower and a cold drink, the first thing he did was phone a courier service to pick up the specimen of Wellington's blood to be sent by pouch that night to his lab in Boston. He wrote out a request to have the blood tested for bacteria and virus and the results relayed to him as soon as the process was completed. He was certain he'd feel better once the blood was out of his possession and on its way across the Atlantic.

The courier showed up on time but the chauffeur that Cage was supposed to send for him did not. At twenty past three Lightman, newly showered and shaven, was still waiting in the lobby, from time to time braving the dismal wind and pollution to take a look outside. He ascribed the delay to traffic snarls at first. As the hour wore on, however, he began to have the feeling that there was a hitch, that something was wrong. Given how the last twenty-four hours had worked out it made sense that something else should have gone wrong. From a public phone he called Mayfair House and asked for Winston Cage's office.

"Mr. Cage is not in today," a woman answered.

"This is Dr. Lightman. I spoke to Mr. Cage yesterday and he said he would have me picked up—I'm meeting Dr. Martindale at four."

"I'm sorry, sir, but I don't know anything about such a meeting. Perhaps I could put you through to Dr. Martindale's office. Please hold."

Another woman answered, "Dr. Martindale's office. May I help you?"

Lightman repeated the story of his plight.

"Oh yes, Dr. Lightman, you were scheduled to see Dr.

Martindale at four. But that meeting has been canceled. I assumed you were told."

Lightman was incensed. "No one told me, no one left any message. When will it be possible to reschedule a meeting?"

"Oh, that's difficult to say, sir. All of Dr. Martindale's appointments have been canceled indefinitely."

"But why?"

"An emergency of a personal nature has arisen," she said delicately.

"And you couldn't tell me what that is?"

"I'm afraid I cannot."

"Is there any way I can reach Mr. Cage then? I need to talk to him."

"No, Dr. Lightman, I don't have that information available. And I suggest that in the future you do not try to reach him through Mayfair House. He is no longer in our employ."

When Lightman hung up the phone he began to wonder what he was doing in London. Had this whole trip been for nothing? At the very least he'd gotten his hands on what he was sure was the virus that had eluded him in Alaska six months before. Though he was still left with the problem of raising money to sustain his lab, at least he hadn't come up completely emptyhanded. He took a seat at one of the small tables in the lobby. A waiter appeared almost instantly. Lightman ordered a double scotch.

The drink still hadn't come when he looked up to see that someone had joined him—a slender, cocoa-skinned man with dreadlocks pouring down the sides of his face, not at all the type of person usually seen in the Grosvenor lobby. He had bright ebony eyes which he fixed in an unsettling way on Lightman.

"Excuse me, if you don't mind, I'd prefer to have this table alone," Lightman said.

"I think we need to talk," the man said. "Do you recog-

nize this?" His accent was Jamaican, but it wasn't thick
enough to obscure the meaning of his words.

Lightman looked at what the man held in his hands. It
was his gold watch, Stephanie's last gift.

"Where the hell did you get ahold of that?"

An appreciative smile formed on the Jamaican's lips.
Before Lightman could get an answer another man pulled
up a chair to the table, a man with a face of a rogue, round
and red, with a cleft in his jaw and a nose that was slightly
misshapen, probably from a brawl fought long ago. He was
better dressed than the Jamaican, in suit and tie, and while
the two would seem to have nothing in common, it was at
once obvious that they were acquainted. "Let us introduce
ourselves, Dr. Lightman. This is Detective Gray and I am
Inspector Finch, and if we could trouble you for a few
minutes, we would like to ask you a question or two about
what you were doing last night at Mayfair House."

SEVENTEEN

How ironic, how ridiculous, Lightman thought, to think
that Stephanie would have had her revenge after all these
years. Her inscription—"to John Lightman on the occasion
of his fortieth birthday from his loving wife Stephanie"—
was all that the Crown would need to indict him, he figured. Although he considered denying that he'd ever been
at Mayfair House the night before, he recognized that he
might only be making things worse for himself.

"Were you at Mayfair House last night?" Finch asked.
Lightman could sense the greed in his voice for an incriminating answer.

Lightman admitted that he was, but volunteered no more. While he'd never been subjected to an interrogation by police, he knew enough not to give away too much.

"Were you in the company of Dr. William Wellington?" Finch asked, undoubtedly aware of the answer in advance. It seemed as though he was to do all the questioning. "Were you aware that Dr. Wellington was not authorized to enter the animal laboratories?"

"No," Lightman said. It was his first deception.

"The fact is that he was not authorized. He is liable to be charged for breaking and entering and for destruction of property."

"Destruction of property? What property? What are you talking about?"

"I am speaking of one Chinese bonnet monkey."

"That damn monkey attacked Dr. Wellington and would have ripped him to pieces if I hadn't done something!" Lightman regretted his outburst and had the feeling he'd just fallen for Finch's bait. But Finch seemed to have something else on his mind.

"Is it true that you were met yesterday morning at Heathrow by Winston Cage?"

Lightman said that he was indeed met by Cage and explained his purpose in coming to London and in setting up an appointment to see Martindale.

When Lightman finished speaking Finch asked, "So you have not seen or heard from Mr. Cage since yesterday morning when he dropped you off here at the hotel?"

"Yes. I tried to reach him this afternoon but I was told that he is no longer employed by Mayfair House."

"The reason you can't locate him is that he seems to have disappeared."

"I don't understand."

"Neither do we, which is why we were so interested in talking with you. Now, we've already established that you participated in a burglary at Mayfair House last night, haven't we? Tell me, what time did you and Wellington enter Mayfair House last night?"

"About midnight, I'd say."

"Could you have been in or around Mayfair House at two in the morning?"

"No, I'm sure that we'd left by then. Why?"

"Because Mr. Cage was last seen at about that hour entering Mayfair House."

Now it became clear to Lightman where this was leading. "My God, you don't seriously think that I had anything to do with his disappearance, do you? That's crazy!"

"Could you provide us with an alibi, a witness perhaps who could account for your whereabouts at that hour?"

Lightman had no intention of bringing Diana into this affair. She'd already become embroiled enough as it was. He hesitated too long thinking of a reply, and Finch had no patience to wait.

"Do you have any idea where Dr. Wellington is at present?"

Lightman said that he hadn't, observing Finch's face carefully to see whether he'd picked up on the lie. But Finch remained expressionless.

Then he put out his hand and said, "I'm afraid I'm going to be obliged to take your passport."

"Now wait a minute, am I being charged with anything? I want to know so that I can get legal advice."

"There's no need for that yet," Finch said. "We are not placing you under arrest. It is just that we would rather not see you leave the country until we can account for Mr. Cage."

"What about the watch?"

"I think we will hold onto it too. Now the passport, if you please."

Lightman reluctantly handed the document over. "There's really little point in keeping me here, I'm not going to be able to assist your investigation. I'd like to find Mr. Cage myself."

"You're associated with Harvard, aren't you?" Finch asked. "And I understand you have also done work for the World Health Organization."

When Lightman confirmed both facts Finch asked, "And your last assignment was in Alaska, is that correct?"

The man had done his homework. "Is it conceivable that your presence here in London might have something to do with that assignment?"

"Let's just say I like to follow through my investigations just as I assume that you gentlemen do."

Finch allowed a small smile, quite a concession on his part, Lightman thought. Then he and Gray stood up. "It's been a pleasure meeting you. Should you ever stumble across any information that might be of use to me, however trivial it may seem to you, please ring me up at the Yard."

"When do I get my passport back?"

"Whenever we're satisfied that there's nothing further to be gained by keeping you here. Don't be unduly alarmed, Dr. Lightman, we'll be in touch."

He remained at the table, expecting the two to return with additional questions, but they did not. So, he thought, this was what it was like to be a suspect, this was what it was like to be a criminal.

EIGHTEEN

Lightman believed he'd succeeded in reaching Diana's Hampstead flat without being followed. He'd gone to great pains to confuse any would-be tail, switching train lines three times, taking a taxi two blocks, then getting out and walking the rest of the way.

It was half past five when he arrived. He rang the bell. Nothing. He couldn't believe that she wouldn't be there if only because Wellington needed somebody to look after him. When again he failed to elicit a response he tried the door more out of frustration than anything else, since it was always kept locked.

Not today. The lock wasn't working. On closer inspection Lightman saw that it had been jimmied. With growing alarm he chose to take the stairs rather than enduring the wait for the lift to the third floor. He knocked on Diana's door before he realized that it, too, was ajar.

He walked into darkness, sure now that he would discover some grotesque tableau—or else that the flat had been ransacked, and Diana vanished. But then he heard the sound of a woman weeping.

She was sitting in the gloom, bare legs tucked under her, a glass of something clutched in her hand. Suddenly aware of him she let out a gasp. Lightman was about to turn on a lamp but she stopped him, shaking her head. Her eyes were glistening with tears.

Lightman sat down next to her. "What is it?" he asked. "Is it Bill?"

"He's gone," she said.

"I'm sorry," Lightman said.

But at the same time he was thinking that at least he'd gotten the sample of blood when he had the opportunity. Lightman held her in his arms.

"I just went out for twenty minutes, there was something I needed to do," she was saying, her voice catching, "and then when I got back he wasn't here."

Lightman was confused. "You mean to tell me he isn't dead?"

"I don't know whether he's dead or not, I don't know. He just wasn't here."

"He was too sick just to walk out of here on his own."

"That's what I thought."

"The downstairs lock—somebody broke in."

She looked at him uncertainly. "I'd assumed that it was an attempted burglary. It's happened before. I didn't connect it with Bill. Do you think that could be it?"

"It's possible. Did you check with any of your neighbors to see whether they saw him?"

"No one's seen anything," she said. "Or if they have, they're not saying. I should never have left him alone. He was sleeping, you see, I didn't think he'd need me." Then she shook her head, utterly confounded. "But why would anyone kidnap him, why wouldn't they let him die in peace?" She lowered her eyes, saying softly, "He was going to die, wasn't he?"

Lightman nodded. "I think so."

"His color was so strange, it was like heliotrope," she said then, as if she now accepted the fact that whatever became of him, he would shortly be dead. "I've never seen anyone with that color before. Even Nicholas, before he died, didn't look that bad. He just withered away. He took such a long time about it and then there were days, even weeks, when he would seem to recover, and I'd think that he'd miraculously recovered."

"How long ago was that?" He was relieved to have the subject changed.

"It's been six months since he died. But it seemed like he was sick forever. I never realized how sick he really was until he began to take an interest in psychic phenomena— it was so unlike him. He was a businessman, a consultant, he disdained anything having to do with ESP or telepathy, to him it was so much trash. He lumped it all in together with gypsy fortune-tellers and daily horoscopes in the papers. But when he got sick it all changed. That was when he found Jonas. He even got Patrick involved with Jonas."

"Let me get this straight. How did Patrick come into the picture? Was he treating Nicholas then?"

"Yes, but all he could do was prolong his life, he couldn't save him. Nicholas began to resign himself to dying, but he thought it might be possible to discover what awaited him on the other side—that was what he called it. Somehow he managed to get Patrick intrigued. And then one day he brought home Jonas Beck. That was about a year and a half ago. Patrick was just going along for the ride, I think. He didn't believe that Jonas would turn out to be more than a source of amusement, a novelty."

"I assume that Jonas surprised him."

"Oh, he surprised him all right. You have to understand that Jonas has an uncanny ability to reach into people's pasts, to know their lives. I never would have believed it myself if I hadn't witnessed it. A group of us would meet every fortnight and he would give readings, tell people about themselves, secrets they didn't want to have known."

"And what was Nicholas' secret?"

"That he was going to die. He knew, you see, but he didn't want me to know."

She fell quiet for a moment and then, giving him a look that was almost reproachful, said, "And now I suppose you would like to know what secret Jonas told me about my past. You do want to know, don't you?" There was something sly and teasing in her tone, but she was right, he was curious.

"He told me that I had a child when I was eighteen—a son—and that I'd put him up for adoption and would do anything to find him again." She said this matter-of-factly as if it were someone else, another woman, she was talking about.

"He was right?"

"Yes." She turned her face away from him. "He knew, there was no way he could have known, but he knew. I'd never even told Nicholas. He did it the same night, gave us both readings, and it was like we'd both been stripped bare, like there was nothing else left, and maybe there wasn't. I suspect that if Nicholas wasn't dying our marriage would have ended then. He was, in a sense, already in the other world, he'd already left me behind. Jonas' revelations told us something about each other that we'd never cared to acknowledge—that we could never share our lives, not really. . ." Her voice trailed off.

"Do you happen to know what he told Patrick?"

"I have no idea except that whatever it was became a bond between them. But neither one would ever say." It was only then that she thought to ask what had come from the meeting he'd had with Martindale.

"There was no meeting, it was canceled. His secretary told me it was an emergency, a personal emergency."

Diana's face darkened, and for a moment Lightman wondered if she might know what that emergency was. He felt cold, as if only now his body had become sensitive to the air conditioning in the flat. As much as he wanted to, he couldn't bring himself to ask her about her relationship with Martindale—not now.

"I've got to go back to the studio and see about my work," Diana announced. "Would it be too much of an inconvenience for you to stay here in case anybody calls with news about Bill? I hate to keep putting you out like this."

Lightman said he was happy to oblige.

"In fact, why don't you stay the night if you'd like? We can eat when I get back. I shouldn't be more than a couple of hours."

She was fully in command now; it was amazing to him how quickly she could pull herself together. He wondered whether she was calling on her skills as an actress with him. He hoped not. It wasn't a kind thought.

She was gone longer than she said she would be. Lightman was too distracted to read, and thinking himself too anxious to sleep, tried watching television. What appeared to be a farce was on; two men, both disappointed in their pursuit of the same woman, were drowning their sorrows in pints of ale. Their plight, however, failed to strike him as funny. Maybe the humor was too peculiarly British. The program did accomplish one thing though: it put him to sleep.

When he woke a commentator, who looked like he might be the older brother of the one who'd read the morning news, was saying that eight people had so far died of the flu and that the outbreak had now spread beyond London proper. But these eight, he said, were all elderly, as if to assure anyone younger in the viewing audience that there was nothing to fear.

It was nearly four in the morning. He called out to Diana but failed to hear a response. Evidently she still hadn't come home. He realized he was more disappointed than he thought he'd be.

Then he remembered the specimen he'd pouched to Boston. It surely should have arrived already. The thought brought him fully awake. Reasoning that he should still find somebody working even at this hour—it was about eleven Eastern Daylight Time—he put in a call to the lab.

The phone rang several times before somebody picked up. It was Stephen Collingwood, sounding out of breath. One of his principal assistants, Collingwood had logged in whole months of sleepless nights pulling together the grant proposal. It was no surprise that he'd been nearly as dismayed as Lightman when the money hadn't come through. Hearing Lightman's voice he grew excited, undoubtedly anticipating good news—or some news. "Did you manage to strike a deal with Martindale?" he asked.

Not wishing to demoralize his assistant more than he was already Lightman said, "We're still trying to work things out, but I'm hoping to have some word for you in the next few days. The reason I'm calling though is to see whether you've received a specimen I pouched over yesterday afternoon. It should have gone out on a four P.M. flight out of Heathrow."

Collingwood said he would check, a procedure that ate up several expensive minutes. When he came back on the line he said, "I looked everywhere. It was never logged in at our receiving department. I called the airline and the courier agency but they say they have no record of any specimen being pouched to us from London in the last week."

Lightman felt a dull throbbing pain in his chest, accompanied by a sharp constriction of his throat, as if he were choking: it was his body's way of telling him that all was lost. He realized that the proof he was hoping for had slipped out of his grasp. With the specimen vanished and Wellington very likely abducted, all evidence directly linking Mayfair House—and Patrick Martindale—with the spread of the virus was gone.

NINETEEN

The news came while Lightman was sitting in a fashionable Hampstead pub eating lunch. The lunch was full of dust, so bad that half the time he felt as though he were chewing his spinach soup. The radio was on, tuned to a station that seemed to carry nothing but unthreatening pop music, interrupted on the hour for news, delivered quickly as if they wanted to get it out of the way.

"Today it was announced in Geneva that Dr. Patrick Martindale was appointed the head of a special commission to arrest the continuing spread of the flu epidemic. Dr. Martindale was quoted as saying that this was the time to act. All the scientific and medical resources available should be applied now to developing a vaccine and curing those people who are suffering the ravages of the virus, he said. Already the London flu has struck in a dozen countries in Europe and Africa, and accounted for some three hundred and fifty deaths. Health authorities here in London are warning of a further rise in the number of cases. So much for the bad news. Now let's get back to something cheerier with the latest from the Blue Angel Boys. . . ."

The news of Martindale's elevation to such a distinguished post in WHO came as a shock to Lightman. If anybody should have had that appointment it should have been him. But what should he have expected? Hadn't Wellington impressed on him just how very powerful his connections were, how they'd even cover up murders for him if necessary? Pulling the right strings in Geneva must not have proven so difficult for them.

Yet it was the temerity of Martindale that troubled him more than his ability to carry out this coup.

From what he could see, it was Martindale who was responsible for setting loose the virus in the first place.

His theory wasn't likely to hold up in a court of law, and probably would be greeted with skepticism by Finch and his colleagues, but it made sense to him.

Although he had to imagine certain steps along the way in the virus' odyssey, he was inclined to accept Wellington's scenario. A flu virus, hibernating in the lungs of a wanted murderer named Joe Taylor, is sent—ostensibly—to the World Influenza Centre for testing. Test results show a mild virus, hardly one capable of turning a victim's blood as black as pitch from oxygen starvation. The courier George Marsh disappears or else never existed in the first place. A switch is made, a benign A virus substituted for a deadly one. The deadly one is instead smuggled into Mayfair House and used in clandestine experiments to which only Martindale's most trusted associates have access. The experiments call for infecting monkeys, one of which attacks and infects Wellington in turn. At the same time Martindale's own family is carried away by an illness never quite specified in the obituary notices.

Almost simultaneously a flu outbreak is reported first in the East End of London—atypical for this season—which is also extremely virulent, striking some victims dead where they stand and giving them no warning beforehand.

That efforts were made to destroy any evidence tying in Mayfair House and the outbreak only further served to convince Lightman that Mayfair House must have been where it had originated.

Yet as plausible as the scenario was, he could do nothing with it, not so long as he was trapped in London, under constant surveillance.

The only thing he could think to do to occupy his time was to sit in the historic reading room of the British Museum and work on an idea he'd long been mulling over and had never found time to develop. It was his belief that the Black Plague of the Middle Ages was not caused by infested rats, as widely held, but rather by anthrax. By devoting his attention to a plague that had occurred six and a half centuries before, he was able—temporarily—to put out of mind the plague that was proceeding around him, unabated.

If there was any subject other than diseases—past and present—which could dominate his thoughts for long it was Diana. He knew what was happening to him; he had only to remember how it was when he'd first met Stephanie. The same troublesome yearnings were present in both cases. They were symptoms of a kind too.

But he was reining himself in, unwilling to let his feelings for Diana engulf him. Her actual connection with Martindale remained ambiguous. She acted as though they no longer had any dealings with each other, seemed to want him to think that she was free and clear. When they were together he believed her. It was only when he was away from her that things became clouded and he was thrown into doubt all over again.

There was only so much brooding over Watney's that it was advisable to do, and so Lightman left the pub. The wind was as forceful as ever, like hot breath against the skin. A green cross, still smelling of fresh paint, was the first thing he noticed on stepping out the door; it was big and clumsily rendered on the side of a windowless facade. Lightman could have sworn that it wasn't there when he'd gone in.

Just a few days ago, for that matter, there hadn't been a green cross anywhere. Now they seemed to be all over the place, on crosswalks, dyed on T-shirts and sweatshirts and running jackets and painted along the sidewalks for block after block, like a trail that was meant to lead to somewhere in particular but never did.

Recalling the procession of flagellants with their crosses and apocalyptic pamphlets he'd stumbled into, he assumed that these crosses were somehow symbolic of the Church of the Redeemed. But he couldn't be sure. Presumably it was necessary to join the church before such mysteries would be revealed.

Fewer people than usual could be spotted on the London streets. Lightman couldn't blame them; why would anyone in his right mind be out in this desolating wind? And while it was still true that the flu was largely confined to the East End, the fear of it had outdistanced the contagion. Public places were shunned as sources of contamination. Even Lightman, who ordinarily escaped the ravages of winter colds and flus and who counted himself lucky to have never missed a day of work for the last ten years on account of illness, was made nervous by this thing. He couldn't quite shake the feeling that he might be next. When he looked into the faces of those he passed in his travels he saw the same terror in their eyes.

Nearing Diana's building he thought he caught sight of Gray.

He looked again. Maybe it was another tall fellow sporting dreadlocks. To be sure, he stopped in a tobacco shop and lingered there, observing passersby in the mirror over the Indian proprietor's head. When his eyes traveled from the mirror to the newspapers and periodicals in the racks below he registered a succession of banner headlines fighting for attention.

SEX SCANDAL ROCKS CABINET

—The *Sun*

MIDEAST PEACE CONFERENCE ENDS IN DISCORD

—The *Telegraph*

NEW ELECTION THOUGHT LIKELY AS LIBERAL-SD COALITION FALTERS

—*Evening Standard*

HEALTH MINISTER RIPTON CALLS FOR QUARANTINE MEASURES TO BE IMPOSED

—The *Times*

Nothing good in any of them, Lightman thought. Raising his eyes to the mirror again and seeing no Jamaican, he decided it was safe enough to venture back out.

He continued on to Diana's building without incident. The downstairs lock had been speedily repaired, but she'd given Lightman the keys, sparing him the necessity of buzzing up. She'd told him he should feel free to stop by whether she was at home or not.

He didn't know what she meant by this gesture, but he appreciated the opportunity it allowed him to see her.

He rang up anyway, not wanting to barge in on her. When he did not hear her respond he assumed she was out and used the key.

But she was in—he heard her as soon as he walked in the door. Or rather he heard the shower running. He made himself at home and waited. He was anxious to find out whether she'd heard the news about Martindale.

When she emerged from the bathroom she was wearing

a loose green shift that only dramatized how bare and wet her legs were. There was a towel wrapped around her hair. The surprise that came into her eyes at seeing him quickly vanished. She smiled. "I was just thinking about you," she said.

"I was in the neighborhood," he said.

She smelled of some scent that Lightman gradually recognized as mint. For a second or two he closed his eyes and breathed her smell in.

He'd never seen her this way, so close to being naked. But what got to him was how easy she was with him, betraying no self-consciousness at all. She walked over and sat down beside him, kissed him glancingly and said, "It's nice to see you."

He could tell she meant it.

She was talking to him but the words weren't penetrating, for what he was really listening to was the tone, the ebb and flow of her voice. He wanted to pay attention, he just couldn't.

When she bent forward the shift fell away so that her breasts came almost into view.

"Are you tired?" These were the first words of hers he registered.

"Yes," he said.

"The heat," she said. "The wind will do that to you."

She got up off the couch and instead of saying good night, as he expected her to do, she took hold of his hand and led him to her bedroom.

There was nothing for her to get out of really. The towel fell off and, with a sweeping motion of her arms, she disposed of the shift as well.

Her skin felt wondrous, like a revelation, like a gift. It had been so long that he'd very nearly forgotten how soft the touch of a woman's skin could be. Her legs scissored him, put him in a vise, and her hips moved slowly, arhythmically at first, lullingly against him.

Her face had vanished, and he was compelled to open

his eyes and look again to square the impression he had of her with the woman who'd gathered him in her embrace with such ardor, with such suddenness. Her eyes were slitted, her mouth hung partway open and her lips were moving silently. This was the face of a woman overcome by longing, by need, but there was no way of knowing how much this need was for him in particular and how much was a need that had nothing to do with him at all.

She was trying to get his clothes off, but his shirt buttons didn't give way so easily and she lost patience and said, "You do it," and he did.

He felt now that he was swimming in mint. Her kisses started quick, teasing, here and gone in an instant, surprising him where they landed. She liked the effect they were having. She laughed and her face changed again.

Everything was happening much too quickly, he had no time to adjust. His whole life had turned so unreal in the last twenty-four hours that he almost suspected that this wasn't truly happening. But her flesh was real, the touch of her lips, her breasts, her thighs was real. How easy it was going to be to get lost in her, he thought, how easy and how dangerous.

She dropped off to sleep in his arms, but Lightman wasn't interested in sleep. He couldn't have slept even if he'd wanted to. He watched the shadows deepening around Diana, gradually obscuring her breasts, her neck, the elegant oval lines of her face, until he could no longer make out her features. The sweat, in drying off of her, left her skin surprisingly cool to the touch. She took in a great breath of air in her sleep, like an enormous sigh, and turned away from him, extending one arm out as if to reach for something.

Lightman looked toward the bay windows. The shutters hadn't been closed so that he could see out perfectly well. Lights were on in the window in the building across the way. There appeared to be people—two, then three—in the window. All women. They were naked, their flesh gleaming, their postures provocative, almost aggressive. Their lips were parted suggestively, but there was nothing at all going on in their eyes.

Lightman got out of bed. Diana shifted position again, bringing one leg up closer to her breasts, but did not awaken. The three women were looking straight at him but there was no reaction on their faces.

Now he realized that none of the three was moving, not so much as a flicker of an eye, a twitch of a limb. Not until he stepped up to the bay window did he realize why they could remain this frozen for minutes on end.

They weren't real. They were a slide projection. He wasn't looking into a room, as he'd previously believed, but was looking at a screen of some kind on which a succession of lurid images was being flashed.

Then, before he could fathom what it all was about, the three women disappeared, replaced by another image, this time of a couple in the throes of passion, entangled on a bed. It took Lightman only a few additional moments to realize that the woman with her head thrown back, her mouth opening to let out a cry was Diana, and the man whose lips were pressed against the base of her neck was himself.

TWENTY

Ezra Omaru shot up, sweat pouring off him. He was shaking but he was no longer feverish. All he had on was a pair of undershorts. There were dark rusty stains on them, dried blood. But that wasn't what shocked him so much. What frightened him a great deal more were the raised purplish blisters that had sprouted out of his body and now covered his chest and arms and legs. A few more he could feel by running his hands along his face. His hands also told him that he was growing a beard; three, four days' worth of stubble, there was no telling. He didn't dare look into a mirror; he didn't think he would recognize himself.

Each step was an ordeal; a baby must feel that way the first few times it tried to walk. His legs didn't want to support him and they wobbled and almost gave way. And when he finally managed to get to the other side of the room he immediately slumped down in his chair, nearly all his energy spent on accomplishing what used to be the easiest thing in the world.

The clock was still working and it said four-fifteen. But what it didn't tell him was whether it was four-fifteen in the morning or the afternoon (the shades were all down) nor did it tell him what day it was.

He didn't know whether he was hungry or not. His body, the whole mechanism that made it work, had become a stranger to him. He felt a loss that wasn't just physical but was something much worse; it was as if somebody had come along and robbed his soul.

When he called out for Nassa and heard no reply he wasn't surprised. He hadn't expected her to be there. Actually he was relieved. Gathering up what little strength he could he rose from the chair and made his way to the other room.

Even before he opened the door he knew that something was terribly wrong. Fear mounted in him that he would find his children dead. Dead of whatever it was that had almost killed him. Nassa he didn't care about. Nassa could die and he wouldn't spare a tear for her.

How many minutes passed before he could bring himself to open the door he didn't know. Then he lost patience with himself. Opening the door he looked in, his eyes widening to take in the dreadful sight that greeted him.

There was practically nothing left. The drawers of the

massively built bureau where the children's clothes were kept were all open—and empty. The mattresses were stripped of their bedding. There was only one pillow left and that had sprung a leak so that when Ezra stooped to pick it up feathers went flying in all directions. It was like snow falling.

Ezra sat down on the floor, covered with feathers. He repeated his children's names—Danny, Benjamin, Elias, Mara, and Cherish—over and over like a litany. There was no litany he could recite, though, that was going to magically restore them to this room.

Their toys were gone. That somehow was a more wrenching absence than the missing clothes. The ten-speed bicycle that he'd scraped together the money for the Christmas past had occupied a special corner all its own and now that corner seemed to mock him with its emptiness. The only thing that had been left behind was the xylophone that none of the children had had any use for.

Without thinking why, Ezra took hold of the mallets and tried to pound the xylophone out of existence. The xylophone could have been his wife; he wished it were. But the xylophone resisted his onslaught and all that he accomplished was to produce a disturbance so shrill that notes lingered on in the air for several seconds afterward. Ezra threw the mallets as hard as he could against the wall, producing two holes in the plaster that gave Ezra an odd satisfaction.

For some while afterward he couldn't move. He remained where he was, inert, giving himself totally to the pain of his loss. Tears dribbled from his eyes and his body was wracked by sobs.

Then he felt an enormous thirst. This very real physical need intruded on his grief. He picked himself up and went to the tap and, unable to find any glass his wife hadn't taken with her, cupped his hands and let the water flow into them.

The water tasted funny, there was even a yellowish tinge

to it, but he didn't know whether this was because something was wrong with the water or because his sickness was making everything taste funny.

He found that he could get around better, that his legs were no longer so wobbly. He made another, closer inspection of his flat. Nassa, he saw, had been kind enough to leave him his own clothes. And the telly; that was still there. Probably because it was too heavy to take.

Thinking to learn what was going on in the outside world he switched it on.

A moment later he was looking into the face of Jonas Beck exhorting those who were still unredeemed to join his church before it was too late. "The great pestilence shall smite you down."

Observing the hideous purple blisters on his skin, Ezra realized he was referring to people like him. He concentrated his gaze on the evangelist's face. How much hatred, how much bitterness, he saw there. It was almost as if he could see beneath the skin to the skull. The man was a corpse, one of the walking dead.

Anger renewed itself in Ezra Omaru. Fury swelled his chest and caused him to put his face so close to the tube that Jonas Beck's face all but dissolved into a sea of electronic dots.

"You stole my children! You stole my Nassa! You stole my soul!" he raved.

Soon he didn't know what he was shouting or what he was doing. His rage, far from abating, grew wilder. He began hammering the television, then, when that failed to appease him, he stepped back and drove his foot through it. Jonas Beck disappeared in a burst of disintegrating glass, some of which struck Ezra and lodged in his flesh. A mystery of coiled wires and transistors came into view.

He paused for breath, wondering whether he'd not been too hasty, especially when he recalled how much he'd had to save in order to buy the bloody thing.

Then it occurred to him that it didn't matter, that he

would never need the telly again, that without his family this was no longer his home.

Although it was sweltering, he put on clothes that would leave the least amount of skin exposed. He decided to let his beard keep growing in hopes that it would hide some of the blisters from view. He was certain that people, after taking one look at his unsightly self, would want to have nothing to do with him.

As soon as he stepped out of his flat he became aware of a terrible stench. Turning on the timed light switch he saw a woman sitting there, with what were probably all her belongings heaped into a wicker basket beside her. It was from her the stench was coming. He couldn't help touching her. Dried flecks of skin came away in his hands.

He pounded at the door next to his. No answer. Without bothering to lock up he descended the stairs. At every landing he rapped on the doors but no one came to answer. It was possible that everyone had fled, that he was the only person—the only person left alive—in the entire building.

His shop was open. The window was smashed, the door hung off its hinges. Inside there was the rich ripe smell of herbs and teas, an aroma that embraced everything he had out for sale. That was all that was left, that aroma; what produced the aroma was gone, looted sometime while he lay unconscious.

All along Buxhill Road, as far as he could see, the shops had been as thoroughly sacked as his. The air was foul with smoke and stank of cinder and ash. Fires were still burning not so far away. A young man came within sight. He was shirtless and his chest, too, was covered with raised purple blisters. He was an African, an Ibo from the looks of him, and when he turned toward Ezra his eyes rolled in their sockets as if he could no longer control their movements. Then, without a word, he shambled along in the direction he was going. Only after he'd passed did Ezra notice that he was barefooted and that he was leaving a trail of blood behind from the glass and debris he kept stepping on. But there was something in him that had gone beyond the sensation of pain.

Alarms were blaring and bells were ringing like mad but there was no way of telling what all the commotion was for. Was it a summons for help? A signal of distress? Or a final convulsive uproar, the plaintive cry of a dying animal, nothing else?

There was no sign of a bobby or a firefighter or anyone in uniform to represent authority. It seemed as if the whole area had been abandoned to the disease and the disorder which followed in its wake. Things had been bad before this; now Ezra couldn't imagine how they could get much worse.

As he walked on he began seeing more bodies. His own loss was such that it had left him numb to the sight of death. The last time he'd felt so numb was when he was in Uganda, escaping Obote's soldiers. He did not want to be this numb, but he knew that to allow the shock and horror to penetrate would immobilize him worse than before. The need to find his children, at least to discover whether they were alive, was what kept him going. That was the only thing that mattered now.

Because there was so much else to capture his attention he did not at first observe the green crosses painted on the walls. Where once there had been hammers and sickles and political slogans now there were only these boldly painted green crosses. Posters advertising Wimpie's and Rothmann's cigarettes and Sanyo video recorders were also covered with the crosses. It was odd, he thought, how so many obvious messages—to buy or to believe—had been cancelled out by a message which didn't make any sense at all. But then he reasoned that he must have been unconscious for four or five days, maybe more, and it was possible that in that time, when these green crosses had appeared, somebody had made it clear what their meaning was.

For Ezra it was like going to bed in one world and waking up in another. He'd heard stories and legends about people who had had such things happen to them, but he had not believed that it would ever happen to himself.

From Buxhill Road he turned north into Caithness Street, making his way into the Pakistani and Bangladeshi district. Here it was no better. The smell of death was democratic; an East Asian stank as badly as an East African. A man he once knew told him that the only people who could be expected to smell good were those who shunned meat. He was a Hindu and he said that a vegetarian diet would guarantee that your shit would smell better. Not that it would make any difference what you ate when it came to what smell you gave off when you started to rot. It was all the same. This excursion in Caithness Street was proof of that.

From Caithness he turned onto Cotswalds where he was obliged to pick his way through the uncollected corpses. They must have been struck down suddenly, allowing them no time to get to their houses so they could do their dying in private.

For the first time since venturing out he spotted people —not just one or two dazed souls—but a whole wave of them, heading in the opposite direction than he, their faces full of despondency and resignation. A few he noticed bore the same stigmata he did, their dark skin covered with raised purple blisters: the mark of the survivor. Some, though, were obviously sick, scarcely able to put one foot in front of the other. There were those who were doing their best to sponge the blood running from their noses and mouths with handkerchiefs and tissue paper.

Seeing Ezra approach, a few of them motioned him to go back.

"Don't bother, man," they said. "Forget it, it's no use."

But Ezra failed to draw a coherent reply from them when he asked them why he shouldn't continue on. He watched as the crowd pushed on along Cotswalds and then disappeared from sight, leaving behind two of their number who had collapsed.

All he needed to do was walk five minutes more to discover why he'd been advised to turn around.

A police barrier, built with just about anything the authorities could lay their hands on—concertina wire, wooden boards, upended trash barrels, sheets of aluminum and tin—had been set down in the middle of the street. Blinding lights, powered by a portable generator, bathed the whole area. Although it was still daylight, there was so much smoke that it was like living in perpetual dusk.

Those weren't bobbies, he saw, but soldiers, cradling automatic weapons, guarding the barrier. Others, out of uniform, continued to buttress the barrier. They were all wearing gas masks.

When Ezra stepped to within a few yards of the barrier, one of the soldiers—eighteen or nineteen years old, he guessed—brandished his rifle.

"You can't go beyond this point," the soldier said.

His voice, from behind the mask, sounded hollow, not exactly human.

"Why? Why can't I go past?"

He wasn't protesting really, he was seeking information although he expected he knew the answer already. "It is by order of her Majesty's Government."

"What order are you talking about?"

"The newly enacted quarantine act." The soldier was impatient.

"How long will this quarantine law be in effect?"

A stupid question. The soldier made a menacing gesture with his gun that convinced Ezra to back off. Noticing that the barricade was being reinforced with concrete, he realized that the answer to his question was nothing that needed to be put into words.

He knew it would be foolish to try other streets that led out of the district. Surely the authorities would have seen to it that all possible exits were closed off. Passing by an underground station he saw that the entrance to it was barred as well. It was obvious to Ezra that the tens of thousands of people in this district of East London known as Limehouse would be left to die on their own. Probably the same held true in Wapping and the Isle of Dogs.

It was only by luck (what little of it he had remaining) that in his wanderings he came upon Mohammed al-Housani, a razor-thin Iraqi who had owned a grocery down the street from Ezra's herb shop. Mohammed had never looked well in the best of times; now he looked no worse.

Though not more than a week had passed since they had last seen each other their greeting was effusive and congratulatory. If Mohammed observed the blisters on his face he did not mention them. What mattered was that they were still alive.

They found some chairs and sat down in front of a shoe store. Like all the other shops around it had been looted. But something very curious had occurred; there were still many, many shoes inside the store and in front of it. But these shoes were all worn and shot through with holes. Clearly their owners had discarded them in favor of the new ones they snatched off the shelves.

Mohammed and he began to catch up on the news. Ezra was so happy to see someone he knew—someone who wasn't ill or dying—that he could scarcely contain his excitement. At last he got around to the subject that weighed most heavily on his heart. "By any chance have you seen my children?" he asked, his voice breaking as his grief reasserted itself.

The question caught Mohammed off guard. He scrutinized Ezra to see if maybe he was joking. But then he understood that this was no joke.

"I saw them yesterday, or the day before—I lose track. I thought that you had sent them away."

"Sent them away—where?"

"They were joining the other pilgrims."

Nothing Mohammed was saying made any sense. "Which pilgrims are you talking about?"

"The disciples of Jonas Beck. Those who declared themselves believers in the Church of the Redeemed were led to a special place—I do not know where this was exactly—and then they were examined by a doctor and allowed to go out."

"You mean they left Limehouse?"

"I hear that they left London."

"My children!" Ezra raised his hands into the air in anguish.

Mohammed tried to console him. "Isn't it better that they have escaped this pestilence?"

Ezra acknowledged that of course it was better. But that Nassa should do this to him, abandon him to this terrible disease and follow Jonas Beck, tore him apart. If he didn't find his children soon then he knew very well what would happen: they would become like their mother, slaves of this madman, this religious fanatic.

When he calmed himself down enough he asked Mohammed, "How is it that these people who believe in this man Beck can go free while we are forced to stay here?"

"This I don't know, my friend. But he must have powerful friends or too much money. What else could it be? It is either one or the other. Always."

History and his own personal experience must have accounted for the conviction in Mohammed's voice.

"Tell me, Mohammed, if I was to go to these people who believe in Jonas Beck and say that I believe in him too, would they let me go free from Limehouse?"

"This is what I am told," said Mohammed. "Are you going to do this?"

Ezra said that yes, this surely was what he would do. He would lie, he would kill, he would declare allegiance to a false god—anything to get his children back.

TWENTY-ONE

The party, if it wasn't growing wilder, was certainly becoming more raucous. The music was a combustible mix of blues, reggae, ska, mento, eskeusta, and inevitably, the Blue Angel Boys. Lightman wouldn't have known what any of the music was except that someone insisted on explaining it to him.

It had been some while since he was last at a party that wasn't confined to a polite gathering over dinner, and so he'd almost forgotten what it was like to have people swirling all about him, their hands clutching glasses of jalapeña vodka, a favorite of this crowd, and small plates cluttered with prawns, salmon, and Persian caviar. Throughout the rooms of this Maida Vale house there was a smell of something that Lightman had never smelled before and which, therefore, he assumed was illegal.

But with all the noise from the music and the raised voices of the revelers trying to talk over it, there was one sound that managed to penetrate: it was the sound of somebody's hacking cough. A dry, dirty cough that at one moment seemed to be coming from the adjoining room and the next from a room overhead.

Only a man who introduced himself to Lightman as Lord Hawthorne hazarded an opinion as to who was responsible for the coughing. "It has to be our hostess," he insisted almost boastfully.

"Our hostess?" Diana, in dragging him off to this party, had neglected to specify who was holding it or even what the occasion was, saying only that it would be fun, and it was about time he enjoyed himself for once.

"Yes, Susan Gately. I would have thought you knew her. Anybody who knows Diana knows Susan."

Lord Hawthorne didn't bear any resemblance to what Lightman had imagined a lord would look like. He was young, with rebellious blond hair, a face unmarked by experience and an air of disdain so pronounced it was almost comical. "You understand that when Susan decides to go ahead and throw a bash she isn't about to be put off by a little thing like a fatal malady."

A buxom, but handsome, woman standing nearby looked shocked to hear him say this. "Oh but it's true, dear Aggie, Susan is on her way out," Lord Hawthorne said. "Perhaps if we're lucky, she'll put in an appearance before the night's out." His smile was full of mock pity for those who were weak enough to fall ill. "But then again she is so very vain that she won't want to show us how poorly she looks in extremis—not unless she dons a mask. I could see her doing that. In fact, I might just go on upstairs and knock on her door and suggest she do just that. There's no reason for her to miss her own party, is there?"

"You don't think that's in poor taste?" Aggie didn't sound like she was very sure.

"Not at all. You know Susan. The idea will be certain to appeal to her, it's so fabulous." Turning back to Lightman, he said, "You know whose fault it is that this has happened?"

Lightman didn't have any idea what he was referring to, and wasn't really interested. He was searching out escape routes with his eyes, hoping to find a way to separate himself from Lord Hawthorne as soon as he possibly could.

"I will tell you since you are an American and cannot possibly be expected to know these things. It is the darker races. They breed faster and live in such squalor that there's no question that they're the ones who are responsible for spreading this monstrous flu. They call it the London flu but we all know that it didn't come from here, it was brought in by the illegals. We should never have let them in."

"But at least they're getting out now," Aggie interjected. "Better late than never."

"You're going to have to make yourself clearer," Lord Hawthorne said.

"Oh surely you know to what I'm referring, Dickie. That man Breck or Beck. It's the coloreds who respond to him more than anybody else. I understand that they're rounding them up and shipping them off somewhere—the farther the better, I say. England's well enough rid of them."

Lord Hawthorne was not impressed. "It will take some doing before the lot of them is gone. If we didn't have this damn Liberal-Social Democratic coalition in power we wouldn't be in a position like this today. It's their policies that are to blame. The best we can hope for is that this bloody flu does the work our damn government should have done long ago."

Lightman resisted the impulse to say that by singling out the so-called darker races Lord Hawthorne had gotten it ass backwards as to who was to blame for spawning this epidemic. Instead he asked where these people were being resettled.

Lord Hawthorne didn't know, neither did Aggie, who simply said, "I don't care so long as it's nowhere near England. Let the Wogs put up with them for a change."

Lightman saw his chance and slipped away without bothering with an excuse. Neither Lord Hawthorne nor Aggie seemed to notice.

He went in search of Diana, pushing his way through the throngs from room to room, from third floor to second and then to first, and failing to locate her was obliged to retrace his steps.

Susan's coughing, through some acoustical fluke, followed him wherever he went. Or maybe it wasn't her coughing but the coughing of someone else, or perhaps of any number of guests who were coming down with the flu.

He found Diana at last, conversing with a group of people, an older couple and a man whose back was to Lightman.

It was the man who arrested his attention when he finally caught sight of his face. It was his eyes that did it. They were fixed in such an unsettling way, and engorged with blood, bulging from their sockets—there was just no way to avoid looking at them. It occurred to Lightman that they might be paralyzed, incapable of movement. His assessment was borne out an instant later when the man held a dispenser over his eyes and squeezed some drops out into them. He was a strangely ugly man, with a long hard face and closely cropped hair. The way his eyes had become locked in place, however it had happened, lent him a peculiar fascination. Lightman could imagine a certain type of woman becoming attracted to him.

Trying not to stare, although doubtlessly this man was used to drawing attention to himself, Lightman directed his gaze toward Diana.

"Oh there you are," she said, "I was wondering what had become of you. John, I'd like you to meet my aunt, Alister Gately, and her companion, Charles Dawes."

Charles was a sprightly graying man in his late seventies while Alister was a diminutive woman of great age and frailty, who Lightman guessed must be related to their secluded hostess.

Lightman smiled and shook hands all around. The gentleman with the immobilized eyes turned out to be a film director, apparently very well-known in certain circles, named Richard Thorning. "Richard's latest picture did an incredible business when it opened in the States," Diana said. "Maybe you recall it, John? It was called *Time, Gentlemen, Please*."

Lightman apologized, saying that he didn't follow films and rarely had a chance to get out and see one.

Thorning said that he understood perfectly. "Diana's mentioned that you are a scientist. Scientists shouldn't be expected to squander time on frivolous things like movies."

There was something in his tone of voice to suggest that, on the contrary, being a scientist was no excuse, and that he greatly resented anybody who had been so derelict as to miss one of his movies—or worse, not have even heard of them.

Lightman was anxious to go although he saw that Diana was enjoying herself, launched into her present state by whatever the pale reddish concoctions she was drinking consisted of. "Richard and I met out at Pinewood when I was contracted to do some costuming for one of his projects," she said. "We got on famously."

He wondered. Thorning was looking at him with those eyes of his and Lightman automatically trained his own eyes on Alister and Charles. They gave him puzzled smiles.

"How long do you plan on being with us?" Alister inquired.

What Lightman wanted to know was what she meant by that. He hoped she was interested in learning how long he intended to stay in London and not on the planet, but since he was equally ignorant in either instance all he could say was, "I don't really know yet."

"Oh, I see." The benign smile stayed on. "I hope it shall be for awhile. I am sure Diana appreciates having you around."

He had no idea what she meant by that either. Exactly what had Diana let on about him? Were these people looking on him as a friend from America or as a new lover who, without his ever being aware of it, was being judged in the context of all those who had preceded him, including Martindale? There was no telling, and that was what made him so nervous. Not just nervous—angry. He didn't know who he was to Diana, nor what she wanted him to be.

Though physically still there he was no longer able to participate in the conversation. He wasn't conscious of what was being said, nor did he hear the music. The only thing that his consciousness was picking up was the coughing, nothing else, not the music, not what Diana or Thorning was saying, just the coughing.

He wanted to be alone with her, he wanted to extricate her from these people and no longer suffer the indignity of being the outsider. Her beauty seemed to be a function of his ability to attain her. He was already feeling proprietary toward her, and this after sharing just four nights together. A mistake, all a mistake.

She was laughing now, her perfect teeth glowing, her African bracelets jangling on her bare arms. The dress she was wearing was like a sheath, all silver and emerald green, molded defiantly to her body.

Suddenly she looked in his direction and motioned to him. "What are you doing over there? Come and join us." She grabbed hold of his arm so as to leave no doubt of her intention.

The night went on. Lightman's longing for departure was turning into a kind of a hunger, but Diana wouldn't think of leaving, not yet, she said, not while life still remained to this party.

While in search of a free bathroom Lightman came on a woman whose voluptuous body would ordinarily have stopped him in his tracks. The only problem was her face; it was so white that it could have been plastered on. On second thought, it might have been a mask. Was it possible that this was the hostess, who having taken Lord Hawthorne's suggestion, had decided to risk an appearance after all? Her lips were purple and they were moving. What was it she was saying? He leaned closer.

"What a nice-looking young man," she said. "And where did you come from?"

Before she could get out another word she was racked by a paroxysm of coughing, and Lightman knew that it had to be Susan Gately. He backed away, not answering the question. He backed away, and then he fled.

When he found Diana again he saw that she'd become more subdued, her attention was wandering, there was a glazed and unfocused look in her eyes. She looked drawn, unsteady on her feet. Lightman had little difficulty prevailing on her to leave.

As they stood outside waiting for one of the valets to bring around the car, she volunteered the information that Thorning had done work for Martindale. "I can't tell you what he did exactly, I think it involved recording his experiments on videotape. I do know that he did at least one promotional film for Mayfair House."

"What about his eyes? How did they get like that?"

"This is the first time I've seen him like this. The poor man must be suffering so, don't you think? Never being able to shut his eyes, it's horrible! Did you see how he has to keep them constantly moistened? I don't know how he gets to sleep. Eye patches I suppose. I'm told that he came down with some illness. I don't know what it could be that could do that to a person."

"Did Patrick treat him for this strange affliction?"

"I imagine so. He was incommunicado in Mayfair House for a week. I'm certain that Patrick would have taken a personal interest in his case."

She broke off her account when her car—a camel colored Bentley—appeared. Lightman, noticing that she still seemed a bit unsteady on her feet, offered to do the driving.

She resented the insinuation that she might be too drunk. "You should see me when I get really pissed," she said. "Believe me, my dear, I could, if I wanted to, drink you under the proverbial table." Then she gave him an appraising glance and, smiling, said, "All right, if you insist, I'll indulge you. You can take me home."

It was an experience, driving her Bentley—like her flat, an inheritance from Nicholas—it rode so smoothly. Diana at his side fell asleep.

But she awoke before they arrived at her building. Walking in she headed straight for the bedroom, flinging herself on the bed, not even troubling to remove her shoes.

Lightman stepped over to the window and looked out across the alley, to the window facing him. It was all in darkness. No show tonight. Nor had he seen anything there the last three nights. Though he'd meant to tell Diana about his sighting he'd held off, thinking she might already know, thinking that in fact she might be a willing collaborator in his perverse voyeuristic fantasy. But finally that wasn't why he'd said nothing to her. What caused him to remain silent was that he was afraid he'd never really seen anything at all in that window, that all he'd been doing was imagining things. He was afraid that he was the one who was going mad.

"Help me off with this, please, will you, dear?" Diana said, raising her arms.

Lightman pulled and the shimmering garment came off of her, leaving her naked. "I'm freezing, do you think you could do something about the air conditioner?"

She huddled up in the blanket. She had gone very pale. Lightman checked the air conditioner but it was already off. It was a little chilly in the room, but nothing that could account for her being as cold as she said she was.

"Can I get you something—some tea, some water maybe?"

"Water would be nice."

When he brought her the water he saw that she was shivering, that the blanket wasn't warming her enough. She took hold of the glass with both hands and brought it to her lips. The water began to dribble, she couldn't control it.

He was becoming worried. He sat at the edge of the bed, looking at her, hoping that it was the drink that was responsible for her plight and nothing more serious.

"I feel so funny," she said, "and it hurts right here." She indicated a point below her diaphragm. "God, it hurts." She winced.

Her mouth was opening, and her eyes widened with astonishment, the way a child might react on receiving an unexpected gift, and then she arched her back, stiffening, and her mouth formed an O, and she asked Lightman a question. "What's happening to me?" But he couldn't tell her. He didn't know.

Then she exploded. Blood flew from her mouth, poured from her nostrils. She managed a strangled, liquid cry. And before he could react she leapt up from the bed, rushing toward the bathroom. But she was arrested by the sight of herself in the wall mirror.

Her face was streaming with blood, her flesh dripping with it. The terror in her eyes mingled with disbelief that this could possibly be happening to her. And then she couldn't see herself anymore; all she could see was more blood. Her reflection in the mirror was blotted out by it. She continued to hemorrhage.

Lightman rushed to grab hold of her, stumbling in her bloody tracks, but before he could reach her she collapsed, falling not toward him but toward the mirror, clawing at it, her nails scraping the glass with an ugly, wrenching sound. Then she slipped to the floor. Lightman lifted her up and called her name. But while her eyes were open, when he looked into them, there was nothing there.

TWENTY-TWO

The worst things were the cries of the sick and the dying. The wards were all filled and so beds had been put out in the corridors. It was impossible to ignore the patients whose faces were fixed in a grimace of pain. Serous fluid dribbled from their lips and oozed onto the sheets—and those were the lucky ones. Others were gushing blood as black as ink, holding their hands in front of their faces—hands that were black and sticky—unable to comprehend how this strange substance could be coming out of their bodies. And everywhere there was the same unceasing racket of coughing, and from the dying a sound that resembled the repeated rustling of wrapping paper.

Doctors, most of them foreign, rushed from one patient to the other, struggling to keep up with the mounting crisis. They themselves, hollow-eyed and drained, looked barely able to keep from falling over. Their white coats were spattered with every type of fluid and serum imaginable. The red blood dried brown, the black dried blacker.

The nurses were more harried, and while they went about their work with brusque efficiency, Lightman saw that they were beyond caring, that they were functioning like automatons, just trying to finish what they had to do so they could take their break. When everything was an emergency then nothing was.

Conditions in Christchurch Hospital might have started out being acceptable, but now, with the staff so strapped, they had deteriorated dramatically. Either the air conditioning system was dead or it was strained to capacity so that it no longer had much of an effect.

There was scarcely any air in the place and it was stifling besides. The stench rising from people's flu-ridden bodies was so pervasive that it was all Lightman could do to keep from vomiting.

It had been one thing to watch BBC broadcasts about the epidemic situation in London, quite another to witness it firsthand. Statistics delivered in a dry monotone by a distinguished looking commentator failed to convey the enormity of the problem. For many, like Lord Hawthorne, the imposition of the Emergency Quarantine Act was an abstraction, meaningless to his own life; even the flu itself was an abstraction for him since he was convinced it would devastate only the darker races, as he liked to call them, and leave him untouched.

But from what Lightman could see now, a quarantine was probably belated and, being only sporadically enforced, too ineffective to be of any use. He could only imagine what it was like in other hospitals in metropolitan London; it couldn't be much better and it was, in all likelihood, a great deal worse.

As he continued through the hospital he kept getting lost. Part of the problem was he couldn't find anyone to give him proper directions. Not being ill himself, he was evidently not entitled to any attention.

Diana, he knew, was in room 640. But when he'd gone to 640A and not discovered her there, he was advised by one of the patients occupying the room that he might try 640B, that there was often a lot of confusion between the two, since the A wing was an exact twin of the B wing. But where was the B wing?

If he'd been permitted to, Lightman would have stayed the night there, but he was told that, under the restrictions of the Quarantine Act, it was impossible. That morning, on his return, there was no one to stop him from going up to the wards.

The one person he had spoken to last night, a Dr. Metha, had told him that a hemorrhage like Diana had suffered might not be such a bad sign, that it might, in fact, represent a "crisis" through which she would have to pass before she could recover her health. It was then that Lightman had pointed out that she'd been in perfectly good health until then. To which Dr. Metha had replied, "Well, you see, this is a very mysterious illness and so we cannot truly say anything certain about it at all."

After searching frantically for several minutes Lightman found the B Wing. It was quieter there, less crowded. The ventilating system functioned. He gathered that it was reserved for patients willing to pay for their care out of their own pockets rather than those relying on National Health Insurance.

He approached the entrance to 640B with trepidation, afraid he would find Diana dying. Or dead. He finally summoned the will to look inside. Then he looked again, thinking that he might have missed something. He checked the room number again. He had the right one.

There was only one person in the room and that was an aged woman, who, with trembling hands, was holding a basin into which she was throwing up.

Panic seized him. He went to the next room and to the next, still believing that he'd made some mistake. But there was no sign of her at all.

He buttonholed a nurse, but she'd just come on duty and had no idea who he was talking about. She did say that Dr. Metha should be somewhere around; if he went to the nurses station, which was back the way he'd come, someone there might be able to locate him for Lightman. It all sounded vague, but he supposed there was nothing else to do.

At the nurses station he was told to wait, that in ten or fifteen minutes Dr. Metha would pass by.

Otherwise nobody had any time for him. The phones kept ringing while the nurses tried to field inquiries from anxious families demanding to know the condition of their loved ones. In many cases, it seemed, the information available to the nurses was outdated or nonexistent. For some patients there was simply no record at all. Among these was Diana Cleary. Callers were advised to call Admissions. If told that this had already been done without achieving any satisfaction, the nurse would recommend ringing back in the afternoon, no doubt when someone else would be at the desk to take the call.

It wasn't until nearly forty-five minutes had gone by that Dr. Metha turned up. He gazed at Lightman in confusion, trying to recall where he'd last seen him.

Lightman reminded him who he was, detecting a glimmer of recognition in Metha's eyes.

"Oh, yes," he said, but tentatively.

"I brought in a patient last night—Diana Cleary."

"Ah yes, I remember now."

"I went to look for her and she just doesn't seem to be here."

"But, my dear sir, she's not."

"Not here?"

"No, not at all. She was transferred out about an hour or two after she was admitted."

Were they talking about the same woman? "Transferred out where?"

"As I understand it, to Mayfair House."

"You're absolutely certain?"

"I thought you would have known about it."

"Nobody told me a thing. Who authorized this transfer?"

Dr. Metha gave a pronounced shrug. "It is not in my capacity to say."

It took an interminable ride in a taxi to reach Mayfair House, but that was by no means the fault of the driver. Everywhere there were traffic jams, commotion, piercing sirens. For the first time Lightman saw people bleeding in the streets, handkerchiefs to their noses and mouths, hurrying to get help. The expressions on their faces reflected embarrassment more than anything else, as if they were deeply ashamed to be caught leaking blood for everyone to see. Sickness, like acts of sex, the faces seemed to say, should be carried out in private.

Lightman spotted bodies, too. Lifeless heaps lying close to King's Cross. Or maybe they weren't dead at all but were ill or drunk. One way or another, they exhibited no movement. Ignoring them, the prostitutes were out in force, tarts with lurid makeup, their dresses designed to reveal the wares they were selling. Taking advantage of the paralysis that had engulfed the traffic they would approach the stalled cars, calling out to the passengers trapped inside, "Sweetheart, darling, what do you say to a date with the likes of me?"

"More of them than ever," muttered the driver, motioning them back. It was a gesture they ignored. "They come out, you know, when things are gone to bloody hell." He said he heard stories he believed were true about men that had gone to sleep one night with these tarts and awakened dying of the flu. "It's them that started it, the same as with AIDS. They're friggin' carriers, but do you think they come down with it? Not a chance!"

Yet in spite of the opinion he voiced, Lightman could see with his own eyes that these girls weren't immune. Some were clearly suffering from the sickness. One, he noticed, had done what she could to wash away the blood on her lips and chin but hadn't done a very thorough job. It had caked into her lipstick and mascara; the result was like some grotesque death mask.

In contrast to the devastation the epidemic was wreaking on the rest of London, Mayfair appeared to have escaped without noticeable effect. There were no bodies in the streets, no one visibly ill attempting to find refuge. On the contrary, there was hardly anyone to be seen in the district. There were more bobbies in sight than pedestrians and the windows in many of the homes they passed were concealed behind drawn curtains.

"All of them skedaddled that could," the driver told him. "You got the bloody money you don't feel obliged to stay and wait for the flu to hit you, do you now?"

Lightman agreed that he had a point. He wished that he, too, could have gotten out. Mayfair House looked untouched by the disease rampaging elsewhere in the city. There was none of the confusion and panic among the people present in the emergency room that Lightman had witnessed at Christchurch. If it was inevitable that those with money had to die, their deaths would be as discreet and clean as they undoubtedly hoped their lives had been.

A magnificent Poussin—a bucolic landscape populated by a great many industrious looking peasants—hung above the admissions desk. A young man sat at a table; he seemed stuporously bored.

Apart from a faintly antiseptic smell, there was nothing about the admissions area to suggest that in the rooms beyond a clinic was to be found. The staff—those members of it whose errands took them by the admissions desk—were neat, their clothes unstained with any unsightly human juices; they were professionals one could put faith in.

"May I help you, sir?"

Introducing himself, Lightman went on to say that he was looking for a patient named Diana Cleary. "I understand she was transferred here last night from Christchurch Hospital."

A console in front of the man lit up, he tapped out a few keys.

"Yes, that's correct. She was admitted here at 12:44 this morning."

It surprised Lightman that this information should have been so easily obtained after his torturous efforts to find out anything at all at Christchurch. He was beginning to think that it was better that Diana was treated here after all. Still, he didn't appreciate the fact that she was under Martindale's control. Who else but he could have arranged for her to come here?

"Can you give me some idea of her condition?"

"That information isn't available to me. Let me see if I can put you in contact with her physician, Stephen Butler. He should be able to tell you what you want to know. Please have a seat."

Lightman took a seat across from the Poussin. There was nothing to read, no sound to heed but the muffled voices of people he couldn't see from behind the wall of the admissions area, nothing to do but look at the peasants on the canvas. The young man made a call to somewhere in the building, then said to Lightman, "I'm having him paged. It shouldn't take long."

An elderly couple, the woman wearing a white fox coat in spite of the heat, walked in. They went up to the desk. The man was in worse shape than the woman was, his shambling step and bent carriage suggesting a debilitating infirmity. From what of the exchange Lightman could overhear they were seeking information about their son. They, too, were advised to take a seat. Their walk back across the length of the room was probably only slightly less painful for Lightman to watch than it was for them to accomplish.

Presently a silver-haired man, really a very handsome man, came out and stood by the desk for a moment, hesitating as he looked from the couple to Lightman and back again.

The young man said something to him. Nodding, he went over to Lightman and identified himself as Dr. Butler.

"Dr. Lightman, how are you?"

"Oh, I'm fine, thank you. Could you tell me how Diana is, if I could see her?"

His face darkened. "I'm sorry to have to tell you this, Dr. Lightman, but Diana Cleary is dead."

TWENTY-THREE

As they were headed out of the Excelsior, the concierge beckoned to Julian in a curiously conspiratorial manner.

The concierge might have wondered at Julian since he gave every appearance of being sober. But the truth was that Julian was far from sober. It was just that when he wanted to act respectable he had little difficulty pulling it off.

But it wasn't his drinking the concierge wanted to speak to him about. He pointed to a copy of *Il Messagario* left unfolded on the counter. Ignoring the headline, which Julian saw had something to do with the election of the new pope, the concierge pointed out a story at the bottom of the page. Since it was in Italian Julian had no way of knowing what it said.

Looking past Julian at his wife, who in her summery confection of lace and cotton was no doubt going to be the cause of a great deal of disturbance once the Roman males got a chance to see her, the concierge said, "Signore, I think it is better for you that you leave Rome at once."

A declaration of this sort from a man whose business it was to encourage the visitor to stay and enjoy the Eternal City Julian found altogether confounding.

"I'm not sure I understand."

He gave Nancy a quick smile to reassure her, then glanced back at the concierge.

"There is an *epidemico* here. A terrible sickness. The influenza."

Julian gaped at him, not clear at all why a bout of the summer flu should so alarm the poor bastard.

"Yes, I'm sure you're right. But what does that have to do with us?"

Everyone in view of him, in the lobby, among all the potted palms, looked healthy enough.

"Many people are dying of this," the concierge went on. "My own aunt, she dies of this."

"I'm sorry, but I've been reading the Rome *Daily News* and the *International Herald Trib* and nothing I've seen in either paper has changed my mind about staying here. Anyhow, I never get sick."

That might be because he was always too drunk to notice whether or not he was sick. He was becoming annoyed that the concierge would see fit to spoil a lovely day by entreating him to pack his bags and blow town.

"This is different, Signore Wilks, this is *il neuro sangue.*"

"The what?"

"The—how you say it?—the black blood."

No, he thought, he hadn't been drinking that much this morning; the problem must be with the concierge, who evidently hadn't achieved enough mastery of the English language to communicate what he really meant.

"It strikes you down where you stand," he continued. "One minute everything is fine, the next you are on the ground. It is the plague returned, signore. Go to the north, to Milano, to the mountains—there it is safer for you and the signora."

The concierge leveled his gaze at Nancy who was tapping her toes, obviously impatient to be on her way.

"Well, thank you very much for the warning. I don't think there's any need for you to worry. We shouldn't be in Rome too much longer."

The concierge looked at him dubiously, already having sized him up as someone of uncertain mental stability.

"What was that all about?" Nancy asked when he rejoined her.

"Nothing, darling. He just wanted to give me some recommendations where we should go tonight for dinner."

Nancy accepted his explanation as she did all his explanations. It was an amazing thing to him, how much she trusted him.

Although Nancy agreed to accompany her new husband to Saint Peter's—she agreed to anything he proposed—it developed that Saint Peter's Basilica was closed to the public. The new pope, Clement XV, was celebrating a special ecumenical mass to give thanks on the occasion of his election.

The closest they managed to get was Saint Peter's Square. It was packed with what Julian observed must have been a couple of hundred thousand people. Not all of them looked like loyal parishioners or curious spectators to Julian. Among them were a good number who sported bizarre costumes and raggedly cut hair and carried green crosses and poster with the picture of an ascetic looking man who most definitely was not Clement XV.

Anyone who came near, Julian would stop and ask what exactly was going on. The meaning of these green crosses escaped him. Nancy kept asking what significance they had, who the man was whose picture people were raising. Julian didn't know what to tell her.

The concierge back at the hotel explained. Scanning one of the afternoon papers, the concierge told him that the new pontiff had just celebrated mass with Jonas Beck, the leader of an evangelical movement out of England known as the Church of the Redeemed.

"Why the hell would the pope be meeting with some crackpot like that?"

The concierge shook his head gravely, and bent his head down closer to the paper so that his myopic eyes could better see. "It does not say here why, Signore Wilks. It states here only that the two men, they find many areas of agreement. They say that there is a great need for peace in the world."

"So what else is new?"

"Julian!" Nancy didn't appreciate his sarcasm.

The concierge went on, "It says here that the pope, he says that there are no big differences between him and this Signore Beck, and that Signore Beck's people are also his people. The pope says that the Church of the Redeemed has the protection of the Church of Saint Peter."

"It says that there? Are you sure you're translating that right?"

The concierge assured him that he was.

"Who is this man Beck?"

"It does not say here, Signore Wilks. It says only that he is a respected religious leader. It says that he has many millions of followers who consider him the redeemer."

"And the pope received this man? I can't believe it."

"This is what it says here, Signore Wilks, ask anyone."

Several hours later, sitting alone at Donney's—still at century's end one of the premier cafes in all of Rome—Julian looked up from his solitary table to see a barrel chested man wearing an electric blue jacket approaching him. "Is that you, Julian? Julian Wilks?"

Julian fought through his alcoholic haze to place him, but couldn't. "I'm sorry, I . . ."

"Oh, it's all right, I wouldn't expect you'd know who I was." His smile grew broader, more familiar. "My name's Jack Brill. There's really no reason you should know who I was. It was a large class."

College? Private school? Or was it a social class he was referring to?

"Haverford," he said, and having established the connection, sat down across from Julian. Among Haverford graduates apparently there was no need to wait for an invitation.

"I was in poli. sci.," said Brill. "You were in what?"

"Literature."

"Oh that's right, I remember. You had something to do with the literary magazine, didn't you?" He was motioning to the waiter for a drink, a pilsner.

"Not very much I'm afraid. I contributed a couple of poems, neither of which was very good."

Brill smelled like a good many pilsners had preceded the one that was now being placed in front of him. That was all right with Julian; he hated it when he was obliged to make conversation with someone who was not keeping up with him.

"You know, I'd heard you were here in Rome."

"Oh? And how's that?"

Since even he hadn't any notion of where he was headed for on his honeymoon, how did this fellow, whom he hadn't laid eyes on in nearly two decades, know where he'd be?

"I'm in the insurance business in Philly these days." He got out his card and dropped it on the table in front of Julian.

> JACKSON BRILL
> Insurance Adviser
> 12th Floor Packard Building
> Philadelphia, Pa. 19102-48
> (215) 569-9011

He scribbled a telephone number on the back of it, saying, "This is my number in Rome for the next several days."

Julian inspected it without interest, then put it into his pocket. Probably weeks later he'd discover it and then have to try to remember who Jack Brill was all over again.

"Well, I'm sure the insurance business is thriving. But that still doesn't answer my question. How did you find me?"

"Actually, Julian, in a way it does. You see, I ran into your cousin and he said you might be in Rome."

"My cousin?" This didn't seem likely. "I don't have any cousins who live in Philly. You must mean my wife's cousin, Larry Deitz. He's in the insurance business too, if I remember."

"Right. I'm sorry, I got confused."

"Did Nancy tell him we were in Rome? She must have called him and let him know."

"I didn't ask. But after I spoke to Larry I thought, why, wouldn't it be funny if I ran into Julian while I was in Rome? I had a feeling, though, that you wouldn't remember who I was."

"I always forget faces, believe me, it's nothing personal."

"I didn't think it was," Jack Brill said. "Could I buy you a drink? For old time's sake?"

Julian didn't see why not.

Somehow, through the magic of alcohol, Julian found himself still in Jack Brill's company many hours later. It was night and they were in a part of the city not far from the Spanish Steps—the ony landmark Julian had been able to identify with any certainty. He really couldn't say what they were doing in this neighborhood of cobblestone piazzas and obscure cafes that all looked empty either because they weren't doing very good business or because the hour was much later than he believed. His Rolex, he realized, had never been changed from Eastern Daylight Time and now he had no notion at all what time it was.

It also occurred to him that Jack was a great deal more sober than he was.

"You have a lovely wife, I'm told," Jack was saying.

"She's a splendid girl. Someday you'll have to meet her."

"Careful, old man."

Julian was weaving. Oh yes, he was very far gone. He would have to find a taxi back to the Excelsior; no way he was going to walk it.

"I'd like that, Julian, I'd like that very much. You wouldn't want to see anything happen to her, would you?"

Julian stopped in his tracks. "No, of course not. Why do you say that?"

"I'm in the insurance business, remember?"

Was all this drinking and banter intended as a way of softening him up for a pitch? "Listen, Jack, I'm sure you're good at what you do, but I don't need any more coverage."

Jack laughed. "I wasn't even thinking of suggesting it. I don't for one minute doubt you have excellent coverage. No, I was thinking about something else."

A solitary man, blind, with a cane, was tapping out a monotonous rhythm across the length of the piazza. He was briefly caught in the lights illuminating the fountain, then he disappeared from sight. The only reason Julian noticed him was because there was no one else in view. The two of them were all alone.

"What is it then?"

"Have you heard of Jonas Beck and the Church of the Redeemed?"

Julian didn't think he was hearing right. What had Jack Brill to do with a weird cult? It didn't make any sense.

"Know what? Look, Jack, it's getting late. Nancy must be worried. I think I'd better be heading back."

There were hardly any cars in the streets and no taxis whatsoever.

"Just wait until you've heard me out. You see, Julian, I have friends—good friends—connected with the church."

"The Catholic Church or this other church?"

"Both really. We're coming to a time when such distinctions aren't going to be relevant anymore. We're all facing a common crisis."

"What crisis is that?"

But maybe Brill didn't hear him. He ʼvent on, "And these friends of mine, these good friends, tell me that it's crucial the message gets out—"

"What message? What the hell are you talking about? Look, can't we discuss this tomorrow at lunch? I mean, right now I'm pretty wiped out and not thinking straight."

"I'm sure I'm getting through to you. Just a minute more, Julian, that's all I'm asking for. Now my friends tell me that what it's come down to is either you change your life—really change it—or your chances will be next to nothing for survival."

No, this was getting way beyond him. He was feeling faint. Part of the trouble was that he hadn't eaten since— no, he couldn't recall when it had been.

"Now part of this change is, admittedly, quite painful. It means sacrifice. But tell me, Julian, would you rather sacrifice your life or Nancy's—"

"Hey, wait a minute, pal, nobody's sacrificing Nancy's life."

He grabbed Brill's jacket but all Brill did was gently remove his hands from it. "If you'd listen to me, Julian, maybe you'd understand. I'm not threatening Nancy's life. I'm not threatening yours. I'm a friend, a good friend, and I don't want to see either of you harmed."

"Harmed by what? Would you make yourself clear, for Christ sake!"

"There's a plague that's coming. It's already here."

He was reminded of the concierge's warning that morning. Or was it yesterday morning? He couldn't keep anything straight. Jesus, what he wouldn't do to lie down and go to sleep.

"This plague is going to sweep away thousands of people—millions—in its path."

"It's the goddamn flu is all it goddamn is!"

What was everybody making such a big thing of it for? He'd gone through countless seasons when the flu would hit and the worst that ever happened was he was confined to bed for a week with a fever. Somehow he couldn't think of it as any sort of plague. A plague was what happened in the Bible.

"You'll see, Julian, it's not quite so simple. It's not just another flu. When it strikes people—those nearest and dearest to you—and you see what it does, how devastating it is, you might change your mind."

"And do what?"

"And surrender your wealth and your property to the Church of the Redeemed. And in that way save Nancy and save yourself. And I'm not just talking about spiritual salvation. I am talking about a very real salvation here on this earth."

Julian gaped at Jack Brill, deciding that he must be mad, that there was no other explanation for it.

"Sure, Jack, whatever you say."

The best thing to do when dealing with a madman, he figured, was to humor him.

"It is no joke. If you wish to save your lives this is something you're going to have to do. Think of it just as you would health insurance. It's a way of protecting your family."

"Yeah, but my premiums usually aren't so high. What do you think I'm going to do, bankrupt myself? You must be out of your mind."

He was still treating it as a joke, hoping that Jack Brill would either acknowledge as much or take his madness elsewhere.

"No, I am not out of my mind. And you won't have to worry about the necessities of life. Believe me, the church takes care of its own. Think about what I've said, Julian. I'll be in touch."

Maybe Julian blacked out for a minute. Or an hour. But however much time had passed, when he looked again Jack Brill was gone and, where before the piazza was empty, it was full of Romans on their way to work.

TWENTY-FOUR

Diana Cleary's funeral was held on the sixteenth of June with as little ceremony as possible. Because of her own modest fashion business and the position her late husband had held in industry the *Times* carried a small obituary. Most newspapers no longer had the space, not with the death toll rising the way it was—144 dead on the fourteenth, 209 on the fifteenth, 294 on the sixteenth. Obviously only a select few were regarded as sufficiently important to warrant a notice. The limitations of space would not permit a total accounting. Only in outlying districts, in villages where everyone knew everyone else, did the local papers record death's daily culling.

Sometimes it was necessary to read between the lines to discern the true cause of death. Often death was ascribed to a bizarre variety of diseases: sandfly fever, scarlet fever, malignant typhus, cholera, diphtheria, whooping cough, even food poisoning. But that was only because the symptoms of this disease were so wide ranging, producing devastating reactions in one victim while barely incapacitating his neighbor. And even a quick perusal of the ages of the victims would serve to disabuse anyone of the notion that only the very young or the very old were the most vulnerable; many were men and women in their twenties, thirties and forties, the majority presumably in good health before the outbreak.

Diana's obituary, however, made no mention of how she had died. It read in its entirety:

> Cleary, Diana, 34, after a brief illness. Founder and director of Circe Fashions, Ltd., Miss Cleary, née Gately, was married to the late Nicholas Cleary, vicepresident of Atlantic Technic Systems, Ltd. She is survived by her cousin Susan Gatley and her aunt, Alister Gately. Funeral services will be private. Donations to the Mayfair House, Mayfair, London are requested in lieu of flowers.

The reference to Mayfair House wasn't lost on Lightman. Who, he wondered, was responsible for placing the announcement? Lightman had assumed that somehow he'd have been let in on plans for the funeral, and perhaps been invited. At the least he'd expected to have been kept informed of what was happening. But that was probably because he hadn't thought it through. Who was he to Diana anyway? A casual friend she'd impulsively taken into her life—and bed—nothing more. Why should Alister Gately give him special consideration simply on the basis of a brief encounter at a party that she in all likelihood had completely put out of her mind?

But he still had the keys to Diana's flat. On the day after her funeral he decided to use them, thinking vaguely that among her effects he would uncover something that might tell him about her link with Martindale—a journal, notes, letters, tapes, photographs—anything really. But he knew that there was more to it than that; he was hoping to learn what had gone on between them in the last couple of weeks. Maybe she'd have left a diary behind where she'd said explicitly what she felt about him. It would be like performing a postmortem examination of a love affair. He realized that it might not do him any good in the end to know, but it was the only thing he could think of to do. In some way it was how he meant to stave off the grief that was sure to follow. Now he was just numb. But he sensed that once the numbness wore off, a terrible paralysis could set in.

He arrived in early evening. Almost from the instant he walked into Diana's flat he realized he would find nothing of value. The smell of air freshener and metal polish that greeted him told him that somebody had already been there to clean up. More than just dust would have been lifted from her home.

Each room he inspected was spotless, everything put back in order. All the beds were made with fresh linens. Lightman almost had the feeling he was in a museum. The only thing missing were velvet ropes to discourage the visitor from getting too close to the artworks and furnishings.

He searched first in her antique desk, but quickly decided that he was wasting his time. Except for blank stationery and stamps he found nothing at all. If she'd kept appointment calendars, tax diaries, business files, correspondence, or even newspaper clippings, they weren't in this desk or anywhere else he looked. Only her clothes and cosmetics remained as mute witnesses to her presence there.

And then he looked across the alley to the mysterious window across the way and an idea came to him.

For anything to come of his idea Lightman needed help. His problem was that he neither had the temperament nor the tools necessary for breaking into buildings. It occurred to him, however, that he knew somebody who probably did—Gray.

Though it wasn't exactly as if they were good friends, Lightman still believed the man could be enlisted in his cause. He called Finch to ask him where he could find the detective.

"Where are you calling from?" Finch asked.

"Diana Cleary's flat."

"I see." He paused, perhaps to consider the implications of that information. "Well, I tell you what you do. Go outside and wait by the door. He should be along any minute."

As Finch had predicted, it didn't take long before Gray showed up, casting Lightman a baleful gaze, shaking his head so that his dreadlocks slapped his cheeks. "You wanted to see me for anything in particular?"

Lightman attempted to explain just what he expected to find inside the flat across the passageway from Diana's, but it was apparent that Gray wasn't interested in the details. "You want to break in, is that it?"

"You could put it that way. I was thinking that you might need a warrant—"

Gray looked as though the suggestion horrified him. "Why do you want me to go wasting my time getting a warrant? There's an emergency on now, we won't be needing any damn warrant!"

Lightman was convinced.

The building that had so long been the object of Lightman's curiosity looked less like a citadel of mystery than a home for businesses that a lower middle class young man might think of making a career in: claims adjustment and insurance offices, loan offices, decorators' salons, travel agencies—and studio photographers.

"Family Foto Celebrities, Ltd., Suite 300. That should be the one," Lightman said, scanning the directory in the lobby. A night watchman observed them with indifference and made no move to ask them where they were going as they started up the stairs.

The door of Suite 300 had a square opaque glass in it under which a sign had been posted: Closed Due to Death in the Family. Gray produced a set of some amazing looking keys, long-stemmed and hooked in a way Lightman had never seen before. "These can open up any door, you watch," Gray said with unmistakable pride in his voice for the miracles they could perform.

Gray was frowning in concentration, sizing up the nature of the locks he was dealing with. Then his eyes lit up and he was rewarded with the snap of the lock.

They found themselves in a long room, constructed like a railroad flat. Along one wall there was a row of equipment draped with sheets. When they removed the sheets they discovered an array of state-of-the-art video hardware, cameras, recorders and consoles with graphic display capabilities.

So, Lightman thought, he hadn't been imagining things: it had been real.

He strode over to the window and raised the shade. Diana's window was in full view, with the drapes down. He turned to see Gray poised over the console, studying the lights and switches before him to find out what kind of magic they were capable of performing. Then he made his decision.

Three video monitors located above the console simultaneously came to life, emitting a dazzling amber glow.

A woman appeared on each of the monitors. At first Lightman thought that they were three different women, only to realize that they were all the same: all Diana. It was astonishing, even frightening, how with the cunning use of makeup and the way she arranged her hair, she could appear so different. On the bottom of the screen dates came up in bold letters—all indicating that they were shot in the previous ten-month period. Gray's expression gave no hint as to what he was thinking.

But then he said, "She was pretty, no? She was Martindale's woman." His eyes fixed themselves on Lightman. "And she was maybe your woman for a little while?" He offered Lightman a sly little smile.

Gray then punched out a series of numbers, another date, and produced on the screen to the right a portion of the tape Lightman had already seen: he and Diana locked in desperate, naked embrace. But before it could run for more than a couple of seconds Lightman killed the tape and punched out another date. Gray's smile stayed right where it was; oh but he was enjoying himself.

Then it was Wellington who appeared on the screen, recalled from the maw into which he had vanished.

"Ah, so it is Dr. Wellington at last." Gray pulled up a chair and settled down to watch.

Wellington looked much as he had when Lightman had last seen him, his face cut and scratched, his eyes incandescent with the fever that was gnawing through him, his body soaking with sweat. For five minutes he did nothing; he just lay there in what appeared to be a semiconscious state. It was like looking at one of those old Warhol movies, Lightman thought, during which nothing happened over an interminably long period of time. The only thing that did happen in this instance was the appearance of a yellowish, gummy substance oozing out of Wellington's mouth.

"We look at something else," Gray suggested.

But Lightman urged him instead to stay with what they had and merely to reset the time. "Make it later that day—

see what happens at four in the afternoon." For that was the day on which Wellington had disappeared.

Gray did as he asked, advancing the tape forward. When they raised their eyes toward the screen they saw that Wellington was no longer alone. Gray pushed reverse, adjusting the tape until they had the exact instant frozen on screen when two men entered Wellington's room.

Wellington was slow to react. It took him several seconds before he could rouse himself out of his stupor to realize he had company. But even then he didn't seem able to recognize the intruders or quite understand what they were doing in the room with him.

Because of the play of shadows and the angle of the camera, it wasn't possible to get much of a glimpse of the two men. But Lightman and Gray had no trouble comprehending what they were up to.

One of the men seized Wellington's arm and plunged a needle into it. All at once Wellington's body went slack and he collapsed back in bed. The two men then proceeded to lift him out of bed. Moisture could be seen trickling from his eyes. But in this case the moisture was blood.

Lightman looked to Gray but he expressed only the faintest surprise at witnessing this scene. "He is just as dead now as he was before we saw this, no?" he asked. It struck Lightman that the murderers had known they were being watched and didn't give a damn.

"Do you know either of these two men?" Gray asked.

One of them looked vaguely familiar, but that was about the only thing Lightman could say for certain.

Gray now proposed to collect all the tapes they could find so he could study them at leisure in a police screening room. But he didn't act very excited at the prospect of discovering any further revelations. "These people are not stupid who did this," he said. "They wouldn't leave such tapes behind unless they were meant to be found. So I say we can expect to find very little. It is even possible they were planted here to deceive us."

Lightman had to admit that he had a point.

As Gray went about his search Lightman continued to stare at the monitors. Diana had come up on all three again. On one she was alone in the bedroom, selecting a dress from among the hundred or so hanging in her closet. He recognized the dress she finally selected; it was the one she'd worn to the party they'd attended together at Susan Gately's.

On monitor two she was with a man. Lightman looked to the bottom of the screen for the date. It wasn't there. The man turned so that Lightman could better see him. He knew who this man was, he would have known him by his eyes alone. It was Richard Thorning. Thorning's dead eyes were staring straight at the camera as if he knew it was there, and perhaps he did at that. Diana stepped in front of him. Lightman noticed how pale she looked, how drawn; there was something hesitant, even fearful in her manner. Her eyes were trained in the same direction Thorning's were. It was as if she knew that the camera was on her too. Then the monitor went black.

What was wrong with that picture? Lightman reversed the tape and played it a second time but still couldn't figure out what bothered him about it.

He wasn't content until he'd played it back a third time. Then Diana's words returned to him. She had told him the night of the party that she hadn't seen Thorning since his eyes had become paralyzed. That meant that this particular fragment of tape could have been shot only later on, at a time when Diana was supposed to be dead. Was there something wrong with his logic? If there was, he couldn't think of what it might be. The only conclusion he could reach was that Diana was still alive. Yet her doctor had declared her dead, the *Times* had announced her funeral, and presumably there'd been a burial. The question was, if it wasn't Diana lying in her grave, who then was it?

TWENTY-FIVE

The next day Lightman was headed out of London on the Victoria line, gazing idly out the window at a landscape that was mostly industrial and unrelievedly bleak for much of the way. Derelict factories and rowhouses were everywhere he looked. The flowers people had put in their windowboxes to bring some color to their surroundings only succeeded in emphasizing just how bleak they were. Low-lying clouds, turgid with the threat of rain, made everything even more depressing.

It was somewhere outside of this town that Lightman was told he could find the cemetery where Diana had been buried. He'd obtained the directions from Diana's aunt, Alister. She'd told him over the phone that she hadn't been feeling up to par of late and consequently hadn't been able to attend the funeral. But she'd been to the cemetery many times before; the Gatelys had once had a country house close to Saint Clement's Wood and a good many of their dead were laid to rest in the local cemetery. Lightman had said he wished to pay his respects. She had no reason not to believe him.

It was already dark by the time he got off at Saint Clement's Wood. The platform was empty. No one else had gotten off with him.

Hard by the railway station Lightman found a pub called the Rim and Roost. Walking in, he could see that his welcome would be a chilly one. The clientele, entirely male, regarded him suspiciously. There was little question in

Lightman's mind that, even in normal times, the appearance of a stranger would be a provocation; but now, with the epidemic, there was all the more reason to fear a person unknown to them. Lightman could be a carrier, leaving disease behind when he left. That he betrayed no obvious symptoms meant nothing. They must have heard about others who appeared healthy one minute and dropped dead the next.

They gave him wide berth, moving down to the end of the bar. The barmaid—the only representative of her sex in the place—was only slightly less intimidated.

After awhile she got up enough courage to speak to him.

"You from London then?" she began.

"Not exactly. I'm an American."

"So," she said, "what in bleeding hell is a Yank doing in these parts?"

"I'm looking to hire somebody for a couple of hours—no more."

Suspicion returned to her eyes. "And what would you want him to be doing for you?"

"I need some help digging."

"Digging? What kind of digging?"

"Just digging up some ground, that's all. I'll pay twenty-five pounds."

She whistled. "That's a lot of money for a little digging, twenty-five quid. You sure that's all it is, just the digging?"

"I don't want whoever I hire to talk about it afterwards."

"I see."

Lightman guessed that her suspicions were now confirmed; a stranger—an American to boot—stepped off the train from London in a town no tourist ever visited and dropped into an inhospitable neighborhood pub; how could he be up to any good?

"It's dangerous then, what you have in mind?"

"To be honest, there may be some danger to it, not the digging part of it though."

"Stolen loot, is it now?"

"What? Oh, no, nothing like that." He smiled as if it was just a joke, but he could see that she hadn't meant it that way at all.

"What is it then?"

"If I find someone who's interested I'll tell him."

She was thinking this over. "Don't budge," she said, "I'll be right back."

She went down to the other end of the bar and conferred with three hulking men, any one of whom were suitable for the job he had in mind. As she talked they gave him questioning glances, trying to puzzle him out.

After five minutes had passed one of the men sauntered up to Lightman. A slovenly fellow, with a bullet-shaped head and a smell of diesel oil about him, introduced himself as Mal. No last name.

"You looking for somebody to do some digging for yer?"

"That's right. Twenty-five pounds."

"What sort of digging you want?"

"Do you know where Saint Clement's Wood is?"

"The cemetery? You want me to dig a grave for yer?"

"No. The grave's already been dug and filled."

Mal studied him for a moment. "You're talking about digging up the dead?"

That was it, Lightman thought, he was sure to back out now.

"Exactly."

There followed a long silence. "All right then," Mal said finally, "let's get on with it."

Mal knew his way around. In fact, he turned out to be more of a help than Lightman ever expected him to be. It was doubtful that he would have been able to slip into the cemetery, particularly with a couple of shovels, on his own.

In the dark there was no way for Lightman to be sure of

the dimensions of Saint Clement's Wood, but it was obvious that it was large. Parts of it looked like a city, not a necropolis, but an actual city whose administrators had gone to great trouble to erect triumphal arches and monuments to foster civic pride. Spires and obelisks combined to form a surrealistic skyline, white against a sky partially shrouded in a moonlit haze.

Then there were sections much older where the stones were so black that the epitaphs were virtually indecipherable. As they made their way along the twisting paths up and down slopes and into sudden defiles, Lightman noticed graves dating back to the 1300's. Certain headstones told their own pitiful stories: B: 1712 D: 1717; B: 11 July, 1668 D: 11 July 1668.

It must have been raining there recently; the way grew slippery with mud as they continued. After climbing over an embankment, they held a vantage point that allowed them to see a generous stretch of terrain; part stubble, part woods. Dominating the landscape was a mausoleum, all of white marble, with seraphs carved into it; the names JAMES AND HELEN GATELY stood out in bold Roman letters. Smaller tombstones surrounded it.

"The one you'll be wanting is down there," Mal said. "All the bloody Gatelys are buried there."

Lightman realized that without Mal he would have been wandering around the cemetery the whole night in an effort to locate Diana's grave. Now that he was there, however, he wasn't sure he wanted to go through with it.

Scientist he might be, but the idea of disturbing the dead wasn't something he could dismiss as mere superstition. The whole history of human civilization, after all, was bound up in the respect and sanctity accorded to the dead.

Evidently no similar compunction bothered Mal. "What's the matter with you? I haven't the whole night to lolligag about. Are we going to do this or not?"

Lightman nodded and allowed Mal to lead the way. "Third row, twelfth from the far end, do I have that right?"

"According to my directions that should be hers."

"A bird, is it?" Mal asked, giving Lightman a funny look. "What do you want to be digging a Gately bird up for?" He gave a vicious little laugh. "You think maybe she'd make you better company than when she was alive?"

"Just find the marker, will you? I don't need your comments," Lightman shot back.

"You're the boss."

Diana's grave was exactly where Alister had said it would be. The marker was almost lost among so many imposing monuments. It was just a cross—a green cross —with her birth and death date stamped into it.

Lightman was conscious of a queasiness in his stomach and a familiar pressure in his chest. His throat was constricted. Really, he thought, this was not such a good idea. He was beginning to believe that it would be Diana he'd find after all. And would he want to look at her now?

But it was too late to turn back. Not with Mal restless to begin.

Throwing off his jacket, Mal scooped up as much dirt as he could fit on his shovel. He looked back at Lightman. "You gonna just stand there and watch me, mate?"

Lightman took hold of the second shovel Mal had brought along and joined in.

"Shouldn't be bad as all that," Mal said. "The new ones, they don't have the time to bury them too deep."

Mal was right. It wasn't long before their shovels met resistence, clanging as they came down on a hard surface Lightman was sure must be the lid of the coffin.

Setting down his shovel, Mal brushed away the remaining dirt with his hands. Polished oak shone through. "Well now," he said, "it looks like where we want to be, doesn't it now, mate?"

Lightman didn't know about that.

The two of them together were able to clear the surface of the coffin in no time. Then Mal used a crowbar to pry open the lid.

Lightman didn't want to look. He looked.

"Well, what do you think?" Mal asked, staring down at the corpse he'd just brought into view.

It was Diana.

Mal shone the beam of his flashlight on her.

Lightman stared in disbelief. It was Diana. How could that be?

Mal was waiting for him to say something. "Is this the one you wanted, mate, or what?"

"Here, listen, why don't you take this? I don't need you any longer." He wanted the man to leave him alone.

Finding thirty pounds in his hands rather than the previously agreed-upon price, Mal seemed not to know what to make of it. "This is too much. You're losing your bloody marbles, mate."

"Take it, please. Just clear out of here."

"Whatever you say, mate. I couldn't be happier."

And with that he was off, walking into the darkness, his step so brisk that he could have been a child unexpectedly released early from school who couldn't quite believe his luck.

Lightman returned his attention to the body in front of him.

In death, Diana's beauty was as much present as it had been in life. But it was another kind of beauty, chilling, passionless and frozen—at least until the maggots got to it and the rot set in.

He couldn't resist putting his hand to her face just as tenderly as he had when he was her lover. It was cold to the touch, of course it was; what could he expect? But there was something else about the feel of her decomposing skin that troubled him.

And then he realized what it was; it wasn't skin at all, not human skin.

Just as he dug his nails into her face and started to peel it away he became aware of movements behind him. He turned, thinking that it was probably Mal coming back again for some reason, but it wasn't Mal. It was his old friends, Finch and Gray.

TWENTY-SIX

What Lightman seemed to have forgotten was that Gray and Finch were in the business of tracking people, allowing them to harbor the illusion that they were free when at any time they chose they could reel them in. It was possible that they'd learned where he was going before he'd even set out from London and so they really didn't have to bother following him to Saint Clement's Wood, they could have been waiting for him the whole time.

Before Lightman had a chance to inspect the corpse he was seized by Gray and an officer with an arm-breaking grip. Finch demanded to know what he thought he was doing, but giving him no chance to reply, went on to say, "You realize that by illegally carrying out the exhumation of a body you are in violation of the Emergency Quarantine Act."

Guilty of yet another crime, Lightman thought almost in wonder. Before he had time to assess his new situation he was forced into the rear seat of a car whose windows were covered with wire mesh. The door slammed shut. There was no way of opening it from the inside.

One of Finch's subalterns was given the responsibility of driving him back to London. Finch and Gray rode in a separate car. So there was no opportunity to discover what was to happen to him until he arrived at his destination, which turned out to be an anonymous gray building, part of a council house apartment complex. The surrounding neighborhood, what of it that Lightman could see in the dark, was drab and lifeless. He suspected that this was a satellite town, neither completely urban nor suburban, that existed on the fringe of London, possibly serving as housing for workers in nearby industries.

The anonymity of the setting made sense only after Lightman had a glimpse of what lay inside. Once he stepped out from the elevator onto the sixth floor he was astonished to find himself in a warren of offices and cubicles. Men and women, some in white lab coats, others in civilian clothes, were in constant motion. Faces were bathed in the bright amber light of computer monitors across which statistics and graphs flickered briefly and vanished.

This wasn't the prison that Lightman had been expecting.

"This way, sir," his guide said, directing him through a honeycomb of cubicles to what appeared to be a central office with its interior windows covered by opaque glass. Lightman could make out shadows behind the glass.

The shadows turned out to belong to Finch and Gray.

"Sit down, Dr. Lightman," Finch said. "Would you care for some coffee?"

Lightman said he didn't. It made no difference to Finch. "I'm certain you'd like some coffee." He buzzed a secretary to bring them three cups.

"Before we begin, just tell me one thing. Am I under arrest?" Lightman asked.

The question seemed to amuse Gray but not a trace of

emotion registered in Finch's face. What he said was, "It all depends on what you mean by arrest."

"I wouldn't have thought that there was anything so ambiguous about it."

"Now, Dr. Lightman, I have the highest regard for your reputation. If I didn't, your situation would now be far from an enviable one. But you do have a penchant for getting yourself into trouble, it seems. You've been here in the U.K. for nearly three weeks and so far you have committed two felonies—acting as an accessory to a breaking-and-entering and exhuming a body without proper authorization. Such a record is not exactly encouraging, especially for a scientist."

Lightman was trying hard to concentrate on what the inspector was saying, in hope of keeping one step ahead. But it wasn't possible; his mind refused to oblige him, his attention wavered. All he could think about was his visit to Diana's gravesite. It wasn't her, he continued to reassure himself. Whoever it was, it just couldn't be her.

"However," Finch went on, "Her Majesty's Government is prepared to overlook these illegal acts if it can be convinced of your cooperation."

"What sort of cooperation are you talking about?"

"It wouldn't do anybody a world of good to toss you in jail, not when there's such a serious epidemic raging. It would be a waste. But I'm prepared to do just that if you refuse my offer."

"And what exactly is your offer?"

"We have in the past several days collected a certain amount of evidence suggesting that the source of this infection may have originated at Mayfair House, and that Dr. Martindale might have had a hand in it."

It was gratifying that the police had finally come to the same conclusion that he had. He might have steered them in the right direction earlier if it weren't for their suspicion that he was engaged in some strange vendetta against Martindale and consequently could not be trusted to tell the truth.

"If it develops that this is the case," Finch continued, "then the implications of such an act would be very serious indeed."

To Lightman's mind, he was vastly understating the case; before the virus had exhausted itself, hundreds of thousands might be dead, millions more debilitated. In essence Martindale was waging biological warfare against the world.

"What would you like me to do?"

"I'm getting to that. Now there are two areas in which you can be of help. The offices here were established only a week ago as a central command post to monitor the health emergency and take measures to deal with it. We chose this site because there are already lab facilities on the premises which we could borrow for our use until the emergency ends."

"From the outside you'd never think there were labs here. What are they used for ordinarily?"

"Let's just say that they are intended for work that we'd rather not have broadcast to the world. It is not something you should concern yourself with. Just be assured that the labs are eminently suitable for the work you'll be doing— should you agree to cooperate, of course."

"And just what kind of work would that be, Inspector?"

"We're looking for answers. First of all, we need to know more about this virus, what is it, why is it proving so lethal, why is it causing such a bizarre range of symptoms, why are some people being exposed to it and not becoming infected."

"That happens with virtually any flu outbreak," Lightman pointed out. "Certain individuals have a natural immunity, others may be asymptomatic but act as carriers, spreading the infection to others."

"I realize all that," Finch said impatiently, "but in this instance we are speaking of one particular category of peo-

ple. You'll see. There's a book I'd like you to take a look
at tonight which bears on this topic. But we can discuss
that later. For now, I want to know whether you're willing
to do this for us."

He found the idea of having a lab to work in again immensely appealing. But he wanted to know how much time
he'd have to do the research. "What you're asking for may
take months."

"We don't have months. You will have to see what you
can do in a week." He wasn't looking at Lightman, perhaps because he understood the impossibility of the task he
was demanding from him.

"A week? That's madness! That's hardly enough time to
set up a protocol and examine the data your people have
already gathered. I can't do it in a week, no one could."

Finch was unrelenting. "You will do what you can. In
the absence of proven facts you will give me reasonable
suppositions. In the absence of tangible evidence you will
give me something on paper I can take to my superiors so
that they are convinced we are getting somewhere. We can
always alter or even reverse our conclusions down the line
if it proves necessary. Look, we are both in the detective
business. I know you need time to develop your experiments and test your hypotheses. I am not unfamiliar with
the scientific method. But you must also understand why I
cannot give you this time. You will have to make do, we
will all have to make do."

"What happens after a week? Why do I have to finish
my work by then?" In spite of what Finch had said Lightman was not persuaded that he had an inkling as to his
needs.

"In a week's time you and Mr. Gray here will proceed to
Geneva. I have reason to think that if we delay longer than
a week Dr. Martindale will have left Switzerland, which
may put him beyond our reach. It is my hope that we will
have collected sufficient evidence to force the Swiss authorities to arrest Dr. Martindale and have him extradited.

Since I expect that much of that evidence will be scientific and highly technical, I'm going to need a reputable scientist who can explain to the Swiss police why they should act."

"You would like me to be that scientist?"

"Correct. May I have your answer?"

"Nothing will give me greater pleasure, Inspector."

"I congratulate you for choosing wisely."

At that moment there was a knock on the door and the same officer who'd driven him in from London stepped in. Seeing Lightman he said, "I can come back later, Inspector."

"No, it's all right, this man is working with us now. He can hear what you have to say."

Lowering his gaze to the yellow form he held in his hand the officer read, "I have just received a preliminary report from the pathologist on the body found tonight in Saint Clement's Wood."

"Go on," said Finch.

Lightman tensed, thinking that if the pounding in his head grew any worse he wouldn't be able to hear what the man said.

"It appears from the extensive adipocere formation that the body was immersed in damp earth before rigor mortis had had a chance to set in," he began.

Lightman was familiar enough with the terminology employed by coroners to understand what was being said. Normally body fat was semifluid in consistency; prolonged immersion in water or damp earth could, however, change that condition so that the watery fat hardened into suet.

"In addition, several bruises were found on the face and arms which were most likely self-inflicted."

"And how does the coroner account for these bruises?" Finch asked.

"Sir, it appears that the victim was struggling to escape the confines of the coffin and sustained those injuries in the process."

The implication was clear to everybody in the room.

"You're saying then that the victim was buried alive?"

"That is what the coroner believes happened." There was more unpleasantness to follow. "The coroner also states that he took a swab from the victim's mouth and rectum and that semen was found in both orifices."

"My God," Finch muttered. Evidently this was a bit much even for him. "Has there been any ID made on the woman?"

"It wasn't a female, sir."

"Now that is a surprise. Not a female? That doesn't leave much of a choice, does it?"

"No, the corpse was made up to resemble a female. A certain kind of waxlike substance was employed. It has been sent to police laboratories in South Kensington for analysis."

What a strange and macabre masquerade, Lightman thought.

"However, we did obtain a positive identification," the officer said. "The dental plates and fingerprints were sufficiently intact. The victim was the man we have been looking for for some time now—Winston Cage."

TWENTY-SEVEN

The room Lightman was given to spend the night didn't resemble a cell. Spartan as it was, and minimally furnished, it was more like a cloister, a monk's dormitory. There was a window which looked out on a gray industrial district; if he leaned out far enough Lightman could make out a glimpse of the Thames and a houseboat with a red roof and a deck splashed with bright yellow paint. Any thoughts of using the window to escape instantly vanished from his mind as soon as he saw just how precipitous the drop was to the ground.

A book had been left by the side of his bed—the one that Finch was so anxious for him to take a look at. It was entitled *Memoirs of the Ariadne Society* and it was by Jonas Beck.

An idealized portrait of Beck dominated the back of the jacket; this was a younger Beck, with all his hair and an unlined face. This was also a more benign Beck than the images of him that Lightman was accustomed to seeing. He looked not unlike a doting uncle, the kind who turned up for Sunday dinner bringing bottles of rasberry liqueur no one would ever get around to drinking.

Lightman opened the volume—published by Heinemann in 1989—and began reading:

It is difficult to say whether one has the gift of prophesy or whether the gift possesses the individual. It is difficult, too, to say whether this gift can be relied upon at all times or whether it comes and goes in response to laws of its own which remain unfathomable to poor humankind. All that can be said with certainty is that the gift does exist and that it can be used—for good or ill.

I recall the very first instance I realized, not that I was necessarily in possession of the gift, but that I could see things other people could not. I was five years old at the time and had just recovered from a serious accident in which I'd fallen out of a car and struck my head. Several weeks passed before I was judged out of danger. All I can remember from this period is like a dream. It was a period when a profound intimacy was achieved between my mother and myself, an intimacy that must have been very much like the first year of life when the child establishes such a fierce ardency for the one who brought him into this world. It was only later that I was told that I was hovering close to death practically the whole time of my confinement, that it was thought that even if I did survive, the severity of the accident would leave me a vegetable, incapable of performing even the simplest task.

But something very different happened, something quite extraordinary.

About a month after I was able to be up and about, my mother took me to see my grandmother. I remember that we were sitting in her living room and that I was drinking a warm cherry soda my grandmother had given me. My grandmother, then a lively, vigorous woman with frosted hair, was in the midst of talking to my mother—her daughter. All of a sudden, prompted by no telling what impulse, I shouted out, "I see Grandpa!"

My grandfather at the time had been dead for close to twenty years, having succumbed to a coronary that struck him on his way home from work. I had never met the gentleman, of course, but I had seen photographs of him and there was absolutely no question in my mind that this was he, sitting next to grandmother, with a contented, faintly amused expression on his face.

I saw him as clearly as I was seeing my mother or my grandmother. I did not perceive him as a ghost; I was not in the least bit frightened, although I must confess I was rather taken aback by this visitation. I recall that he was wearing a meticulously tailored suit with a striped tie and a vest, what I imagine he was wearing on the day he passed from our midst.

My mother responded to my cry with a chastening look and an expression of shock. "What on God's earth made you say a thing like that, Jonas?"

It was astonishing to me that she couldn't see him because he was as clear as day to me. I suppose I expected that everyone would be able to see him. My grandmother, however, didn't react the way my mother had. On the contrary, she smiled sadly at me and asked me to describe her late husband. This I proceeded to do, all the while ignoring my mother's indignant stare. As I spoke I noticed a tear falling from my grandmother's eye. It occurred to me that something beyond my understanding must be happening, that I was being used as a vehicle or an instrument, although those were not the terms that I was thinking in at that tender age.

When I had finished, my grandmother directed her gaze at the space on the couch her husband was occupying. "I wish I could see him now," she said then, "but it doesn't matter. I know why he is coming." She paused and then said in a voice that was nearly inaudible, "He is coming to tell me that it's my time."

Until my mother admonished her, saying, "Don't talk such nonsense, Mama!" I hadn't quite caught the implication of her words. Then I realized what I had done. I had just predicted my grandmother's death. It was to be the first of many. Not more than a week later she died—peacefully—in her sleep.

What Lightman had read made sense—some sense anyhow—to him. Other people claiming psychic powers had also reported that they became aware of their special gifts shortly after suffering a severe childhood illness or a particularly bad head injury. But how this happened, how a blow to the skull could cause someone to see into the future or experience visions was unknown.

Too exhausted by the events of the night to continue reading, he dropped off to sleep.

He was awakened while it was still dark by Finch. Finch

held *Memoirs* in his hand and was leafing through it. "This is the part I wanted you to have a look at," he said, opening it to page 248. "Second paragraph from the top."

Lightman read.

What especially fascinated me about the work of Jewish mysticism known as the Kabbalah was an obscure but tantalizing notion fostered by followers of the Kabbalist Isaac Luria.

According to scholars of the Lurianistic movement it was not enough to be patient and wait for the Messiah to appear. One needn't wait for redemption to come at some distant future. The Messiah's appearance could be accelerated; the process didn't have to take millenia. Lurianism encouraged an ascetic life, a life lived in accordance with the rigors of the law. But as I studied the relevant texts I became convinced that this doctrine did not go far enough.

It seemed to me that we already know from the Bible what conditions must obtain for the Messiah to return. We know from the Books of Daniel and Revelations and from the Apocalyptic Books of Ezra and Baruch that chaos will descend on the earth and that an antichrist will appear; we know that the forces of evil will be vanquished by God's shock troops—the Elect— who to achieve their end are given sanction by God to devastate the lands they cross, to overthrow the nations and destroy the cities.

At the end the antichrist will have fled in terror and his followers put in shackles and made into slaves of the Hidden, Holy people—that singular and virtuous community altogether immune from fatigue, sickness and premature death.

When Lightman had finished he understood why Finch had wanted him to read it. "The part about a virtuous community being immune from sickness and free from premature death is interesting."

"And it also happens to be true. The people who join the Church of the Redeemed simply don't come down with the flu. From all reports this is as true abroad as it is here in the U.K."

Lightman was skeptical. Of course, it was often the case that certain groups had a predisposition or a susceptibility to diseases while others remained relatively unaffected. Sickle-cell anemia struck predominently black males; hemophilia avoided women although they could be carriers; before AIDS made it more widespread, Karposi's sarcoma by and large only attacked elderly Jewish males. But he'd never heard of a group of people enjoying an immunity simply on the basis of their beliefs. When had only Presbyterians been spared the ravages of a pestilence while Episcopalians, Universalists and Seventh Day Adventists fell ill with it? No, it just didn't make sense—not unless the members of the Church were receiving a vaccine that no one knew about.

"There's no evidence that church members are being inoculated against the flu," Finch said. "We've already investigated the possibility. We've spoken to a few people who've defected from the church and they insist that at no point were they inoculated."

"What about an oral vaccine? Something that could be slipped into their food or drink without them being aware of it?"

Finch said they'd examined that possibility too. "Most of their food is pretty tasteless, organic rot. We've subjected it to every test we can think of. On what really was a flimsy pretext we staged a raid on one of their gathering places while they were having their meal. We confiscated every dish, we went through their whole kitchen, even investigated as much of their food suppliers as we could."

"And you found no trace of any vaccine?"

"Mouse droppings, yes, but no vaccine."

"Then it must be a statistical fluke, some coincidence. Or else the church is covering up the incidence of illness and death."

"I'd like to think so, it would be a convenient explanation certainly. But I fear that the truth of the matter is that you stand a far greater chance of survival if you join the church than if you don't."

"Maybe somewhere along the way I'll turn up something to explain how Jonas Beck has acquired this phenomenal power of his."

"You can start now. I'll show you to our laboratory as soon as you've washed."

TWENTY-EIGHT

Experiments to fathom the mysteries of the virus and measure precisely how lethal it was had been under way ever since the devastating nature of the outbreak was recognized. The anecdotal evidence alone was sufficient to convince researchers that they were contending with something far more virulent and far more enigmatic in its variations than they had encountered before. By the morning of the nineteenth of June when Lightman started work at the Quarantine Control Center, as it was officially designated, more than seventy thousand deaths had been accounted for in eighteen countries. All but one of them were located in Europe, the Middle East and the northern tier of Africa. The exception was Bolivia. There was no reason to believe that the infection would restrict itself to Bolivia; one had to assume that the pandemic would presently spread throughout the Americas.

Tissue and blood samples from all affected areas were being tested, just as they were at the World Influenza Centre and in similar facilities elsewhere in the world, including one of Lightman's home bases, the NIH in Bethesda.

But the process of testing the virus was much the same in any lab. To determine whether a virus was present in the blood and tissue samples technicians would rely on what was called a hemagglutinination test. A broth consisting of a fixed dilution of particular samples and mixed with red blood cells of chickens would be prepared in shallow wells set into clear plastic plates. Progressively higher dilations of the samples would be added to other wells. What was left over in each of these wells at the end of a half hour was what counted. In those samples without any virus researchers would find a compact red button of blood cells. But in those samples where the virus was present they would discover, depending on the concentration of the virus, either a thin film or a diffuse mat. The mat consisted of red blood cells involuntarily bound together by viral particles. Which was exactly what happened when the virus succeeded in getting inside a human body.

The infectious process of influenza proceeded in two stages. In the first the virus attached itself to cells in the upper respiratory tract—the nose, the mouth, and the throat. This represented only the infection, not the disease itself. The disease resulted from the second stage when the virus, not content to linger any longer in the upper respiratory tract, moved to attack the whole body. In its relentless odyssey from cell to cell, the virus created havoc, destroying each cell as it went along, hijacking its cell-making machinery for its own devious ends. It was the substances released from these damaged cells, not the virus itself, that caused the misery associated with the flu: the headache, the fever, the weakness.

But what had stumped researchers until now was why

this particular virus was responsible for symptoms which commonly were even seen in such devastating flus as the B/Hong Kong/72 or the A/Victoria/75, both of which had taken thousands of lives.

Lightman was given eighteen hundred and forty pages of documentation related to the outbreak to examine. It was crammed full of statistics. Because not all cases of the flu were reported, especially in Third World countries, the pandemic was tracked in other ways—through hospital surveillance, through industrial and school absenteeism, and through pneumonia mortality rates. If the statistics gathered here were reliable, and Lightman had no reason to believe they were not, then the outbreak was far worse than the media was saying.

In addition to the statistics there were hundreds of pages devoted to the manifestations of the disease. It was a litany of horror, a kaleidoscope of pathology. Lightman devoted nearly three whole days to studying the documentation.

Here was a virus that could blacken blood from oxygen starvation and turn victims cyanotic because it interfered with the passage of blood from the heart's right ventricle to the lungs. This was a virus that could cause the victim to expel blood from his nose and throat up to thirty times a day, threatening to choke him. Victims had been known to go into cataleptic states and trances and suffer from amnesia or to become delusional. One coroner reported dissecting a victim's heart that weighed thirteen ounces, four ounces heavier than normal; it appeared that this unusual dilation was caused by the virus. In other corpses, lungs were found to be blue and swollen. There were reports of people falling stone deaf. Certain victims had ruptured their rectums because they were coughing so hard. Others were afflicted with such acute nephritis that they discharged ten ounces of smoky blood-streaked urine a day (three pints were normal); still others couldn't urinate at all, the retention accountable to muscular flaccidity brought on by the virus. On many, but by no means all, victims raised purple blisters appeared. They seemed to indicate acute septicemia, but nobody knew for certain. Others discovered inexplicable lumps on the right side of their necks; no one knew what they signified. For certain victims even the slightest movement was dangerous; some would begin hemorrhaging if they stood up while others might find themselves leaking serous fluid from their mouths and nostrils if all they did was move their heads too suddenly. There were people with such intense diarrhea that they were forced to take twenty intense bowel movements a day while there were others, equally unfortunate, unable to pass anything for ten days straight. Pregnant women were particularly at risk, suffering spontaneous abortions, miscarriages, and premature labor, all precipitated by the flu. Then there were those who recovered from the flu only to discover that their sexual organs had turned gangrenous.

One symptom especially sparked Lightman's interest as he consumed the reports that had been prepared for his benefit. Apparently the infection, being so democratic in selecting the organs it struck, didn't spare the eyes either. There was one account of a twelve-year-old girl in Saint Albans who'd developed cataracts after she'd been stricken by the flu. A twenty-five-year-old carpenter in Frankfurt had become totally blind from it while a sixty-six-year-old housewife in Lyons suffered a paralysis of the eye muscles.

Now he was sure he knew what the mysterious ailment was that Thorning had been afflicted with. Lightman was willing to bet that he'd become infected at Mayfair House, perhaps as a result of an accident while filming one of Martindale's riskier experiments.

But that still did not tell him what the virus was. It was definitely an A influenza virus but one which behaved far more aggressively, far more obscenely, than any he'd ever done research on.

To begin with, it was even hard to say whether a virus was alive or dead. Scientists generally settled for the term chemically inert to describe this paradoxical state of being. It was like sugar or table salt in that respect. It could lay dormant for years, waiting in ambuscade as it were, until an unsuspecting victim came along. And it had a wide choice of victims too: humans, animals, even plants could do. Once it found its victim it went to town, full to bursting with vitality, anything but chemically inert. Lightman thought that viruses and vampires had a great deal in common.

While every virus was made up of a protein or fatty protein overcoat wrapped around a sliver of either DNA or RNA, each strain had its own particular configuration. Some resembled space ships with four-pronged landing gear attached; others were more like spherical globs which, if greatly enlarged by clever special effects people, might scare the bejesus out of twelve-year-olds in a movie. Many, however, took more pride in their appearance and were really quite beautifully geometric in shape. But not this one; this one was an ugly son of a bitch, spherical and covered on its outer surfaces by spikes. A billion times a billion of them and you might be able to fill up a salt shaker.

Because of the complexity of these viruses, and because there were three distinct strains—A, B, and C—each with its own variants—A/Chile, A/Mississippi, B/Ann Arbor, etc.—it was a considerable challenge to identify each virus and compare it with others that had been preserved from pandemics past—even with the assistance of computers. The question researchers were hoping to answer was whether the virus was new or was it something that had previously appeared. Or if it wasn't the same then was it a close cousin to a known virus.

Another possibility was that it was a new virus altogether, one that, like the HTLV-3 virus responsible for AIDS, was in all likelihood without precedent in human history.

In Lightman's reading he'd come across many diseases

like this. What, for instance, was the cause of the purple fever of 1780 that killed off hundreds of Parisians? Nobody knew.

And what was the French plague of 1558 that began with fever and spitting up of blood and culminated in abscesses and pulmonary weakness? Nobody knew.

What was the disease called ladendo which broke out in Europe in 1447 and caused back pain, shivers, a bad cough, and eight straight days of misery? No one knew.

What was the catarrh of 1595 that disfigured the face and caused people to die without warning? Was it gone forever? Would it ever return? No one knew.

And what was the unidentifiable disease that broke out in Madrid in the summer of 1597 that caused the groin and throat to swell up and either killed its victim or went away and left him in peace? No one knew.

And how to account for the English sweating disease which turned up nowhere else but in London five times between 1486 and 1551, attacked the heart and lungs, caused severe rheumatic pain and intense shivering—and sweating—and often left its victim dead within hours of striking them? No one knew.

Without the technology to record and capture the organisms responsible for these afflictions, all these diseases were apparently lost, like mammoths and carrier pigeons. They were, Lightman thought, like any extinct species. Or to put it another way, perhaps they were extinct species themselves.

Lightman had a feeling that the virus that they were fighting, just like the English sweating disease or the catarrh of 1595, had been considered extinct. Not that anyone had ever proven that it wasn't hiding out somewhere, waiting for the right moment to strike. Yet so many years had passed since its last occurrence that people could be forgiven for thinking it was gone for good—that was, if they gave it any thought at all. But he needed to find out one thing before he was ready to venture an opinion as to the identity of this virus.

He instructed one of the technicians assigned to him to run a computer check on a viral strain baptized A/New Jersey/76. It had claimed exactly one life, as far as was known, a soldier at Fort Dix named David Lewis. David Lewis' death had caused a panic among public health officials who feared that the flu that struck him was so virulent that a vaccine should be readied at once. Lightman was anxious to know whether the Lewis viral strain and the one from Taylor might be related.

As soon as he had the report in hand he would arrange to meet with Finch. With the computer analysis of the A/New Jersey/76 swine flu virus, he'd have gone as far as he could in the lab. To learn more about the virus, he suspected, and how it was spread, he might have to temporarily abandon his test tubes and centrifuges and go out into the world. The world, after all, was the theater where the great drama of the virus was being played out.

TWENTY-NINE

Finch occupied the eye of the storm. While the air around him was charged with urgency he maintained a deliberate calm as if to serve as a reminder that panic wasn't necessarily the appropriate response to crisis. However, it didn't look as though he'd gotten much sleep in the seventy-two hours since Lightman had seen him last, and his clothes were rumpled and interestingly stained.

In the isolation of his lab Lightman hadn't kept track of the events in the outside world. Perhaps he was better off;

nothing good was happening beyond the cloistered walls of the Quarantine Control Center. In suppressing renewed rioting in the East End, police had killed nine and wounded another twenty-two. The government claimed that the shooting was in response to violence by demonstrators against the Emergency Quarantine Act but promised an investigation anyway. "It was a matter of the people wanting to break out of the contaminated areas and the police trying to keep them in," Finch explained.

Why, Lightman asked, was it necessary to confine the population of the East End when it was clear that the infection had already spread so widely? "Isn't that a little like shutting the barn door after the horses have gotten out?"

"I'm not in a position to comment on the law. My job is to enforce it," Finch replied, taking refuge in his role as a loyal, unquestioning subordinate of the Crown. "Now tell me what you've found. Just what are we dealing with here?"

Lightman didn't need to look at his notes although he'd brought them along for reference; what he had to say was all in his head. "Ever since this outbreak began to reveal its full dimensions I've had an idea what was happening. But I had to have some way of verifying it. The conclusion I've reached is still tentative, but I think it pretty much conforms with the facts as we know them."

"Go on. We won't string you up on the gallows if you're wrong."

"There is only one virus that bears any resemblance to the virus currently in circulation. It is, if you will, a close relative. That virus is called A/New Jersey/76. All the thousands of other viruses we've compared it to differ enough so that we can rule them out."

"Is there anything significant about this A/New Jersey virus?"

"It occurred only once in the spring of 1976 and killed just one soldier at Fort Dix. But administration officials, taking note of how deadly it was, were afraid it was the

same one that struck in 1918—the virus responsible for
the Great Influenza Pandemic. The Ford administration
launched an emergency campaign to produce a vaccine.
The vaccine was introduced but over a hundred elderly
people were paralyzed by an unusual side effect and ninety
million doses of the vaccine were left over. The virus itself
never reappeared."

"But you're implying that this A/New Jersey isn't what's
out there now."

"No, what's out there is the virus the U.S. government
was in a panic over in 1976. The problem is that the virus
that caused the pandemic in 1918—popularly known as
the Spanish Lady—was never properly identified. It was
too infinitesimally small to be viewed through the microscopes of the time. If they'd had an electron microscope to
use they would have been able to see it, only it took them
another fifteen years or so to get around to inventing one.
By then the virus had disappeared so there was no way of
knowing what it looked like."

"How did you decide that it was the Spanish Lady?"

"My suspicion was first aroused by a coincidence of
dates. It's my belief that the virus now spreading originated
in the body of a man wanted for murder in Alaska named
Joe Taylor. He probably died sometime between 1918 and
1919—the years in which the Spanish Flu was raging. His
body was recovered last winter and while it was subsequently cremated, it's my belief that infected specimens
from his body were somehow transported here."

"Can you prove that?"

Lightman allowed that he couldn't.

"But you're positive this body was infected by the flu
virus now in circulation?"

"It's a reasonably good hypothesis to go on." Lightman
wished he could present the inspector with the kind of hard
evidence he was seeking. But the truth was, he just didn't
have it. He continued, "When I went over the literature, I

realized that most of the symptoms recorded in victims in 1918 are showing up now. One of the most striking aspects of the Spanish Lady was its propensity to attack just about every vital organ in the body. It happened then and it's happening now."

"Let's say it is this Spanish Lady. How bad do you think it can get?"

Lightman was hesitant to say. "One of the most puzzling aspects of the 1918 pandemic was that it didn't obey the rules that most other flu viruses do, it didn't follow any geographical axis—north to south, say, or east to west. It seemed to break out everywhere at once. For example, it appeared in one week's time in Freetown, Sierra Leone, in Budapest, in South Africa, and in Portugal. It even managed to reach a lighthouse off the Tasmanian coast. That was an interesting case because neither the lighthouse keeper nor his wife had seen a soul for the preceding six months."

"How *did* it get there?"

"There's no telling."

Finch frowned; by profession he didn't like unsolved mysteries, especially those that remained unsolved for eighty years. "So you're saying that this virus—if it is the Spanish Lady—is going to spread fast and in nearly every quarter of the globe?"

"I think it would be foolish to expect otherwise. And keep in mind that communication is much faster and the world far more interconnected than it was in 1918, so the rapidity with which this can spread will be significantly greater."

"Is there any glimmer of hope, anything we could look forward to?"

"The pandemic lasted for just about three months ending in late November and early December of 1918. There was a less severe recurrence in the spring of the following year, but those 120 days saw the worst of it. By that time it had pretty much exhausted the human reservoir available to it."

"You don't hear much about it, though."

"Partly I suspect because it was overshadowed by the ending of the First World War, partly because what people do you know who like to remember bad times? But it might interest you to know that it took more lives in those three months than World War One did in four years."

"You're joking."

"Look at your history books. In fact, it's judged to be the worst pandemic since the Black Plague of the fourteenth century. If you're looking for something else to compare it with you have to go all the way back to the Plague of Justinian in 542 AD. Estimates of how many lives that carried off go up to 100 million."

"And how many people did the Spanish Lady kill?"

"Twenty-one million."

Finch looked understandably aghast. He was more accustomed to dealing with murders that could be counted on one hand. And murder was what this very likely was.

"In one way or another it affected approximately a billion people, which in 1918 was half the world's population."

"And you believe that it could do the same again?"

For the first time in their meeting Lightman consulted his notes. "If this outbreak is in fact caused by the same 1918 virus, and if the same proportions hold up, I estimate that close to three billion lives will be adversely affected, if not by the virus directly than by the loss of family members and by economic and political dislocation. What you're already seeing in the East End is a harbinger of what may happen throughout the world."

"And how many dead would you estimate?"

"Again this is if the proportions hold up. Each outbreak is different even if the same virus is present."

Finch repeated his question, more irritably now.

"I estimate sixty-three million deaths," Lightman said.

THIRTY

He was alone when he saw her. Her face was not clearly in
focus, but he could tell by her posture, by the way she was
moving, by the way her skin shone that it must be Diana.
Someone else was materializing from out of the dimness, a
man, naked just as she was, his eyes drinking her in, his
arms extended to her. There was an early evening stillness
about the tableau, a sense of pastoral calm. Diana's eyes
were searching out someone else, another man. And then
he, too, came out of the dimness. And then Beck knew
who it was; it was Patrick, naked just as the other two were
naked. And so he understood who the other must be—John
Lightman. The bed was large enough for the three of them.
As Lightman reached for her she arched her back, stiffening, for his touch surprised her even though she'd been
expecting it. His hands traveled to her breasts, cupping
them, and she leaned in toward him, her hair skirting his
chest. But what he failed to realize was that Patrick was
watching and allowing his hands to wander up her legs.
Diana could see but Lightman could not. What neither of
them knew was that she was beyond them both, rising out
of her body even as they claimed more and more of that
body for themselves. They were possessing her just as she
slipped from their grasp. And then it was just the two of
them, locked in a terrible embrace. Each man, only then
comprehending what was happening, that they were alone,
and that the woman was gone from their midst, attempted

201

to disengage. But the more they struggled to tear apart the
more they were pinned together. One looked into the face
of the other and they knew that finally there was no escape.

He could never tell in advance when the visions were
going to come, they would just happen. But they usually
came in cycles, one right after another in an explosive
frenzy of mental energy. Then they would subside and
leave him feeling strangely bereft, deflated; it was like
being abandoned by parents or a lover, knowing that it was
the last one would ever see them again. People who observed him at the time of these trances said that he would
sink into a semiconscious state, that he would often cry out
as if he were enduring great agony. It was true; he would
experience pain and heat and cold and all sensations which
the body was capable of registering, but in a heightened
form while he was experiencing his visions. And yet when
he emerged from these energized states he was surprised to
find himself back in the world, surprised to learn that only
a few minutes had passed when to him it had felt like hours
or longer.

God was speaking through him—that was what he'd
thought at first, ever since his first vision, of his dead
grandfather, as a child. But a year before Jonas Beck had
begun to see that it wasn't this way at all; God was *in* him.
After a month of fasting and meditation he understood
what was wanted of him. It had come in a vision more
powerful than any he had undergone before. It was a vision
of the world to come. It was, he believed, like the vision
that Noah had seen before the flood, like the vision Moses
had seen before God laid to waste the land of the Pharaohs
and destroyed the first-born of the Egyptians, like the visions of Isaiah and of Mohammed and Jesus Christ: a
vision of fire, pestilence, and the death of the cities of
man. It was the vision of all the calamities that must by necessity precede and pave the way for the final days of awe.
And in this great vision Jonas Beck had seen the man

who would act as the vehicle to hasten the time when these days would arrive. He saw this man without knowing his name or anything about him other than that he was a physician, a scientist. Into this man's hands would come a treasure, more precious than the gold and jewels that other people coveted, so small as to be invisible but capable of releasing power as destructive in its own way as the atom when split. God intended this man to help his church, to cast out the wicked and unrepentant and save those who submitted themselves to His judgment.

But even Beck was surprised when this man actually appeared, introduced to him by Nicholas Cleary. He rejoiced at seeing him, he told him at once that honor and fortune would be his inheritance, but that these things were as nothing in comparison to the love of God he would earn.

Naturally Patrick believed him mad. It was the case with most of those who sought him out. But he didn't mind, he was accustomed to their skepticism, their contempt and mocking laughter. For he knew how easily their defenses would collapse and their skepticism fall away. Patrick was no different. He affected an attitude of disdain but he did not stop listening. Beck told him about his life, dissected his soul, exposed his deceits, laying bare secrets that Patrick had labored for years to conceal, elaborating ever more labyrinthine fictions to cover his tracks. And cover them he did; but such tactics availed him nothing against a person who had the ability like Beck to peer into the heart and read it as clearly as if it were a children's book which, often, of course, it was.

Yet Patrick would have fled from him, petrified at being found out, had he not given him the secret keys to the treasure. He told him where to look. To the north, to the frozen wastes, to Alaska. And he told him how to obtain it. But he reminded Patrick that it would cost him enormously to steal this treasure and that he would suffer, like Prometheus did for his theft of fire. But Beck knew the

warning wouldn't deter him; the treasure was too desirable.
As Jonas Beck needed it for the mission God had commanded him to undertake, so Patrick Martindale needed it
to stop history in its path and alter its course just as if it
were a churning river he could dam. But in the end, as
Beck knew, it wouldn't be the flesh of women or the
money or the power even to fashion history according to
his design that mattered to Patrick Martindale. It would be
one thing only: absolution.

BOOK TWO
Gifts

"Men who had hitherto concealed their indulgence in pleasure now grew bolder. For, seeing the sudden change, how the rich died in a moment . . . they reflected that life and riches were transitory, and they resolved to enjoy themselves while they could, and to think only of pleasure."
                                        —Thucydides on the plague of Athens

"This scourge had implanted so great a terror to the hearts of men and women that brothers abandoned brothers . . . In many cases wives deserted their husbands. But, even worse, and almost incredible, was the fact that fathers and mothers refused to nurse and assist their own children, as though they did not belong to them."
                                        —Boccaccio

"The plague only exaggerates the relationship between the classes; it strikes at the poor and snares the rich. . . ."
                                        —Jean-Paul Sartre

ONE

Ezra Omaru had no idea where he was going. Not since leaving London had anyone bothered to inform him. He, along with three hundred others, was herded from one point to another, obeying instructions from members of the church known as captains. His captain was a scrawny young man named Ken Snape.

Curiosity was not encouraged. Everyone was given a copy of a book by Jonas Beck called *The Holy, the Hidden* which was filled with quotations from the Bible and sayings from the Apostle Beck himself. Snape said that they would all be obliged to memorize it eventually because the words in this book were the way to God. Ezra, however, wasn't interested in the way to God so much as he was in the way to his children.

Now, crammed into a seat inside what must have once

been a military transport plane, he didn't know whether he was getting closer to his children or farther away from them. There were no windows, so he couldn't even gaze out and see whether they were passing over ocean or land, flying toward the sun or away from it.

The only thing that he could say for certain was that the journey from England to wherever it was they were descending to had taken about five hours.

When they were down, Ken Snape appeared from the cockpit and declared, "This is where our journey ends, this is where the Apostle Beck wants us to be, this is where we will spread the holy name and witness in safety the passing of wickedness from the earth."

Yes, Ezra thought, but would this be where he found his children? He looked to the sides of him and saw with dismay that the faces of the other passengers were rapt with attention, their eyes lighted up with excitement. The fervency of their belief, however expected, was revolting.

"Please assemble in single file," Snape instructed, "and leave the craft in an orderly manner."

Still no indication where they were.

While it was certainly a great relief being liberated from the confines of the transport plane, the passengers had no more way of knowing where they were once they'd debarked and were standing on the tarmac than they had when they were thousands of feet in the air.

All that anyone could say with assurance was that they were in a country where it was mercilessly hot. The heat was dry, though, desert dry.

The airfield on which they'd landed was no larger than the one they'd left in England. What appeared to be a small terminal building, glinting in the morning sun, was at the other end of the runway so that if there was any sign to orient them, it could not be seen.

There didn't seem to be any town or even a village nearby. This might be as close to the middle of nowhere as Ezra was likely to get in his life. Mountains, with parched slopes strewn with rocks, stretched across the western horizon. Not a cloud was anywhere in sight.

More than an hour passed without anything happening. The members of Ezra's battalion—the church used military jargon in classifying their membership—milled around in the scorching sun, uncomplaining as always.

All that Snape would tell them was that they were waiting for ground transport. Sparing as he was with information, he responded to Ezra's question—the only question asked by anyone—by saying that he had no idea how long they would have to wait.

Although Ezra was determined to keep up this masquerade, at least until such time as he found his children and freed them, he would forget himself occasionally and act in a manner that invited skeptical looks and sharp rejoinders from Snape. He knew that he ought to watch himself.

Having survived the flu unaided, he had to keep reminding himself that the people around him believed that their lives were saved by the church. Their allegiance was total.

Then, all at once, emerging from a cloud of dust in the distance, a convoy appeared—a dozen troop carriers, their chassis painted the colors of the landscape surrounding them, all browns and tans.

They loaded onto the carriers in the same unnerving silence that they'd boarded the plane back in England. Chatting among themselves was discouraged; whenever people did speak it was to mouth phrases derived from *The Holy, the Hidden*. All things being equal, Ezra preferred the silence.

The canvas flaps in the back of the carrier weren't completely secured and so Ezra could see out. It was not much of a freedom when compared to those he'd given up, but it was all the freedom he had right now and he was grateful for it.

What he saw, though, didn't tell him a great deal. His original impression at the airfield was being borne out; they seemed to be in a desert. And the desert showed no sign of ending. The only vegetation he could see were stunted palms and Joshua trees and dull green cacti springing up alongside the road. The desert floor, by turns gray and brown and ochre, was shot through with veins of red and black; it extended in every direction Ezra looked; only in the east did it stop, to then give way to the rugged chain of mountains Ezra had seen earlier.

Strangely enough, at no time did Ezra have a glimpse of any other traffic on the road or hear the blast of the horn. What he did hear were the carriers' motors and the clatter of stones striking metal, only that and the eerie silence from those forced to endure the racket.

And then the gradient of the road changed dramatically, growing steeper. Although they still had no way of knowing where they were going, the change at least was welcome.

The motors strained against gravity; they were going up, up. And then they seemed to have reached the summit. One by one the carriers drew to a halt. This was accompanied by a confusion of voices and cries.

A moment later the back flaps were loosened and the battalion members began to clamber down.

"We're here," a young man with fire in his eyes declared to Ezra.

"But where's here?"

The young man looked blank, as if he couldn't comprehend why anyone would be asking a question like that.

As the battalion gathered, massaging their legs to relieve their cramps, the captains moved among them, shouting orders.

But Ezra wasn't listening. His attention was fixed entirely on the sight that presented itself to view.

Below them was a city that Ezra never believed he would see in his lifetime; even now it was difficult for him to absorb the reality of it. Apparently the others around him felt much the same for they were all agog, their mouths hanging open, their eyes bulging in disbelief.

Shimmering in the summer haze, just as golden as song and legend had promised, was the city of Jerusalem.

When Ezra recovered from the shock of finding himself in Jerusalem he became aware of the tolling of bells—church bells—coming from every quarter of the city.

The more he looked the more he could see that there was almost no movement at all in the streets. He observed a camel making endless circles, around and around and around, unable to strike out in any direction. He could see no people, though. He couldn't believe that they had all disappeared like that. But there was no doubt that they weren't anywhere in sight.

It then dawned on him what he was seeing. The city that he had never dreamed he'd ever set his eyes on, this beautiful, fabled city, was dying.

TWO

After nearly two weeks Lightman was beginning to think that if he expected to make any progress at all in his investigation it wasn't going to be in Geneva.

It was apparent to Lightman that Finch was hoping for far more from him than he had any realistic chance of delivering. What Finch wanted was hard facts, indisputable proof clearly implicating Martindale, proof that would leave the Swiss authorities with no other alternative than to send him under guard back to England for trial. Under the provisions of the Emergency Quarantine Act Martindale would have faced arrest—even in the absence of proof—were he still in England. But this was Switzerland. Clearcut evidence was necessary for the police to act, and given

Martindale's connections, perhaps not even then. More-over, the sense of urgency present in countries ravaged by the flu was missing here. God either loved the Swiss or was just taking his own good time about getting around to them because, apart from a scattering of isolated cases, there had hardly been any incidences of the flu in the country at all.

Finch had gone ahead with his original plan nonetheless, dispatching Gray and Lightman to Geneva in the belief that the evidence needed to make his case could somehow be gained from the people working under Martindale at WHO. He reasoned correctly that Lightman enjoyed a number of contacts at the health organization he could enlist to help him.

But however well-founded the inspector's assumption it wasn't working out at all the way he'd intended. Of the twelve members of the expert committee on the flu outbreak serving under Martindale, not a single one would agree to talk to Lightman. Some politely declined, citing the press of work while others simply refused to return his calls. What was infuriating was that he was personally acquainted with seven of the members and had always gotten along well with them. Certainly they had no cause to rebuff him like that. The person who infuriated him the most was Geoffrey Hopkins.

He had always regarded Hopkins as a friend. He could remember nothing about their last meeting in Hong Kong that could justify this silence from him, but each message he left at his office went unanswered all the same.

The only explanation that came to mind, and the most obvious one, was that Martindale had instructed the expert committee members not to talk to any outsiders, or perhaps just to him. He didn't know how much of a threat Martindale believed him to be: a nettlesome pain or a diabolical antagonist.

Gray, who was obliged to brief Finch on a daily basis as to what progress was being made, grew increasingly anxious. "If you're supposed to do something, then you do it, and don't be jerking everyone around," he kept telling him.

Lightman got nowhere trying to make him understand the kind of roadblocks he was running into. So far as Gray was concerned, Lightman was being deliberately obstructionist. No longer sporting dreadlocks and a slight goatee, he now wore his hair shorn nearly to the scalp and carried on like a panjandrum from some indebted Third World country. He repeatedly dangled in front of Lightman the threat of a long prison sentence back in London should he fail to make headway. Relations between them, never too good to begin with, soured further.

What was particularly frustrating to Lightman was the enforced inactivity. He'd hoped that when he left London there'd have been a change. But now, two weeks later in Geneva, he seemed to be no better off than before. He should have stayed in the lab at the quarantine center; at least there he could be doing some good. Finally an idea came to him. If he couldn't get Hopkins to return his call, he would find him in person and corner him.

There were just so many hotels in Geneva, and of them only a select few that WHO delegates and consultants generally stayed in. A couple of phone calls were all he needed to locate him.

Before venturing over to the President Hotel, situated on the north shore of Lake Geneva—the shore with cachet as opposed to the less desirable south shore—Lightman called ahead to see if he should bother. Without giving his name he asked for Hopkins' room. But Hopkins wasn't picking up.

Lightman then asked to speak to the house manager. Explaining that he was with WHO he said it was imperative that he get in touch with Hopkins, that it could not wait. The manager was sympathetic; he understood that there was a health emergency even if it hadn't gotten its grips on Geneva yet, and he was anxious to cooperate. "Dr. Hopkins is attending the Théâtre de Poche tonight," he told Lightman. "If you go there you should find him."

Lightman left Gray at their hotel. It was called Le Jardin Anglais and so was presumably located near an English garden, although Lightman had never seen it. It was a small unfashionable hotel, but Finch's budget for this expedition didn't allow for the extravagance of a hotel like the President.

While there was no question in Lightman's mind that Gray didn't trust him, it was also apparent that he felt no special urge to follow him as he did in London. Lightman's passport was in Gray's possession, after all; so it wasn't as if he could suddenly take off to another country even if he had it in his head to try to escape. It seemed that he preferred to stay in the room and watch Swiss TV.

A musical version of Boccaccio's *Decameron* was being presented at the Théâtre de Poche. From time to time, as he waited out in the lobby, Lightman could hear the swelling strains of the orchestra and the occasional sound of applause. But when the audience began to file out Lightman noticed that people mostly looked confused. It didn't appear as if Boccaccio, at least in musical dress, had gone over big with them.

He was hoping that Hopkins would be alone; it would be awkward to have to confront him with someone else present. But when Hopkins materialized, looking vastly relieved to have escaped, he was with a pretty young woman, Swiss from the looks of her.

Lightman positioned himself so that Hopkins would have no choice but to see him as he approached the exit.

Hopkins saw him without any problem. But he didn't react at all as Lightman had anticipated. His eyes brightened and he threw his arms open, calling out, "My God, John Lightman as I live and breathe!"

He encompassed Lightman in his arms and then turned excitedly to introduce him to the woman whose name was Gerta.

"This is my good friend, Dr. John Lightman," he told her before turning back to him and asking what the hell he was doing in Switzerland.

"You mean you didn't know?"

"Know? How was I supposed to know?" He motioned Lightman toward the door. "Come on, there has to be a place around here we can have a drink. What did you think of that piece of excrescence?"

"I didn't see it."

This puzzled Hopkins greatly. "Well then what were you doing at the theater? She's my excuse." He indicated Gerta beside him who merely blushed and said nothing.

"I was waiting for you."

"I don't understand. How did you know I'd be here? You never told me you were psychic, John."

Lightman explained why he'd resorted to waiting for him in the theater lobby.

"But that's crazy, I never received any messages that you'd called. Why wouldn't I return your calls?"

Lightman tried to mollify his bruised feelings by buying Hopkins and his date a drink once they'd found what might have been the darkest bar in all of Geneva. Lightman had a feeling that it was a place where lovers came when they didn't want friends of their spouses spotting them.

Hopkins promised to talk to the secretary Lightman had given the messages to. "I can't fire her because she's a member of a permanent secretarial pool. We're the ones who are temporary—or as temporary as this outbreak turns out to be." Then he nudged Gerta playfully and said, "My friend Lightman is a very serious man. Don't you ever relax? Jesus, you're driving yourself too hard. People like you keel over of coronaries before they hit fifty. So what is the call for such alarm tonight? You're itching to say something, so say it."

Lightman began by asking him how he liked working for Martindale.

"He runs us ragged, this is the first night in three weeks

I've had off. But the way he's delegated authority among all of us, I couldn't tell you what's really going on, whether we're getting anywhere on this or not. If you want my opinion, I don't believe he really gives a shit about the expert committee. We take up space, we make calls, we move paper. But it doesn't add up to a whole hell of a lot. You ask me, the real work is being done elsewhere—he's got another chain of command, his own personal organization, operating on this outbreak. We're there for show if you ask me."

None of this particularly surprised Lightman. "Where is Martindale now?"

"That's a good question. Nobody I know has seen him in over a week. The Great God Patrick we call him. We feel like we've been blessed if he puts in an appearance. Not that the memos and directives from him ever cease flowing, it's just that he rarely cares to honor us with his presence. So I really can't tell you whether he's here in Geneva or Rome or wherever."

"Rome? Why Rome?"

"I hear he's opened a clinic there like the one he has in London. Now maybe you won't mind telling me why you're so interested in Martindale."

Lightman knew that if he attempted to explain he'd be with Hopkins all night. Hopkins wouldn't settle for a brief accounting, he'd want to know every last detail, and besides, Gerta was growing impatient to leave. So Lightman tried to be succinct, saying that his interest in the Great God Patrick stemmed from the investigation he'd begun seven months ago in Alaska for the National Institutes of Health.

"The one you told me about in Hong Kong?"

"That one, yes. The investigation is still continuing."

"Pretty far afield, isn't it—Alaska to Geneva?"

"It surprised me, too."

"And Martindale's a target of this investigation?"

"I wouldn't go so far as to say he's a target, but I'm anxious to talk to him, ask him some questions."

Had it been Hopkins alone Lightman might have been more forthcoming, but as pretty and innocent as Gerta looked, he didn't feel inclined to elaborate. Paranoia wasn't his style, but taking certain precautions couldn't hurt.

In any case Hopkins seemed to accept his explanation. "If there's something I can do to help you out, I'll be happy to, you know that, John."

"As a matter of fact, there is."

"Shoot."

"In your work for the expert committee, anything that strikes you as well . . . unusual, a little off-base I'd like to hear about."

"Like what for instance?"

"I can't tell you because I don't know exactly how your committee conducts its work. But I'd say that you should keep a lookout for any data that doesn't quite correspond to what you think it should be or that just seems completely out of whack."

"I think I get your meaning. It's one of those cases where you'll know it when you see it."

"You'd be doing me a great service if you let me know, whatever it is. Even if it seems barely worth mentioning. Mention it anyway. Right now I'm staying in a hotel on the south shore, but I don't know how much longer I'll be there. I assume, though, that I can always reach you at the President."

"Just so we won't run into any problems like before, why don't you give another name when you ask for me."

"How about if I call myself Joe—Joe Taylor?"

The Hotel Le Jardin Anglais closed early, a little after ten, and so it was necessary to ring a bell and summon the porter to open it up. He was an aged man with a bad leg who made it clear that he didn't like being disturbed from his sleep. A tiny elevator brought him to the fifth floor and his room.

The quiet in the hotel was of a distinctly different kind than the quiet that reigned at night in the streets of Geneva; it was a hollow, unhappy quiet which gave Lightman the feeling that there was nobody else staying in the place. He'd seldom seen another guest and from the rooms he'd passed not a sound ever emerged.

He was surprised to find that the ordinarily security conscious Detective Gray had failed to lock the door.

As soon as he stepped inside the room he stumbled over something. It was dark and he groped for a light to see what it was, even at the risk of rousing Gray from his slumber.

The light on, he looked to see what he had tripped on. It was Gray. Obviously Lightman didn't have to worry about disturbing him.

THREE

Gray was bleeding onto the carpet from the back of his head. His eyes were open and in the process of glazing over. Not so his mouth; his lips were vised tight.

Lightman was torn between running out and staying put. He shut the door behind him, though, and then took a look in the bathroom. There was a lot of blood there, and brain tissue staining the tiles of the wall and floor. It appeared that Gray had been shot there and had somehow survived long enough to make it into the adjoining room. Whoever had shot him was gone now—luckily. Lightman went back to take a closer look at the body.

There was of course nothing to be done. But as he knelt down beside the body he discerned, very faintly, a curious ticking sound coming from Gray. He dismissed the notion that what he was hearing was caused by some peculiar postmortem metabolic process. No, this was a mechanical sound, not a sound any body would produce, alive or dead.

With his fingers Lightman pried open the lips. Something gold glinted within his mouth. Overcoming his revulsion he grabbed hold of it and lifted it out. Now it was clear what it was; his watch—Stephanie's gift—smeared with Gray's blood. He wiped the blood away. The time the watch told, he saw, was precise.

This ghoulish joke immobilized him for a minute. He continued to stare at the watch as if he was preparing to put himself under. Then he forced himself to move. He knew that he couldn't very well stay there. Not only would he have to face questioning by Swiss police, he would doubtless have to endure an even more intensive grilling by Finch on his return to London.

He was sure that anything of value Gray had owned was taken. He recalled specifically a miniature tape cassette Gray employed to record his observations, always out of his earshot. Naturally that was gone. Hunting through the drawers of the bureau and the single drawer of the bedside table he found nothing but dust.

Yet curiously, certain things of value had been left behind. Gray's gun, a Baretta with every bullet still in its chamber except for one. It wouldn't be difficult to guess where the missing one could be found. The gun felt heavy and strange in his hand. The last gun he'd used was a .22 on a rifle range when he was a teenager.

He also was gratified to find his passport. The blood on the back of it had left a stain, but it wasn't so conspicuous as to alert the suspicions of a customs inspector.

And there was something else he came across: it was a letter crammed inside the back pocket of the trousers Gray had on. Lightman unfolded it. It was crumpled and the handwriting was scrawled, suggesting that it had been written in haste. But it was legible enough. What was so astonishing was that the letter was addressed to him.

> Dearest John, if you have it in you to forgive me I
> need all the forgiveness that you can summon.
> There were things beyond my control—that are
> still beyond my control—you must believe that. I
> am at the Villa Pilatus, ten kilometers west of
> Fluelen on Lake Lucerne—Alpenrose closest
> station. If you don't come I'll understand. Love,
> D.

There was no way of knowing when, in the last couple of weeks, this letter had arrived for him. Upon intercepting it Gray must have suspected him all the more, perhaps thinking that he was secretly an accomplice of Martindale's, and that Diana was acting as a go-between. What was so unsettling was the possibility that she was in fact working for Martindale.

A hundred questions cried out to be answered. Who had delivered the letter? Had the murderer, in lifting what he wanted from the room, overlooked it—and his passport? Or was it left there intentionally as bait? It was obvious that answers to none of these questions would come by remaining there soaking up the smell of Gray's death.

It took a determined effort on his part to stay composed in front of the porter, whose scowl suggested how unhappy he was at being woken up again, this time to transport Lightman back to the ground floor.

Lightman realized that he couldn't spend the time reflecting on the alternatives, to weigh which course of action was the most sensible. He had made up his mind: he would go to the Villa Pilatus and hope that it wasn't a trap and Diana was actually there. Aside from Hopkins, she might be the only person in the country who could help him.

It was only in the taxi on his way to the railroad station that he realized how much he wanted to see her. It was as if the unknown murderer had acted not so much to kill Gray for any information he might have gotten ahold of, but for the express purpose of bringing Lightman and Diana together again.

FOUR

Lightman arrived in Alpenrose in the middle of a blazing July afternoon. Had he been in a more relaxed frame of mind he might have stopped to admire the view, which at every turn of the road proved ever more majestic; it was almost too much for the eyes to bear, the optical equivalent of indigestion. The horizon was defined by white-capped mountains that presided over a landscape of valleys and shimmering lakes.

There were only two others who'd gotten off the train with him, a man in a gray jacket that looked too warm for such a lovely summer afternoon and a youth whose step was so hurried that Lightman imagined he was on his way to see a girlfriend after a long absence.

Neither of the two struck him as the type he needed to be concerned with. If he was followed here it was not done in such an obvious manner.

The village was located behind a cluster of pines and the

dirt road turned into a paved street that led past a succession of brightly colored wooden houses and somewhat more elaborate structures where the village's commerce was conducted. Flowers were everywhere, sprouting out of windowboxes, climbing up trellises, blossoming in planters on the narrow sidewalks.

There wasn't much doing here nor had Lightman expected there to be. A village the size of Alpenrose, from what Lightman could see of it, couldn't have contained more than a hundred—maybe a hundred and fifty—people. Most of them were inside somewhere, dozing through the long, hot afternoon.

But walking along the street he was drawn to the sound of men's voices. Looking to his right he saw that the voices belonged to the customers of the local tavern. They were sitting at tables, throwing back large steins of amber brew. Lightman walked in.

Not only men were present, he saw, for in the recesses of the place, not quite submerged in the gloom, was a large, really very corpulent woman, whose features were so coarse that her face was as masculine as those around her. It was she Lightman remarked on first, possibly because of the intensity of her gaze on him. Almost automatically he went over to the table that she alone occupied. It was just a feeling he had that she might be able to help him.

"English?" she asked, raising her eyes toward him.

"No, American."

"Ah, American." She beckoned him to sit down.

Her face was full of flesh that drooped off the anchor of her skull. A conspicuous mustache defined her lips. Her eyes were wary in her appraisal of him.

"They call me Marthe."

"I'm John."

She wasn't drinking anything, she just seemed to be sitting there taking everything in.

"I'm looking for—"

"For what?" Her tone was accusatory.

"Somewhere to stay for a few days."

"You've come to the right place. There are rooms upstairs. Six francs a night with breakfast."

From the size of the village Lightman gathered that there would be only one bed and breakfast; there was no sense in asking to inspect the rooms. It was either that or nothing.

"That will do fine."

"What else do you want in Alpenrose?"

"Just passing through."

A glimmer of a smile came to her lips. "You wouldn't come to such a village like this if you did not have another purpose." She scrutinized him. "You do not look like a climber." She reached for his hands, turning them over to inspect them. "You are not a worker. You must be a professional, yes?"

"A scientist, a researcher."

"Tell me, what is there to research in Alpenrose?"

He decided he had nothing to lose by stating his purpose. "I'm looking for a friend who owns the Villa Pilatus. Do you know it?"

The old woman studied him, suspicion coming into her eyes.

"Who is this friend?"

"Dr. Patrick Martindale."

"I see." After a pause that went on for too long she said, "Yes, I know this place. It is too far for you to get to now. Tomorrow I will direct you."

"Is it possible to go there by car?"

She frowned. "But you have no car. You come here by train, no?"

Just as it was in villages everywhere, it took no time at all for news to get around.

"I don't suppose there's one I could rent."

The woman shook her head, a patronizing smile playing

on her lips. "You go by foot to the villa or else you find someone generous enough to give you a ride. Most of those who make the journey to the villa already have their own cars, they do not bother stopping off in this place."

"All right then, I'll go tomorrow. Who do I see about the room?"

Pointing a stubby callused finger toward her pendulous breasts, loose under the floral design of her shift, she said, "Who you see is me, Marthe."

Before he went to bed Lightman began to have second thoughts about what he was about to do. He reread Diana's letter. Not that he expected to find in it something he hadn't already learned, since he'd read it over several times already. No, it was more that he regarded the letter as a cipher which careful study might ultimately unlock. What he needed to believe most of all was that the words were heartfelt and that they were in fact Diana's and not dictated to her. Of one thing he was certain; it was her handwriting.

He couldn't let his doubts get the better of him; he reminded himself that if an experienced detective like Gray could be surprised and killed, so could he—easily. Why would Martindale or his devoted followers feel the need to lure him into a trap when they could eliminate him without going to the trouble?

Unfortunately he was applying his logic to a situation which seemed to have nothing logical about it. One way or another, he knew, he would be leaving tomorrow for the Villa Pilatus. But he decided that he ought to take the precaution of alerting somebody as to his whereabouts in the event that he didn't return.

He couldn't think of anyone better to notify than Hopkins. Reaching the President Hotel he identified himself, as agreed, as Joe Taylor, and was immediately put through.

"Where are you, John?" Hopkins demanded. "Have you got yourself into some kind of trouble again?"

"It seems I'm acquiring quite a reputation."

"I don't have anything new to tell you, if that's what you're calling about."

"Not exactly. I wanted you to know where I'll be for the next day or so."

"Oh? You're not in Geneva?"

"No, I'm in a village called Alpenrose not far from Lake Lucerne."

"Touring the country, are you? Taking in all the scenic vistas?"

"I wish. No, I'm on my way to Martindale's private villa—it's located not far from here."

"Has the Great God Patrick issued you a personal invitation?"

"I wouldn't put it that way."

"Am I supposed to be reading between the lines here?"

By not answering his question Lightman figured he was answering the question. "I'm now at an inn called the Paradise. It isn't really, but let that go. Any message you have for me you can leave here, and they'll know how to reach me. If I don't contact you in forty-eight hours, by Friday night, you might think of notifying the police."

"You're in trouble. Would it be fair to say that you're in deep shit?"

"It's one way of putting it. Will you do that for me, Geoff?"

"Absolutely. Friday night the Alps will be swarming with cops if I don't hear from you."

It wasn't the screech that roused him from his sleep but the frantic flapping of wings that did it. For a second Lightman thought he still must be dreaming the owl, with its black eyes and speckled body, a symbolic creature dredged from his subconscious.

But then he saw that it was as real as any owl ever got. Perhaps in reaction to his sudden wakening, the owl, with a shriek of protest, flew off the windowsill and soared into the morning sky.

Later, over breakfast, he mentioned the owl to Marthe.

"Yes, they come here all the time, those owls," she said.

There was no visible reaction from the other boarders eating at the breakfast table, three of them elderly gentlemen and one spinsterish woman. They might not know English or maybe they'd seen enough owls alighting on the windowsills of their rooms not to take notice of the phenomenon any longer.

"Oh? Is this common in these parts?"

"Since a month ago. It is a sign."

"A sign?"

"The plague comes here soon." Marthe spoke these words evenly, without the slightest inflection in her voice. "The last time the owls came to this village the plague followed."

"The flu, you mean?"

Ignoring him she said, "The leaves of the trees are turning white with mildew, did you see?"

Lightman said that no, that wasn't something he'd observed, though he'd yet to see much of the village and nothing at all of its environs.

"And the winds, the winds came the way they did before."

The winds. Lightman knew something about the winds, but not what they portended, if anything.

"It was like this in 1918, the white leaves, the winds, the flowers withering out of season."

Under different circumstances Lightman might not have paid any attention to the voicing of such superstitions. But he was more convinced than ever that the Spanish Lady was back. And against such a threat as this pathogen presented, superstitions were as effective as any drug prescribed to suppress it.

"It is because of the malefacs," Marthe continued.

"The what?" Maybe he hadn't heard right.

"The malefacs. The sign of Leo is occupied by Saturn and Neptune. The vibrations are out of tune."

"I see." Lightman didn't want to offend the woman.

"It was terrible, how many died the last time. Karl, he died."

"Karl?"

The kitchen girl, a strapping blonde with not a bit of intelligence in her eyes, set a plate of eggs and sausage in front of him.

"My mother was a widow at an early age," Marthe explained. "My father was dead, killed in the war. He was a German patriot and a fool. So she chose to marry a young man, a farmer whose name was Karl."

An unexpected smile lit Marthe's face as she recollected the young man. "I was only a very little girl then. But I remember how Mama was so happy to have found him.

"For awhile everything went well, the preparations for the wedding were made, you could feel the excitement in the house. And then—then the Coquette came."

"The Coquette?"

"It is what we called the influenza. Here in Switzerland it is the Coquette because it shares its favors with everyone. It makes no distinctions."

It was another name that Lightman would have to add to the list he'd been assembling. It seemed to have had as many aliases—or perhaps they were noms de guerre—as symptoms: the Cubans called it *trancazo,* meaning blow from a heavy stick; the Siamese the *Kai Wat Yai,* the Great Cold Fever; the Poles, with no love for the Russians, named it the Bolshevik Disease; the Ceylonese referred to it as Bombay Fever while in Penang it was known as Singapore Fever. Some, however, just called it the disease of the wind.

Marthe went on. "Suddenly Karl fell ill. The doctors came, they looked at him, they could do nothing. But Mama refused to call off the wedding. Love was love.

People asked her, Why do you want to be twice a widow? But she would not listen to anybody. She pretended to be brave. She made her wedding dress herself. But the doctor said that he would not permit the marriage to take place unless everybody wore a mask. Karl too, even the minister, they all wear masks.

"So they hold the wedding and they exchange rings. But right at the moment Mama slips the ring on Karl's fingers he expires. Nobody but Mama seemed to realize this, because he went so quietly."

"Just like that? Right after the ceremony?"

Marthe nodded. "Just like that. Mama couldn't speak. She couldn't believe that this had happened. Even though she knew that there was no other outcome she could not believe it. Right away, before anyone could stop her, she threw off her mask and leaned down and ripped Karl's mask off so that she could kiss him. The doctor tried to pull her off. But she resisted.

"Later on, she became sick also. I believe that it was from her kiss. But maybe not. She died and then I had no Papa and no Mama. The war takes one, the Coquette takes the other. It is like this always."

A long silence ensued. Finally Lightman broke it. "Marthe, I need to be on my way. Will you show me how I should go?"

With a groan the old woman rose from her chair, at the same time shaking off the memory that had temporarily held her in its sway.

When Marthe escorted him out of the house she asked him again why he wished to go to the Villa Pilatus.

Was it such an unusual destination? he wondered. "I told you a friend of mine may be there—Dr. Martindale."

She gave him the same intense look as she had the previous afternoon. "You seem like a nice gentleman," she said.

"Well, thank you, I appreciate it."

"I don't think that a nice gentleman should have anything to do with such a place."

That caught Lightman off guard; he didn't know how to respond. "Why is that?"

"Because the people who go to the Villa Pilatus are terrible people." She made a face. "They are degenerate!" She literally spat the word out, getting half of Lightman's cheek wet in the process.

"How do you mean degenerate?"

A proper Swiss matron, Marthe seemed not to want to say. She swallowed hard, her eyes narrowed, her voice dropped. "The people who are invited to the Villa Pilatus, they do all sorts of unspeakable things. Right in the backyard!"

It was the setting as much as the unspeakable things that seemed to cause her such great distress.

"Are you sure of this?"

"Ja, I am very sure."

Recalling the surreptitious videotaping of Diana's flat he had no doubt that, even if this woman was exaggerating, something must be going on at the villa, something freakish and licentious.

Now he understood why Marthe had acted with such an air of reproach toward him. Anyone inquiring for directions to the Villa Pilatus naturally invited suspicion.

"I assure you, my intentions are wholly honorable."

He realized he sounded as if he were asking for permission to marry a daughter of hers.

"Maybe so," she said, "maybe so." She was still dubious.

"Do you know whether Dr. Martindale himself participates in these—unspeakable things?"

She shook her head, rolling her eyes up in their sockets. "I know nothing else. Nothing else."

"Let me ask you this. Do you know who's up at the villa now?"

"No, Herr Doktor, this you will have to discover on your own."

It wasn't a difficult climb, it was just long and took more out of him than he imagined it would. The problem was that he was out of shape.

Along the path he kept looking for mildew on the leaves but saw none. Nor did he spot an owl. It was a fine summer day and whatever omens and portents might be present escaped his attention. He preferred to think about nothing, not about his circumstances, not about the flu, not about untimely death. And certainly he didn't want to think about what would happen once he got to his destination.

Reaching the summit, he saw it. There could be no mistake; the architecture was Moorish, with cupolas and spires rising from the roof and high arched windows decoratively outlined by pastel colors. It was strategically situated so that it overlooked the Vierwaldstaatersee, which shone a silvery blue in the clear light. Lightman started toward it.

There was a gate in front of it. Finding it open, he continued on up a set of stairs. The entrance to the villa was marked by high drama; the visitor was obliged to ascend to it. Lightman imagined dazzling, dissolute parties being held there, the lights and shadows in the arched windows enticing the guests to quicken their pace.

But now, obviously, no party was going on. It was difficult to tell whether there was anyone inside at all.

When no one responded to the bell he didn't know whether to be disappointed or relieved. He went around toward the back, toward the lake.

Then he stopped, his eyes caught by the sight of a woman emerging from the water. The sun burnished her with light, she was naked. He didn't move, his breath caught in his throat, he couldn't move.

It was Diana.

FIVE

There was still time to change his mind, to turn around and go back before she had any idea he was there. Happy as he was to see her, he was still afraid that he'd done the wrong thing by going there. What would he do if he discovered Martindale with her?

But by not moving an inch his decision was made. As soon as she put on her robe and started back toward the house she spotted him. Her face registered confusion, then delight. After a moment's hesitation she rushed toward him.

She embraced him and he felt the dampness of her body through her robe. The kiss she gave him was almost enough to put to rest any doubts he had about what kind of reception he'd get. "You came," she said, "I can't believe you're actually here." There was wonder in her voice.

Drawing away from him, studying his face for some sign of what he might be thinking, she said, "I didn't know whether you got my message. Pilar said she'd get it to you but I wasn't certain."

"Pilar?"

"One of the servants, but all that can wait. You're here, that's the important thing."

Only then did she become conscious that her robe had fallen open. She met his stare and said, "Come with me."

He started to ask her how she'd known where to find him but she hushed him. "Later, it can wait until later."

She led him up a set of stone steps to the portico, then

into the house itself. It was dark and cool inside. Lightman had a momentary glimpse of walls full of veined marble, of framed paintings, of a stained glass window ignited by an amazing violet light as the sun hit it. Before he could really get a sense as to what he was seeing she was guiding him down a spiral staircase, down and around, a quick, dizzying descent.

And then they were in a bedroom.

She was kissing him, frantically, desperately. He reached under her robe, exalting in the alternating sensations of expensive silk and wet flesh.

They sank to the bed. Though it was dark and windowless, untouched by sun, he didn't believe that they were safe, that the dark afforded them any protection from the cameras. He had to assume that they were being watched and taped, but for once he didn't give a damn.

Her hips bucked, rose and fell and rose again to meet him, while she tore at his clothes. Whenever he could, he'd steal a glance at her face, hoping somehow to catch her unawares, as if he might have a chance of seeing something in her eyes, in her expression, that had escaped him before. He didn't want her to remain unknowable, he didn't want anything in his life to remain unknowable.

She kept surprising him, slipping out from under him and clamoring on top of him, her hair partially obscuring her face and dripping drops of Lake Lucerne all over him. The tips of her breasts grazed his chest. A smile played on her lips; she liked what was happening, there was the sound of her laughter in his ears.

Lightman kept his patience at bay only for so long, and then, though he realized he was going to dispel the languorous mood they'd achieved, he had to ask her where Martindale was.

The mood was broken as he suspected it would be. She moved away from him and didn't immediately reply. The silence between them, however, was suddenly electric with tension. He was beginning to think she might never answer, but at last she said, "I don't know. Maybe in Geneva, maybe in Rome. I never have any idea. He disappears for weeks on end and then one day he comes back. He's fascinated by you. I know you won't believe me but he really is. He's been reading your papers. When I mentioned I met you in Hong Kong and talked to you about your thesis on how the Indians were wiped out by the flu and not smallpox he wanted to know all about it. He says he can't understand why you're so opposed to him. He insists he had nothing to do with what happened to your grant money, and he says that he's terribly sorry you misinterpreted his offer to help you as some form of bribery or blackmail. The reason he had Winston ring you up was because he felt that you and he might someday be able to collaborate. He was anxious to meet you and if possible give you a boost."

As Diana spoke, her eyes were searching out the ceiling, then the walls; they were anywhere but on Lightman. Her voice had a peculiar flatness to it as if she were reciting lines whose truth she couldn't quite buy herself.

Lightman was appalled by what he was hearing. That Martindale had ever entertained any notion that they might work together was preposterous, absurd. "You don't really believe him, do you? Aren't you used to his cons by now?"

"I don't think he was lying when he said he wanted to work with you."

"You're still lovers, aren't you?" He didn't mean to sound so accusatory.

"It's not like you think."

"But when he comes back here what happens?"

"Sometimes, yes, we sleep together. But it's not the same as it was."

"How was it?" Lightman asked.

"I don't have to answer to you," she retorted angrily. "I wanted you to come here, I risked a lot sending for you. Doesn't that say something to you, John? Doesn't that count for something?"

He supposed it did. But it wasn't enough. "Come away with me, Diana. Why don't you leave here and come away with me?" In that instant it was suddenly very clear and simple. They would go back to Geneva together and expose Martindale. Once Diana was able to accept the possibility that Martindale could in fact be brought down then surely she'd agree to help him.

"I can't."

"What do you mean you can't? He's not here now, is he? I didn't see any guards. Is there anyone to stop you from leaving?"

"No." Her voice had gotten very soft. "But it doesn't matter. He'll find me wherever I go."

"Not if he was in a prison he couldn't."

"He won't go to prison." She sounded more confident about that than anything she'd said so far.

"Between us we could piece together enough evidence for the police to arrest him and extradite him back to England," he said, entreating her. "Even if we can't prove that he deliberately leaked the virus from Mayfair House I'm certain we could tie him to the murders of Bill Wellington and Winston Cage."

She didn't like that at all. "Bill died of the damn flu. You said yourself he was going to die. Why would anybody want to murder him? And where did you get it into your head that he killed Winston? Maybe Patrick's right about you, maybe you do have this vendetta against him. Is it because of the grant money not coming through? Or is it because you promised your dear Inspector Finch you would give him Patrick on a silver platter? If you hadn't been such a bloody fool and gone in on that burglary with Bill, maybe you wouldn't be in this fix."

"Who are you to be talking about fixes? Not only is Winston dead, he was in your grave—buried alive."

She winced and turned her face from him. When he took her hand she drew it away. He was enraged by her obtuseness, her stubborn refusal to acknowledge the truth. But at the same time he recognized how much pain she was in.

"There's no way you could understand. I can't leave, John, I can't. What happened in London . . . he bailed me out of it."

"Who? Martindale? Bailed you out of what?" He hated her evasiveness, her unwillingness to come clean with him.

"If it wasn't for Patrick I might be sitting in one of Inspector Finch's jail cells right now."

"For Christ's sake why? What have you done?"

She didn't say anything for awhile. Then she spoke so softly that he could barely hear her. Yet when he asked her to repeat her words she received only silence in response. Still, he could have sworn she'd said, "If you knew what I've done you'd want to kill me."

SIX

In the morning he woke to the sound of Diana's laughter. Next to him the bed was empty. Voices mingled with her laughter. A man was speaking. Lightman feared that it was Martindale he was hearing.

Throwing on his clothes, he mounted the stairs, hoping to trace the voices to their source. Vast white rooms he'd had no idea were there offered themselves to him. The ambience was Mediterranean and elegant. Highly polished silver gleamed from tabletops and mantels. Paintings by Magritte, Chirico, and Matisse—or their very clever imitators—looked down at him from the walls. Splendid tableaus of gardens and snow-capped peaks were visible through the open windows.

As a result of the villa's devious acoustics the voices alternately receded and grew louder. But once he stepped out into the garden the voices died, and he was left only with the incessant buzzing of insects among the anemones and roses.

Turning the corner he caught sight of Diana. She was alone, sprawled on a red blanket, her head in the shade of a floppy straw hat, topless.

Raising her eyes toward him, she gave him a smile and a warm greeting. If she was still angry about their talk last night she didn't show it.

"Were you talking to someone just now?"

"No, why do you think that? Maybe what you were hearing was the servants. They come up from the village every morning."

"I could've sworn it was your voice."

"No, darling, I've just been out here reading, waiting for you to wake up. Are you feeling better today?"

"I suppose so."

"Good. Then we mustn't talk about anything bad today, nothing that will put us out of sorts. Not a word about Patrick or about any dread diseases, promise me?"

He hesitated.

"Promise me, John, or else I'll have nothing to do with you."

He promised. She kissed him and laughed as though she'd just won a carnival prize no one thought she could have.

"Today we're going on a picnic," she announced. "Today we will indulge ourselves completely. You mustn't protest, it doesn't become you."

When they set out she was wearing a red button-down dress and a pair of white sandals. She was in such exuberant spirits that it only caused him to feel more downcast. He felt as though he were missing the point of something very important. One day with her, no matter how idyllic, wasn't enough. He had to get her away from the villa, had to convince her to go with him. Nothing else weighed on his mind so much as that. His desire was so strong for her that he was ready to carry her off right then and there and the hell with her objections.

Noticing how glum he was looking she chided him, "Damn it, you're not going to act gloomy and spoil this lovely day, are you?" She took him by the hand and quickened her pace as if to suggest that what was wrong with him could be cured by getting his circulation going.

A film of perspiration had gathered over her face and down her arms. It was growing hotter with the approach of midday. Idly Diana undid the top buttons of her dress. Now, depending on how she moved, her breasts would float in and out of focus.

They took a path that led along the lake. At a clearing near two oak trees that at the trunk had somehow become melded together into one, she laid out the contents of her picnic basket. A sumptuous feast of salmon mousse, Persian caviar, smoked salmon, lobster tails, shrimp, truffles and cheeses took form in front of them. To wash it all down she'd brought along a bottle of Italian chianti.

It was the combination of the food and wine and the torpor of the afternoon that finally lulled him into thinking that maybe things weren't so bad after all. And what good was it going to do him to worry anyhow?

He was lying on her blanket, looking up at her, communicating his desire to her with no need for words. He reached for her and she responded. She seemed only to have to shrug for her dress to slip off. Her body glistened with sweat. They were in no rush now, and so they eased into each other and proceeded to make love slowly, languorously, fused by desire and the enfolding summer heat.

Much later, after a long silence, she said to him, "If you still want me to, I'll go."

He looked at her in astonishment, not certain he'd heard right. "Do you mean it, Diana?"

She nodded. "I've thought about what you said and decided that perhaps you're right. Wherever you go I'll go with you so long as it's not back to London."

London seemed to terrify her, and Lightman wondered why. But he'd be damned if he'd object to the one condition she'd imposed. "Love," he said, kissing her, "you'll never have to see London again."

They agreed that they would leave early the next morning. She assumed he'd want to go back to Geneva, but he didn't know. The more he considered it, the more Geneva seemed out of the question. The police were undoubtedly looking for him in connection with Gray's death. If he wanted freedom of action there was no way he could allow himself to be the object of a police investigation. He would have to determine how to carry out his plan elsewhere. Maybe Italy—someplace where the authorities didn't have a warrant out for him. One way or another he'd figure everything out. What counted was that Diana would be with him. It could all be made to work, he kept thinking, it could all be made to work as long as she was with him.

As they approached the villa a woman came running toward them, calling to them.

"It's Pilar," Diana said.

Pilar, close up, proved to be a pretty but buxom young woman with dark hair and a certain Arabic cast to her features. She was eighteen or nineteen, and from her heavy accent he guessed she was Spanish. Probably a migrant worker.

She kept her eyes only on Diana, shyly averting them from Lightman. The way she referred to him was as if he wasn't there at all. "This man John, he is to phone the Paradise. It is urgent, he is wanted."

Diana shot him a questioning glance. But Lightman was

equally confused. It occurred to him that maybe the police had traced him all the way there. But there was another possibility. "Do you mind if I use your phone?" he asked Diana.

"Not at all."

Relief swept over him after he confirmed with Marthe that it was indeed Hopkins who'd called. Lightman phoned him at the President.

"John, thank God it's you," Hopkins said. "I was beginning to wonder what happened to you. Are you okay?"

"Just fine, Geoff. I'm sorry it slipped my mind to give you a call."

"Well, just so long as you're all right, that's what matters. But to be honest with you, I wasn't calling just to find out how you were doing. Remember you asked me to check out the data we're getting in on this pandemic? You said you were interested in anything unusual or out of whack, as you put it."

"Did you find anything?" All at once Lightman was alert, his whole body tensed with anticipation.

"Let's just say that I think I did. One way or another, I'd like your opinion on it."

Lightman was about to press him for details when he remembered whose phone he was using. Better wait until they could talk in person.

"I'd be happy to take a look at whatever you've got, but I have a problem. I don't know when I'll be going back to Geneva. Could you get a car and meet me in Alpenrose?"

"I don't know, I'm not much on driving. I'm so exhausted these days I don't think I could keep my eyes open. Are there trains that go there?"

"Absolutely. You can check the schedule, but I'm pretty sure there's one that will get you in around ten-thirty. There's a tavern downstairs at the Paradise—you can't miss it. Let's say we meet there around quarter to eleven."

It was only when he put the phone down that he realized

Diana had been there the whole time listening to him. Her expression betrayed her anxiety. Having her heart set on him spending her last night at the villa she was visibly dismayed by the change of plans. "It's important that I see Geoff tonight," he told her. "We can still leave tomorrow at the same time. It will be just like we planned. The only difference will be that I'll meet you at the Paradise—say at eight. Then we can go to the station together. It will be all right, Diana, really it will."

She looked skeptical. He took her in his arms but that didn't help; she still looked skeptical.

"I wish you'd stay with me. Couldn't this friend of yours wait?"

"No, there's no other time, I've got to see him tonight."

A sigh escaped her. She wasn't convinced.

"Where are you going?" he asked.

"I'll go tell the servants you'll be going down with them now, that way you won't have to walk."

Lightman worried that by leaving her he'd be giving her the opportunity to change her mind. But he had to trust her; he couldn't see any other way around it.

He walked outside to find her standing with Pilar who was leaning out the window of a green Renault.

He understood what he was trying to do as he stared at her; he was memorizing her, hoping that in the future he would remember her exactly as she was now, how her hair had all tangled up, blond and red from the sun, with a blade of grass still resting in it, how her eyes were so dazed and moist, how her skin held such luster, how the buttons of her red dress strained futilely to contain her nakedness.

He wanted to prolong their departure but he couldn't, not with the Renault's horn blaring to summon him. "Quickly now," she said. Her kiss didn't last. He squeezed in the back of the Renault and turned to look at her, but she wasn't there to see anymore.

SEVEN

Hopkins was late and for several minutes Lightman sat in the tavern agonizing over whether he'd made the right decision to leave Diana. And then Hopkins showed, flushed, out of breath, and obviously uncertain that he had the place he was looking for until his eyes fell on Lightman.

"Goddamn," he said, sitting down and then putting his overnight bag on the floor. "It's good to see you. I almost got lost."

"Impossible, this town's too small to get lost in."

"Well, I went the wrong way when I left the station."

"Didn't you notice there weren't any lights?"

"John, there weren't any lights in either direction."

"Oh, I see." He'd gotten off in daytime so he didn't know. "Look, Geoff, why don't we get you settled and then afterwards you can come up to my room and we can talk?"

"Sounds good to me, but first do you mind if I order something to drink? I'm dying of thirst."

Once Marthe had given Hopkins a room he joined Lightman in his room one flight up. He brought with him a printout that opened like an accordion and spilled to the floor when fully extended. "This is what I'm talking about. This is where it gets weird," he said, pointing to all the paper that covered nearly half of Lightman's floor.

"Well, what is it? Tell me what you've found." Lightman could barely contain himself. It was just possible that Hopkins had located the chink in Martindale's armor, hit upon the one thing that would prove his undoing.

"To begin with, are you familiar with the way WHO uses outside contractors?"

"Which outside contractors are you referring to?"

"I'm referring to the ones that WHO engages to deliver drugs and medical equipment to any country where there's a critical medical emergency. Say Guyana or Togo or Iraq is hit by cholera, WHO will contract a company to airlift the necessary supplies of Chloroquine to them, bypass the bureaucracies, fuck the red tape."

"That makes sense. But what relevance does it have?"

Lightman was concentrating with difficulty—and no wonder, with his mind still back at the Villa Pilatus—trying to figure out what relevance these outside medical suppliers had to the outbreak.

"Of course there are several such suppliers," Hopkins continued, "but only one caught my eye—Obelisk Medical Services." He scanned the length of the printout until he found it.

From what Lightman could see, Obelisk, more than any competitor, had been contracted to make deliveries in several countries over the last month and a half.

Hopkins explained how he'd examined all the relevant epidemiological studies, focusing his attention primarily on isolated communities—island villages, harbor towns, desert settlements, etc.—which in addition had little intercourse with the outside world: few tourists, minimal trade, no major transportation arteries running through them. He'd concentrated on five such communities scattered on three continents, Europe, Africa and South America, all of which had recently experienced outbreaks of the flu.

From the available field reports, put together by physicians, paramedics and churches, he was able to rule out a number of possible sources of contamination, vectors like insects or potable water.

"This is where it starts to get interesting," Hopkins said.

"I started looking for any other factor that these isolated communities might have in common. Since the dozen or so I found were spread so far apart—ranging from the Hebrides Islands in the South Pacific to a village like Pampa Libre in the desert outside of Lima—I had to rule out any common host such as an indigenous animal, and certainly I had to rule out most products imported from abroad. In some cases, most of what the people consumed was home-grown, they couldn't afford to import anything."

"What did that leave you with?" Lightman asked.

"It was only by chance that I decided to take a look at the contracts various medical suppliers and pharmaceutical houses have executed in different parts of the world on behalf of WHO. I was actually trying to find out what kind of vaccines were being sent to these locales so I could factor them in. And you know what I found?"

"Let me guess. The one thing all of them had in common was a shipment of medical supplies from Obelisk."

"Exactly. But the interesting thing is that the supplies are almost always different and seldom include any vaccine for Type A viruses."

Hopkins consulted his printouts. "Listen. On June twenty-ninth Obelisk delivered a shipment of rehydration fluid to Oddur, Somalia to combat a cholera outbreak there. Up until that time there were no reported cases of the flu. On July second the first cases of the flu were reported in Oddur.

"On July third Obelisk delivered a supply of benza-thine penicillin and penicillin aluminum monostearate to Matthewtown on Great Iguana Island in the Caribbean where there were several cases of yaws. Again there were no incidences of the flu on the island prior to the Obelisk delivery. On the sixth of July there were three cases of the flu in Matthewtown and several more subsequently.

"Also on the third of July Obelisk delivered Amphoteri-cin B as well as Ketoconazole to desert communities outside of Lima to arrest an outbreak of Lobo's Disease which

is caused by a fungus. Before that date there were no cases
of the flu in any of those villages. On the eighth of the
month outbreaks of the flu were reported in every single
one of them.

Before he could go on Lightman interrupted him. "How
many instances have you come up with altogether?"

"Eleven that I could make a good case for, another seven
that are probables."

Lightman was stunned; he hadn't imagined that the virus
was being spread in such a calculated manner.

"What you're telling me is that at the same time WHO is
trying to halt the pandemic it's responsible for spreading
it."

"Not WHO directly," Hopkins was quick to point out.
"Obelisk. Of course, if the flu is being introduced by these
shipments into a region, the infection begins to spread on
its own. So then it becomes nearly impossible to trace it
back and prove precisely where it got its start."

Lightman lifted the unwieldy printout into his hands and
began to read.

PORT OF ENTRY	PRODUCT	DATE OF DELIVERY
Cairo, Egypt	Tetracyclines; Flagyl	June 16
Khartoum, Sudan	Chloramphenicol; Amphotericin B; Oral Nystatin; Oral-5 Flurocytosine	June 18
Kingston, Jamaica	Atabrine; Flagyl	June 18
Port Saint Louis, Mauritius	Immune Gobulin	June 19
Managua, Nicaragua	Draprim; Camolar; Glucantime	June 20

But it was the next one down in the list that Lightman found especially interesting:

LaPaz, Bolivia   Yellow Fever Vaccine   June 20

Now he thought he understood why LaPaz had been struck by the flu when there had been no outbreaks anywhere in the entire South American continent until then.

The manifest went on and on; there was even a schedule of deliveries that were to take place in the next several days—to Manila, Kuala Lumpur, Dar-es-Salaam, Belize, Beira in Mozambique, and two locations in Zaire—Kinsasha, the capital, and Kisangani, the former Stanleyville in the north of the country.

"That doesn't mean that the flu will necessarily break out in the ports of entry listed here," Hopkins said. "Once they're off-loaded at the airport they're usually sent right to wherever in the interior they're needed."

"Were you able to find out who was responsible for contracting Obelisk?"

"I've done better than that, I've gotten ahold of the documents authorizing Obelisk's services and renewing its contract. From everything I can tell, there were two principals involved in the arrangement. There was a letter of intent dated the eleventh of November and signed by Patrick Martindale and George Marsh."

Lightman sat up. "What name did you say?"

"George Marsh. He was the one who signed the original letter of intent. Why? Does that mean anything to you?"

It was too complicated to explain. "No, not really. Is his name on any other documents?"

"That's it. All the contracts were signed by various executives on behalf of Obelisk. Marsh's name never appears again."

"Where are these documents?"

"They're safe, don't worry. Tomorrow we can have them copied if you'd like. I've got to get the originals back to

Geneva before anyone finds out they're missing. I'm telling you, I'm going to get myself in as much trouble as you're in at this rate. But I had a feeling that you should look at this material. We should talk to somebody, a good lawyer we can trust if there is such a thing, then when we know where we stand, go to the director-general."

"And the police."

"If you think it necessary, why not?"

It they could prove that Obelisk was circulating the virus throughout the world and supply the incriminating documentation to back them up they could immobilize Martindale. Thoughts of taking the documents to the media flashed through Lightman's mind. Finally Lightman saw a way of redeeming himself in Finch's eyes.

Tomorrow, he thought, Diana would join him. Tomorrow he would have the evidence to put away Martindale. No wonder he had such difficulty sleeping.

Something was wrong. Even before Hopkins set foot into the room he knew it.

The room had been thoroughly ransacked, the drawers pulled out, the bureau overturned, his suitcase emptied of its contents which now lay strewn over the floor. The sight of all this mess so astounded him that it took some seconds more before he realized that the person responsible for it was still there.

"What the hell are you—" His words died in his throat, not because of the gun the intruder was holding on him but because of his eyes. They didn't blink, they weren't moving at all. There was nothing remotely human about the stare he fixed on Hopkins.

"Would you be good enough to sit down?" he asked quietly. "And then let us see just how well we can dance together."

EIGHT

Marthe woke Lightman in the morning. "It is six-thirty, Herr Doktor," she said.

Groggy, Lightman stumbled out of bed. He'd asked Marthe to rouse him early so he could have the time to pack and talk to Hopkins before leaving. There were certain things they needed to clear up. Having had the chance to sleep on what he'd learned from Hopkins, Lightman had concluded that Hopkins should immediately go to the director-general and present his findings to him. He believed that, at the very least, all further deliveries of supplies by Obelisk Medical Services should be halted and that an exhaustive investigation should be initiated to determine whether previous shipments of medicine were contaminated intentionally, as he believed, or accidentally.

After dressing, Lightman proceeded downstairs and knocked on the door to Hopkins' room.

No answer. He knocked louder, risking waking up the people in neighboring rooms. Still nothing.

The man must be an incredibly sound sleeper, Lightman thought. He tried calling out Hopkins' name through the door. But this, too, drew no response.

The door was locked. While he didn't like the idea of barging in on Hopkins this wasn't something that could wait. It was already a little after seven, and with Diana due to arrive in an hour, he needed time to copy down the relevant data from the printouts, something he'd been too tired to do at two in the morning when they'd finished talking.

He descended another set of stairs to the ground floor where Marthe was presiding at her usual table.

Once he'd explained his problem—without, however, going into any detail—Marthe said she would open the door for him. Apparently she'd gotten over her suspicion that he might be a disreputable character for wanting to visit the Villa Pilatus. Now he was Herr Doktor, worthy of respect and consideration.

For a woman of her bulk she moved with surprising agility up the stairs.

Lightman was right behind her when she unlocked the door and stepped into Hopkins' room. But she was so big that she made it all but impossible to see much of anything beyond her.

Suddenly she slapped a hand against her brow. *"Das ist nicht richtig!"* she cried out.

"What is it?" He stepped around to the side of her so that he might have an unimpeded view.

Hopkins wasn't there. The room was empty.

"Herr Hopkins leaves and he doesn't pay his bill." She shot Lightman a reproachful look as though he were responsible for Hopkins running out.

She's lost a few francs, Lightman thought, but he had lost a great deal more. Without asking Marthe's permission he began to search the room. She regarded him with dismay but did nothing to stop him.

Not that it would have mattered; the printouts—all the documents he'd brought along to implicate Obelisk—were gone.

"Where did he go?" Marthe demanded.

"I wish I knew."

He walked into the bathroom though he certainly didn't think he was likely to find anything there.

Nothing.

He was about to turn away when his eye was caught by a flash of pink in the toilet bowl. He looked more closely and saw, floating lazily in the dull grayish water, something not quite identifiable, but definitely organic. He used the plunger to turn it right side up. An eye stared back at him—Hopkins' eye. He vomited violently.

Eight o'clock according to his gold watch. He was waiting downstairs in the tavern which was about to open for business. Even now, though, the smell of beer and lager permeated the room.

Lightman was crazed with fear and guilt. If he'd never sought Hopkins' help and involved him the way he had, he would still be alive. He was being allowed to live while the people around him were dying. Why?

Eight-fifteen. Diana wasn't coming, he was sure. Yet what else could he do but wait? He called but received only a persistent busy signal. He toyed with the idea of starting out for the villa but if he did that he might miss her.

Eight-twenty. He walked out into the street, blinking furiously in the sun. There was no sign of her.

Then he heard the phone ringing inside the rathskeller. His heart drummed wildly, he was sweating all over.

"Herr Doktor!" Marthe called to him. "It's for you."

Diana.

"John, everything's changed. I can't get away just yet." Her voice was rushed, breathless. "Do you think you could meet me where we had lunch yesterday?"

Where we made love yesterday, he thought.

"Yes, but when?"

"How long will it take you to get here?"

"Give me a couple of hours. I'll see what I can do about getting a ride."

"Say eleven then. But make sure you don't come anywhere near the villa, all right? I'll explain when I see you."

"Whatever you say. I love you, Diana."

There was a small silence. "Eleven then. Good-bye, love."

He kept looking behind him. But there was no one he could see following him. Retracing his steps of the previous morning he kept driving himself harder, pausing only as long as necessary to catch his breath.

It was possible that if he'd spent more time at it he might have found someone to give him a ride. But he was so anxious to be on his way that, after a few unsuccessful attempts, he gave up and elected to make the journey on foot.

He was so gratified to have heard from her that he scarcely gave any thought as to why her plans had changed. Nor did he care to dwell on Hopkins' fate or whether he could reconstruct the information about Obelisk from his memory. All these things could wait. What mattered now was to get to Diana.

His worst enemy at the moment wasn't Martindale; it was his own body. He was growing increasingly winded. His head was spinning and his eyes clouded over. He removed his glasses to see if maybe the problem was with them. It wasn't. His limbs felt heavy; gravity was pulling him down, sucking him into the earth.

Still, he was making progress. He was familiar enough with the landscape to know when he was beyond the half-way point.

He was drenched in sweat and becoming so nauseated that he wondered how he could continue putting one foot in front of another. He was gasping for breath; the distances he could go before resting were diminishing the farther up he climbed. He couldn't go for more than two or three minutes without stopping. He couldn't believe that he was feeling so rotten. He realized he wasn't in terrific shape, but he had managed this same climb two days before and suffered nothing more than aching muscles.

It was the anxiety that was doing it, the panic, the fear, all weighing him down.

Somehow he pushed on. As soon as she was in his sight, he could allow himself to relax. He was sure that with some food and something cold to drink inside of him he'd feel better.

Over the rise he saw the villa. His vision was faltering so much now that it had the aspect of a hallucination, at one moment receding into a haze, the next resolving itself with astonishing clarity.

He skirted the grounds of the villa, relying on the poplars and evergreens to navigate. Instinctively he found the path headed in the direction of the lake.

There was a harsh, acrid taste of bile in his mouth. He realized that he might feel better if he surrendered to the urge to vomit, but he restrained himself, swallowing down what was threatening to come up. There was no food in his stomach, just coffee. But it didn't want to stay put.

He quickened his step, but the exertion was ill-considered; he stumbled, neglecting to observe a fallen branch in his way. The dizziness was more acute; everything he tried to focus on danced and gyrated or floated out of his visual field. Still, he believed that it was Diana he saw, approaching: blue top, yellow dress, bronze skin.

Scarcely able to breathe, he hurried toward her—if it was Diana he was actually seeing.

And then he registered in the back of his throat a sudden nauseating sweetness that replaced the metallic taste that had been there before. Blood.

Suddenly it was as if someone had punched him hard in the solar plexus. His whole body convulsed and he began to vomit. Blood rushed into his hands. He tried to see Diana but could only see a blur of trees, foliage, and lake. An instant later he pitched forward and the world went black.

NINE

"Really, it's nothing, I wish you wouldn't make such a fuss. I'll be better tomorrow, I promise."

Julian would have liked to believe her, but one look at her and he knew. Her face was waxen, her eyes bloodshot. The fever attacking her had drained so much energy from her that to do more than prop her head up with her hand was a terrible strain for her. Yet he would not say anything to alarm her.

Sitting down beside her in bed, he told her he was certain that by the morning she'd be fit, but just to be on the safe side, he wanted to call the embassy; someone there would be able to recommend a good doctor.

"I feel so awful about getting sick on our honeymoon, sweetheart, whatever will you do?"

He held her hand. It was cold and clammy to the touch. "For God's sake, Nancy, I'll be fine. It's you that concerns me. I just want you to get well."

In spite of her protest he phoned the embassy. Apparently he wasn't the first to request the name of a doctor.

"We've had lots of calls like yours," the official who answered told him, "both from tourists and Americans who live here permanently. The problem is there just aren't enough doctors to go around."

Julian, who was on his second gin and tonic of the day, grew indignant. "Look, my wife is seriously ill. I'm not interested in excuses, you hear me? If you'd rather talk to Senator Bob Matthieson I can arrange it. But if that has to happen, I doubt whether you'll remain much longer at your post."

Evidently his words, or maybe it was the vehement tone in which they were delivered, had some effect. Around nine that evening a doctor turned up, a gray-haired Italian gentleman whose face rather resembled the marble busts of Roman emperors Julian had seen on his wanderings through the city.

Nancy was barely awake when he examined her; it was difficult for her to keep her eyes open.

Listening to her heart, the doctor assumed a thoughtful pose, his face darkening.

"What is it?" Julian asked, trying to keep his voice as low as possible.

"Let me complete the examination," the doctor said, removing the stethoscope from his ears.

The doctor woke her so that she could respond to his commands. He peered into her eyes and down her throat, felt her glands, observed the discoloration of her skin which, over the course of the last twenty-four hours, had turned from a mottled pink to heliotrope, a strange and frightening shade.

After ten minutes the doctor motioned Julian into the adjoining room.

In excellent English he said, "Her respiration is now close to forty and her heart is beating at a rate of 120."

"What does that mean?"

"It means she is seriously ill. Normal respiration is twenty. A normal heart rate for a woman her age should be approximately 72. I have also discovered a lump on the right side of the neck that I have seen in other patients who are down with this flu, but regrettably I can offer you no explanation as to what this lump means."

"Wait a minute. I thought you were supposed to know these things. How can you stand there and tell me you can't offer me any explanation? Who the hell can then? Give me his name!"

"I am afraid that I am only a physician, not a miracle worker. You can get any doctor you wish and he will tell you what I am telling you."

His drunkenness was like a mist, enveloping him while at the same time putting a great distance between himself and this calamity; he could almost believe it wasn't happening.

"At least she isn't coughing. Isn't that a good sign?"

He didn't like to have to implore this man—his only hope—to give him reason, any reason whatsoever, to believe that she would recover.

"I have seen this in others, they do not cough, there is no dilation of the heart, but . . ." He didn't think it was necessary to finish the sentence.

"Shouldn't we take her to the hospital?"

"The hospitals are very crowded, signore. In any case, there is nothing that can be done for her there. I will write you out a prescription. It is an antibiotic, it may be of help."

There was nothing either in his voice or manner to give Julian encouragement. It was with despair that he took the prescription from him.

"I will come by tomorrow to have a look at her."

"Isn't there any vaccine, some drug that can make her well? If it costs money, I've got it, I'm willing to pay. I don't care how much it is."

There was no change in the doctor's expression. "In this instance, signore, you are better advised to save your money. There is nothing that can make her better except for God. Put your faith in Him."

Once he'd filled the prescription and administered the recommended dosage to his wife Julian went down to the bar and began to think of what he could do.

But no plan came to mind. More gin would be necessary, he decided, before something would suggest itself. But he couldn't believe that the Italian doctor's was the last word, that he had to resign himself to fate or the hand of an inscrutable god.

He cursed himself for dragging Nancy along on this protracted binge. The indulgence and the jet lag and the lack of sleep all undoubtedly had contributed to the lowering of her resistance. But, Julian wondered, why hadn't he been struck down. He guessed he'd just been lucky.

As the hours dissolved and Julian descended into an alcoholic haze, it occurred to him that maybe it wasn't blind chance at work. He recalled his strange encounter with Jack Brill and the thinly veiled threat he'd delivered in that empty piazza. While Julian couldn't possibly imagine that Brill, or the church—whatever its name was—he claimed to represent could have been responsible for infecting Nancy, he couldn't entirely dismiss the possibility, either.

But maybe the insurance salesman had been telling him the truth, that his fault wasn't that he'd lowered Nancy's resistance by keeping her up late in two or three countries drinking but that he'd neglected to heed sound advice.

He knew it was ridiculous, he knew that he wasn't thinking straight, but he was seized by the idea of locating Brill. Here was a man he never wanted to lay eyes on again in his life, but if he could help him, Julian swore he'd do whatever he asked.

He began to search for the card Brill had given him, but couldn't find it. It was nowhere in his wallet. Back up in his room he went through everything he owned looking for it, but it was gone. He'd probably lost it or, more likely, torn it up in disgust after they separated.

He got out a phone book—it was all he could think to do—and called more than a dozen major hotels listed in it. In not a single one of them was a U.S. citizen by the name of Jack Brill registered.

Maybe he'd left town, Julian thought. Or had he conjured him up out of one of his drunken reveries to begin with?

He slept badly, and not for long. In the morning, around

six, he abruptly woke up, only mildly surprised to find himself sprawled on the floor of his room, still in his clothes.

Nancy didn't stir. For a moment Julian was afraid that she'd died. He saw her calling for him in the middle of the night, unable to rouse him from his stupor.

But when he approached the bed he was relieved to see her chest rising and falling—not much, though. Her breathing was shallow, desperate. The heliotrope tinge in her skin seemed deeper this morning, but maybe that was only his imagination. He uttered her name but failed to evoke any response.

When the phone rang he was certain it must be the doctor, checking up on Nancy.

It was not, it was the hotel operator. "Signore Wilks?"

"Yes?"

"You have a visitor waiting to see you in the lobby."

"Who is it? I'm not expecting anyone."

"A gentleman, he says that you know him."

If it were the doctor he wouldn't have hesitated to come directly to the room just as he had the previous evening.

When he got down to the lobby he was astonished to find Jack Brill waiting for him. So, Julian thought, he wasn't a creation of his drunken mind, he was flesh and blood, substantial as the couch on which he was sitting.

Now that he was sober, though terribly hungover and badly in need of a drink, Julian wasn't certain that he wanted to see Brill. The very sight of him made him queasy, or queasier than he would otherwise have been.

Brill, impeccably groomed, outfitted in an electric blue jacket and white slacks, gave him a practiced smile. They shook hands.

"You don't look at all well, Julian."

Julian ignored the comment. "How did you find me?" he asked.

"Weren't you looking for me?"

"Yes, I was, but—"

"So now I'm here."

The man was scary, Julian thought. He buried his shaky hands in his pockets.

"Nancy, my wife, she's very sick."

"I told you that something like this might happen." Brill sounded relaxed, as if it were all the same to him whether she was dying or not.

"The doctor tells me there's nothing to do but pray."

"And have you?"

Julian didn't answer, catching the sarcasm in his voice. "You said that if I signed over my wealth to that church you told me about this wouldn't happen."

"I see that you remember, I wasn't sure you would. But apparently you failed to act on my words."

"Look, you could hardly expect me to give you every last cent I own just on the basis of a warning, could you? I thought you were full of shit, frankly."

"Is that why you wanted to see me, so you could tell me that?"

"No, no, it isn't. I'm sorry." Julian realized he couldn't start insulting the man if he expected to ask him for assistance. "I want to know whether it's too late to do something."

Brill deliberated for a few moments. "You'd be willing to sign the papers I'll have drawn up turning over your wealth and future earnings to the Church of the Redeemed?"

Julian felt a stab of pain in his chest at the thought of doing that. Yet he felt that maybe, later, after Nancy was better, he could find a way to back out of the agreement, have the contract nullified.

"If you can guarantee that Nancy will recover, I'll do it."

Brill surprised him. "I can't guarantee anything. I could before, but not now. However, what I can guarantee is that she will receive the best care in the world. If you'd like, we can compromise. Half of everything now with a proviso that, should your wife recover, the remainder of your wealth will automatically become the sole possession of the church. It's the best I can do for you."

After taking a deep breath Julian said, "All right, we have an agreement. You can draw up the papers."

"Very good, I'm happy to welcome you aboard."

He insisted on shaking Julian's hand again.

"It is possible," Brill continued, "that your wife will have to travel to receive the necessary treatment."

What was this? "She can't be moved. You're crazy."

"I am not saying that it's definite but you must be prepared for that eventuality."

"You'll kill her. You kill her and you get nothing."

"That's not our agreement, Julian. But be assured that we will do nothing to jeopardize your wife's health."

Julian was dubious. "Who the hell is going to be in charge of Nancy's care?"

"He's the best man your wife could hope to get," said Brill. "His name is Patrick Martindale."

TEN

His illness was like a landscape that he could move in and out of; it was always there, but occasionally he seemed to be able to rise above it. There was him and there was the fever, two separate entities; at such times he felt insubstantial, like a ghost must feel, detached from the body, floating and hovering. But then his body would want him back again and he'd be yoked to it for days, feeling suspended in time.

He didn't know where he was. Or rather he would find out and then forget or else confuse his surroundings, mistaking the bedroom where he lay for another bedroom in another house, another part of the world. When clarity did return to him, though, he realized he was in one of the great white Mediterranean rooms of the Villa Pilatus.

The pain was interesting; it assailed him with varying degrees of intensity depending on which part of the body it assaulted. It ranged from a throbbing sensation that could almost be ignored to a feeling of being seared by a hot poker thrust deep into his vitals. His tongue was thick and heavy and coated with a whitish, gummy substance; it didn't feel like his tongue, actually, but rather like some foreign object he could neither swallow nor disgorge from his mouth.

There was pain behind his ears and behind his eyes. The pain behind his ears was accompanied by a constant ringing; the pain behind his eyes kept his vision blurred more than it ordinarily was.

Worse, however, was the heaviness in his chest and lumbar region. He reasoned that this was due to the buildup of fluid in his lungs. He realized that, if it continued unabated, it would leave no room for any oxygen to get in. Then he would begin to die.

The hemorrhaging had ceased. But he didn't know whether that was a favorable sign or not.

There was a blurring of night and day; one minute he'd open his eyes to find the room bathed in sunlight, the next it was all darkness and the sound of cicadas.

It was hopeless trying to make sense of the sounds he heard: the hushed voices, the footsteps echoing on the parquet floors, the opening and closing of doors, shutters, windows, and the music, Handel, Mozart and Scarlatti alternating with Viennese waltzes and oompah bands.

Maybe it was a bad dream. Maybe there were no voices, footsteps, doors opening and closing, no music. There were times when Lightman would wake to find the room, and the rooms beyond his room, amazingly still. Outside in the windless heat it was just as still; perhaps the heat had stunned even the insects into silence.

There was a woman who came in to check on him and take his temperature and give him water and juices; she was the only living thing he could be sure existed in the house, in the entire world for that matter. She was Italian and middle-aged and smelled like fresh strawberries. Her face was round like the moon and brown and her hands were strong and callused. She must have been someone's mother—it didn't matter whose; she was his mother now.

From time to time she would pull up a stool by his bed and begin talking to him; there was a musical quality to her voice that he enjoyed listening to, although not once did he comprehend a word she was saying for she spoke nothing but her native language.

While he assumed she was one of the servants who came each day to the villa he had no way of being sure. And if she was, what did it matter? She never failed to appear; her very robustness was a guarantee for him that she would be there the next day and the day after, that the virus would not strike her, too.

It was strange how sometimes the fever would rage and then all at once abate, giving him the illusion that he was on the road to recovery, and in those rare intervals everything would seem to become immensely clear, his life no longer an unfathomable mystery. His senses would also come alive in a way that he'd never experienced; even lacking glasses, his eyes could see objects all the way across the room, sharply focused, almost too finely detailed, too brightly colored. Titles of books stood out, entirely legible, whereas before he couldn't see even the books themselves. Though he couldn't prove it he had the feeling that he was picking up sounds, no matter how muted, from parts of the villa that ordinarily would never reach him.

But these lucid periods didn't last for long; afterward, in fact, he would descend deeper into delirium, his fever spiking alarmingly, and, whatever he thought he had grasped ahold of would slip away.

Whole days and nights must have gone by while he struggled for sleep. One night he discovered that he'd rolled out of bed and was lying on the floor, tangled in sweaty sheets. He was cold and hot simultaneously. Picking himself up, he became conscious of a commotion originating from the loggia. He somehow managed to walk halfway across the bedroom to the window.

At first, from where he was standing, he could make out nothing, just hedges, shadows and sky. Then he spied a figure, a man, naked, strolling across the lawn. Seconds later a woman, materializing from the nearby woods, rushed toward him, naked or nearly so. Her breasts shimmered, her unbound hair swung from side to side and fell into her face. They came together. The woman pressed herself against the man, clung to him, drew him down. She began to laugh, a boisterous, coarse laughter. Then another couple came into view, two women this time, one stout, with immense hips and knobby legs, the other elegantly shaped, with small breasts that she was offering to the other's greedy hands.

There were more people, cavorting and coupling, wherever he looked, suddenly emerging from the darkness. It was as if they'd been there all the time, only he hadn't been able to see them.

A woman wandered onto the loggia, briefly caught by a light that might have come from one of the villa's upstairs rooms. Turned from him, she could have been Diana. Same sweep of hair, same strong tanned back, same muscular buttocks, same legs, same stance. He was sure it was her though he'd been under the impression that she was long gone. He was paralyzed, fearing that it was Diana, fearing that it wasn't.

She opened her arms, spreading them in a welcoming gesture. But a welcoming gesture for whom?

Then he saw him, a man, distinguished from the others

by the fact that he was fully dressed. His eyes were concealed behind polarized lenses, his face half submerged in shadow.

All Lightman could think of was that it was Martindale, Diana's lover, her true love.

Lightman struggled to get the window open but either it wouldn't budge or else he was so enfeebled by his illness he couldn't maneuver it. He wanted to call out to her, to draw her attention to himself before the man got too close to her and gathered her up.

But then the man stopped a dozen paces in front of the woman and began to disrobe. First the tuxedo, then the black bow tie. The excesses continuing all around failed to distract the man; his concentration was focused entirely on the woman who remained still, waiting, anticipating what would come next.

The black pants fell into a heap at his feet. The underpants came off. Something was wrong; the genitals weren't those of a male but of a female. The shirt was quickly unbuttoned to expose some kind of white frilly undergarment; that, when loosened sufficiently, allowed two breasts to pop out. Last to be discarded were the polarized lenses. Lightman recognized who it was; the servant girl, Pilar.

The woman stepped down from the loggia to join her. There was a sharp, ecstatic cry when they met. They tumbled onto the grass, shrieking, rolling, rolling, but there was no way for Lightman to get a glimpse of the other woman's face.

What followed was like a ballet, the sexual acrobatics synchronized—or so it seemed to him. And what he felt was less lust, being in no condition to feel anything like lust, than awe. If he was surprised at all it was not by what was happening so much as by the fact that he was witnessing it.

In the swarm of flesh he began to see people he knew. But there was still a part of his mind that held back, that told him no, what he thought he saw was not what he was seeing, and certainly there was no way that he could continue to spot Diana; she couldn't be everywhere at once. And yet it seemed that she was.

It was when he saw Winston Cage and Geoffrey Hopkins, and finally when he saw Stephanie that he realized he must be delirious, that his mind was a prisoner of the fever.

And yet he stayed where he was, unable to tear himself away, wondering at the same time whether there really was anything out there.

Then the door opened behind him. Or he heard a door, turned and saw someone entering, knew at once who it was.

"Enjoying the show, are you?" Thorning asked, his eyes watering from the drops he'd just put in them.

Lightman shifted his gaze back to the window and saw nothing but blackness there. He looked toward Thorning and saw the same blackness. Pain exploded in his head; it was as if every blood vessel had burst. Blind, deaf, dead to the world, he was catapulted to a place far away.

ELEVEN

When he woke in the morning he found he'd broken out in an icy sweat. The sun, divided by slats in the shutters, formed a series of bars on the tile floor. It took him several minutes to understand that the icy sweat didn't represent yet another stage of his illness but the end of it. His fever had broken at last.

Lightman experimented. He got out of bed and planted both feet solidly on the floor, attempting to stand without support. His legs were wobbly, like a one-year-old's, and he had to throw out his arms to steady himself. But he could do it, that was the main thing; he could do it.

The swelling of his tongue had lessened and the heaviness in his chest had diminished considerably. He took a step forward and didn't fall. What a triumph! Nothing he could remember doing, not in his adult life anyway, no award for scientific achievement had ever gratified him so much as his ability to take a step forward without having his legs give way under him. He felt ravenous, as if his stomach were crying out for all the food his body had rejected during his siege of illness.

Another step. And another. He was alive, he thought, he was alive. He couldn't help laughing. The laughter engulfed him, his whole body shook convulsively with it. Good God, how delicious the morning was.

It was only when he started out to the corridor and toward the bathroom—as monumental a journey as he'd ever embarked upon after relying so long on a bedpan— that he became aware of how very silent it was in the villa. Only an enormous black fly was making itself heard as it explored the ceilings and walls.

"Hello!" he called out. "Hello!"

The faint echo of his own voice was all he got by way of response.

At least he would have expected the Italian woman to turn up, as she had every day, but there was no sign of her. For the hell of it he tried the phone. Dead.

The man who appeared in the wall-length mirror hanging behind the toilet was someone Lightman didn't recognize.

Face drained of color, ribs prominent against shrunken flesh, half his head of hair gone, he could have been someone thirty years older than he was. His eyes were still bright with the fever that had been burning in him all these days.

How many days? he wondered. What date was it? It

wouldn't even come to him which date he'd been struck down by the flu.

He was happy to put his own clothes back on, though. He was happier still to discover that his money and passport hadn't been touched. He felt as if he'd regained at least some of his identity.

It was only when he walked outside that he remembered the spectacle he'd seen the night before. He thought it was the night before. He was standing on the lawn where it had taken place. While it was true that the grass was flattened and gouged out, there was no way to judge, on the basis of this evidence alone, that this had been the setting for any wild display of passion. The images that floated into his mind caused him to shudder.

When he drew far enough away from the villa he turned back toward it. No longer did it give the appearance of Moorish splendor. On the contrary, it already had begun to assume an air of emptiness and disuse. There was something sad about it, with its shutters hanging open, squeaking with the wind, and the flies and mosquitoes getting in, and the poisonous silence impregnated with the disease that had nearly taken his life.

He began down the mountain toward Alpenrose, reaching the village late in the afternoon. It was still furiously hot and at first Lightman believed that it was the heat that had driven everyone indoors. But then he understood that the silence prevailing there was the very same silence that filled the Villa Pilatus. Although there wasn't a single body in the street—it was Switzerland, after all—he realized that death was there, death was everywhere around him.

The tavern below the Paradise was closed; there was a sign in German hanging on it he couldn't decipher but he had an idea what it meant. Raising his eyes, he saw that all the windows were boarded up as well.

Even so, he was resolved on reclaiming his possessions should they still be on the premises. He banged hard on the door, eventually hearing footsteps and coughing in response.

An old man who looked like he was related to Marthe appeared at the door.

"I need to get my things," Lightman said.

The man mumbled some words in a language that might have been English and motioned Lightman in. There was a smell of antiseptic and something overcooked inside, more powerful than the customary odor of stale beer. Most of the lights were off. Aside from the old man there didn't seem to be anybody else present.

"Marthe? Is Marthe here?"

The old man ignored him. Lightman could see he wasn't about to get any satisfaction from him. He continued upstairs on his own. The door to his room was open. His suitcase was exactly where he'd left it. If he never had come back he doubted that anyone would have gotten around to doing anything about it for a long while.

The first thing he checked for was the Baretta. It was still there, hidden underneath his shirts. For someone who'd never fired a handgun in his life, this Baretta was assuming ever greater importance. Keeping the gun where it was, he gathered up his belongings and left.

Back on the street he became aware of a dull, monotonous rhythm: hammer against metal, hammer against wood, hammer against metal, hammer against wood. It was coming from somewhere near the end of the street in the direction of the railway station. Curious to see what was going on, he set out toward the source of the sound.

All the hammering, he saw, was coming from a garage which previously had escaped his notice. It was dark inside and smelled strongly of oak and turpentine and shellac. He peered in.

Two men, stripped to the waist, with sweat dripping off them, were hard at work driving nails into wooden frames on which a dark brown finish was beginning to dry. They scarcely glanced at Lightman; he might not have been there at all.

It was obvious to Lightman what they were doing, though. They were in the process of making coffins, the last and certainly the most productive business operating in all of Alpenrose.

<u>TWELVE</u>

Lightman could only credit God or the natural resilience of his own body for his recovery. Moreover he'd come through without suffering from the aftereffects reported in other cases: cardiac disorders, pulmonary tuberculosis, nephritis, deafness, or a weakness of the muscles so pronounced that a person could end up hobbling like a cripple for the rest of his life. The disease wasn't one that simply ran its course, predictable in all but a few obstinate cases, but instead attacked or abated at will. What it did in a great many cases, however, was reach a crisis, sometimes marked by terrific hermorrhaging, challenging the victim to overcome it. Those who despaired and cashed in their chips too soon died. Those who fought back stood a chance of emerging victorious.

But what kind of victory was it that left Lightman stranded in a remote Swiss village where half the population, alive a week before, now awaited burial? His was becoming a journey where there was no way back: in Boston his lab was in the process of shutting down for lack of funds; in London he was likely to be thrown into prison for running out on Finch; in Geneva the police would be looking for him in connection with Gray's murder, undoubtedly interested in learning why he was carrying around the murder weapon.

His only hope would have been the documents that Hopkins had found. But they were gone, and Hopkins was gone. And Diana too was gone, again she was gone. He felt bewildered and lost.

From an open window of a house he walked past he heard the familiar sounds of the Blue Angel Boys' latest hit. There was a stink of decaying flesh and that was coming through the open window as well. He walked on.

A man was coming from the other direction. Lightman vaguely recalled him from the rathskeller. "Excuse me," he said, "but would you mind telling me what day it is?" He knew by his watch that it was three-twenty in the afternoon, but otherwise he didn't know. It could have been any hot afternoon in summer.

The man looked at him uncomprehendingly. Lightman said that he'd been sick, using the French and German words for it.

"It is today sixteen July," he said.

He'd been sick for over a week, eight days lost. No, not lost: lived in another time, sick time.

No other destination suggested itself than the railway station; he couldn't very well stick around this dying village.

But when he arrived at the station he found it deserted. The ticket office was closed. There was, oddly enough, a television on, presumably for the entertainment of passengers waiting for the train. Only there were no passengers, and there didn't seem to be any trains. The schedule posted had become theoretical. The 4:28 P.M. to Basel, for instance, never arrived. That was totally unlike the Swiss. Lightman imagined that there were some people in the country who regarded a violated timetable as a greater disaster than the deaths of their neighbors. But still there were no trains.

Had he felt better and had more energy he might have

done something decisive. But he was too weak, too depleted from his bout with the flu, and the only thing he
could think to do was sit down on one of the benches and
rest.

Now and then he dozed, and when he would come
awake it was to find himself looking up at the television.
Scenes of immense disaster flickered on the screen. The
commentator was speaking in German, a language Lightman could not understand, but the images needed no trans-
lation. Bodies piled up on corners in some part of the
world were being bulldozed into trenches. Then skulls decorating a fence in a country far away stared back at him.
They might have had some ritualistic purpose, but again
Lightman had no way of telling. Once he woke up to see
what appeared to be a before and after picture frozen on the
screen. A girl of about eighteen was smiling at him in a
turtleneck sweater; the face of the girl next to her, though,
was so contorted, so twisted out of shape, that he had to
look at it closely to see that it was the same girl. And she
was virtually bald besides. The flu, Lightman gathered,
had done that to her, made her unrecognizable in death.

It got so that he didn't know if he were sinking back into
a delirious state or actually seeing the grotesque scenes that
were passing in front of his eyes. There were hospital
wards full of black faces, death announcing itself in their
eyes. A bus was drawing to a stop in a city which seemed
to be composed largely of cinderblock buildings and badly
designed skyscrapers of chrome and glass. And when the
door of this bus hissed open a woman of about fifty years
of age tumbled out and lay still on the sidewalk. The camera zoomed in on the fallen woman. But there was little of
her face to be seen; it was covered over with blood, black
blood. Meanwhile police began pulling other bodies out of
the bus. There didn't seem to be anybody alive left inside
it. It must have been a strange route that bus had taken.

There was no way that Lightman could see to shut the
television off. Evidently the controls were located where

only the station master could get at them but there was obviously no station master to appeal to to at least change channels.

It might have been the same night, or the next one, but suddenly Lightman awoke with an incredible thirst. As he began to quench it from the water fountain he became aware of voices and brisk footsteps. Looking through the window at the platform, he could see several people gathering. There was no reason for anyone to be on the platform unless there was a train coming. Clearly they knew something he didn't.

As he made his way out of the station a cloyingly sweet scent hit him. It was awhile before he realized that it was coming from sticks of incense the people were burning. There must have been twenty of them, equally divided between men and women. They didn't look like they were from around Alpenrose. They were young, and people in Alpenrose weren't young—those who were left alive. Nor did any of them seem to be suffering from the effects of the flu. On the contrary, they were vital and in seemingly good health. Lightman felt as if he'd been dropped down from another planet. He might have been invisible; no one paid him any attention.

And then he understood who these people were. They carried with them the green crosses of the Church of the Redeemed, each one of them glowing with fluorescence. A few moments later he saw somebody he knew. It was the Spanish servant girl, Pilar. She failed to see him, though, occupied as she was talking to her friends.

Nor did he want her to see him. But there was little danger of that happening. Five minutes later a train pulled in. The church members began to clamber on board. Lightman asked a woman of about thirty where the train was bound.

"Rome, we're all going to Rome. Come with us, we're on a mission to Rome."

Lightman had the passport and the money. This train was

going somewhere the police weren't looking for him. All those things spoke in favor of getting on board. But more than that he was anxious to see what Pilar was doing among these people, where she'd go once she detrained in Rome. It was just possible that she might lead him to Diana.

The woman he'd solicited the information from insisted that they share the same compartment. She was determined to convert him, that much was obvious. But Lightman played along with her, deciding that if she became too wearying he would simply close his eyes and drop off to sleep and that would be the end of it.

She wasn't unattractive, just sort of antiseptic and sex-less in a way that he found almost aggressive. She was in her mid-twenties and her eyes were bright and she was full of energy. "I went to England to be a nanny," she started to tell him, determined to fill him in on her life story whether he was interested or not. "And I didn't do so badly at it except that I understood that my life wasn't what I wanted it to be. And I looked around at the people I was working for, most of them were very rich, and I saw that their lives weren't what they wanted them to be either. And I thought that there ought to be something more. I think we all feel that way, don't you? But how many of us do anything about it?"

The train was picking up speed, and in the darkness the Swiss countryside could have been any countryside and they could have been going anywhere.

"I am telling you the truth when I tell you that I commit-ted some unpardonable acts."

Lightman looked at her freshly scrubbed face and won-dered just what kind of unpardonable acts she was capable of imagining, let alone committing, and decided that it wasn't worth questioning.

"I became pregnant and had an abortion, I took drugs

and would have died if I hadn't entered a rehabilitation program. And all the time I was searching, searching."

No, he couldn't quite believe that this woman had lived as dissolute a life as she wanted him to think.

"And then I was led to discover Jonas Beck. I never missed a single one of his broadcasts. He promised salvation to those of us who joined his church, he predicted what would happen, what *is* happening. He said that only those who were members of the Church of the Redeemed would escape the pestilence, and you can see for yourself he was right."

She leaned toward him, her hands in motion, more excited all the time, and burning with the conviction of the saved. "I can tell you have suffered the pestilence, you may be suffering it still. Am I right?" But she didn't wait for an answer from him, she knew what the answer was. "But you could have spared yourself this ordeal of fire if you'd only accepted God's word."

She was busy in her vast and bulging pocketbook, extracting another stick of incense and putting a match to it.

Lightman thought he was going to be sick all over again from the smell. "Excuse me, is it necessary you burn that in here?"

She looked at him, aghast, incredulous. "You shouldn't complain, sir. The burning of the incense is a beautiful and healthy thing, it purifies the air, it purifies the soul."

"It does what?" Lightman was suddenly interested.

"I said it purifies the soul."

"How do you know this?" The moment he'd said it, he knew it was a ridiculous question.

"How do I know it? It is the Lord's scent, it is the sweet smell of Christ Jesus on the cross, it is the sweet smell of the body uncorruptible."

"Does every member of the church receive such incense?"

The question seemed to baffle her. "Of course. Why should it be otherwise?"

"Do you all receive a certain number of sticks? So many a week or a month, let's say?"

She screwed her face up, not sure what he could possibly be driving at. "Sir, we are given this incense to use as the Lord sees fit. I don't know how else to answer you."

"Would you mind if I ask you for a stick for myself?"

What he would have thought a simple request, however, drew a strange response. It was as though he were asking her to renew the life of depravity she claimed to have escaped. "I cannot do that, sir. I am sorry. You are not a member of the Church of the Redeemed."

"But maybe if I could get ahold of a sample I might grow accustomed to the scent, I might be able to appreciate it more."

"No, I'm afraid I can give these sticks only to other members of the church. I truly am sorry."

"It's all right," he said.

"But I have some pamphlets you might like to read. I'd be happy to give you those."

He accepted the pamphlets, assuring her that he would read them carefully.

"There's a telephone number you'll see listed on them. You can call it twenty-four hours a day from anywhere in the world, free, and you will be told where the nearest church is located so that you can go to it and find salvation."

Lightman thanked her and said if she didn't have any objection he'd like to sleep for awhile.

He didn't sleep. He waited until she herself had dropped off and then reached into her bag and slipped out one of the sticks of incense. He concealed it inside his jacket, next to his gun.

It was possible he was mistaken, but he had a feeling he'd just stumbled on the means the Church of the Redeemed employed to immunize its followers against the pandemic. A vaccine injected into the body had its greatest effect in the bloodstream. But a vaccine introduced directly into the upper respiratory tract—the initial site of the flu's attack—had already shown itself to be more effective in experiments. In addition, if this vaccine relied on live viruses modified in the laboratory rather than the inactivated viruses more conventionally used, it could have even more impact. The most common means to deliver such a vaccine were through nosedrops or a nasal spray.

He would have to find some way of getting this stick of incense chemically analyzed. If his hypothesis was right, then it would be found to contain the vaccine that had rewarded the followers of Jonas Beck and the Church of the Redeemed with the heaven on earth that had been promised when they'd joined—life now being more precious and more real than life promised them in the hereafter.

THIRTEEN

From a window of the Lombardi Castle, built between 1347 and 1350 and completely rebuilt in 1995 at his expense, Patrick Martindale looked out over the city of Rome and contemplated the end of mankind. He was inclined to think that Rome was a beautiful place to watch the world die.

In the castle, a miraculous structure with a hundred or more rooms, halls, passageways, courtyards, cellars and servants' quarters, all surrounded by great crenellated walls, Martindale worked and studied and pondered the course of the pandemic that he'd set loose on the world.

Below his personal apartments there was a fully outfitted clinic, almost an exact replica of his facilities at Mayfair House. Occupying yet another floor was a laboratory where many of the top researchers in the world were hard at work trying to understand and defeat the virus that he took credit for discovering.

It wasn't his intention to preside over the defeat of the virus. After all, by creating a vaccine for it he'd already accomplished that end. No, what interested him most was whether it could be contained once it had taken hold in a human body. A vaccine was only preventative; without it there was nothing to stop the infection from doing what it wanted. The therapies available were virtually powerless to do more than mitigate its effect and lessen the pain.

But Martindale was obsessed by the virus. The virus offered him an unprecedented opportunity. Could the virus be conquered or at least blunted in its attack? He was still a scientist, still curious. But he loathed the regulations, the endless delays that had to be endured before a new drug was allowed to be marketed. Tests run on mice and primates needed to be done, studies carried out, officials and experts won over, and all while people were dying. And that was why he'd established his base in Rome. Here he had the freedom to experiment; here there was the possibility of developing a therapeutic drug without going through all the formalities—a drug that, once marketed, would not only earn him an immense amount of capital but could bring him honor and the gratitude of millions. Of course, he had to do this on his own; his unorthodox methods would never meet the approval of his colleagues in the World Health Organization.

For those privileged patients admitted to his clinic at Lombardi Castle he and his staff spared no effort. Near death, they eagerly signed release forms for experimental remedies that might carry them off quicker than the disease itself: dangerously toxic antiviral drugs, strains of genetic material derived from mice and cows, even newly discovered plants found in tropical rainforests in the Amazon. Sometimes the therapies worked, sometimes not. But even those that did work with one patient failed utterly with another. It baffled Martindale just how mysterious—and mischievous—this virus was.

Parts of the castle were still undergoing restoration so that all during the day there was a constant clamor of wood being pounded echoing through the passageways. Should Martindale decide to step out of his study his nostrils would fill with the smell of dust. The foreman couldn't tell him when the work would be done and held out the possibility that it would never be completed. Too many of the workers had fallen ill with the flu; some, master craftsmen, masons and artisans, could not be replaced at all.

It was unfortunate that the work was slowing down like that, an unforeseen consequence. But it couldn't be helped. The disease had spread enough, even without the assistance of Obelisk Medical Services, that it visited whomever it wanted, striking the hardiest and sparing the weakest with a capriciousness that Martindale associated with the deity. The only ones who had a chance of escaping the scourge were the rich since they could always pick themselves up at a moment's notice and fly off to another part of the world that the flu hadn't yet reached. The strategy worked only so long as there remained areas that were still untouched.

When Martindale wearied of reading or gazing out the beveled windows on the Tiber he would switch on Thorning's video monitors and study the progress of the disease as it burned through its victims lying in the clinic one floor down.

Most of these patients, whose number ranged anywhere from a dozen to thirty, were young women, young attractive women—at least before they were struck by the virus. They were selected by his agents from thousands who were in the same desperate circumstances. Beauty alone did not confer such a privileged status on them, of course; it was necessary that they come from money, a great deal of it. These were people who had not been prescient enough to bolt before the flu caught up with them; these were people who had scoffed at the promise of redemption offered to them by Jonas Beck. Some would live; some would not in spite of the best efforts of Martindale's staff.

In the past three days Martindale had taken special interest in one of the newer arrivals, a woman just recently married named Nancy Colville Wilks. While her dissolute husband drank himself into melancholy oblivion in the cafes in Rome she hovered between life and death, seeming at one moment to prefer the former and the next the latter.

The disease had naturally made her drawn, thinned her out, pared her down to something essential, something even pure. Martindale liked seeing how a woman looked when her energy was sapped, her body at its feeblest. He liked having the capacity to sometimes restore that woman to the full bloom of her health and to receive in turn a gratitude much greater than what she would ever give to any husband or lover.

Nancy intrigued him; there was something about her that conveyed the impression of untested sexuality. Struggling against the disease in her dampened bed, writhing and thrashing, throwing off her sheets, mindlessly exposing herself, the johnny hiking up with her frantic, heaving motion to reveal her suntanned legs and the promise of her pudendum, she might have been with a lover—a lover only she could see.

When the struggle grew too much for her she would sink back into the bed and lie there quietly, breathing rapidly, gasping for whatever breath her fluid-filled lungs would permit her. Martindale imagined that this was how she would be with her passion sated, surrendering herself to her lover, who in this case was death, the most possessive lover of all.

This was not a woman who could ever wholly capture his heart, who could ever seize it with such a frightening grip as Diana had done, was doing still. But this was also not a woman he would allow to return to her husband if she survived. And if in some dim future she should ever find her way back to Julian it would only be with the smell of Martindale on her skin.

It was a rule of his, in this Roman interlude, never to leave his private apartments until night. Night induced in him a strange restlessness; he needed a respite from his daytime solitude. Not until close to dawn did he sleep, and then only for four or five hours.

Night was when he would slip into his clinic and pay a call in person to whatever patient he'd been watching on the monitor during the day. As each patient had a private room with its own private entrance only the patient he visited would know he was there. He took every precaution that the staff wasn't aware of his nocturnal visits, although even if they were he could justify them on medical grounds.

On day four of Nancy Wilks' treatment she was still failing to show satisfactory progress. Her temperature hadn't come down significantly, there was marked prostration, a hint on the EKG that she might be developing a gallop rhythm: a sign of myocarditis. She was receiving antibiotics to combat a slight streptococcal pharyngitis; her cervical lymph nodes were enlarged and the elevation of her diaphragm was compromising pulmonary function. Antipyretics to reduce the fever and analgesics for pain were being administered to her regularly, accompanied by oxygen therapy to assist her in breathing. Her prognosis was listed as poor.

The protocol that Nancy was receiving was conservative and, in fact, nothing more than she would have gotten in any major hospital in the world. What distinguished the clinic in Rome, like Martindale's clinics elsewhere, was the use of experimental medications. The drugs the laboratories produced in one facility could be applied almost immediately in the other. The only one whose approval was necessary to initiate the experiment was Martindale himself. Although it was by now an open secret that his procedures were highly questionable, he continued to deny doing anything improper or illegal. Reports that his experimental therapies had not been adequately tested, certainly not approved by any government agency, he dismissed as vicious rumors and threatened to bring suit against anyone claiming otherwise.

One of the substances, still in the experimental stage, was known as Interleuken. It was derived from a natural growth factor found in the human thymus. Shown to have had success against AIDS, leprosy, and genital herpes, Martindale was interested to see how it would fare when administered to the victims of the virus.

There was an unusual side effect associated with Interleuken: people to whom it had been given often maintained that it left them with a feeling of general well-being, a kind of euphoria.

It was Martindale's drug of choice for Nancy. He hoped not only that he would cure her but that he would forge a bond of intimacy between them, heightened by the pleasurable feeling brought on by the drug.

She was raving, in the throes of delirium, crying out the name of her husband when he entered her room. He didn't turn on the lights.

She saw him. Or rather she saw that somebody was in the room with her. She extended her arms. "Julian? Is that you, Julian?"

Martindale, the hypodermic needle in hand, approached her bed and sat down on it. She smelled of sweat and disease but it was something he was accustomed to.

He took her hand, clutching it. It was so cold. "Dear Nancy, I am Dr. Patrick Martindale and I am going to make you feel much better."

She tried to smile back at him. The sting from the needle caused her to wince.

"There, that's all there is to it."

Her head lolled about, she was talking underneath her breath, inaudible most of the time and incomprehensible when audible.

After several minutes had gone by her mouth fell open and her head stopped its restless motion. She was asleep. Her breathing was so shallow that he could scarcely see the rise and fall of her breasts.

He drew his hand under the johnny; wet warm skin welcomed him. He moved his hand up until he found her breasts. And then down until he found her center. While she didn't wake she began to respond to what he was doing inside of her, probing the walls of her vagina, back and forth, and up, and then down.

Then her eyes came open and it seemed from the glimmer in them that she understood what he was doing. He leaned over and kissed her, leaving his hand where it was. And into her ear he whispered, "Nancy, darling, forget about Julian, forget about anyone else. You have only me, Patrick Martindale, to love now."

FOURTEEN

There was an amazing din—unspeakable confusion—throughout the Stazione Termini. Everywhere Lightman looked people were screaming madly or talking excitedly in a babble of tongues, gesticulating and slapping their hands against their brows, their faces flushed. People were either trying to get to or from the trains; it was hard to tell which. Small children, dark urchins, five, six years old maybe, ran from one person to the next, palms extended. When they were ignored they'd spit and curse. There were sunken-eyed women and men bent with age and derangement wandering through the crowd, altogether oblivious of the uproar, talking to themselves. There were people with the stigmata of the pandemic, the raised purple blisters on their faces and limbs. There was even one man Lightman thought must be Thorning, but it was not. Yet the man's infirmity was the same as Thorning's: a total paralysis of the eye muscles.

A woman whose age Lightman guessed to be close to forty passed immediately below the window of his compartment. A handkerchief was pressed to her face and it was becoming so saturated with blood that it would soon be useless. Suddenly she raised her eyes, meeting Lightman's gaze. He read embarrassment in her eyes and astonishment, too. Why, she seemed to be asking him, should this be happening to her?

Then all at once she threw out her arms, her hands clawing the half open window before she collapsed. No one reacted. It was as though nothing remarkable had happened at all. Lightman sprang from his seat but the Beck disciple sharing his compartment gripped his hand to restrain him. "There's nothing you can do. She is among the unredeemed."

Lightman tore himself free but when he looked out again there was no sign of the prostrate woman; it was as if she hadn't been there at all.

There was undoubtedly some reason to explain why the conductor wasn't allowing them off, but whatever that reason was no one was bothering to announce it.

At last the doors of the train opened and stairways were lowered to the platform. Making his way out through the crowd, Lightman began to look for Pilar. She was standing not far away, surrounded by other members of her sect.

But then, as he watched, she separated herself from the group of Beck adherents and started out of the terminal. Lightman followed.

The district bordering the terminal was derelict, in an advanced state of decomposition. The shops and taverns were boarded up; green crosses were painted on many, possibly to signal the victory of death over the faithless. Stray dogs with their ribs showing through prowled the streets and barked fitfully at any passerby.

Pilar proceeded with a brisk, certain pace, as if she knew exactly where she was going. The streets kept narrowing and filling with smoke from smoldering rubbish. Breathing became more difficult.

And then suddenly, beyond a crumbling wall whose masonry had all but turned to powder, Lightman found himself in what appeared to be a thriving commercial district. But it was a commercial district totally unlike any he'd ever seen before. For one thing, it was ramshackle, jerry-rigged, its shops and cafes assembled out of wood, sheets of corrugated metal and cannibalized auto parts. Crowds moved through the district languidly, like somnambulists. The music was more alive than they were, pulsing with alien rhythms and unidentifiable instrumentation. Prostitutes were especially conspicuous as they circulated among the cafe tables, bald or sporting iridescent hair, full of leather and tattoos, often naked but so cunningly painted that he had to look two or three times to realize it.

But that was only a small part of it. Beyond the row of cafes there was a warren of stucco and stone structures where the air was ripe with the smell of hashish and spermicides. Laughter and music mingled with screams that could have meant either agony or passion. More prostitutes loitered in doorways, doing their nails or primping when they grew weary of opening up their dresses to exhibit their genitals. Through these doorways, even in the gloom,

Lightman could sometimes distinguish a leg, an arm, a breast, a buttock, rarely anyone's face, just these bits and pieces of human anatomy, of bare sweaty flesh.

Where was Pilar? He would catch a glimpse of her only to lose her, give up all hope of finding her and then suddenly see her again, walking with a determined stride among the twisting passageways.

Lightman began to notice headstones. More graves wherever he looked. It occurred to him what purpose these stone structures must have served before the whores and the cafes moved in: they had housed the dead. He was in a necropolis, a city of the dead that the living—the survivors of the contagion and those who, for one reason or another, hadn't been struck down by it—had usurped for themselves.

There was no discernible borderline between the living and the dead that Lightman could see. One overlapped the other.

Some distance away, thrown into silhouette by the glare of the sun, was a castle, its turrets surrounded by scaffolding.

But what good had it done him to have penetrated from one end to the other of this curious, corruptible place when all he'd succeeded in doing was losing Pilar? She had vanished completely. It was useless to remain where he was, constantly accosted by whores with lurid tattoos and rings through their nipples and buffeted by men conducting a listless search for pleasure.

A small cafe offered the only spot available to sit and rest. Even if he'd managed to keep sight of Pilar he wasn't certain he could have continued following her, not in his depleted condition.

The woman who took his order was a whore like the others; she'd strung a gold chain from her earlobe to just inside her right nostril. Where her eyebrows should have been were two tattoos, each one a blue rising sun; the effect was to give her a look of permanent surprise. Lightman asked for a cold beer. When she returned with it she intimated, in bad English, that he might like her after he'd done with the beer. He declined.

"But I am disease free," she said and, reaching into her tangle of red hair she gave a tug. The hair was not her own. Her scalp shone brightly in the sun. "Immune," she said, "immune, immune, immune."

How strange, he thought, that this should be her pitch. Or maybe not so strange at that. He shook his head and waved her away.

"She's full of shit, they're all full of shit. You're crazy if you believe any of them."

Lightman turned to where the voice was coming from. The man who had just addressed him was sitting at the next table over. Three empty glasses and another couple of empty beer bottles were in front of him. His ashtray was too full to accommodate so much as another butt.

"You're American, aren't you?" he asked. "I can tell. I didn't even have to hear you speak and I could tell." His words were slightly slurred, but not so much that he couldn't make himself perfectly understood. Lightman decided that he'd had long practice being drunk.

Lightman admitted that he was an American.

"See that castle?"

"Yes, what about it?"

"That's where my Nancy is, my wife, Nancy." He drew his chair closer to where Lightman was sitting. "You know, the people who come here, most of them aren't American. Too fucking fastidious, Americans. Sometimes." He paused and looked thoughtfully at Lightman. "Julian Wilks," he said.

"I beg your pardon?"

"That's my name, Julian Wilks." He seemed disappointed that Lightman didn't respond with more enthusiasm to the announcement. On the other hand, he didn't bother asking Lightman who he was. Instead he said, "So what the hell brings you to a pit like this? I myself come for the view." He again gestured toward the castle. "And," he added, surveying the parade of whores, "the atmosphere."

"I'm looking for someone," Lightman said, thinking there was no reason to elaborate.

Julian appeared to be in his early thirties, but Lightman suspected that he was older by ten years. Some alcoholics seemed to preserve their youthful looks long after their sober contemporaries grew aged and gray. Of course, inside their bodies it was constant decay and corrosion, but the facade lasted.

"You see, what happens is that I wait here," Julian went on, clearly uninterested in what had brought Lightman to the place, "or maybe not, maybe I don't wait here, I wait back at my hotel or sit in a cafe by the Spanish Steps, it doesn't matter. Because wherever I go, they find me. I stay here mostly because here I'm closer to Nancy."

"Who finds you?"

Again Julian made a vague gesture toward the castle. "Those people. Jack . . . Jack Brill. He tells me what progress Nancy is making. Nancy's my wife."

"Yes, you told me."

His voice suddenly fell. "I don't think she's making any progress, to tell you the truth. I don't care what fucking Jack Brill says. I think she's dying."

Lightman felt a pang of sympathy for the man. But how much sympathy was there left to go around when so many were suffering his wife's predicament? Hers would be another, more or less anonymous, death.

"She might pull through. People I know have. I did."

Julian looked at him with renewed interest. "Oh? Yes, I can see where you might have at that. Yet sometimes, you know, this terrible feeling comes over you where you think nothing, no matter what you do, will come out right. You know what I mean?"

Lightman said he was familiar enough with the condition.

"It was our honeymoon. Not the kind of honeymoon I would have planned."

"I don't imagine it would be."

"They say she's being treated by the best specialist in the world, that if anyone can save her it's him."

"Who?"

"Martindale, Patrick Martindale."

Lightman could scarcely believe what he was hearing. He asked Julian to repeat the name, wanting to make sure that there could be no mistake. He had found him, Lightman thought, he was that close to getting him.

"That castle is where Martindale runs his clinic?"

"They say he's gutted the whole interior, remodeled it so that you'd think you were inside a spanking new hospital."

Closer than he'd thought. He wondered if Diana was inside there as well.

"How can you get inside?"

"You can't," Julian said simply. "They won't let you in unless you are an authorized individual." He pronounced these last two words scrupulously, as if he were afraid of tripping up on one of the syllables.

"Well there must be some way to get in there besides walking straight up to the front door and ringing the bell."

Julian cast a skeptical glance at him. "Why would you want to get in there so badly?"

"I have reason to think that a friend of mine may be there and I'd like to see her."

"A woman then." Immediately Julian warmed to him. Because they suffered from the same plight there was now a fraternal bond between them. "You know, there may be another way in," he said. "I don't know for certain but I've heard talk around this cafe that you can get in through the sewer system. The Romans, you know. It's still around from their time. Goes underneath this cemetery. Maybe if we follow it far enough we can find a way in. Only one problem."

"What's that?"

"We need a guide. We'd be fucked if we tried to do it ourselves. I don't have any idea where you even enter, let alone where you come out. No question, we do need a guide."

"And how do we find a guide?" One step at a time with someone this drunk, Lightman thought.

"We have to hire one of these kids. They're all cheats, they all figure you to be some fucking rich American who wants to get high or get laid before your number comes up. But without one of these kids to show you where you're going, forget it."

"How do you go about finding one of these kids?"

Lightman figured that if Julian was too damn loaded to acquire the services of a guide he'd do it himself.

"You use your intuition, you use your sense of smell. You see what's available, then you make your pick. You wait here, I'll go see what I can dig up."

"You don't want me to come with you and help?" What Lightman was afraid of was that Julian would disappear for good, and with him any chances of finding his way into the castle.

"No, no, no, you stay there and drink. I'll be back, count on it."

A moment later he plunged into the labyrinthine district of quick fucks and quicker death and was lost from sight.

Lightman looked up to see a woman looming over him, her face splashed with some lavender dye that gave her the appearance of one of the plague victims, whether out of mockery or sympathy Lightman couldn't tell. Reaching down to his crotch with her bejeweled hand, she asked in an insinuating voice that could have aroused the dead, "What do you say, American, do you want to have some fun before you die?"

FIFTEEN

Diana waited until it was night. The part of the castle she was living in was cut off from the area devoted to the clinic and the laboratories. Patrick's apartments were situated on the opposite side. There was a security presence in Diana's wing but nobody had ever told her that her movements were restricted.

Immediately outside her suite stairs descended to an atrium. The atrium was bathed in a soft beige light during the days when the sun streamed through the tinted glass that enclosed it. There was a fountain there, designed to imitate the famous one at Trevi, but not nearly so filled with coins and wishes. Potted palm trees were there as well as towering dieffenbachia whose leaves had the capacity to deaden a man's throat. Several pre-Raphaelite paintings of Madonnas and tormented saints were set into niches on the veined marble walls. Expensive black leather chairs and couches were positioned at great enough distance from one another to make conversation virtually impossible. The atrium had been meant as a waiting area for guests and distinguished patients of Patrick's but in the end another area, built on a more human scale, was employed for that purpose. So the atrium went unused.

A guard was patrolling the area when Diana passed through. He was a local, perhaps recruited from one of the museums that had closed since the outbreak began. He only smiled in greeting at seeing her, his eyes closely following the movement of her hips. He didn't ask what she was doing with her jacket on or why she was carrying her handbag. That wasn't his concern.

A small elevator led further down to a dining room for fifty, then to a dining room for twelve, then to a private screening room established by Thorning where the only movies to be seen were movies that the studios had kept shelved, never released to the public.

She knew that what she was about to do was dangerous, and that it was possible it wouldn't get her anywhere.

The door she walked up to led to the record room. There were stored, on CD-RAMs, the entire account of Martindale's operations over the years: the records of every patient he'd treated from the first days of Mayfair House; a complete listing of every financial transaction; copies of Martindale's correspondence; any contract he'd ever entered into in the last fifteen years, including those that he signed with Obelisk Medical Services; finally, a catchall catalogue of confidential memos, operational plans, eyes-only analyses of unregulated drug experiments, and a series of secret agreements between Martindale and Jonas Beck on behalf of the Church of the Redeemed. What Diana meant to do was steal whatever she could of the documentation.

Diana hadn't fully thought her plan through. Had she, she might not have had the courage to go through with it. But she'd come to realize that she had to do something decisive, if only to allay her own nagging conscience. For months now she had felt as though she were in a trance, mesmerized by Patrick and Jonas Beck, incapable of exercising any control over her life. A desperate action might prod her awake.

Her objective didn't quite coincide with John's; she had no desire to destroy Patrick. Rather she hoped to use the stolen documentation as leverage—really as blackmail—to force his hand. She knew that John was right, that Patrick was responsible for perpetrating, or at least condoning, terrible crimes. He could not be allowed to continue; he must be made to see that he should give up, take his wealth and steal away into suitably luxurious retirement. What more did he want that he didn't already have?

There was no guard at the door of the record room. More surprising still, the door was unlocked.

She walked in. The room was in darkness except for a bright greenish haze produced by the gas plasma display monitor hooked up to a computer. The screen was blank.

Diana groped to find the light switch.

"Don't bother," a familiar voice said.

"Patrick!" She spun around to see him, virtually indistinguishable until he was standing right next to her. He must have tracked her through his surveillance system; she could think of no other explanation.

Her heart thumped insanely and she felt all control slipping away.

"It wouldn't have done you any good," he spoke gently. "The information on these compact disks will be automatically destroyed if you try to read them off unauthorized equipment."

Everything was anticipated, everything predictable. She despised him.

"What are you going to do to me?"

His eyes were almost luminous; no light was needed to interpret the look he was giving her. She felt his arms gather her in; the press of his hands against her buttocks caused her to hold back her breath. He moved one leg between hers and said, "Whatever you want me to do, Diana, that's what I am going to do to you."

SIXTEEN

The boy that Julian brought back with him was about ten or eleven. His name was Emilio. Short and emaciated, he had beautiful eyes that seemed to be continuously passing judgment on his prospective employers. Lightman doubted that he much cared for what he saw, but the sight of Julian's money—U.S. dollars—certainly brought him great pleasure. After Lightman deposited his few belongings with the proprietor of the cafe, parting with some money of his own for their care, they set out.

They entered the sewer system through a sepulchre whose contents must have long since been looted. Built of stone it was now turning to dust. Darkness ahead of them soon became darkness all around. On looking back, they observed that there was nothing to see of the lights burning in the makeshift cemetery town.

From time to time Emilio would make some garbled sound, exhorting them on, but otherwise they had to rely on his white T-shirt to navigate by.

It was wet down there, and rank, and the darkness was a different kind than any Lightman had experienced before.

Sometimes they would hear noises, absolutely incomprehensible, reverberating against the walls of the sewer. At one point it would sound like metal gnashing and clattering, then it would sound like a platoon of soldiers proceeding in a fast, deranged cadence, booted heels clicking along the passageways. But there was no way of distinguishing with any precision what was going on, or even where the sounds were originating. It was possible that they came not from anywhere in the sewer but above-ground, amplified and distorted as they were routed below.

"How much farther on do you think it is?" Julian's voice was edgy and quaking. For him it was probably worse than it was for Lightman.

The question he'd put to Lightman was patently ridiculous since he had no idea what distance might remain. For that matter, he hadn't even considered what he would do once he reached the castle. What mattered most of all was finally having the opportunity to confront Martindale. Something, he felt sure, would occur to him once they met.

The passage would narrow, then broaden again, but it continued to turn more and more. Even in the murk Lightman could make out the eyes that were watching them, the eyes of rats that made their homes there. And every once in awhile he would feel one brush against his pants leg. Their squeaks and odd little rustling sounds followed them; it was like a running commentary on their progress.

The smell was growing worse. It was a stench of rot. And there was an unsettling noise, too, that sounded like several people whispering at once. To this was added the shrill squeaking of rats drowned out only by the sound of Julian screaming in terror.

"What is it?" Lightman demanded.

But Emilio saw what had made him so crazed with fear. Not more than a dozen paces in front of them nearly a hundred rats were feasting on an unidentifiable carcass. They were so intent on gnawing it apart that they gave no notice to the three interlopers approaching them. Emilio glared at Julian and addressed him harshly in Italian.

Lightman imagined Emilio was telling him to shut up. What had he expected to find down there—a pleasure palace?

Taking hold of Julian's arm Lightman guided him past the macabre scene. Only then could he see that it was a human being they were consuming. But that wasn't what troubled Lightman the most. It was the size of the rats; they were so fat they could hardly move.

But they hadn't seen the worst of it. More corpses littered the passage, obstructing their way, so many that even the rats were ignoring them, choosing only the best parts —the eyes, the earlobes, the penises—and leaving everything else to waste in its own good time. It probably explained why they expressed so little interest in the three living humans.

Julian was still screaming—or at least he looked like he was still screaming. No sound, however, emerged from him. His eyes were gaping, his mouth hung open, sweat bubbled from out of his face. And when finally he did make a sound it was to gag. His body shuddered and he vomited long and noisily, winning a contemptuous stare from their guide.

Lightman, too, was gagging. Nothing he saw was quite as bad as the stench. Only Emilio, amazingly enough, seemed immune to it. Maybe he'd been down there so many times it failed to make any impact on him.

Suddenly Emilio turned back to them, his hands outstretched as if he expected more money before he went on. But that wasn't it at all. His lips were quivering, he was breathing quickly, painfully, and then his face sagged and he fell helplessly at their feet.

Lightman stooped down and as he did so, a rat shot out of the darkness and took a big bite of the boy's exposed ankle. It knew better than he did that Emilio was dead.

SEVENTEEN

In the dimness Diana's flesh shone. She slept. Martindale was lying in his commodious bed next to her, wondering at the mystery of his passion for her.

He wasn't surprised that she'd tried to escape the con-

fines of Lombardi Castle, nor was he surprised that she'd
intended on stealing the CD-RAMs. Rather it was that she
believed she could ever get free by leaving him. It wasn't
so simple. He'd be with her wherever she went.

They were bound—he and Diana and Beck—by a destiny that Jonas Beck had discerned long ago, that they were
to be instruments of history; their personal desires, satis-
factions, and passions were of no relevance.

What Diana had never understood was that the virus was
their gift to the world. But then he didn't expect most people to understand. How could he inflict such devastation
and misery on the world? they would demand to know. But
it was just as Beck had said: the devastation and misery
were inevitable. Millions would die. If history were permitted to lurch and stumble along its own blind course then
any possibility of man taking control would slip away. A
nuclear war, the proliferation of holes in the ozone layer,
the inexorable annexation of the earth by the sea and the
desert—these catastrophes or others as yet unforeseen
would eventually account for man's sorry end. But by allowing the virus to do its work unfettered they were reas-
serting control, becoming masters and transformers of
history. And it was this that mattered, far more than the
abundance of money eagerly pressed on them by people
willing to endure the poverty of a religious calling in exchange for their lives. It was the ultimate power that Beck
and Martindale held; prime ministers and potentates of oil-
rich kingdoms alike, even the new pope, all had been eager
to cut deals with them. Like anyone else they wanted to
live and were willing to go to great lengths to guarantee
their survival. That was why the Church of the Redeemed
could establish itself in any country in the world and enjoy
the protection of its rulers: none dare oppose it.

But always there was resistance, people who for one
reason or another believed that they could do without the
church, confident that their natural immunity would keep
at bay the scourge of the virus. Diana had resisted, refusing

the offer held out to her by the Apostle Beck, and refused to join the church. He and Beck had argued about what should be done, he insisting that Diana be vaccinated anyway and Beck arguing that it would be better if she underwent the baptism of the infection. "There are only two ways one can come through fire," he had told Martindale, "by donning a suit of asbestos or by God's will. Let us discover how deep her faith goes."

She had come through of course, she'd survived the test. And because she'd survived Martindale loved her all the more; little by little she was becoming his equal.

He kissed her on the nape and she stirred, but it wasn't his kisses that wakened her; it was the ringing of his private phone.

Stephen Butler was on the other end, calling from the lab. "Dr. Martindale," he said, his voice catching in his excitement, "something's happening with the virus. The reports we're getting are really disturbing. I think you ought to come and take a look at them yourself."

Setting down the phone Martindale felt something he hadn't felt for a great many years: fear.

Diana turned and opened her eyes at him. "What's wrong?"

"Nothing," he replied, "nothing's wrong. It's just some business I have to look after."

EIGHTEEN

Using his private elevator Martindale hurried to the laboratory where Butler was waiting for him. Martindale read dismay in his eyes. Butler thrust a sheaf of papers into his hands. "It's all in there."

The data contained in the pages had been collected from five of the eighteen communities the Church of the Redeemed had set up in various parts of the world. Populations of these communities ranged from several hundred to ten thousand. They were modeled on the religious communes of nineteenth century America, like the Shakers, and governed by strict codes of behavior. They were intended to appeal to those followers of Jonas Beck who needed authority imposed on them. Not everyone who joined the church elected to uproot themselves and settle in the communities, and practically speaking there wouldn't have been room in them for the millions who now counted themselves members. But for thousands of others—particularly the impoverished peoples of the world who could never hope to share the benefits of capitalist society, who were doomed to a life of subsistence, malnutrition, and disease—the communities were truly refuges. Unlike the wealthy who had to buy their way into the church, they needed to do no more than declare their faith and accept the word of the Apostle Beck.

The nineteen communities were monitored routinely for outbreaks of the virus. Any incidence of the disease was promptly investigated. Usually it was a new convert who had been infected prior to receiving the vaccine. From time to time someone who had been vaccinated would fall ill, although the episode was seldom life threatening. Far more than any vaccine administered orally or by inoculation the use of a nasal spray delivered by the incense had proven remarkably effective.

But for some reason the data assembled on the pages indicated that it was no longer.

The data, collected from settlements in El Oued, Algeria, Jerusalem, Israel, Salvador, Brazil, Barranquilla, Colombia, and Savannah, Georgia, were showing that incidences of the flu were up markedly. In the Barranquilla settlement alone—in just one week—cases had soared from eleven out of a total population of 4860 to 634. Half the victims had died and the majority of the others were in critical condition. The statistics relating to outbreaks in the other four were equally alarming.

"Have you checked at the other settlements?" he asked Butler, his mind working frantically to reason out an explanation.

"We've conducted spot checks on eight other settlements in Europe and East Africa. Except for the Uganda settlement, we're seeing the same thing happening. Then we compared incidences of flu cases in surrounding areas using the WHO Weekly Epidemiological Reports and our own surveillance. The pattern we found emerging indicates that even individuals who have already had the flu are coming down with it a second time. And the vast majority of them, weakened to begin with, are dying."

Martindale was stunned. All this demanded further verification, a reassessment of the data. "Let's get back to the settlements for a minute. Have you checked on the dosage levels of the vaccine? Is it possible that they're too low or that somehow the batches of vaccine have been contaminated somewhere in the pipline?"

Butler nodded. "I didn't want to bother you, sir, until I was absolutely certain of my facts. We've run tests at Obelisk, we've run random tests on sample batches of the vaccine in different locations. The results have all been negative. The vaccine is, if anything, more potent than previous batches have been. But it's failing to have any major therapeutic impact. On the basis of the projections we've drawn up, the infection rate should treble within two weeks in the settlement alone. It looks as if members of the settlement are spreading the infection faster than anywhere in the outside world. It's possible the new virus even started with them. In zones outside the settlements the infection rate can be expected to be six to ten times greater owing to the general disability of the affected population groups."

Martindale remained silent while Butler went through the reports prepared for him. But there was nothing in them that would cause him to question Butler's conclusions.

"There's only one explanation I can think of to account

for this phenomenon if this same pattern continues to hold true," Martindale said.

"Antigenic drift," Butler suggested.

Antigenic drift described the action of viruses as they mutated from one strain to another, a fairly common occurrence. That was why there were so many different types of viruses: A/Hong Kong, A/Russian, A/Taiwan, etc. If a virus did mutate—or drift—it could easily strike an individual for a second time. But Martindale didn't believe that they were witnessing an instance of antigenic drift here.

"If it were antigenic drift then we shouldn't be seeing such a fantastic fatality rate. The second strain would be a close relative, a half brother, let's say, to the initial strain. Antibodies built up after exposure to that first strain should mitigate the impact of the second. I could see the church members coming down with a mild fever, but nothing they should have any difficulty recuperating from."

"So what do you think it is then?"

"Something else altogether. What we're very likely seeing is a case of antigenic shift."

Antigenic shift was an entirely different, and far more dangerous phenomenon. It meant that the virus hadn't just transformed itself from one strain into a close relative, but that it had turned into a new virus altogether—one that nobody in the world had built up any resistance to, one for which there was no vaccine, no protection whatsoever.

How this might have happened was a mystery even to the top people in the field. Scientists theorized that the initial viral strain, having exhausted most of the available human pool, took haven in swine. The swine population then contributed its own genetic contribution to the makeup of the virus. The result was a totally new virus, an unknown quantity, part human, part swine, loose in the world.

Martindale had no way of knowing whether something like that had in fact occurred. That determination awaited another day. What mattered most was that no one, least of all he or Beck, had any control over the virus.

After instructing Butler to continue monitoring the situation and to keep him informed of any new developments, he returned to his office and telephoned Beck. He had to be told immediately what was happening; they would have to arrange to meet. It was possible that not all was lost, that Beck would have foreseen this happening in his visions and that his visions had told him what was to be done.

But Martindale had no way of finding out whether or not Beck had received any visions relating to this unwelcome catastrophe. He was not where he should be, he wasn't available at all in fact. His representative said that he was on retreat in an unidentifiable location, presumably communing with God. There was no way of reaching him by phone even in the event of an emergency. Nor was there any way of knowing when he would reemerge and resume his ministry.

Martindale couldn't afford to wait. Days, even weeks might be lost while Beck was meditating. He decided to leave that very night. It was likely there were places in the world that the mutant virus hadn't gotten to yet; a careful study of the relevant data would give him the answer he needed—and his destination. Rome was finished; he'd leave only a skeleton crew of researchers and physicians behind. Everyone else would accompany him. If he couldn't defeat the virus the least he might be able to do was outdistance it.

NINETEEN

Lightman slept. When he finally awakened it was morning and he felt like shit. He ached all over. He forced himself to get out of bed, no matter how weak and wobbly he was. He didn't like the idea of indulging himself. When he was more fully alert he realized that he was in a hotel room. A lavishly appointed hotel room from the looks of it.

All sorts of memories rushed into his mind then. It occurred to him that the stink and the rats and the young boy pitching over in front of his eyes were not some bad dream he'd had. It had all happened. He remembered Julian. While there was no sign of him Lightman had a feeling that he must be in some way responsible for Lightman being at the hotel. But that part wouldn't come to him; the last thing he recalled was running pell-mell out of the sewer, frantic to escape the contamination and death. He got dressed and went out to discover where exactly he was.

When he reached the lobby the concierge hailed him. "Signore Lightman, please to go to Donney's," he said. "Signore Wilks is waiting there for you. It is just a few blocks from here to your right."

Donney's was practically empty at that hour of the morning. Julian sat, looking miserable in the bright sunshine, staring desolately off into space. A snifter of brandy was on the table in front of him. Seeing Lightman he gave a wan smile that was quickly gone.

"Did you sleep well?" he asked.

"Soundly," Lightman answered, "though to tell you the truth, I don't know how much good it did me. I still feel fatigued."

"Well, you were out for almost three days."

"Three days? You must be joking."

"Today's the twenty-second of July," Julian said.

Lightman supposed that between the ordeal he'd undergone in the sewer and the lingering effects of the virus he'd needed the rest. But he resented the demands of his body on his time. He didn't feel as if he had so much of it left to spare. Nor did anyone else in the world for that matter.

"I want to thank you for all you did," Lightman said. "How much do I owe you for the room?"

"I didn't do shit. You saved my life down in that damn sewer. When that kid dropped dead I couldn't bring myself to move. I might still be there if you hadn't forced me to get my ass in gear. Besides, I have more money than I know what to do with, the least I can do is pay your room. As a matter of fact, anything you want is on me." His voice was flat. He looked haggard, worse than when Lightman had first met him by the cemetery.

"What's wrong?"

"Nancy."

"Your wife?"

"Last night that bastard Brill came to tell me that she died."

"Jesus, I'm sorry. Have they let you see her?"

"No. Brill says that the Italians have made laws because of the epidemic, you have to cremate the body right away to avoid risk of infection. Fucking Italians."

That sounded suspect to Lightman. "I don't want to get your hopes up, but it's just possible your wife is still alive."

Julian gave him a reproachful look, as if he believed Lightman was making him the butt of an inscrutable and tasteless joke. But once Lightman had told him what had happened to Diana, and how the body he'd disinterred in Saint Clement's wood wasn't hers, Julian began to see things differently.

"You're not lying? This actually happened?"

"I swear."

"My Nancy's alive." It was amazing to see how the exhaustion fell away from his face, how spirited and boyish he suddenly seemed.

"It is possible that Nancy has died, don't forget," Lightman said. "I don't want you getting your hopes up on account of me. All I'm saying is that you shouldn't take this clown's word for it, you should confirm it for yourself if you possibly can."

"I have an idea." Julian looked as though he'd become divinely inspired.

"And what exactly is it?"

A waiter finally appeared at their table. Julian would have liked Lightman to order a drink, but all Lightman thought he could stand was coffee, if that.

Julian continued. "My idea is this." He held up a wad of money pulled out of his billfold. "When I run out of this stuff I have credit cards. I have letters of credit. There are banks here I can walk right into and come out with whatever I ask for. So the two of us—"

All at once he looked blank; maybe he'd forgotten what it was he wanted to say.

"The two of us what?"

"The two of us can find them together, your Diana, my Nancy. We'll find them with this, with this money. There's always somebody that can be bought. Haven't you found that's the case?"

"I don't doubt it, it's just that I've never had the means to prove it myself."

"We'll find Brill, we'll talk to him, we'll give him money, we'll see what he says when the money's for him and not for the fucking Church of the fucking Redeemed. What do you say?"

It turned out that, while Julian wasn't permitted to view the body of his wife, a memorial mass at the church of Santa Trinita Dei Monti was scheduled that afternoon at three for all the families of the dead. Brill had given Julian the impression that he would be attending it.

Lightman wasn't counting on anything, not with Julian, but he saw no reason not to play along. He was beginning to like the man, and besides, there was something to what he said about the ability of money to favorably influence behavior. Ironically, Julian had more money than he would have had had Brill come to him to say that Nancy had pulled through. His bargain with the church called for her being restored to health. Failing that, he was permitted to keep half his fortune. As Julian admitted, "I can either drink it up or else do something useful with it. I think doing something useful would be a change, don't you?"

Not that he was prepared to eschew drinking altogether. Told that the church had been filled up by others mourning the deaths of their loved ones, Julian proposed that they adjourn to a nearby cafe.

They sat in a silence that was, at intervals, broken by the lugubrious toll of church bells throughout the city.

It wasn't burning rubbish that Lightman was breathing. The smoke that hung in the lifeless air contained in it the stench of human flesh turning into cinders, bodies incinerating, the virus being expunged.

Before an hour had passed the doors of the church were thrown open, releasing the mourners into the clouded air. Most of them seemed to be older women in black with reddened eyes who looked as if they'd been weeping over generations of dead.

Julian was watching out for Jack Brill with expectant eyes. Lightman could almost tell what was on his mind: money must be able to resolve this problem, money must be able to find Nancy for me, money must not let me down.

And then Julian pointed him out. He was a balding man, on the plump side, wearing an electric blue jacket. A woman was walking alongside him. Not as old as the other women, she had on dark glasses obviously intended to hide her tear-stained eyes. A new widow, Lightman suspected. Brill was trying to console her, no doubt assuring her that her future would be a great deal happier than she could possibly imagine at the moment.

Julian stood up from the table and motioned frantically to Brill, who pretended not to see him. For several seconds he was lost in a knot of mourners carrying crosses who made scarcely a sound as they proceeded along the cobblestones at their suitably doleful pace.

But Julian wouldn't allow Brill to hide from him. He

hurried over in his direction, breaking through the mourners, indifferent to their grief. And why not? He had his own to deal with.

From his table Lightman watched the two men converse, first in full view of everyone, then off to the side in the shadows of a building where they would not be quite so conspicuous.

Several minutes went by. Lightman began to think that maybe he'd been wrong, maybe drunk or not, Julian might prove competent and accomplish what he'd set out to do. If Brill didn't want to deal with him surely he would have sent him packing before this.

Finally Julian returned to Lightman's table.

"I need a drink," he said. Once he'd insured that the drink was on the way he related to Lightman how his conversation with Brill had gone.

"He doesn't know."

"Doesn't know what?"

"Doesn't know whether Nancy's alive or not. But he did say she might be. It happens, he says, that mistakes are made. See, he wasn't willing to say that he was wrong, but he said it wasn't out of the realm of possibility. He swears he doesn't know what goes on inside the castle, he's not one of Martindale's confidants." His eyes were becoming inflamed by the drink.

He wasn't interested in weighing the odds. He'd wanted to be convinced that she was alive and he'd heard all he needed to allow that to happen.

"Did Brill give you any idea how to get inside the castle then?"

Concrete information, something that they could use, was what Lightman was hoping for.

"Well that's the thing. He says it won't do us any good. Martindale's gone. Just about everyone's gone. They left Rome a few days ago."

Lightman despaired. The idea that he'd come so close

only to let Martindale—and Diana—slip from his grasp again was almost unbearable. "Did he tell you where they'd gone?"

"He told me they headed south—to Africa."

TWENTY

No one could say what had happened. But one day there were only the dead to occupy the former hotel that had served as home for the members of the Church of the Redeemed. The living had scattered throughout Jerusalem or found refuge in the caves dotting the mountains that surrounded the city.

And except for Ken Snape, who had appropriated a house for himself in the Arab quarter, the captains were making themselves scarce. Those who weren't ailing or dead, Ezra suspected, had probably deserted, their faith shaken to the quick. For if it was faith that had protected the devout of the church until now, that faith was no longer enough.

In place of the Mirages and Phantoms and MiG fighter planes Ezra saw when he first got here, the skies were now filled only with carrion, their sharp eyes picking out their next meal. It seemed that everyone in the region had been preparing for war but there were no longer enough people well enough to carry it out.

What the carrion missed the stray dogs and the rats—especially the rats—claimed for themselves.

Rats were everywhere, no longer intimidated by the few humans able to get around. They prowled the passageways of the Old City with bloody teeth and greedy eyes, probably amazed at the luck they were having.

There wouldn't have been so many rats if the cats were still around. Ezra remembered from his first days there seeing dozens of cats everywhere. They belonged to no one but themselves; they especially favored the district by the Damascus Gate. All night long he could near their unceasing laments, worse when they were in heat.

But one day they were gone. Ezra wondered what had become of them. He asked Ken Snape, but Snape thought he was crazy. People were dying all around them; why was he so worried about the cats? But Ezra was curious. It was something he wanted to find out.

It remained a mystery. The fact was that they'd disappeared, leaving the city to the depredations of the rats.

Ezra was one of the last to depart what used to be called the Intercontinental Hotel. It had once been a luxurious establishment whose windows held a beautiful view of the Old City. But it had fallen on bad times and its rooms were in shambles, windows broken, plumbing nonfunctional when it was there at all, the smell of refuse pervasive. The hotel had been selected by the church because it occupied a position at the summit of the Mount of Olives.

There were already a great many dead on the slopes of the Mount of Olives; it was, Ezra learned, a popular place to be buried. The Jews believed that when the Messiah returned the first people to be resurrected would be those whose graves were there. But if the Messiah had come, he hadn't gotten around to raising them from the dead. All that had happened was that there were more dead to join those already in the ground.

A sweet, sickly odor, like smoke, lay over the whole city; it was the odor given off by people in their last stages of illness. They were dying behind shuttered doors and windows. The hospitals were too crowded to admit more than a few every day. Dying had to be done at home.

The one place to which all the disciples of Jonas Beck would go was the Church of the Holy Sepulchre. People believed that it was on the site of this church that Jesus had been crucified. At one time many religions—Copts, Armenians, Roman Catholics, Greek Orthodox—shared this church, dividing it up, staking out small dominions in chapels and sacristies, sometimes growing violent as to who got what.

But things had changed. It was now the church where everyone went to petition their particular brand of god to halt the plague in its tracks and spare them and their loved ones.

It was there that even Ezra, who swore by no god at all, went to pray. It made him feel better, eased the pain. He sank down on his knees in front of an altar draped with bloody vestments of a dead priest and recited the names of his lost children: Danny, Elias, Benjamin, Mara and Cherish. Over and over. It was his litany, his prayer. He knew no other words.

The Church of the Redeemed had other settlements scattered around the world and it was possible that his children were in one of them, still in good health. But if there was anyone who knew which settlement it was, Ezra was at a loss to find him. He supposed that all such information was maintained in the memory bank of some computer, but again that was only his guess, he didn't know.

On all sides of him in the candlelit gloom of the church people were chanting and keening, their bodies wracked with sobs. Everyone was asking for surcease from pain. Their voices echoed and rebounded against the walls of the nave.

Hooded figures circulated in the midst of the mourners, their faces submerged in shadow, their trembling hands clutching plates into which people would drop coins. These were survivors of the virus, like Ezra, who no longer wished their faces or their bodies to be seen. They relied on alms to get by. They'd assumed the role of messengers, a constant reminder that those who were healthy today might well be in their place by tomorrow.

One of them came close enough to Ezra so that he could feel his breath brush against his cheek. "I am one touched by God," he whispered, thrusting his plate in front of Ezra's face.

Ezra unbottoned the top of his shirt so that the scars left by the blisters would be in plain sight.

The hooded figure nodded. "You are one of us, brother," and then, before Ezra knew what was happening, he pressed his lips on his.

Ezra's stomach heaved. He pushed the alms seeker aside and rushed out of the church, spitting in hope of ridding himself of the poisons the kiss had left on his lips. It wasn't enough. He bought a soda from a vendor outside the church. Still not enough. The taste persisted, the taste of corruption and death.

It was in front of the church that Ken Snape found him. He walked unsteadily on his feet, looking paler than usual. He'd allowed his ginger hair to grow so that it now trailed down his back. He might be sick himself but his voice remained firm.

"I need you to come with me," he said.

Although there was hardly anyone left to issue commands to the battalion, with its ranks so decimated, Snape wouldn't relent. He was one of those people, Ezra thought, whose life would have been played out in dull anonymity: a cleric's job, a wife of indifferent looks he could never quite get up the courage to cheat on. But chaos and destruction had allowed him an opportunity to take power. The Church of the Redeemed had embraced him and ratified that power, and now he couldn't get used to the idea that it was no longer his to exercise.

Ezra regarded him sullenly. "I'm not going anywhere with you, Snape."

His insolent response failed to make any impression. "It's vital. There are very few I can rely on. We are shutting down operations in Jerusalem," Snape said. "The church is threatened here. We have received instructions from the Apostle Beck. We are to leave as soon as possible."

"Leave for where?" Even with the pestilence Ezra wasn't certain he liked the idea of being sent to some new destination.

"I can't tell you that," Snape said, looking somewhat apologetic. "I can't tell you because I don't know myself. But I can tell you this much: you have been chosen for something very special."

He reached into his pocket and produced a photograph which he showed to Ezra. It was a photograph of a woman —a pretty woman lying on a blanket in bright sunlight, her head in the shade of a straw hat, her breasts bare and clearly visible.

"Her name is Diana Cleary. She is English. You will be assigned to look after her, make sure no harm comes to her."

Ezra didn't want anything to do with this. But Snape anticipated his reaction and added, "You will be out of the reach of the infection, don't you want that? You'll be safe." Seeing that Ezra didn't buy this line completely, Snape offered him more of an inducement. "Do you know why the church selected you, and only you?"

Ezra shook his head.

"Because the church wishes to reunite you with your family. If you perform this service for us and guard Miss Cleary, we can guarantee that your search will come to an end." He looked Ezra squarely in the eyes. "Now what do you say?"

But he knew his answer already, he knew he'd won.

TWENTY-ONE

The visions wouldn't come anymore. Try as he might to get them back nothing worked. He couldn't trick them into coming, his dreams showed him nothing, and on waking he saw only what everyone else did: devastation and waste.

He had made certain before he went into seclusion that even his most trusted associates wouldn't be able to find him. As far as anyone in his organization knew he was on retreat and would return when his meditation was finished. In fact, he was in a private hospital in Berlin, in a room high enough so that he could see over the wall and into the eastern sector.

He'd chosen the hospital because it specialized in the care of people who would just as soon keep their illnesses to themselves. Established during the early years of the Cold War to care for operatives and defectors who required anonymity as much as medical care, it now took in ailing dictators and celebrities suffering from AIDS. Important people died, and sometimes recovered there.

Jonas Beck was very sick; existing in a perpetual twilight state, he regularly went in and out of a coma. It surprised him to find that each time he returned to consciousness another part of his body had failed him. A tube was removing pus from his lungs but it didn't seem to be doing the job fast enough; there was too much of it. His lungs felt heavy, as if slabs of stone were weighing down on them. His X-rays were revelations: his lungs looked like maps of forgotten countries, strewn with oddly shaped little islands, some as small as a chestnut, others as large as a hen's eggs.

His bedpan, meanwhile, continued to fill up with smoky, blood-streaked urine draining day and night from his catheter. His ankles were swollen, his legs looked like they belonged to an old woman. His doctor, a scrupulous, blunt talking Prussian, told him the swollen ankles were a sign of acute nephritis.

Worse than suffering the indignity of these symptoms was the shock of getting sick at all. He had taken his immunity for granted, not because he'd received the vaccine but because he felt that God wouldn't allow him to come to any harm. God had commanded him to go out among the masses and bring them his message. God was in him, God was in his blood, in his every movement, his every word. What he'd done he'd done without reservation. Surely God would want the wicked to perish, and all Beck was was an instrument to see that it happened.

But why should he and his disciples be struck down too? The church could no longer keep its promise, could no longer offer deliverance. There were diabolical forces loose in the world who didn't want to see him complete his mission. He would know what would have to be done if only his visions would come back to him.

That night—the night of the twenty-second of July—he did have a dream that carried through to his consciousness the next morning. In the dream he'd seen several dogs, a dozen or more, gathered in a circle, all of them scrawny, with hunger in their eyes, and they were making queer little whistling sounds through their lungs. That was it; he could remember no more. When he told his doctor this, though, the doctor scoffed at its significance. There were dogs like that everywhere in Germany, he said, and probably throughout the world. Those queer little whistling sounds he spoke of were the sounds they made when they were starving. They would eat anything, he said, even human flesh if it came to that.

In the nights following Jonas Beck saw those dogs again and again, always collected in a circle, always breathing in that funny way they had, their eyes transfixed by something they could see but he could not. Every night he would fall asleep wondering if this time he would discover what it was the dogs were waiting to pounce on and devour.

BOOK THREE
Findings

"The influenza viruses that cause disease in man appear to be peculiar to man, although some strains isolated from swine and horses are antigenically related to human strains. It is not known where influenza virus is harbored between interepidemic periods. Moreover, the mechanism of the transequatorial shift of occurrence of influenza, apparently in accord with the season, is not understood. The simultaneous eruption of influenza in many areas distant from each other is also intriguing."

—Chien Liu, "Influenza," from *Infectious Diseases*

"The Spanish Lady inspired no songs, no legends, no work of art. Even fundamental facts were meagre. To this day, no one can say with certainty where the disease began, where it ended, or even which virus was at fault. As one leading authority has summed it up, 'The resemblance to the disappearance of the Cheshire Cat in *Alice in Wonderland* is striking.'"

—Richard Collier, *Plague of the Spanish Lady*

"I can believe that the virus goes 'underground,' and perhaps does so all over the world . . . that it can persist in an area without causing outbreaks . . . but able to become active and epidemic when the time is ripe."

—Dr. Christopher Andrewes,
member of 1933 team that isolated Virus A

ONE

Just about every night there was screaming aboard the steamship *Lahadi* as it traveled up the Congo River from the capital Kinsasha. Headed north toward Kisangani, thirteen hundred miles into the interior of Zaire, the *Lahadi* was taking Lightman and Julian Wilks along the same route that Martindale and his entourage had traversed a few weeks before. The only difference was that Martindale had somehow secured the use of a plane while they had no alternative to this torturous form of transport. Even with all the money at his disposal, Julian had been unable to find a plane anywhere in Kinsasha. Invariably they were told that all available planes had been appropriated by the government. Whether these planes were used to deliver medical supplies and doctors to the interior or for use in combat against rebels was another story entirely. The fact remained that it was either this steamship or nothing.

The nightly screams were constantly intruding on Lightman's sleep. Sometimes they seemed to be coming from the deck above his, sometimes from the barge the *Lahadi* was pushing ahead of it. Although there were animals kept on the barge—goats and chickens mostly—the screams were not from them. Even a goat getting its throat slit couldn't produce such an agonized cry.

And then they would cease, leaving in their place the throb of drums from along the riverbanks signaling the approach of dawn and the reassuring rhythm of the steamer's churning engine and the plow of its paddle through water, and finally, the uneasy breathing of Julian sleeping off his latest binge on the other side of the cabin.

There was no way he could get back to sleep and it was probably better that he didn't even try. A few moments later there was a hard rapping on his door.

Silhouetted by the ship's lamps, the man standing in the doorway wasn't immediately identifiable. But he knew who Lightman was all right.

"Monsieur le Docteur, come quickly," he said.

It was Julian who had let it slip that he was a doctor. Now there was no explaining that he was a researcher—a scientist—not the kind of doctor who treated patients. They wouldn't understand. There were nearly two thousand people crammed on board the six-deck steamer, more maybe. And as far as he knew, he was the only doctor of any kind among them.

It wasn't just that he had no experience practicing medicine that made it so difficult; he had almost no medicine to practice with. His improvised doctor's bag contained only what he could purchase from the merchants who came out to meet the steamer in dugout canoes called pirogues: bandages, Necko medical soap, Vick's cough drops, ether, tins of aspirin, quinine water, antibiotics and herbal teas which were supposed to have miraculous healing properties. For victims of the Hebiesso—which was the name the flu went under in these parts—no tea, no aspirin or herb was likely to do any good.

But at the very least Lightman could see to it that the patient was isolated to help minimize the possibility of infecting the people around him. Why the outbreak wasn't worse on board Lightman couldn't understand. With so many thrown together, and generally in such unsanitary conditions, hundreds should have been stricken by now. He couldn't rule out the chance of that happening, however; it would be four more days before they reached their ultimate destination of Kisangani.

Although it was still dark the heat had settled in, crowding out the air. Much of the river ahead was indistinguishable with the haze that grew thick along the horizon. A cluster of thatched huts was visible on the right but there was no sign of any life.

Lightman's guide moved nimbly, fast, able to do what Lightman could not, avoid stepping on the sleeping forms of passengers who lay sprawled everywhere on deck.

Just ahead of them the lights of the closest barge were burning, emitting a ghostly red glow. As they approached it the music became louder, more emphatic, a pulsing dancebeat with a brooding Arabic melody running through it.

There were three barges altogether being pushed ahead of the steamer; those who traveled on the barges slept on deck for there were no cabins on them.

His guide, a tall man with a small gold ring dangling from his nose, with skin black enough for him to blend easily into the darkness, spoke some French, a lot of lingala, and practically no English whatsoever. Lightman really had no idea what the trouble was but he had to assume it was the flu.

They proceeded from the deck of the steamer onto the barge. There was an unceasing clamor of cocks, chickens,

pigs, and goats, all of which seemed to be stirring in anticipation of the sunrise. Meanwhile the night's revelry was
continuing as frantically as ever. The music was being amplified, Lightman saw now, by placing the speaker cones
into empty oil drums. Scores of men and women, their skin
glossy with sweat, were dancing, driving themselves as
hard as they could. At small tables gambling was going on,
cards and roulette and games of chance unfamiliar to
Lightman.

Smoke was everywhere, dense and sooty; there was
smoke from marijuana and smoke from cooking. And
there were smells—smells of brios and grubs and
smoked bats and smoked fish and maniac flour, smells of
the live animals and the stench of the dead ones. It was
overpowering.

Eventually they reached their destination. Inside a
room that had been created by the ingenious use of
canvas, cardboard and old newspaper, a woman was
stretched out on a pallet, her eyes so luminous that they
seemed to give off more light than the kerosene lamp set
over her head.

In the cramped space there was another smell, a smell
of death taking its time about finishing what it had started.

Another man, whom Lightman guessed was the woman's
husband, sat with quiet, sorrowful dignity at the foot of
her bed. Six children, ranging in age from two to
twelve, were gathered around the pallet, seeming more
curious about what was to happen than anything else.

"*Sauter, sauter*," said the man who'd brought him there.

Lightman, stooping down to inspect the woman, rum-
maged through his memory, trying to recall from his high
school French lessons what the word *sauter* might mean.

Taking the lamp and holding it closer so he could better
see, Lightman noticed that the woman was wet, not just
from perspiration; the smell of the Congo was on her, too.

After five days on this river it was an odor he'd become intimately acquainted with.

"You mean she jumped?" He made a diving motion with his hands, eliciting a smile of recognition from both the husband and the man with the ring in his nose.

It wasn't the first time he'd heard of someone attempting suicide. Reports had reached him that others had done so. Apparently it wasn't despair over having the disease that prompted people to resort to such a drastic remedy. It was the disease itself doing it, ravaging their minds in such a way that they had no idea what they were doing when they decided to take their own lives.

Hope filled the eyes of the husband, hope that Lightman could do something, find in the bag he'd carried some medicine, some cure, that would restore his wife.

Gingerly, Lightman drew the sheet away from the woman. The body he revealed—naked, wet, smooth—wasn't just thin, it was bones, it was virtually nothing at all. She was making a tremendous and mostly futile effort to cough; she hadn't the energy even to do that much. Her teeth, what of them hadn't rotted, were flecked with blood.

While Lightman continued his examination, one of the children tapped him on the shoulder. Turning, he saw that the child, a boy of about seven, was holding out for his inspection a tin can with a Nestle's chocolate wrapper pasted on it. Lightman was sickened by what he saw when he peered inside the can; it was pus, at least a couple of pints, yellowish green in color.

The small boy pointed to his mother and then to the can so that Lightman would have no doubt where the pus came from. What struck Lightman was how impassive the boy was, how his expression showed no emotion at all.

Lightman returned his attention to the woman. Having seen enough victims of the Hebiesso, a name he understood derived from an especially fearsome Voodoo god, he doubted that the woman would last another twenty-four hours. Her listless stare, shallow breathing, the puffiness in her face were all signs that the end couldn't be far off.

Still, he did what he could, providing her family with aspirin and antibiotics. It didn't matter that he could not communicate very well with them; they were delighted to have anything at all to give the dying woman. They wouldn't let Lightman go without thanking him vociferously, a show of gratitude he'd rather have done without. The truth was he'd done nothing, could do nothing, and no thanks were due him.

The same child who'd displayed to him the pus approached him again; in his small fist was clenched something he wanted Lightman to have. He pressed the object into Lightman's hand.

Opening his palm Lightman saw that his gift was a small green cross on which was impressed the image of Jonas Beck. He wondered whether they thought that this talisman would do him more good than it had them. He smiled to show how much he appreciated the gift, thrust it into his pocket, and quickly stepped out onto the deck of the barge. He heard the man with the gold ring in his nose calling out to him, but he hurried on without responding. As soon as he was close to the edge of the deck he took the cross out of his pocket and dropped it into the water below.

He was headed back to the steamer when he felt a hand grasp his arm. He looked to see an ungainly woman with so much flesh hanging off her face that it was a wonder her skull could support it all. Her skin was café au lait in color but her eyes were almost Chinese. A kerchief was wrapped around her head, a brilliantly colored smock drooped over her massive body. "Docteur," she said, her eyes drinking him in, "you must come with me."

Another patient, he thought, another poor bastard on his last legs. He didn't know how much he could stand.

But it turned out that that wasn't what the woman wanted to see him about at all. She led him by the hand to her table. A deck of well-thumbed playing cards lay on it.

Realizing what she was he said, "Sorry, but I'm not interested in having my fortune told."

Shaking her head, she said, "No, this is not why I wish to talk to you."

"Why then?"

"You are looking for another docteur, no? Docteur Martindale?"

True, Lightman had been making inquiries after Martindale and Diana ever since he and Julian had gotten on board the steamer at Kinsasha, but he hadn't expected news of his interest to have penetrated so far afield.

"Yes, I understand he's somewhere beyond Lualaba."

Lualaba, he'd been told, was full of papyrus-choked marshes. There was a train that ran from there to the east, through Zambia and down into Mozambique. Or maybe not. No one was certain. It was possible the train didn't run anymore. Nor was there any way of finding out until he actually got to Kisangani which lay 1300 miles upriver from the capital.

"I can tell you where he is gone. I am Mamissi." The way she pronounced her name it was as though she expected Lightman would identify it immediately.

"How do you know this?" Lightman had a feeling he was about to let himself in for a confidence game, that in exchange for some useless information he'd be asked to part with as much money as he had on him.

"I know this," Mamissi said almost vehemently. "I will tell you because the English woman came to me. You know her." Her eyes bore into Lightman. "This woman's name is Diana."

Lightman didn't move, couldn't move. A familiar pain gripped his chest.

"Sit," she commanded, "and I will tell you what you want to know." Then slyly she added, "But maybe not what you wish to hear."

TWO

The dream was one of the most disturbing Julian had ever had, not because of its content but because it had left him so convinced of its reality. Coming awake was like returning to hell. Nancy was gone. He was staggered to realize that she was never there to begin with. His arms held a pillow, not his wife. In the cabin was the same dull gray light that he'd learned to expect from every morning on this river.

He couldn't bear to keep his eyes open, it hurt too much, even in the grayness. Above him, on deck, he heard the sound of people stirring. Outside the cabin there was more fitful commotion. A new day. One, he imagined, which would be as wearying as the last.

Still on this damn river, he thought. He hated the Congo, hated this steamer and its tedious, plodding pace. And he hated the passengers, their body fluids, their unceasing chatter, their smell. He hated the traders who came in pirogues to barter and palm off on the passengers the detritus of Western civilization: scratched records, motheaten magazines, aspirin, condoms, cigarettes, chewing tobacco, Sony Walkmans, tape cassettes, and porno movies on videotape that found ready buyers even among those who had no equipment to play them on.

He had to trust that Brill was right and that Nancy had come this way with Martindale. But to pursue them in this fashion was like putting the nineteenth century to work trying to catch up with the twentieth.

Hearing somebody at the door he assumed it would be Lightman returning from his nocturnal rounds, tending to the feverish and dying.

But after a moment went by Julian began to have the sense that it wasn't Lightman at all. Whoever it was stood over his bed. He looked up.

He was right. It wasn't Lightman, it was a man whose unblinking eyes met his own. There must be something wrong with his eyes, Julian thought, they were not moving at all. Only then did he realize that there was something else odd about the man. He was white. There were scarcely more than half a dozen whites aboard the steamer, including himself and Lightman, and surely he would have spotted the man before now if he'd embarked in Kinsasha.

"Julian Wilks?" the man asked agreeably.

Julian managed to prop himself up in bed, trying to puzzle out why the fellow should want to invade his cabin.

"Yes. Who are you? What do you want?"

"My name is Richard Thorning and I'd like you to answer a couple of questions for me."

Before Julian could ask him why he expected him to comply he felt pressed against the base of his neck the sharp edge of a gleaming blade, something he'd failed to notice until now. It was an adze, he knew, a tool the locals used to cut wood. He didn't like to think what it could do to him.

"What is it you want to know?" he asked.

THREE

The way Mamissi described Diana was so accurate that Lightman was convinced the two had met. The old woman —old for that part of Africa although she might not be past fifty—told him that Diana had called on her at her shop in Kinsasha. She was in the company of another young woman and it sounded like she might have been the servant girl, Pilar.

"I am sure this other woman spies on her. She is not free to do as she likes."

"Did she say that?"

"Oh no," Mamissi said, "This whole time this other woman, this Spanish lady, she stays very close to her. I also see, standing outside my shop, a man. It is his job to watch her, too. This I think is true."

Mamissi's voice had a singsong quality so that even though she could speak English well enough Lightman had to listen carefully to understand everything she was saying. Leaning closer so as not to miss a single word, he was forced to endure a powerful odor of garlic and tobacco that accompanied the words from her toothless mouth.

"This man is African man but not from West Africa. He speaks with a British accent. Maybe he is from Tanzania, maybe from Kenya."

Lightman had no idea who it could be. "How long ago did you see her?"

For so many weeks now he'd had to content himself with his memories of Diana, repeated over and over in his mind like a video loop. Hearing news of her was like a tonic, renewing hope in him, hope that he wasn't sure was better abandoned.

"This is maybe two weeks, three weeks ago."

He had the feeling that time with her meant something completely different than it did to him.

"She comes to see me because I am famous everywhere in Zaire, in Brazzaville, in Ghana, in Nigeria. . . ."

It seemed she was about to go on and enumerate every country in West Africa in which she'd achieved a favorable reputation. Lightman said that he, too, was honored to meet her, causing her to break off before she went on any further. "What did she want to consult you about?"

"The future." For an instant Lightman thought that that was all the answer he'd get, but then she began to elaborate. "I could see that she was in difficulty. It was on her face. I could see that she was in danger from a man."

"What man?"

"This docteur you look for. It is a danger of the heart." Mamissi planted her hand on her pendulous breast to emphasize her point. "She loves this man for a time, then the love changes."

"I'm not sure I understand."

"She feels . . ." Mamissi's eyes narrowed and her great brow rippled as she hunted through her mind for the precise word in English. "She feels obligated to this docteur. She is bound to him."

"In what way?"

"Because she has done something terrible for him."

"What? What kind of terrible thing?"

He was on tenterhooks; at that moment he felt as though there was nothing holding him together, that this love he carried with him for Diana might kill him. He didn't wish to hear anything more from this woman, but he couldn't tear himself away from her. He needed to find out everything.

"Sometimes the penalty of the law is nothing when weighed against the penalty of the heart."

Mamissi seemed to be Kinsasha's Delphic Oracle, spouting cryptic sayings and enigmatic phrases.

"Could you tell me what exactly she did for Martindale that was so terrible?"

Mamissi looked at him long and hard. Then she said, "I cannot tell you this, I do not know."

He couldn't figure out whether she was being honest with him or not. But then, when did he ever give any credence to someone who professed to be a fortune-teller?

"She asked me to tell her whether she would be reunited with her son."

"Her son?" Then he recalled that there had been a son, given up for adoption at birth. At the time he hadn't realized it was so important for her to find him. Certainly she'd never mentioned him again.

"What did you say?"

"I told her no. I couldn't deceive her. As soon as she heard my words the blood left her face, she gasped like she couldn't breathe. She asked me, 'Mamissi, tell me, is he all right? Is he alive? Is he healthy?' She asked me, 'Mamissi, what is he called now? What is his name?'"

It was eerie because as she uttered the words it was as though Lightman were listening to Diana. All the Zairian inflections and lilt to her voice fell away, even the accent was momentarily gone; the mimickry was astounding. Frightening too.

"I said to her his name. 'He is called Thomas,' I said. I tell her he is healthy because I see that she cannot stand another shock. I must lie now, I think. The truth is not so good to her." She fastened her eyes on Lightman. "He is dead. Like so many others." She held up her hands to the gradually brightening sky, maybe to her gods. "It is the Hebiesso. It comes to take him away. But better that she thinks he lives."

"Is there anything else you told her?"

"One thing more, yes. She asked for you. She asked me,

'Is he well?' And I said yes. She asked me, 'Will I see the gentleman again?' "

She fell into a calculated, mischievous silence.

"And how did you answer her?"

He produced a twenty dollar bill and laid it on the table. A smile came first, then the answer.

Julian stared at Thorning, wishing that his brain could be made to work. But nothing would come. He was blank. Blank and numb. The unreality of the situation was what got to him. While he understood that terror was the most appropriate response he couldn't manage it. Too much Dao wine the night before maybe. He wasn't conscious enough to deal with this. "Do you think it'd be too much trouble if I had a drink?"

Many, many times in his life Julian had requested a drink without needing one. This time was an exception.

He was heartened by the withdrawal of Thorning's blade from its precarious position below his Adam's apple.

"Certainly," Thorning said, handing him the bottle of Johnny Walker Black Label.

It tasted hot and deadly going down but it was quick to take effect which was, after all, the point.

Maintaining his grip on the adze Thorning moistened his engorged eyes with drops. "Why are you on this river?" he asked. "Do you actually expect to find your wife this way?"

Julian didn't know whether he was surprised or not that Thorning had discovered his purpose. But he didn't give him an answer; something in Thorning's tone told him that none was really expected.

"Did you think that your money alone could do the trick?"

Julian stayed quiet, listening to the sound of his breath coming in rapid spurts. Sweat was pouring off him. Maybe the liquor wasn't doing the job it should have.

Thorning seemed to read his thoughts and held out the bottle for him a second time.

"Tell me, Julian, what will you do if you do see Nancy again?"

"Take her back," he said. "I'm in love with her."

"And she's in love with you, is that it?"

"Yes, that's right."

Julian felt as if he were being led somewhere, and that it was somewhere he didn't want to go. But he was helpless to do anything about it.

"And what will happen, Julian, if she doesn't want to come back to you?" His voice was soothing. It was the voice somebody would use to read a bedtime story to a child.

"But that's impossible! Of course she'll want to come back. Damn it, we were just married, we were on our honeymoon." For an instant he was so incensed that he forgot the danger he was in. Feeling the adze against his throat he was quickly reminded. He shut up.

"You might be interested to know that she's in love with Dr. Martindale. She will never go back to you. You are a drunk and a buffoon. Your money is useless to her. Dr. Martindale has far more wealth than you can imagine." He fixed his unmoving eyes on Julian and said, "Don't you understand? You're wasting your time in pursuit of her. She is lost to you forever."

Julian was shaking his head. "You shit, you're out of your mind. You don't know what you're saying. Nancy's in love with me! And fuck your Dr. Martindale."

His outburst succeeded only in causing Thorning to increase the pressure of the adze against his throat. Skin broke, a bit of blood flowed. Truth, Julian realized, must now be what Thorning said it was.

But then Thorning relaxed his hold and the adze dropped away from Julian's neck. It seemed as if he'd suddenly become bored with Julian. All his attention went into putting more drops into his eyes.

"Is that it?" Julian asked.

"Almost."

With Thorning so preoccupied Julian decided that this

might be his only opportunity to escape. He sprang up from the bed and darted toward the cabin door.

At first the searing pain in his right shoulder seemed a thing apart from himself and he had some difficulty understanding what had happened. But then he found himself spun around—he wasn't sure how—and he saw the adze, sopping wet with blood. Only then did he realize it was his blood.

His mouth opened with amazement. But he couldn't speak, couldn't get out much more than a strangled cry. It was too much, it was what he got for agreeing to go up the damn Congo. There ought to have been an easier way. Fuck Brill, fuck Lightman, fuck Martindale, fuck Nancy for that matter, fuck them all.

Thorning seemed to do a strange little dance step, swinging the adze around at the same time. Julian watched it coming, but couldn't quite move fast enough to avoid it. God, it took forever to arrive at its destination. That was what they meant when they talked about time standing still. It was the Dao wine from last night and the Johnny Walker slowing him down, dulling his reflexes.

He felt the same hot pain as before, only it was in his chest. His shirt was ripped apart, his skin sheared off, and when he looked down he could see for half a second what might have been a layer of muscle and a glimpse of something white that might have been bone. Then blood rushed in to fill the wound and that was all there was left to see. Blood everywhere, all over him, all over the floor—and still he couldn't believe it, couldn't absorb the actuality of it. The pain was taking awhile to assert itself. He still felt as though there was a way out, that the wounds could not be that deep, that everything could be put right if he could just escape the confines of the cabin.

But the trouble was that no matter where he went, no matter how close the door seemed, he couldn't quite get out or avoid the reach of the adze.

Nor could he any longer detect what it was doing to him

when it struck his body; the pain from one wound would merge so swiftly into the pain from another that he had no idea what was happening. He was filling up with pain, that was all he knew. Blood was in his eyes, a blood mist was what he saw when he tried to see Thorning.

He was doubling over, throwing up everything he'd put inside him since the previous night. The Johnny Walker Black was what he tasted most of all.

He was dying, he thought, he was dying. It was still impossible for him to conceive of it, it remained a bad dream, stirred up in his unconscious by too much local booze drunk too fast. Surely there was a way he could wake up from it.

For the first time he wished that Nancy was truly dead because otherwise he didn't think there was any chance of ever seeing her again.

Not since leaving Switzerland had Lightman felt so close to Diana. Mamissi's words had succeeded in conjuring her up more vividly than his own imagination. Yet at the same time he couldn't escape the feeling that he'd been had. He didn't doubt that Mamissi had at some point met Diana, but whether their conversation bore any resemblance to what Mamissi told him he couldn't possibly judge. She was a crafty woman, no question, adept at discerning the vulnerabilities, the pain, the suppressed yearnings of those who came to her for advice and a glimpse into their future. Diana obviously had a weakness for such people; that wasn't a surprise. What Lightman found surprising was that he seemed to have the same weakness.

He was so intoxicated by what Mamissi had said that he resented being pulled back to reality. As he proceeded on his way to his cabin, he was dimly aware of the looks he was drawing, neither friendly nor antagonistic, but filled with intense curiosity. All these people, first- and second- and third- and no-class passengers, knew who he was,

identifying him easily as a white American and a "docteur," while he had no idea who they were, scarcely able to
distinguish one from the other. It seemed to him that they
had all the advantage. Yet he was trying to help, trying to
do some good, and he knew that they knew it, too.

He was so preoccupied that he failed to notice anything
awry as he approached his cabin. There might have been a
funny smell but then there were always so many unusual and
often unpleasant smells that he didn't pay any attention to it.

The door was unlocked. He walked in. And then it hit
him just how very wrong things were. But by that time it
was too late to turn around and leave.

FOUR

What struck him right off was the blood. There was no
place that it didn't seem to be. Blood was even spattered
on the cabin's ceiling, enough of it so that it was dripping,
slowly, down to the floor. It was as if the cabin itself were
hemorrhaging.

Lightman looked for Julian. There was no sign of him
but he was under no illusion that this was his blood and
that it was impossible—or nearly so—for anyone to suffer
such an enormous loss and survive.

The stink of it caused him to retch. But nothing came
up.

Thorning, meanwhile, observed him without reacting.
He seemed to be waiting for Lightman to say something
before he would deign to speak himself.

"My God, what did you do to him?" Lightman cried out when his voice returned to him.

"Consigned him to the oblivion he was seeking his whole life long," came the reply.

Thorning was covered with blood, Julian's blood. But he seemed unconcerned.

Madness was present in those paralyzed eyes of his. Lightman realized he could expect no mercy. What had he done with the gun? He cursed himself for failing to keep it with him. But it was such an alien object, so fearsome a thing for him that it was no wonder he continued to leave it behind.

It was, he remembered, packed in his suitcase. It lay by the side of his bed, far out of reach.

"Where is he?" Lightman's voice was thin, barely audible. But Thorning heard what he said.

"Providing the crocodiles with their breakfast."

"God." It was all that Lightman could get out.

"It was a mistake," Thorning said.

"A mistake?" At first Lightman believed he was referring to what he'd just done to Julian, but then he understood that Thorning had something completely different in mind.

"A mistake for you to come this far. You should have left well enough alone. Dr. Martindale is a good man. I don't know what you have against him."

There was in his voice genuine puzzlement. Lightman knew it would be useless to attempt to persuade him otherwise.

"I would have died without him," Thorning said. "I owe my life to him. Everyone else had given me up for dead, but he never did."

It was likely that Martindale had been responsible for infecting him in the first place, but Lightman refrained from pointing that out to him, afraid of inflaming him more.

"You should have never come this far," Thorning said

again. "I thought you were an intelligent man. I gave you warning. I could have finished with you at any time. I was that close." He indicated with his fingers how close he meant. "Dr. Martindale didn't wish to see any harm come to you."

That surprised—no—shocked Lightman. Somehow he almost could believe it was true.

"You, too, owe your life to him." There was a certain pride in his voice. It was as if they were joined together in the same brotherhood of those who were forever indebted to Patrick Martindale.

"Why would he be so concerned about me?"

"Because, in spite of all that you have done against him, in spite of this terrible vendetta that you've undertaken, he admires you. It is the admiration that a man has for an enemy he can respect."

Thorning seemed dazed, caught up in one of his own movies, except that this time the movie wasn't on celluloid. "I suppose you thought you could steal Diana away from Dr. Martindale."

"I don't think what I was doing was stealing her from anybody." Lightman felt strangely calm; maybe it was numbness, though, not calm at all.

"Oh no, no, you've got it wrong. You were trying to steal her away from him, you were doing everything you could to ruin him. But it wouldn't work, you see. There was no way that it could work. What Dr. Martindale and Diana have together is so strong that no outsider can destroy it. They have a love that surpasses anything in your imagination, a love that you do not have the soul or the capacity to equal."

The man might be raving, he was clearly demented, but all the same Lightman couldn't quite discount his words as much as he would like. What did he know about her? There was the Diana he remembered and the Diana Mamissi described and the Diana Thorning was referring to. They seemed like completely different people.

"Don't forget that I watched her, I tracked her, I recorded her so that, even when she was out of Dr. Martindale's sight, nothing she did was ever lost to him."

Moisture from the drops oozed from his eyes. "He watched you with her, nothing escaped him."

Lightman knew that he had to do something. He sensed that Thorning was winding down, there was less energy in his voice. He was visibly tiring, his shoulders sagged, he leaned against the blood-spattered wall for support. He said something.

"I'm sorry, what was that?" It was important he hear every word. Miss one and he might be dead.

"I said that nothing escaped me, either."

And then Lightman understood what he really should have known all along: that this obsessed voyeur, this unhappy director of forgettable films had been in love with Diana too.

"I must . . ." Thorning said.

Lightman felt himself choking. It was approaching an end. And while the need to take action asserted itself— painfully—he couldn't get it straight in his mind just what he should do. He'd be dead by the time he opened his bag and found the gun. There was only a slightly better chance that he could reach the door. He looked frantically about the cabin for some object, a lamp, a deadweight, anything that could be used to defend himself, but nothing in view seemed right. A sense of futility engulfed him.

"You must what?"

"I must," Thorning repeated, the adze swinging gently, almost imperceptibly in his hand. He sounded oddly sorrowful, melancholy, defeated in a way. "I must finish this now. The scene must end."

Lights, camera, action, thought Lightman.

Thorning took a step forward, another step, another.

Lightman glanced toward the door, one way out. Thorning anticipated him, though, planting himself in Lightman's path. It was then that there was a sudden shift in the rhythm of the ship's paddle. The engines groaned, the steamer lurched leeward, and everything in the cabin went flying.

FIVE

Lightman found himself flat on the cabin floor, his face wet either from the blood already there or from a cut that had been opened up in his own skin. As he began to get up he saw that Thorning had been thrown against the bulkhead. He appeared a little stunned, for the moment unable to comprehend what had happened. His weapon lay midway between the two of them. Lightman grabbed hold of it.

Outside there was a tremendous commotion, voices, footsteps marking a furious tattoo along the deck.

Then the door to the cabin was flung open and a man in a camouflage uniform stood there, brandishing an automatic rifle.

Before Lightman could react to this latest intruder Thorning brushed by him and shot past the soldier, vanishing instantly from sight. The soldier shouted after him but made no attempt to set off in pursuit.

Returning his attention to Lightman he barked out a command which might have been in French. The gesture that the soldier made with his automatic, however, left no doubt that he was to leave. He betrayed no interest in the

blood that was everywhere, nor did he raise any objection
when Lightman indicated he wanted a few moments in
which to pack his things.

"*Cinq* minutes!" the soldier said, withdrawing.

Five minutes was sufficient. He took what he felt he
needed, most importantly the gun and Julian's cash. Then
he went out onto the deck.

Other passengers stood in bewilderment on deck, directing their eyes toward the banks of the river where a town
was coming into view as the steamer moved along. It was a
town of white and faded pastels which seemed to be
drowning in vegetation. Wherever one looked giant palms
and banana trees protruded from among the cluster of
houses and roofless emporia. Western technology had met
its end here; old tramps, run aground, lay rusted in the
shallow water near shore. Where the jungle parted it was
possible to make out an abandoned railroad, its turntable,
winches and cogs similarly rusted and decayed, overrun by
high grass and the omniverous tendrils of the wild plants
that grew there.

People could be spotted on the banks and rotting jetties.
Big-boned women with shiny skin, bare to the waist,
wearing linen smocks were doing their wash in the greenish water. Small children watched the approach of the
steamer with their eyes agog. What a spectacle they must
be making.

Above the nervous murmur of the crowd assembled on
deck the harsh, violent voices of the soldiers could be
heard. There was urgency in their movements but no hos-
tility.

For his part Lightman was just thankful that he was
alive. Whatever reason these soldiers had come on board
they had saved his life. He was breathing hard, like he'd
come through an amazing marathon, and his heart was taking its time to slow down.

When at last he felt sufficiently composed he turned to

one of the crewmen and asked him in something vaguely resembling French what was going on.

From what he was able to understand the ship's captain was under orders to dock at the town of Coquilhatville and that it was possible they would not be allowed to continue the journey any farther up the Congo River.

"Combien de temps restions-nous ici?" Lightman thought that sounded right.

A shrug was all he got in response.

"Pourquoi restions-nous au Coquilhatville?"

"Personne dit. Mais c'est certainement parce que d'Hebiessso."

"Le quarantine?" He wondered if it was the same word in French.

"Peut-être, monsieur." Another shrug. And then the crewman was gone.

If what this man had told him was true—or what he believed the man was telling him was what he had in fact said—then it meant that he might be stuck in this place for days, even weeks on end.

Combating swarms of mosquitoes and tsetse flies that had made a home on the banks of the river, the passengers debarked. While Lightman was aware that a great many people had been crammed on board, seeing them en masse caused him to wonder why the steamer hadn't simply sunk into the Congo from their collective weight. But nowhere he looked among them could he see Thorning. And for that he was grateful.

It wasn't long before it began to rain. It started as a fine drizzle, then graduated to a downpour. All the while the soldiers were shouting exhortations to the bedraggled procession coming off the boat. It was a bad enough that the red soil streets were turning to mud and that no one seemed to know where he was supposed to go, but the ordeal was made far worse by the sheer amount of baggage that was being borne along with the human tide. Some of the baggage was very much alive, chickens, squealing pigs, goats, cocks, all protesting the unexpected exodus as vigorously as the people to whom they belonged.

The only favorable aspect of the whole business, so far as Lightman could see, was that the entire town of Coquil-hatville was not so big that wherever they were headed could be very far away.

The passengers were divided up, half being sent to the old mission station and the other half to what might once have been an elegant, or at least a decent hotel called the Bienvenu Hotel Afrique. It was now a ghost of its former self, with walls peeling off layer by layer from the incredible humidity, and a pervasive smell of wood in the process of going rotten.

Without explanation Lightman was given a room all to himself in this run-down colonial outpost. It wasn't much of a room—a part of the floor had to be avoided because there was a gaping hole which gave a view of the room underneath—but it did afford him some privacy, which was more than most of his fellow passengers could claim for themselves. He didn't know whether this "luxury" was his because he was foreign or because he was white or because he was a "docteur."

Downstairs in the lobby, which was still adorned with fading posters proclaiming what a wonderful country Zaire was to visit, a kind of office had been established. A man with a goatee and tortoiseshell glasses, wearing a uniform, but conveying an air of authority that distinguished him from the other soldiers, sat at a table, a mountain of passports, identity papers, passenger manifests, and international health certificates spread in front of him. Another man, a subordinate, was busy scrutinizing all the documents, every so often jotting down a note on a pad of paper. From time to time he would get out a rubber stamp and ground it down, wet with purple ink, into one of the documents that had come under his scrutiny. Lightman had the feeling that if he turned over his passport to these people he would never lay eyes on it again. So far, though, no one had requested it from him.

The officer in charge glanced up at him with a touch of annoyance.

"S'il vous plait, pardonez-moi—" Lightman wasn't allowed to get any farther.

"Engleesh?"

"American."

"American." The officer frowned. Americans were not what he was expecting to have to deal with in Coquilhatville. "What is it you want?"

"I'd like to know why we're being kept here and how long we're going to have to stay."

Behind a dead potted palm there were anywhere from a dozen to twenty people crowded around, waiting for their cases to be heard. A couple of soldiers kept them at bay. No one had thought to stop Lightman. Curious.

"I cannot tell you."

The officer, no longer interested in Lightman, refocused his eyes on the papers in front of him.

"Why are we being kept here?"

"You are not being kept here." This officer didn't seem to be constrained by the truth.

"Well, we're obviously here," Lightman pointed out. "Do you mean to say that we're free to go?"

"Yes, free to go, of course," the officer implied impatiently.

"Go where?"

"To Kinsasha."

"But that's where I came from."

"Yes, this is where you came from," the officer repeated. "Tomorrow, maybe next day, steamboat goes back. You go back."

With that the officer waved Lightman away. Lightman didn't want to leave, convinced that if he didn't get some straight answers then, he was never going to get them. But he had no chance to ask any further questions. A soldier

who might have been half Lightman's age stepped up to
him and yelled something which, while neither in English
nor in French, he had no trouble understanding. He re-
treated behind the potted palm; its fronds were the same
rusty color as all the disintegrating machinery he'd seen
earlier.

He turned to his room although there was no solace to be
obtained there. He thought. The prospect of spending an
indefinite time in this benighted place made him disconso-
late. But the idea of getting on board the steamer and sail-
ing back downriver was equally as dismal. He couldn't
quite believe that he'd come all this way for nothing. Julian
was dead, uncounted millions around the world were dead,
and he was in that backwater, helpless to do anything at
all.

If Diana were with him, he thought, he could get
through it. Whatever she'd done, whatever sin, whatever
crime, against the law, against him, he would be perfectly
willing to forgive her so long as she could be made to
suddenly appear. The one thing he might never bring himself to forgive her for was the one thing he'd had to endure
the most: her absence.

The next morning he woke to find that the rain hadn't let
up. There was a leaden light in the sky that promised more
of the same. A puddle was growing on the floor—that part
of the floor that wasn't caved in—from the rain leaking
through a hole in the ceiling.

He'd made up his mind that he was going to spend the
day searching out someone in command, a man with more
authority than the goateed officer he'd tried talking to in
the lobby the day before. There was always the possibility
that there was no one with more authority than he, in
which case he was in trouble. Well, he supposed, he was
already in trouble, no matter whom he succeeded in finding.

There was something like breakfast being served, buffet style, but it was the most perfunctory food available in that part of the world: manioc, bananas, white cabbage, paw-paw, avocados, and some items which, even after days on the river, were still a mystery to him. He could barely get anything down.

No sooner had he set out from the Bienvenu Hotel Afrique than he heard someone call out to him, "Hey, Monsieur le Docteur! Américain!"

Turning, he saw that it was the man with the gold ring in his nose. He was running toward Lightman, not such an easy thing to do with so much mud everywhere.

There was an enormous smile for Lightman followed by a furious pumping of hands. Two old friends meeting after years apart was what it was like. Lightman was bemused.

With the feeling that this man might be in the habit of turning up in the future, Lightman asked him for his name.

The question seemed to take him by surprise. He looked momentarily stumped. Then a smile flashed across his face. "Call me Willy," he said.

It was probably just something that had sprung to mind, but it would do just fine.

It was strange how Willy was acting with him; he regarded Lightman with reverence.

"You miracle man," he declared. He didn't have enough English, however, to explain why.

But Lightman wondered; was it possible that the woman he'd seen on the barge the day before and given up for lost had actually pulled through? He could scarcely believe it. But then who could tell? The flu didn't follow any logic in pursuing its destructive path. Or maybe it was governed completely by logic, only the logic was altogether alien to human conception. Pandemics played by God's rules, not man's.

"You no bag?" A look of dismay clouded Willy's face.

"Bag upstairs." Lightman gestured back toward the hotel.

"You go get?"

Lightman deliberated for an instant. "Sure, I'll go get."

Lightman wanted to ask Willy if he knew where he was going. They were threading their way along a muddy path leading out of town. But of course, Willy knew where he was going. There was such a purposefulness to his stride that he'd be foolish to doubt it.

With all the rain, everything around them grew thick and lush and tall. Palms and plants Lightman didn't know the names of towered over them, making him feel as if he'd wandered into an outsized world, one constructed on a scale whose proportions had little or nothing to do with the one that humans ordinarily dwelled in. There was a pungent smell in the air of ripeness and endless rain and flowering plants.

Then all at once they confronted what appeared to be a corral made out of thatch and wood that might have been used to keep cattle or goats. But there were people inside —thousands of them. Those who lacked for tarpaulins or sheets of aluminum had to endure the rain unprotected. Everywhere Lightman looked there were fires burning: brackish smoke trailing up from piles of rubbish. Families hunkered around these fires, doing their cooking or trying to keep themselves warm against the chill of so much rain coming down.

There was a lot of crying and wailing, the cries of children. Dogs barked loudly and unceasingly. Lightman knew, without Willy saying anything to him, that the flu had arrived there and was making its rounds of the encampment.

Two bored looking soldiers stood guard at the entrance, their mission evidently to bar those inside from getting out.

"Les réfugies," said Willy. "From Upenba, many kilometers away."

Willy had what looked like a laissez-passer, signed illegibly by someone presumably in authority.

The sentries barely glanced at his papers or at Lightman's. They opened the gate and allowed them in.

The sight of Willy and the American doctor with his magical bag elicited some curious glances but nothing more. There was the same terrible blankness on the faces of the people they passed, a sense of resignation and defeat.

Small naked children with their ribs showing through and their faces drawn tight like paper against their skulls scampered at their feet, crying out in lingala. Willy kept having to shoo them away.

At one point they came on a woman who had just given birth. Her eyes were so lost in the hollows and her features so ravaged that Lightman could easily have mistaken her for a woman of eighty. Her breasts were shriveled and drooped down to her stomach. From underneath a frayed green blanket something pinkish lay in the mud. It took Lightman a few moments to realize that there was also an infant in this tableau and that it was the placenta he was seeing. But the mother was not alive. Nor was the newborn infant. The Hebiesso had killed them both.

It seemed to Lightman that everyone there needed him. Or rather they needed someone who had the cunning and power—and magic, too, perhaps—to deliver them. He felt like nothing, like a fraud. But to Willy he was a shaman, a miracle man. He didn't want to disappoint.

They entered a shed, a frail, jerry-rigged structure. A little boy lay on the pallet, a mother and her uncountable brood all around him.

"Maintenant," Willy said, *"vous commence."*

And so Lightman stepped over to the little child and did what Willy wanted him to do. He began.

* * *

Ironically, Lightman was probably the only person who was anxious to continue upriver, whatever the perils that awaited him there. But even if he could elude the squad of soldiers deployed in town—something that he didn't imagine would be hard to do—he could hardly expect to go in on his own. He had no transportation, no guide, no provisions.

On the other hand, even if he should have decided to abandon the whole enterprise and return to Kinsasha, he found that he couldn't do that, either. For all the assurances the becalmed passengers had been given that only a day or two would have to pass before they could get back on board, nothing happened. The steamer remained docked at the jetty, going nowhere.

When Lightman sought out the same goateed officer he'd spoken to the day of his arrival, despairing of ever finding someone in a position of higher authority, and asked him when the steamer would leave, he was informed that it would most certainly be tomorrow or the next day at the latest.

"But you told me that three days ago!" Lightman pointed out.

The officer peered skeptically at Lightman through his thick tortoiseshell glasses.

"It can't be helped," he replied. "Tuesday or Wednesday, no later."

But then Tuesday would come, and Wednesday, and nothing would happen.

"This is Africa," Willy explained in one of the only full-length English sentences Lightman had ever heard from him. *"En Afrique tout c'est plus tard toujours."* In Africa everything is always later.

Or never, Lightman thought to correct him.

Lethargy was setting in; it seemed that the same rot that was all around him had begun to seep into his blood. A week went by, a week of rain and mud and fever. There was no way of getting dry. Even when it would stop raining for awhile, never longer than an hour, the moisture in the air was so pervasive that it scarcely made any difference.

The mood among the several hundred people trapped in Coquilhatville was souring. At night tensions brewing during the day would spill over. Above the relentless patter and drum of the rain Lightman could hear the agitated voices, then the clatter of bottles being broken preliminary to their being turned into weapons.

From time to time when he went down to the banks of the river, he would see bodies drifting by, bloated and filled with disease. Maybe it was because of all the gas in their stomach or the action of some parasites, but occasionally they would burst apart and, while the corpses themselves would sink almost instantly, their intestines would remain floating on the surface, carried downriver on the jacinthes d'eau—the mats of hyacinth plants that were pretty to look at but hell for boats to plow their way through.

The claustrophobic atmosphere was made even worse by the absence of news from the outside world. Lightman had been told that all the radios had been confiscated and destroyed and that it had been done so no one could listen to any subversive broadcasts. All he could do was wonder and imagine what was going on beyond the perimeter of town. For everyone else—soldiers, refugees and people in transit—Coquilhatville was all the world there was.

Lightman's only salvation was the work he was doing in his newfound capacity as doctor. While under no illusion that he could do more than console the sick and offer them temporary relief, he still found a purposefulness in this enforced limbo that otherwise would have been lacking.

One day, late in a sodden afternoon about two weeks after his arrival in Coquilhatville, Willy found him in the lobby of the hotel. He was more excited than usual, his words coming as fast as shells spat out of a machine gun.

"What is it, Willy? Calm down."

"You come quick, man sick, *très malade,* white man."

"A white man is sick?"

"Yes, yes. I go get your bag." For Willy, everything powerful, everything miraculous, was in that bag of his.

"What white man?" There being so few of them from the steamer, Lightman was acquainted with them all.

Willy didn't know or else he wouldn't say. Lightman followed after him.

They arrived at last at a small thatched roof house a block down the street from the mission house. Willy entered first, saying to the patient within, "I bring help, I bring le docteur."

Lightman's eyes took a moment to adjust to the dimness within. Lying stretched out, shivering, on the mattress in the corner was Thorning.

SIX

Thorning didn't know who he was since his paralyzed eyes were shielded by black patches. He was saying something. Lightman, conscious of Willy's expectant look, leaned closer to him to catch what it was.

His voice was shaking almost as much as his body.

"Wasn't supposed to happen, not again. My eyes last time, what this?"

Lightman lay his hand on Thorning's brow. Burning up. He said nothing.

Don't look at me that way, he had half a mind to say to Willy. There's nothing I can do for this man, there's nothing I want to do.

In the back of his mind he realized that there was another virus, or another mutant of the same virus, at work. Whatever the case, immunity to one clearly did not guarantee immunity to the other. Which meant that he, too, was equally at risk.

But he couldn't think about that now. He had to concentrate on the problem at hand, which was Thorning.

Willy was frowning, unable to puzzle out why Lightman should seem so hesitant about doing something for this ailing man, especially since he was like him, a white man and a foreigner.

Let him die, Lightman thought. It was a situation he didn't believe fell even under the most compassionate interpretation of the Hippocratic Oath. Save a man who would just as soon murder him if he could? Save a man who had chopped up a friend? He wasn't a saint.

"Monsieur le Docteur!" There was a scolding tone in Willy's voice.

"Attendez-vous!" Lightman said.

He stepped back outside. If he was a man who smoked, he would have gotten out a cigarette right then.

Willy knew better than to follow him, remained inside. Thorning was raving, words tumbling out of his mouth nonstop.

"Monsieur le Docteur!" Willy called to him.

"What is it? *Qu'est ce que desirez-vous?"*

"Regard ce radio!" He appeared at the entrance holding the device in his hands as gently as if it were a child.

Lightman was elated. A radio, particularly if it was in working order, was more welcome than a steak or a cold shower at this point. At last he would be able to find out what was happening in the rest of the world.

But when he took a closer look at it his heart sank. The radio seemed to be operating on some kind of shortwave band that produced only coded transmissions and a great deal of static. Willy, who might have been anticipating music or news, was clearly disappointed.

"He must use it to communicate with Martindale," Lightman said.

"What is it?"

"*Rien*—nothing at all."

Lightman went back inside, Willy following right behind.

"Thorning, it's me, John Lightman."

All at once the man's delirious babbling ceased. Lightman removed the eyepatches. The pupils were dilated, the whites filled with broken blood vessels.

"Lightman?" He was looking at him kneeling by his side but he didn't appear to recognize him.

"Listen to me, I am going to help you."

Thorning groaned in pain. Willy began smoothing his brow with a sponge dipped in water.

"But you'll have to help me in return."

Silence. Then Thorning began raving again.

Lightman grasped hold of his arm to bring him back. "Do you understand me?" Without waiting for a reply he placed the radio in front of him. "What do you use this for?"

Thorning said something inaudible. Lightman demanded an answer.

"Transmit, receive," Thorning mumbled.

"Martindale? Do you contact Martindale with this?"

Thorning nodded. The effort needed to respond seemed to have exhausted him. He pressed his hand to his eyes, blocking out all sight of Lightman.

"Before I do anything you're going to have to relay a message to Martindale, you're going to tell him that you want transportation out of here as soon as possible—tonight, tomorrow morning at the latest. Can you do that?"

He lifted Thorning's hands away, exposing his paralyzed eyes, and repeated his question.

"Water, please, something to drink, so dry, can't swallow."

Ignoring the look of bewilderment on Willy's face,

Lightman said, "First you transmit, then you get something to drink."

He proceeded to help Thorning into a sitting position, then set the radio in his lap. With a trembling hand Thorning began slowly adjusting the dial to the designated frequency. And as he did so, the static yielded to a steady hum, like the sound of a note lingering in the air long after the music was finished.

The plane was arranged for that night. It would be a seaplane, there being no available place in or around Coquilhatville to land. All Thorning had said, when relaying his request to be evacuated, was that he'd be accompanied by a doctor. No mention of names.

Although Thorning never said why he'd delayed so long before seeking assistance, Lightman suspected that he was still holding out hope for recovery. He wouldn't want to go back to Martindale with Lightman still alive.

There was no mistaking the plane when it came. It was heralded by a faint rumble and an eerie greenish light that shortly resolved itself into twin crosses shining on either wing.

A drizzle was falling, creating a fine mist, so that the plane didn't become really visible until it was almost upon them. It came down in a graceful sweeping descent, its pontoons churning up the water and leaving behind a foamy trail.

Willy was waiting with Lightman and Thorning. Unhappiness distorted his features. Monsieur le Docteur was deserting him and the many sick people of Coquilhatville. Though their ability to understand each other had vastly improved in the two weeks they'd worked together there was no way for Lightman to convey to him just why he was going. It was especially hard because he had no idea *where* he was going. Either Thorning himself didn't know or else the information had become lost somewhere in his delirious mind.

Thorning was in a stretcher, shivering continuously no matter how many blankets Willy draped over him. His mouth was askew, his whole face in fact twisted out of shape so that it was virtually unrecognizable. His speech was garbled. There was no world he belonged to anymore except the world of fever and pain. Lightman was upset with himself for feeling any sympathy for the man. But there it was; he couldn't help it.

Between Willy and him they succeeded in getting the stretcher on board the plane.

Then Lightman turned to Willy to say good-bye. "I'm very grateful to you," he said.

Willy was puzzled. "It is we who are grateful to you, Monsieur le Docteur." He stated these words in a slow, solemn manner that made it sound like he'd been practicing them for days.

They shook hands and then Lightman stepped up and into the plane. When he looked again Willy was gone. The darkness seemed to have swallowed him up.

A few seconds after the seaplane was in the air Lightman gazed down at Coquilhatville through the rain-streaked window by his side and saw not much of anything at all: a few feeble lights, whorls of mist, and a terrible blackness where the jungle lay.

He dozed off. When he came fully awake again it was because the sun was hitting his eyes. He looked out. They were over water. Not a lake, a sea, an ocean—most likely the Indian Ocean. The water was endowed with the most amazing color, all blue and jade green. No land was in sight.

When he directed his eyes toward Thorning he detected no movement. When he checked his pulse he found none. Sometime while he'd slept Thorning had died. The copilot just then emerged from the cockpit. He read Lightman's expression without any trouble.

"Dead?"

"That's right."

"He somebody special to you?"

Lightman wondered what relevance that had. He was somebody special, but not in the way that the copilot meant.

"No," said Lightman, "I was just taking care of him. I did what I could."

That much was true.

"Then you don't mind if we...uh...dispose of the body now?" He seemed nervous. "See, with this flu, I'd rather not run the risk of the infection—" He broke off.

"You'd like to throw the body out, is that what you're saying?"

"If it's all right with you."

"I have no objection."

Relief came into the copilot's eyes. "I'll open the door here, you can just...uh...give him a push."

Obviously the copilot wasn't anxious to have any physical contact with the body.

"No problem." Lightman and the copilot lifted the stretcher up and placed it by the side of the emergency exit. The copilot began to unlatch it.

"Wait a moment, would you?"

Leaning over, Lightman placed his fingers on Thorning's unseeing eyes and gently closed them.

Cold air shot in the instant the door was opened. Lightman gave a push. Thorning dangled for half a second, then went out. Lightman watched his body recede until it plunged into the ocean.

When the copilot had gotten the door secured again he said, "You ought to strap yourself in, Doctor, we'll be making a landing in the next ten minutes."

Lightman had seen islands when he'd looked out—one especially large island he'd identified as Madagascar—but mostly all he'd seen were the emerald blue waters of the Indian Ocean.

"Where exactly are we landing?"

The copilot seemed taken aback by the question. "I

would've thought somebody had told you. We're landing at Plaisance Airport, Mauritius."

In his travels through the years Lightman had often thought of visiting Mauritius. Located about two hundred and fifty miles off the east African coastline, Mauritius was reputed to be an island of captivating beauty and seductive climate. As it wasn't on the beaten path, it remained largely undiscovered by tourists. But he doubted that it was the lush scenery that had drawn Martindale there.

"Where is Plaisance Airport in relation to the capital?" Lightman asked, wondering what he'd do once he stepped off the plane.

"It's not far," the copilot assured him. "But you won't have to worry about transportation. Dr. Martindale will have somebody waiting at the airport to pick you up."

Another surprise. "You mean to say he's expecting me?"

"Yes, of course." Again the copilot was startled by Lightman's ignorance. "I understand he's been looking forward to meeting you for a long time."

SEVEN

It was Ezra's understanding that the virus hadn't spread to the island of Mauritius. It was his understanding and his hope. At first sight the island had seemed to him like a paradise, Eden transplanted. How, he'd wondered, could a place so idyllic be cursed with the pestilence that had lain low so many millions around the world—more all the time? Here, surely, he would find his children, safe and in good health. That was all that he prayed for, all that he wanted: to find his children again, Danny, Elias, Benjamin, Mara and Cherish.

But they were already in the third week in August. Nearly a whole month had gone by since their arrival and he was no closer to getting his children back than he'd been in Jerusalem, or London for that matter.

Despair had begun to gnaw at him. How could his children have survived so long? He'd seen what the telly had said, he'd heard the statistics—eight hundred dead each day in England, two thousand dead each day in France, double that number in Punjab, in Afghanistan, in mainland China. Three million six hundred eighty thousand dead; then it was five, six, seven million dead. It depended on which source one believed. A distinguished white-haired man speaking from Washington was quoted as saying, "If the rates of death continue to spiral the way they've been going we will see the death of Western civilization before the year is out."

Nine million dead, some people had said. Fourteen million, others declared. It was just that the officials in each country had gotten together and made an agreement not to announce the true figures for fear of causing panic. An emergency meeting of the United Nations General Assembly had been called in New York to cope with the crisis. The Soviet ambassador to the UN said that he hoped the pandemic would bring the survivors closer and pave the way for a lasting peace.

Eighteen million dead, some people insisted. It had gotten so bad in Mali and Senegal and Mauritania that coffins were at a premium. A man could be buried in one but just as soon as he was in the ground the coffin was taken away and sold on the black market to another bereft family so that they could repeat the process for their deceased.

In Tibet lamas danced around the sick with drums pounding and cymbals clashing. Ezra had seen pictures of them. They did it because they were convinced that the sick were inhabited by devils and that all one accomplished by sleeping too much was allow more devils to invade.

All over the world fetuses were dying in their mother's wombs. All over the world fields of wheat and corn and rice were lying fallow, with no one to work them. Tin and copper and gold and diamond mines went untapped. All over the world people were starving. They marched from one border to another, from one country to another, hoping to find food, prepared to kill if necessary to get at it. Ezra had seen pictures of those people too. All over the world officials were appealing for families to adopt children who suddenly found themselves without parents.

So how in this chaos and decay could Ezra ever hope to lay eyes on his children again?

And where, he wondered, was Jonas Beck? They continued to put him on the air. But Ezra, having heard his broadcasts so many times, began to realize that many were repeats or else were spliced together from programs that had been aired before. Members of his church were dying just the same as everybody else, so Ezra could understand why he might not wish to expose himself too much to the public eye.

There was nothing for him to do, nowhere to go—certainly not back to the mainland where whole cities had been emptied by the flu. All he could do was stick it out in the Mauritian capital of Port Louis, living in a place called the Everyday Hotel, waiting for the day when he would hear word about his children.

The only thing demanded of him was that he look out for the English woman who occupied the room next to his. Hers was far more luxurious, redecorated and upholstered for her benefit. She favored reds, pinks, startling shades of blue. Her days were spent sunning or snorkeling among the coral reefs. At night she only rarely visited the casino La Mouche or L'Amicale where the Chinese went to do their gambling. Mostly she stayed in, painting intricate designs with enamel paints on the wall of her room. She'd asked for one wall to be left blank so that she could decorate it herself. Gradually, Ezra observed, faces were emerging from the swirl of colors. The face of a child, a young boy, was especially conspicuous.

Even after spending weeks in her company, Ezra didn't feel as though he knew her very well. It was his sense that she didn't want to be known, not to him, not to anybody. She was polite to him, casually friendly, not much more. But he didn't take offense; often she didn't seem to be there for anybody. He had observed her carefully enough, however, to realize that she had once been Martindale's mistress. There was a look they exchanged that Ezra had no trouble interpreting. Oh, he knew that look and all the past intimacy, past secrets, and dead love that was in that look. Because it was the same look that Nassa had given him. It was the look that asked what have you become? It was the look that said I am free to hate you now. It was the look that said only you have the capacity to take away this hate from me and you are forever to be cursed for failing to do so.

Ever since this calamity had begun Ezra had kept his own counsel, saying as little as possible, asking questions only when it was obvious to him that he would obtain the information he wanted no other way. He placed more faith in his eyes and ears than in other people's words anyway.

But one morning, as Diana was preparing herself for the beach, he couldn't resist asking her about the face of the boy whose face she had painted on the wall.

"My son," she said simply.

"I didn't know. He is a beautiful child."

"I don't think it's a very good likeness." Her smile held deep sadness in it.

"Why do you say that? I have seen the pictures you've done of others. You represent them accurately enough."

"But you see, I don't know what my son looks like. I can only imagine this is how he turned out to be."

Ezra was about to ask her what happened to him, but

realized that there were places with people one didn't go if he didn't know them well. Even if he did know them well. He let the matter drop.

She went back inside the bathroom. Over the sound of running water she called out to him, "Are you coming swimming with me this morning?"

"If you want me to."

"Yes, I do very much. I appreciate your company."

She'd told him many times, with a certain wonder in her voice, that he was not like the others, by which he assumed she meant the followers of Jonas Beck and all those sycophants of Martindale's—especially them.

Ezra didn't know whether she was aware that his true role was not to be her bodyguard or companion but to spy on her. And while it was to Pilar that he was supposed to report he didn't doubt for one moment whom the information was intended for. It would have to be Martindale.

He had to tell Pilar something though. If he didn't, he knew, they would replace him with someone else, someone more compliant. He liked this English woman and he wanted to make sure that no harm came to her—no more harm than had already been done. And so he told Pilar things, meaningless things, and occasionally he told them things that weren't true just to shake off Martindale's suspicions. Even so he felt dirty doing it.

When Diana came out of the bathroom she said, "I've found a car we can use for the day. Would you like to do the driving?"

Ezra said that it had been years since he'd sat behind the wheel of a car and he wasn't sure that what people said was right, that it would come back to you.

"All right then, I'll drive. Actually, I think I'd like it."

Over a one piece suit that was partly black latex and partly black mesh, a suit intended to keep the eye deceived as to what it was seeing and what it was not, she threw on a silk robe. Her hair was clasped and drawn up to expose the nape of her neck. It would be very easy to succumb to her, Ezra thought. He avoided her gaze whenever possible.

Ezra thought it was an odd feeling being in a car, a silver Porsche that she drove along the narrow roads that led out of Port Louis along the coast. Monkeys scampered for dear life out of the car's path. Other vehicles swerved sharply to avoid hitting them. Tired men, full of sweat and dust, with horsedrawn carts swore at them as they raced past.

"Don't you think it would be safer if you slowed down?" Ezra ventured.

Diana, eyes hidden behind lenses in which Ezra could only see his own face, shook her head, saying, "This is how I like it." Then she thought to add, "Anyway, I'm not sure I would mind. . . ."

"Mind what?"

"Mind it if I crashed."

If anything, she was increasing speed, her bare foot pressing harder on the gas.

"Why would you want to do that?" The idea that such great, sad beauty might be destroyed pained him.

"Because my life's a shambles. Because, Ezra, it could go on like this endlessly."

"But it will end, the pestilence will end. It always does."

"But it doesn't end for me inside." She put her hand over her heart.

"That is no reason. Whatever the hurt, it is no reason." He told her about his own children, about how they were gone and how he could not find them again. "I believe that I will find them one day. It is what keeps me going."

"He won't let you leave this island, don't you see, Ezra? You'll never find your children, I'll never find my son. They said I would, they promised I would. Jonas assured me he had. But it was all lies, all lies." Her voice rose and fell. It didn't sound quite like her anymore. "Ezra, he's mad, deranged. He wants us with him. There's no out for him but death, a horrible, hideous death, and when he dies, he will make sure that we die, too. You see, he doesn't want to be alone in dying. That is why we are here on this island."

Ezra couldn't believe what he was hearing. He wanted to point out that the island, of all places in the world, was one spared the onslaught of the disease, that until it vanished altogether from the world it was possibly the safest spot to be. He was sure that she was exaggerating, that her loathing for Martindale—he had no doubt it was Martindale she was speaking of—was what had set her off. But the passion with which she spoke was so strong that he knew better than to disagree with her. He stayed quiet.

They were taking a route through a landscape that could never seem to make up its mind what it wanted to be. It was barren volcanic rock, then it was full of bottle palms and traveler's palms and lipstick trees and rose of Venezuela and flowering reed, then it was flat, then it was mountainous. The climate, too, kept changing; at one point it was as scorching as a desert, at another it turned into a monsoon season, and then, as they once again descended onto the coastal plain, it was a warm, windless day.

There was a beach in view that hugged the shoreline as far as they could see. There were cottages and buildings off to the right that belonged to a famous resort.

Diana pulled off the road and parked. They got out and began walking toward the beach. The smell of the ocean was wonderful.

To get down to the beach they first had to climb over a bluff that had formed from lava long ago.

From the bluff they could look down and see sunbathers, thirty or more of them, lying sprawled in the golden sand, their bodies bronzed and glistening in the midday sun. Men and women, even some children. Seen from the high vantage point they looked beautiful and ripe. The women in particular caught Ezra's eyes, their bodies, mostly topless or entirely nude, were so well-toned, so elegantly fashioned, that it practically took his breath away.

Who were those people to have inherited such beauty?

Without either of them saying a word, they continued down until they were on the beach, the fine powdered sand seeping between their toes.

It was only when they were closer to the sunbathers that Ezra sensed that something wasn't quite the way it should be. There was no movement at all from them, no shifting of positions so that another portion of their flesh could bake, no change in posture whatsoever. Ezra cast a sidelong glance at Diana and saw that she, too, had noticed the same thing.

Stepping up to one leggy woman, with long blond hair streaming down her naked back, Ezra called out to her.

There was no reaction. He knelt by her side. He touched her. The skin was warm but that could well have been because of the sun on her.

Then he saw that the sand was being stained, a little at a time, by blood. Lifting her face up he saw further that the blood was oozing out of her nostrils and her mouth.

Diana inspected another woman. The same. All of them, the same. All bleeding into the sand. All dead.

If Mauritius had been free of the pestilence until then, it was no longer.

EIGHT

A car and an ambulance were waiting on the tarmac when the seaplane landed. The ambulance was not needed. Lightman was instructed to take the car, a Lincoln with a sunroof. The ride seemed to take forever. The driver said that they were going to have to travel through a good part of the island before they arrived at their destination. Lightman kept trying to get some sense as to what the landscape was like through the Lincoln's tinted windows. Mostly he had the impression of palm trees and sugarcane fields dominated by a backdrop of mountains on one side and an endless vista of sea on the other.

He was tired from the flight and would periodically drift off to sleep, only to be jolted awake whenever the driver failed to slow down sufficiently to avoid a deep rut in the road. One moment he was looking out at lush countryside, the next he was in a city, being conveyed through neighborhoods that changed dizzyingly from Chinese to Hindi to European to nothing he could distinguish one way or another. When finally the car came to a stop he saw that they were in front of a mosque, white-walled with green trim along the edges. A sign proclaimed it was the Mosque of the Martyrs, erected in 1678. Several pairs of well-worn shoes were visible on the steps leading to the entrance.

The driver directed him to a building across the street from the mosque. It too was white, its architecture echoing the mosque's. Narrow arched windows ran along the upper floors; lower down there was only a blank wall and an entrance composed of twin wooden doors. Above the doors was intricate calligraphy, letters formed so that they were designs as well as words.

Although there were signs saying that the building had served as a religious school, apparently it was one no longer. As soon as Lightman entered he was greeted by the sight of men in lab coats making their way across a mosaic floor, their faces lit up like beacons from rays of the sun filtered through a translucent dome. With scarcely any furnishings in the room save for a couple of cushioned benches their words reverberated against the stucco walls.

"Dr. Lightman?"

Lightman saw a petite woman of Indian extraction standing by his side. "This way, please."

Lightman hardly dared think that, at last, he would actually come face-to-face with Martindale. He decided not to ask but wait and see what happened. He was afraid, but no more so than he'd been before on his journey to Martindale.

They proceeded down a corridor that led past a succession of rooms he guessed once held classes in Koranic teachings. In some computers had been installed, in others there were centrifuges, electron microscopes, refrigeration units, cylinders of liquid nitrogen, and rows of test tubes, a whole arsenal of lab supplies and equipment.

They ascended a series of steps. At the top was a window from which Lightman could look out and see the ocean, more lavender than blue now with the sun going down.

Through a slightly ajar door, on his right he had a momentary glimpse of a bank of video screens emitting a cloudy bluish light. Then they were in a small, dark room with rugs everywhere, on the ceiling and walls as well as the floor. There was a low, elegantly wrought mahogany table on which was set a brass pot and two cups. A smell of mint tea reached him as he took a seat.

His guide asked him if she could hold his suitcase for him. He saw no reason not to hand it over to her for safekeeping. The one thing he might need he'd made sure to carry on him when he came: his gun.

<u>NINE</u>

The hours dragged on. Lightman waited because he hadn't anywhere else to go. He waited because he was anxious not to lose this opportunity to meet with Martindale.

It was early evening. He'd long since finished the mint

tea. The same woman who'd met him earlier brought him
dinner. She apologized for Dr. Martindale, explaining that
his obligations were detaining him. "Please," she said,
"just be patient. He should be with you soon. Is there anything I can get you to read?"

Lightman accepted some magazines, an international as-
sortment: *Quick, Paris Match, Bunte, Oggi, Time, Saturday Night, The Economist*. Martindale, he found, was
mentioned in all of them, his picture staring up at him from
the pages he flipped through. Often he was photographed
in the company of extraordinary looking women—none of
them Diana. The way the articles read Martindale was the
only person who could arrest the pandemic. Amid the
gruesome statistics cited in the pages—two hundred eighty
thousand dead in Bombay alone, seven hundred fifty
deaths a week in Lagos, two and a half million confirmed
dead in the U.S., eight million thought dead in the Soviet
Union, nearly twelve and a half million reported dead in
China—Martindale emerged as the hero, the white knight.
His staff at WHO received only passing credit; a photograph of a man or woman with an eye glued to a microscope sufficed for them. Over and over Lightman read
Martindale's confident statement: "The pandemic has already run its course, it is now in its final days. We've seen
the worst."

What Lightman failed to see mentioned was any reference to a second virus. It must exist. Thorning had been
afflicted with something to which he'd gained no immunity. It was unlikely that his was an isolated instance. People whose resistance had been lowered by the first virus
might easily succumb to the second. In fact, it was possible
that a second outbreak might prove more devastating than
the first. He was so occupied by these thoughts that it
nearly slipped his mind why he was there, what he meant
to do. But he was reminded of his purpose when he shifted
position and felt the pressure of the gun against his chest. It
was, he thought, a measure of just how far he'd come, not

just in geographical distance but in his heart, that he could contemplate the notion of going through with this.

Yet it was still an abstraction, still something to be imagined, until the door to his left opened and Patrick Martindale walked in.

Once he was actually in Martindale's presence he didn't quite know how to respond. Even the photographs hadn't quite prepared him for the reality.

For one thing he was shorter than Lightman had anticipated, five-seven, five-eight maybe, and he was more ruggedly built with a certain propensity to put on weight. He wasn't as handsome as the photos had suggested; his features were somewhat coarse, in fact. His hair was longer than when the pictures had been shot and grew in unruly curls at his neck. Gray was at his temples and peppered his hair. A beginning of a beard wreathed his lips. His eyes were amazing, a moist bluish gray flecked with green. He was wearing a white jacket, his collar was loosened. He was exceedingly tan.

"Dr. John Lightman," he said and held out his hand.

Lightman didn't know what else to do; caught off guard, he took it.

"I hope you find that I was worth coming all this way for." There was nothing the least bit sardonic in his voice. "Have you ever been to Mauritius before?"

They could have been two old acquaintances newly met the way he was talking.

Lightman said no, this was his first time on the island, a fact he was certain Martindale already knew.

"Well, you'll find it a most unusual place. Just about everyone you can think of has settled here—Chinese, Hindus, French, Dutch, the British who ruled it before independence. And the Creole population, of course. They speak a kind of localized French, a patois, if you will. It's rather like a microcosm of human society. He glanced at the table where the remains of Lightman's dinner were in

evidence. "I see that you've already eaten. I must apolo-
gize for having kept you waiting. You weren't terribly in-
convenienced, were you?"

"Having waited this long to see you I can't say that another few hours, more or less, could make much difference."

Martindale gave him a quizzical look, then smiled.
"Good," he said. "I suppose you could use an after dinner
drink—a cordial? I have some rare eighty-year-old brandy
I've been anxious to try. You'll join me, won't you?"
Without allowing Lightman a chance to reply he pressed a
switch on the wall that must have activated a hidden intercom. "Drina, would you mind bringing Dr. Lightman and
myself some of that special Napoleon we've been saving?
We'll be in the library." To Lightman he said, "Please come
with me."

He was all motion, this man, clearly someone who could
not remain long at rest.

They went in through the door that Martindale had just
emerged from. A dimly lit corridor yielded to a spacious
room lined with books, many of them with Arabic titles.
Maps of Mauritius and the world were hung on the wall.
There were, in addition, several graphs in view, each with
dramatic crests and troughs interrupted by a succession of
spikes. While Lightman was too far away to read them he
had a good idea what they represented: deaths. Deaths by
city and deaths by country, deaths predicted and deaths
recorded, deaths by the first virus and deaths by the second.

The far end of the room was dominated by a painting
Lightman guessed might be by Velásquez. If it in fact was,
it was certainly worth millions of dollars. A long-dead per-
sonage, depicted in brilliant detail by the great Spanish
painter, was staring back at him with an expression of
barely concealed disdain.

Martindale invited him to have a seat and then dropped
into a rattan chair right where the last few minutes of sun

could get to him, spilling over his face so that his skin assumed a bright orange shade.

"Nervous? You should be nervous. I'm nervous. Do you think I'm made of stone, so hard as all that? Yes, I'd expect you would. Following me all this way, of course that was what you'd think. Do you know that I have been studying you." He knitted his fingers together and leaned back. "Oh yes, studying you, observing you from afar, taking your measure. Reading up on you." He smiled. "It's true. I've read many of your papers, and do you want to know what I think of them? Well, I think they're quite excellent, quite excellent indeed."

Almost from the start Lightman picked up on how his accent would change from purely American to high-flown English, beautifully rendered Oxbridge, then back again. His eyes shifted, then all at once locked on Lightman which might have been his way of saying I've got you!

"What you said in your talk in Hong Kong about the Tanios Indians—I completely agree. It must have been the flu, not smallpox, that killed them off. And what you wrote about the English sweating sickness struck me as unusually incisive. How you intended to develop your thesis that it was anthrax, not the bubonic plague, has me curious. I don't know whether I would agree, though I would be anxious to see how you adduced your findings."

This caught Lightman completely off guard, having forgotten about the plague thesis he'd been writing in London to pass the time. For that matter he hadn't any idea what had become of the notes. Now he knew.

"We are locked in this same terrible struggle with this disease, terrible that it should have turned out this way." He looked up. "Ah," he said at seeing Drina, his diminutive Indian woman, enter with a tray on which were set two handsome snifters and the bottle of promised brandy.

Going down, the brandy tasted molten; Lightman could almost savor every one of the eighty years that had been waiting to pass before it would be consumed.

"And now you want to kill me."

Lightman didn't think he heard right. Or rather he knew he'd heard right but would rather not have believed it.

"What did you say?"

"You came here to kill me. Shoot me with your gun. Nothing escapes me. You'd be mad to think anything does. I know you backwards and forwards. It was wrong."

"What was wrong? I'm afraid I don't understand."

Lightman was growing edgier, not sure what he should do. He felt naked, exposed. How did he ever expect to take Martindale by surprise? And yet, if Martindale sensed the threat to his life, why had he allowed him to get so close without even having him frisked?

"Wrong for Richard to try to hurt you. Damn fool, Thorning. I gave clear instructions you weren't to be hurt. I put the word out. Could you catch up with me, what were you made up of, I wondered. But it wasn't my idea you should be killed. And see how it happened that you weren't. Damn fool Thorning. He never had the chance he needed to film that great movie of his. He was nothing but a high class pornographer. Years ago what he used to do was snare young lasses with fabulous sets of knockers, walk up to them right on the street and convince them that they ought to have a career in the pictures. The tarts went for it of course. For a few bob they'd throw off whatever you asked them to, buck and pitch and yaw under any bloke Thorning picked out for them. But he had talent, Thorning. I miss him in a way."

As Martindale spoke it became more and more apparent to Lightman that he was raving, that he was mad. It was just that he couldn't puzzle out the logic of the madness. It was his experience that all madness responded to certain rules. What Martindale's were he couldn't imagine. But he just stayed where he was, quiet, thinking that he couldn't possibly shoot the man. What sense would it make? How could he have ever considered doing it? This wasn't a sewer, or some back alley where he had no choice if he was to defend his life.

"We find each other," Martindale said now. He cast a baleful gaze at Lightman as if he fully expected Lightman to know what he was driving at.

"Find each other, I see."

"Don't humor me, Dr. Lightman, I don't like people humoring me, thinking I've gone around the bend. Not true. Not true."

Strange how the prospect of Lightman's judging him insane seemed to frighten him more than the possibility that he might pull out a gun and shoot him.

"What I am referring to, sir, when I speak of how we managed to find one another is that we are linked, you and I and Diana. And even poor Jonas Beck who failed to see far enough ahead. A failing in most of us, I grant you, but in him an especially grievous one. More brandy?"

He got up and, like any gracious host, poured out another shot for Lightman, who decided that he could probably use it. His head was swimming, but that was all right with him. The brandy was giving him the distance he needed from Martindale. Not all of his words were penetrating any longer.

"But we are joined, united, linked, bound. Imprisoned. One to another. We cannot escape one another. The virus is the destiny of us all, and who knows but that if you handle this right, you may achieve the fame you are searching for, funds to keep your laboratory going, even the woman you imagine as your lover, your wife, our Diana."

He was waiting, but Lightman maintained his silence, drinking faster.

"You want to find her, yes, of course, find her you shall. It is a small island, a small city. Inquire enough and who knows but that she might come to you. Dear Diana is half in love with you, but uncertain of how strong her connection is with me. She hangs on for all sorts of reasons, but the point is she hangs on. Here is what you do, sir, here is what you do. Are you listening?"

"Yes."

"Good. You find her, you take her away if you can. But first you must ascertain the truth from her. What she's held back from you so far. Ask her to tell you about George Marsh."

Lightman flinched. Martindale saw it and smiled.

"Oh, yes, she knows very well who he is. You hear what she has to say, and mind you, she'll put you off if you let her, so be firm with her. And then make your decision."

All sorts of notions shot through Lightman's mind. Maybe Martindale was truly mad and was just saying all this without thought, without reason, just to provoke him. Or perhaps he was posing another test to Lightman. It was as if he were saying you've come this far, can you go the next step?

"All right, I'll ask her." Lightman was anxious to escape; the man's presence was growing oppressive. He'd come all this way hungering for a confrontation, ready to square off, only to end up drinking eighty-year-old brandy and listening to the ramblings of someone who was scarcely in touch with reality. He felt deflated and confused.

"Of course we all may die. Beck was mistaken, thinking that he was God or God was in him. His actual thoughts on the matter were somewhat contradictory, you see. He didn't do such a bad job for a time, did he? I'll be the first to admit that I believed as much as the next fellow. He knew certain things about me that I'd never told a soul, so why shouldn't I take into account his visions? He liked to call them that, *his* visions, very proprietory about them. You would, too."

"What?"

"Believe him if, back in the old days, he'd gotten ahold of you. He'd have done a job on you, I'll tell you. I had to rely on the more immediate senses to ferret you out, sir.

Why else would I use Thorning but to be my eyes in places I couldn't conceivably get to? His eyes, you remember I'm sure, never stopped seeing. Like a Greek curse, like Oedipus reversed. One becomes blind by seeing too much, I suppose. Poor dear Thorning. Ah, but forget Thorning. What a job Beck could have done on you. You'd convert to the Church of the Redeemed without a moment's hesitation. Don't believe me, I know you don't want to believe me, but it's true. But of course poor dear Apostle Beck is all washed up. Beached whales couldn't get any more beached than he is right now. He's one of the survivors who's now saddled with the burden of living life as an ordinary human being, more's the pity. How many job openings do you think are available for ex-visionaries? 'Failed prophet wanted for intriguing situation.'" He experimented with a laugh. "No, he had it all wrong. He wasn't God, not at all. You know it I'm sure, you've understood it this whole time, sir. The virus is God."

Lightman left Martindale, shaken, if anything more nervous than when he was waiting to meet him. He wasn't certain what to do next. All this way, he kept thinking he'd come all this way. Now what?

Making his way out of the reconverted mosque he heard his name being called. Turning he saw somebody he recognized, whose white coat identified him as a doctor. Then he knew. It was Diana's doctor, the one who informed him of her purported death, Stephen Butler.

Not wanting to have anything to do with him he resumed walking, pretending not to have heard.

"No, please wait. Please, Dr. Lightman."

Butler ran up to him, out of breath. "Did you just come from seeing him?"

"Martindale?"

"Yes, did you talk to him?"

Lightman acknowledged that he had. He continued to

walk, quickening his pace. Butler hastened to keep abreast of him.

"Then you've seen for yourself that he's mad."

Somehow, almost from the beginning, Lightman had assumed him mad, but he had envisioned the madness of the twisted scientist, the diabolical genius. Yet the madness Martindale had just exhibited was more like the insanity encountered in a psychiatric unit. What it came down to was that he didn't seem dangerous. That was what got to Lightman most of all: he didn't seem dangerous. More than that, he almost emerged as a victim himself. But he said nothing like that to Butler.

"Listen to me, please, Dr. Lightman. I know you have good reason not to like me or any of us here. But you have to realize that ever since Dr. Martindale arrived in Mauritius he's been like this. He won't see me, he hardly sees anyone at all aside from a few women."

Lightman wondered if Diana were among them. "He did see me," he pointed out.

"Yes, but that's because you evoke his curiosity. He's fascinated by you. I think he believes that you're what he could have been just as he believes the reverse to be true. But I really couldn't say what's motivating him any longer. All I know is that we're essentially rudderless here. There's no one in charge. We have an excellent setup here, Dr. Lightman. We essentially airlifted most of our laboratories from Rome and brought them here. There's no reason we couldn't continue our research except that we don't have the qualified personnel. People have died or gone off."

Lightman understood what was happening. "I'm not interested." He kept walking.

"I'm not sure you understand. You've heard the death rates have skyrocketed? The mortality rates were leveling off for awhile and now they're back up there—worse than ever."

"I've been out of contact with the world for a couple of weeks. I haven't had a chance to catch up, I'm afraid."

"What we seem to be experiencing is antigenic shift. There's a desperate need to develop a new vaccine and do it quickly. We have the facilities, we have the necessary specimens to work with, and enough competent personnel. It's just that we have no one of your caliber who can orchestrate the whole thing. With you on board we could speed up the process by months."

"Certainly there are other people working on this at the WHO in Geneva and London and New York."

"Where do you think we've gotten all our specimens from? Where do you think all our personnel are from? Dr. Martindale borrowed—"

"Borrowed?"

"Well, took . . . He took whatever, whomever, he needed. And he was the first to perceive what was happening and identify how the virus had changed. Only now he's lost all interest in it. We could use you, Dr. Lightman. It wouldn't be for us. It would be for the millions of people out there that we might be able to get to with a vaccine before the virus does. I'm not going to say more. It's up to you. But if you just want to stop by and see the lab, you'd be warmly welcomed, I promise you."

TEN

Butler's proposition proved irresistible. The challenge of deriving a vaccine was too enormous to pass by. So long as he wasn't working for Martindale Lightman could justify it in his own mind. And it also presented the additional advantage of buying him time. He knew that Martindale wasn't so far gone that he would permit him to leave the island. Because he seemed to have the liberty to move about on the island as he pleased he could be excused for thinking that he was free. But he wasn't free. As soon as he tried to board a plane or a boat he was sure he'd be stopped. It was just a very capacious prison, that was all.

But he couldn't discount the opportunity he was being presented with: he'd have a chance to see how the island worked and what influence Martindale actually wielded there. And if luck held with him he might succeed in finding Diana. This time, he swore, he wouldn't let her slip away from him.

As much as he might detest Martindale and want to see him destroyed Lightman had to acknowledge that there was something to what he'd said. True, by agreeing to work for him he was running the risk of becoming his collaborator. But that didn't take away from the fact that a vaccine for this mutant viral strain was desperately needed. Better to be a collaborator than to stand by and do nothing while hundreds of thousands of people died.

Beyond that, he had a personal stake in discovering a cure. Like everyone else in the world, he was at risk from the virus. The person he saved might well turn out to be himself.

As promised, the facilities were superb, occupying two floors of the religious instruction center. It was an environment of glacial white walls, antiseptic and sparsely appointed. In its own way it was a shrine for the virus. Those who were there had no interest other than in the virus, no desire other than to understand the virus; even in their quest to defeat the virus, no weapon was more important than the virus.

The virus was present everywhere in the lab, all the more so because it could only be seen through high-powered electron microscopes or inferred from the damage done to the cultures exposed to it. The virus was there in the bloodstreams of the monkeys in the Hosfall isolators, and it was there in specimens contained in Roux bottles, French Square bottles, in test tubes and plaque bottles. It was there in the cell lines taken from animals and humans that had the look if not the smell of Lavoris. It was in the cell lines that the virus was nourished so that it could prosper and divide and divide again and again, forcing technicians to transfer it to other petri dishes where the process would repeat itself. And it was by the endless cycle of division and subdivision that the virus achieved what its human hosts could not: immortality.

In the lab there was no past nor future, no Martindale, no Diana, only the test tubes, the microscopes, the centrifuges and the cell lines. In the lab there was only the virus.

Day after day through August Lightman continued to oversee efforts to produce a vaccine. First it meant producing a virus that was a hybrid of the various strains that were sweeping through the world: a super virus. Then they would try to develop a vaccine strong enough to resist it.

It was painstaking labor. It meant candling fertilized chicken eggs, holding them up to the light so that the embryos revealed themselves, and with such clarity that it was possible to view the blood vessels. Attenuated strains of the flu would later be injected, the eggs would be placed in a warm room to be incubated. The incubation period over, a circular, spring-driven blade would be used to cut off the small ends of the eggs so that the amniotic fluid could be removed and tested for the presence of the virus.

The new virus they were creating was in part drawn from the influenza virus in circulation, and part from the porcine form of the virus similar to the A/New Jersey/76. Other strains were mixed together—an exacting and time consuming procedure—to produce brand new strains known as recombinents.

Almost as important as developing the most effective recombinent strain of virus was to make sure that it was a strain that could be used to make a plentiful supply of the vaccine.

The procedure might have been complicated, but the theory behind it was relatively straightforward: to fool the body into believing that it was being attacked by the virus so that it could generate the antigens that would give it the immunity necessary when the real thing came along.

Two teams of eight researchers and technicians were put to work on the vaccine. But as head of the project only Lightman actually knew what progress they were making. He preferred to operate like that; it was one of the conditions he insisted upon before he agreed to undertake the project.

He did whatever he could think of to throw off the spies he was certain Martindale had put on him, carrying out experiments that were deliberately designed to fail or were, in some instances, irrelevant. He mislabeled specimens and entered data into the computer that could only have the effect of confusing it. Yet at the same time he was careful to do nothing that would undermine their efforts to derive a vaccine; he just wanted to make sure that he'd know when it happened first.

After two and a half weeks, on a night shortly after the beginning of September, Lightman had ready a small batch of vaccine that he was prepared to secretly test.

Making his way down the corridor from his own offices he slipped into the primate room. Six Mauritian monkeys were housed there. Three he inoculated with pink nutrient broth, his controls. To the other three he gave the vaccine that his colleagues had been led to believe was still weeks away from creation.

In all six he injected a dosage of pleural serum, infected with both the original Joe Taylor and recombinent strains of the influenza virus. Then they were all infected. There was nothing for him to do but to wait and see what became of them.

* * *

The apartment he was given to use for as long as he worked at the laboratory was spacious and comfortable, and provided with a sumptuous view of the Indian Ocean. It had the added benefit of being situated near the lab so that Lightman didn't think twice about walking back and forth.

But on this particular night just as he was getting ready to leave, one of his technicians stepped up to him and, in a voice more in keeping with an exchange involving black market transactions, asked him if he was thinking of going back on foot.

Since Lightman hadn't considered doing otherwise he naturally wanted to know why the technician had asked.

The technician was surprised, even a bit annoyed, that Lightman was so ignorant. "Haven't you heard what's going on out there?"

"I'm sorry to say I haven't."

"People are rioting, they're going berserk. Gangs are roaming the streets, breaking windows, breaking heads. You're taking your life in your hands if you go out there without protection. Why don't you arrange to get a driver?"

Lightman couldn't believe it was that bad. And hiring a driver for six or seven blocks struck him as ludicrous. Only when he gave it some thought did it occur to him that perhaps, after all, there was a darkening mood in the city. It was just that he hadn't paid any attention to it. His mind was elsewhere.

He decided that the least he could do was take the gun out of its locked drawer in his desk. If it came to it, he supposed, he could bring himself to actually use the damn thing.

Thanking him for the warning, Lightman left, heading along a street that, if taken far enough, would lead into Pope Hennessey Street and the Creole quarter. Perhaps because of the technician's words he was more conscious of an air of menace. A fire was burning somewhere in the distance. He could smell the smoke and his eyes stung from it. Loud, clamorous, jarring sounds broke the silence in the streets about the Mosque of the Martyrs.

Those still on the streets at such a late hour had the wary, expectant look of people barely able to keep their panic at bay. Maybe there was the same look in their eyes every night, but it was only tonight that Lightman noticed it. They transmitted their fear to him, another contagion.

Like them, he began to quicken his step. The sweet smell of fish and curry wafting out of the cafe at the corner of his street failed to arrest his progress as it had on other nights. Better to get home, do without the snack.

Turning down his street the smoke was suddenly thicker. A siren wailed.

Before Lightman could quite get a handle on what was happening, a group of men broke from out of the swirl of smoke, bottles blazing in their upraised hands. They were running. Their faces were streaked with soot, sweat and blood. One toppled over, didn't move again. There was a crackle of gunfire, so many reports at once that there was no telling where the shooting was coming from. Another man fell. Blood washed all over his chest, but he was still moving, thrashing, like a praying mantis that had just been crushed but couldn't believe that there was no possibility of getting itself whole and moving again.

The men were rapidly approaching Lightman, desperate to escape the gunfire. Flames leapt up behind them, silhouetting them in its Halloweenish glow.

Lightman sprang out of the way, taking refuge in the shuttered doorway of a moneychanger's storefront. His limbs were slow to respond to his mind's commands; it was as if there was nothing he could do quickly enough.

Something struck his leg and it burned like hell. In the dark he couldn't see what it was, thought that maybe he'd been shot, felt blood right above his ankle, but thankfully, not a great deal of it.

Then there were more sirens, shrieking in an unceasing, maddening din. It was impossible to consider going the way he would have ordinarily; the violence was moving in his direction. For a few seconds longer, though, he stayed where he was, as if it were a heavy downpour he was waiting out in hope that it would abate. But it was clear his position there was untenable. He bolted.

The fire could have been in his leg, radiating out from the wound, but the pain wasn't so bad that it could cause him to slow down.

For a minute, probably less, he was caught up in the midst of the fleeing men, as much at risk as they were from the bullets. Then they were gone, enveloped once more by the smoke they'd come out of.

And Lightman found himself on his own without any idea where he was. If he could have had a glimpse of the harbor at least he would have been able to orient himself. But with the pall of smoke that hung over the streets he couldn't see more than a few feet in front of him.

It seemed that he was in a Creole district where the houses were distinguished by iron balustrades and louvered shutters, almost all of which were closed. On both sides of the street—whichever street it was—the windows were like blind eyes, so he had no way of knowing whether anyone was inside.

The gunfire and sirens began to sound like they were growing farther away, and at first that was really all that concerned him, to escape from the danger. But on the other hand, he was dead tired, anxious to be in bed, asleep, and the idea of walking around aimlessly throughout the night was hardly something he wanted to be doing. He thought that if he could at least find his way back to the lab he'd be all right. But when he tried circling back he succeeded only in becoming more lost. Signs in Chinese, with English and French equivalents, leapt out of the darkness at him. He didn't know where he was at all.

He regretted not having taken the time to acquaint himself with the city. It wouldn't have taken too long, it wasn't such a big city. But all he knew was the route to and from the lab and his apartment.

It was possible that the heat from the fire had made the night hotter than nights were ordinarily. The humidity was murder.

There was more activity in this quarter. Through open windows he would see Chinese men, some looking very old, seated around tables playing cards and dice and ob-scure games of chance. In the light from one of these win-dows he stopped to inspect his leg.

The blood had stopped. There was an ugly abrasion but nothing serious, no evidence of a bullet wound. It was more likely that a stone ricocheting off the street had hit him. It still burned, but the pain was dying off.

He encountered a pregnant woman with two toddlers and asked the way back to Jummah Mosque Street, thinking that this would be something anyone might know.

Either she couldn't understand his pronunciation or just didn't know where it was. All she did was to shake her head, her eyes suddenly wide with fear as if he'd just prop-ositioned her. She hurried on.

The next person, a man with an opium glaze in his eyes, was no more helpful. He made some mumbled response and gestured vaguely behind him. Altogether it wasn't much to go on.

So he kept on the way he had been, suspecting, how-ever, that the direction he'd chosen was sure to lead him further astray. But he knew how these things worked: if he turned around and went in the opposite direction then *that* would prove to be the wrong one. There was, unhappily, no right way. Or rather the right way was inevitably the way he'd rejected.

Within twenty minutes he was convinced he'd taken the wrong turn. Nothing appeared remotely familiar. He seemed to be somewhere close to the harbor—the smell of

brine and seawater alone could have served as his guide—
but it wasn't a part of the harbor he wanted to emerge at.

He was in a commercial district. Banks and airline offices presented themselves wherever he looked. There were
buildings that looked official as well, presiding over small
parks and wide, depopulated plazas.

A sanitation truck was making its way along the street,
which he saw now was called Rue Royalle, a broad avenue
that followed the length of the harbor. Water spurted out
from underneath the chassis; thick, coiled brushes attached
to its bumper were pushing aside the scattered refuse of the
day. Then the truck came to a halt and two men jumped
down from its cabin. As Lightman watched they gathered
up three large trash cans and emptied them into the rear of
the vehicle. Compacters, with an infernal racket, began to
go to work on the contents.

In removing the trash cans from their place on the sidewalk the sanitation men exposed what at first looked to
Lightman like a large sack or a beaten piece of luggage
somebody had discarded. But then he realized that it
wasn't a piece of luggage at all but a man—a corpse—in a
tattered jacket hiked up above his waist and mud-smeared
pants.

For an instant the sanitation men hesitated, clearly surprised by their find. But only for an instant. Then, with
their gloved hands they scooped him up and tossed him,
along with everything else, into the compacter.

Lightman couldn't believe his eyes. In some way it was
scarier than stumbling into a riot and nearly getting himself
killed. It was the casualness that these men displayed in
disposing of the body that he found especially disturbing. It
suggested that this had happened before, that there were
other bodies they'd come upon at night in carrying out their
duties. And it stood to reason that they were only following
orders from superiors. While he wasn't about to ask the
sanitation workers, he was certain that this man was a victim of the flu. Sooner or later, he suspected, there would

be too many deaths to cover them up so simply, so conveniently.

He went on. He turned a corner and then spotted a woman whose form, even from the back, was eerily familiar. She was alone and walking quickly, in a rush to get somewhere.

Lightman darted across the street, running ahead so that he could steal a glimpse of her from the front. She was so intent on her mission that she failed to see him.

Now there was no question. It was Pilar. The pursuit he'd been forced to break off in Rome was resumed. This time, though, he swore that he wasn't going to lose her.

This time he was luckier. There being so few people in the street he had little difficulty in tracking her. About ten minutes later he saw her enter a hotel, the Everyday Hotel. He went in after her.

A desk clerk looked up as Lightman entered the lobby, regarding him with skepticism.

"The bar's closed, sir," he said, diverting his attention from Pilar who was walking in the direction of the elevator.

"Visiting somebody," Lightman muttered without stopping.

"What guest are you seeing, sir?"

When he neglected to reply the clerk began after him, but by then Lightman had already stepped inside the elevator. The door slid shut in the clerk's face.

Pilar, standing next to him, didn't react to him at all until they were passing the fourth floor. Then her eyes took him in. Recognition entered her eyes. "You," she said.

She said it like an accusation.

She'd already pressed the sixth floor so he knew very well where she was getting off.

"Are you here to see Diana?" It was a guess, but not, he thought, a wild one.

The moment in which she hesitated told him what he needed to know. "No," she answered. "No Diana."

He'd forgotten how crabbed her English vocabulary was.

"Then you don't mind if I come with you?"

She shrugged and averted her eyes. She might not have understood him.

Sixth floor. The smell was new there, unlike the lobby, suggesting that there had been renovation done, new paint, new carpeting.

Rushing out of the elevator, she tried to escape him. Her dress was long and tight and didn't allow for much freedom of movement. There was no way she could outrun him.

She pounded frantically on a door. What did she think, that he was going to rape her?

The door swung partway open. In the gap he had a glimpse of Diana—he was sure it must be she. Pilar shouted out a word in Spanish, full of urgency.

Before she could get in Lightman was there, his hand on the door to keep her from shutting it.

Pilar's face turned ugly, the way she'd most likely look when she was very old. With a shriek she attacked Lightman, her astonishingly sharp nails digging into his cheeks, attempting to claw out his eyes.

Diana was shouting something he couldn't quite hear, he was too preoccupied getting the girl off him.

Just as he managed to pull her away he felt two hands clamp hard around his waist. Before he could get a notion as to what was happening he was thrown to the floor, the wind knocked out of him. The door slammed. He raised his eyes to see who his assailant was.

There was a black straddling him, looking as if he was about to throttle him. His English, when he spoke, had an African lilt to it. "What the hell are you doing, man? What do you want with Diana?"

It must be her bodyguard, he decided. He couldn't hope to answer the man until he recovered his breath.

"I'm going to kill you, you don't tell me what you're doing here."

Lightman succeeded in getting his one free hand down to where he'd hidden his gun. The bodyguard grinned.

"This what you're looking for, man?" he asked, placing the gun to Lightman's head.

ELEVEN

Pilar stood in front of Martindale, her hands clasped like a schoolgirl approaching the headmaster, and said, "I did as you asked and led the American to her."

"You did well."

"That black bastard interfered, but it's all right now." Actually, it wasn't "black bastard" that she'd said but an even more opprobrious term in Spanish that worked out to about the same thing.

"And he is with Diana now?"

She nodded.

"Thank you, Pilar." He stood up and walked around his desk. "You won't say anything about this to anyone." He pressed his hands against the softness of her buttocks and drew her in. She gasped hard, surprise registering in her eyes. And there was a question there too. He let one hand wander. She was wearing nothing underneath the skirt. There was a familiar damp smell on his hand when he took it away. "We will speak later," he said, dismissing her.

She was still standing there as if there might have been

something she'd missed. But Martindale was through with her for now. "That will be all, Pilar."

This time she understood. As she left he could see that the question he'd failed to answer was still there in her eyes.

Behind his Velásquez a panel opened into another room, a room which, whether it was in London or Rome or Port Louis, remained forever the same; it was a room where he could watch to see how his experiments were turning out. A bank of screens faced him, all controlled from one console, a streamlined operation of Thorning's devising.

She would know he'd be watching, she'd always known he was there. Whatever words of love or desire she'd breathe to Lightman would make no difference; the words would be intended for him. And if she went to Lightman, and if she gave herself to him, it would still be a lie: the man she would truly be giving herself to could be no one other than Martindale.

They were seated across from each other in her room in the Everyday Hotel; she was on the bed, the red silk robe she had on open enough to reveal a narrow stretch of skin from the base of her neck to her navel. Her hair was down, darker because it was wet. She must just have emerged from the shower. In this place people took showers all the time. Lightman was sitting in a big, embracing wicker chair, trying hard not to look at her as intently as he was doing.

They were talking animatedly, flushed with excitement. So much to catch up on. How had he gotten there? she asked, and at once he set off on his journey again, unfolding his tales of Rome and Julian and slow-moving steamers up the Congo River. He told her about Thorning, and his account of his savagery made her cringe and look away. And perhaps it was her reaction that caused him to offer an excuse for his actions. "The disease," he says, "can drive people mad. Somehow it triggers a part of the brain—a part of the self—that we usually keep buried, locked away."

But her only response to that was, "I could never imagine Richard doing anything like that."

"There are others like him too," he said. His meaning was clear to her.

"Yes," she said, "I know there are."

They shared a bottle of wine, and then another: a beaujolais first, a burgundy second. Diana began to recount her adventures, leaving out mention of Martindale as much as possible, as if he played no important part in her life, as if he no longer existed.

"My fault," she said. She had had enough wine so that she was dispensing with complete sentences. "I should have gotten out before, but at each point I would think, no, this isn't the right time, I should wait. And then it got worse, and much harder."

As she talked, and as she continued drinking, more passion came into her voice. Her eyes were burning, her hands moved through the air, her robe was falling open but she seemed not to realize it. "You've always wanted to know what hold he had over me." She couldn't get herself to pronounce his name.

Lightman was tense, his body held rigid in the chair as he braced himself for what was to come.

Diana began to tell him about the son she'd put up for adoption and how Beck had seen him in his visions and promised that she would find him again. And she'd believed him because Beck had known so much else about her, because, as she said, "he could read my depths." So she had listened to Beck, taken into account what he'd said—up to a point. She'd refused to join his church, after all, but she did oblige him by taking up with Martindale.

It was then that Lightman said, "But maybe that was because you fell in love with him, not because of anything Beck told you."

She didn't reply.

He then said, "I've met him."

"Then you're one of the few who have. Since we've arrived in Mauritius he's gone into seclusion. Hardly anyone sees him any longer. What was he like when you saw him?"

"He was raving, almost unintelligible, leaping from one thought to another, making references that I could follow only with difficulty. I don't know what I was expecting, but it wasn't that. He doesn't seem to have a grip anymore —not over his lab, not over himself. He just seems to be in a free fall."

"I'm not surprised. There are some people who say he'll never come out of it."

Lightman decided it was as good a time as any to spring on her the news that he was now working at the lab, in effect assuming the position that would otherwise have been Martindale's.

"I don't know, John," she said. "It could be dangerous to count him out. You mustn't let yourself be deceived. He may be insane but it could be an act, a performance he's putting on for our benefit. He's more cunning that you could possibly realize. He knows how to play on our vulnerabilities and cons us into thinking we're acting independently when in fact we're doing what he wants. I've seen it happen before. He works in lies, he deals in them like currency. After all, he succeeded in turning my whole life into a lie."

Tears were in her eyes. She brushed them away with her hand. "Don't pay any attention to me. I'm feeling sorry for myself, an unflattering trait in anybody."

But he was paying attention. He walked over to the bed to sit by her, to comfort her. There would be no difficult questions about George Marsh, not then.

Consolation was turning into something else. He embraced her. She seemed to collapse against him, her head dropping on his shoulder, her face suddenly lost to sight. His hands were stroking her back, up and down, up and

down, down farther to the curve of her buttocks. Stiffening, she drew herself closer to him, moving against him.
One of her legs shot out from the folds of the robe, sweeping over Lightman's back. They began to roll on the bed,
and he was on top, and then she was, and then he was
again. And the robe was gone.

She lay stretched out on the bed, magnificently naked,
needing to use her body to express herself, words no longer
capable of doing the job adequately. He was kissing her
methodically, her face, neck, ear. Oh, he knew what would
happen when he slipped his tongue into her ear. It did
something extraordinary to her. She could not bring him
close enough to her. Skin against skin, and still not close
enough. Her head was turning this way and that, eyes closing, opening, closing, then becoming wide open again,
gaping, real surprise in them at what he was doing. Too
dark to tell actually. All those sounds he was getting from
her were sounds that came from her at no other time. She
gasped as he moved into her, her hips entering a rhythm
that began to match his own.

Across the room the son she would never find seemed to
be watching them, his eyes fixed, drinking everything in
with the same implacable, yearning, sorrowful gaze of
voyeurs the world over.

TWELVE

Early the next morning there was a frantic pounding on the
door to Diana's room. Lightman stirred, struggling to remember the events of the night before. Diana, gathering on
her robe, went to answer the door.

Lightman began to scan the floor for his clothes. He was certain it had to be an emissary of Martindale's.

It was Ezra.

Looking past Diana toward the bed, but betraying no reaction, he apologized for intruding at such an hour. "I'm afraid it's an emergency. Martial law has just been declared. All foreign residents have been ordered to be ready in half an hour downstairs. I hear we are being moved to a residence on Deforges Street."

There was nothing to do but comply. Although Diana complained to Lightman that half an hour hardly left her time to pack he assured her that, at some point, she would probably be allowed to return and do a more thorough job. He pointed out that all he had on were the clothes on his back and, unless he somehow got back to his apartment, that would be his state of affairs for some time to come.

The lobby of the Everyday Hotel was packed with groggy people exchanging rumors and secondhand information over cups of tepid coffee. The only evidence that martial law had been declared was provided by an anxious looking soldier who stood by the entrance of the hotel with an automatic rifle in his hands.

At half past six a bus pulled up and an officer with epaulets on his shoulders got off.

"I deeply regret the inconvenience," he said. "But it is for your own protection."

The foreigners, grumbling and pushing their luggage ahead of them, filed out of the Everyday and onto the bus.

It wasn't just that martial law had been declared overnight; something else had changed in the city. The pandemic—known in this part of the world by its Swahili name, *Hamu Ya Mafusa*—seemed to have gotten much worse.

All along the road that took them from the hotel to their destination they could see bodies, often lying in heaps, on the sidewalks and in the gutters. Some had obviously been collected in one spot to await removal. Others appeared to have fallen right where they lay. There were far too many of them to be easily disposed of. And in the fearful humidity they were decomposing fast. What damage the heat and moisture didn't do to them the vermin did. Clouds of black flies buzzed over the bodies, blotting out all sight of them.

Among the passengers on the bus there were murmurs and an occasional muffled cry, but that was all. Nobody dared react too violently; they seemed to be taking assurance that most of the dead were unknown to them, of other races and tribes. Lightman suspected that they were clinging fast to the idea that the fate visited on these poor souls might be something that they yet could avoid, particularly if they were behind the walls of a protected compound.

Their new home turned out to be a modern apartment block, all of white stone, big and slapped together with module units. There was nothing remarkable about it at all. Yet those who were ready to take up residence inside were thankful that there were no bodies lying anywhere close by. Spared that embarrassment, they were also buoyed by the sight of the uniformed guards outside the entrance, as if their guns would be able to keep out the flu when it came.

No choice was permitted about the selection of apartments. Three young men with long lists clutched in their hands were giving out assignments to the hundreds of people who'd congregated in the glass-enclosed foyer, shouting over the din to make themselves heard.

It took nearly forty minutes before one of the men called Lightman's name.

When Lightman identified himself, the man said, "C-32," and handed a coded slip of paper to him. "Present this at the concierge's desk and he'll give you the key."

Next he called out Diana's name. As soon as she stepped forward he gestured toward Lightman and said, "You're with him. C-32."

He took no notice of the surprise that registered on her face.

It occurred to Lightman that Diana was right. Martindale was giving them what they wanted. It wasn't just the lab and the opportunity to develop a vaccine; it was Diana, too. He was making her a gift to him. She didn't say anything to him, she appeared to accept her new circumstances with equanimity, even with gratitude, delighted, she said, that they could be together. But he knew what she was thinking: They were being seduced into betraying themselves.

When Lightman reached the lab around noon he sensed that something was wrong. Not that the lab's routine had been disturbed; on the contrary, work seemed to be progressing normally. It was just a feeling he had that there was greater disorder even in the rarefied atmosphere of the facility, that overnight entropy had managed to make more headway. And it had nothing to do with what was going on outside in the strife-ridden streets; no, it was different.

Even the way the technicians and researchers were looking at him reflected a disturbing change. Their smiles had a falseness about them, an exaggerated quality that Lightman picked up on right away. It was as if, after all his time working there, he was finally seeing what was truly going on. The bonhomie, the solidarity that the people had displayed toward him until now, he understood, were all for show. All their professions of loyalty meant nothing; their allegiance was still to Martindale, no matter how sick the man might be.

Somehow he knew that, even though nothing on the surface had altered. There was a distance the people were keeping from him that, however subtle, was detectable nonetheless.

An hour after he'd walked in Butler came by. He seldom visited that part of the lab in deference to Lightman's wishes. His appearance now, he explained, was due to concern. "I wanted to make sure you were all right," he said.

"And why shouldn't I be?"

"Well, with martial law declared and the relocation, I thought that there might be some problem. I was going to suggest that if you were anxious to have your old quarters back I might be able to arrange it."

"No, I'm happy where I am."

Did he know about Diana? There was no way to be sure.

"And the work on the vaccine, how is that coming along?"

"I expect we should have it developed and ready for testing in a couple of weeks." It was a lie he'd been ready to deliver whenever anybody asked.

Butler nodded as if he found it to be satisfactory, but there was something about his expression, a way he had of narrowing his eyes that indicated he knew Lightman was not telling him the truth. "It would be to everyone's benefit if we could accelerate the process," he said.

"How do you mean? Are we supposed to grow the cultures faster? You know we can't just eliminate steps so we can get results." He hadn't meant to snap at Butler, his reaction had been too hasty.

"Just try to do your best," Butler said.

But Lightman realized that he knew, that somehow he'd found out that there was already a vaccine and that tests were being run on it.

Later, when the opportunity presented itself, Lightman checked to see whether the vaccine he'd prepared—falsely labeled as a serum containing a PR 8 influenza virus—was where he'd left it. He'd placed it in the refrigeration unit with hundreds of other tubes of serums, specimens, and test vaccines they'd been working on, thinking that it would be as well hidden in their midst as it would be if he sought to conceal it by itself.

It was still there, sealed and untouched.

He then walked down to the primate room. The woman in charge of the room that afternoon exhibited little interest at his appearance, and why should she? Researchers were coming and going all the time.

Careful not to show an excessive curiosity in cages twelve and thirteen, Lightman observed the condition of the six Mauritian monkeys he'd inoculated, the controls and the three to which he'd administered the vaccine.

Two of the three controls, the monkeys in twelve, were

in bad shape; their hair was matted to their bodies, their eyes were yellowish, and they were both shivering. Both of them sat in a corner, hugging themselves, looking like nothing so much as balls of fur from which a pair of hopeless eyes were peering out. The third control didn't evidence such distress, but it demonstrated little movement and the brightness had gone out of its eyes.

Then he stopped by the cage next to the controls. They were chattering and screeching and jumping about in their cage, none too happy to be where they were but apparently in robust health all the same. Though there was still a chance that they, too, might fall sick, that the vaccine was only delaying the onset of the flu and not protecting them from it, Lightman was hopeful. The vaccine just might be taking.

But he knew that if he didn't move soon to remove the vaccine from the premises Butler would discover its whereabouts. Maybe it was like what Diana had said: Martindale had only pretended to be mad so as to deceive him. Butler had played the shill. Having succeeded in using Lightman's knowledge and skills for their own ends, they could soon dispense with him. The only leverage he had was the vaccine. He had to get it out but not until he'd laid the groundwork and thought this whole plan through. Merely to carry the vaccine out of the lab and into the streets of Port Louis wouldn't be enough. Martindale or the people who acted in his name ruled Mauritius. His only chance was in getting himself and Diana off the island.

The sun, slipping into the Indian Ocean, briefly painted the water a lurid turquoise. With the approach of night, Lightman knew, there was certain to be more trouble in the streets, martial law or not.

Although the newspapers and the radio were making appeals for calm, there seemed little reason to hold out hope for it, not so long as the Europeans were blaming the Creoles for infecting the island, nor so long as the Creoles were blaming it on the Indians, and the Indians were blaming it on the Chinese, and the Chinese were blaming it on the Europeans who, they asserted, had brought it with them from their own devastated lands to the north.

Factored into the equation were the criminal elements and anyone tempted by the opportunity to loot abandoned shops and pilfer the dead. It was amazing and quite frightening, longtime residents of the city said, to see how quickly civil order had given way, how easy it was for the social fabric to become unglued.

If Lightman was to get what he wanted done it would take him the better part of an hour, maybe longer. Although a driver was now at his disposal he chose to do without one; he did not want Martindale to learn his destination.

He told his assistants that he was tired and leaving early, assuring them that he would spare no effort to get ahold of Martindale and rescue their experiments from destruction.

There was no bus, no taxi, no public transportation whatsoever, to be had. And no wonder, since few people cared to be out at this time. Lightman began to walk.

This time he carried a map with him so he would have a better idea where he was going than he'd had the night before. His step was hurried but not panicky. To keep his mind off the danger he thought of Diana and of the Mauritian monkeys in the primate room. He prayed for the two he'd given the vaccine to; he was becoming a believer in something.

Very nearly every shop he passed, every place of business was shut down or was scarred by broken glass and splintered wood.

From time to time he looked behind him to see whether anyone was following him. But for long stretches he had the streets all to himself.

The market, not far from the harbor, was boarded-up and rank with the stench of fruits and vegetables gone rotten in the sun.

Accelerating his pace, Lightman reached the Place des

Armes and, continuing across it, found the office he was seeking.

It was the only airline office still functioning. A line trailed out from the door. Inside a mob was assembled, everyone desperate to book passage off the island as soon as possible.

Lightman didn't want to wait. He figured that all the cash and credit he'd recovered from the cabin in the aftermath of Julian's death ought to do him some good. He pushed his way through, ignoring the protests and curses directed to him.

Getting to the counter where the reservations were being made wasn't easy. "Wait your turn, wait your turn," people kept telling him.

"Pardon me," he addressed a woman wearing a navy blue uniform of the airline. "I need to book a flight for two."

"I'm afraid you'll have to wait your—"

She got no further. Her eyes fell on the bills in his hand.

"Would you mind waiting here for a moment, sir? I'll see what I can do."

A few minutes went by during which Lightman began to think that the ruse had failed. Then the woman materialized, closing a door marked AUTHORIZED PERSONNEL ONLY behind her.

"Sorry for the delay, sir. When did you wish to leave?"

"The next available flight out."

"I see." There was a huge commotion in back of them with so many people pressing forward, hollering and gesturing frenziedly, fearful that they wouldn't have a chance to get their business done before the office shut its doors for the day. The woman ignored them. Lightman too ignored them.

"That will be for two, sir?"

"That's right."

"What destination did you have in mind?" Under normal circumstances, that might be the first question she would ask. Now it was a matter of secondary importance, even a little irrelevant. The crucial thing was to get somewhere relatively safe.

"Europe somewhere, Paris, London, the States, whatever you have that's convenient."

The woman nodded, expressing no surprise. Lightman surmised that she was accustomed to such vagueness and indifference on the part of prospective customers.

"I think that we can accommodate you. We have a flight out of Plaisance Airport at 10:40 tomorrow night."

"Don't you have anything leaving tomorrow morning?"

"I'm afraid not, sir. The best I can do is tomorrow night. You're luckier than most people." Her gaze rested again on the cash in his hands. "Believe me, I had to pull a lot of strings to get this for you."

"All right, tomorrow night will have to do."

Her smile returned. "It's Flight 408, stopping in Nairobi and concluding at Heathrow in London. Shall I reserve two first class seats for you then?"

"No economy?"

She shook her head. "First class or nothing, sir."

"First class then."

The bills disappeared from his hand. It was better than magic.

"Follow me, sir, and I'll make out the reservation forms for you to sign."

He went back with her through the AUTHORIZED PERSONNEL ONLY door. People waiting in line looked at him with a mixture of indignation and envy, wondering what it was he had that they didn't.

"It's fixed. We're leaving Wednesday night."

It was night, but not dark, not with the sky so pink from the fires burning throughout the city. Of Diana he could discern only her eyes and the profile of her face, nothing else, no matter that she was lying next to him in bed.

When he spoke it was in a whisper, almost inaudible, and he indicated that she should do the same.

She was confused, naturally. "What are you saying, John?"

He explained the best he could. "We can't be much worse off anywhere else. And no matter how bad it is back in England, we'll be far from Martindale."

"I don't think I can go back there."

"Then we'll get off in Nairobi and make connections for another city." It occurred to him that, by returning to London, he might be putting himself in as much danger as she would be. No telling how Inspector Finch would react if he should suddenly reappear on English soil. Even now.

"I don't know."

"Diana, we can't stay here. You told me yourself he'll do something drastic. And it's sure to happen soon, you know that."

Distantly, if he listened hard enough, he could hear the sound of glass shattering and the hoarse exhortations of the rioters. Even keeping the windows closed and the air conditioning running on high couldn't black them out entirely.

"Maybe," she conceded. "Maybe you're right."

Lightman was certain they could carry it off. It would mean taking precautions, and doing nothing to alert Martindale's spies as to their intentions. He'd booked the flights under another name, that was a start. What mattered now was that they continue to act normally.

"What about Patrick?" she asked. "I thought, when you came here, it was to put a stop to him."

He had thought about that long and hard and concluded that there was nothing he could do. It was not in him to shoot Martindale and it was absurd to think he could prove to the satisfaction of the authorities here or abroad that Martindale was guilty of murder, although murder, in some sense, was the least of it. What mattered was getting his hands on the vaccine he'd created and spiriting it away from the island.

"God will deal with him."

"How strange that you should say that." She turned toward him, her eyes wide and luminous.

"I can't do more than I'm doing."

As much as he wanted to, he didn't dare mention the vaccine to her. For one thing he suspected that every word he spoke in this place was being recorded. For another— and this he had a hard time admitting to himself—he didn't quite trust her.

"All right," she said, "I'll come with you—but on one condition."

"What's that?"

"That Ezra come along with us."

"Ezra?"

"I don't think I would have made it without him. He's a friend. I can't leave him behind."

It would take some doing and more of Julian's money, but it was, Lightman felt, feasible. "Agreed," he said.

A smile flashed in the semi-darkness. Then the smile became a kiss.

THIRTEEN

"Ezra Omaru?"

Ezra looked up from the table toward a man wearing a blue jacket and white slacks. White loafers too. There was an overpowering odor of men's cologne surrounding him.

"Yes, what can I do for you?"

"My name is Jack Brill. I'd like to have a word with you for a moment if I may."

Uninvited, he sat down. His eyes traveled about the tables of the bar. A certain disapproval registered in his eyes. The kind of people who went there, Creole mostly, dark-skinned mostly, were obviously not the kind he was used to associating with.

"Nice morning, isn't it?"

It was a hot, humid morning full of death, and Ezra, for one, couldn't see what was so nice about it. He mumbled a response which Brill seemed to interpret as corroboration.

Glancing at Ezra's empty glass he asked if he could buy him another drink.

"That's all right, I'll buy my own."

Brill signaled to the waiter: two more. He seemed not to have heard what Ezra said. "I understand that you were with Ken Snape's battalion in Jerusalem."

Ezra nodded.

"So you're a devotee of the Church of the Redeemed?"

Ezra decided that there was no point in lying. "No, I don't give a shit about the Church of the Redeemed."

Brill laughed. No sooner was the dark rum planted in front of him than he took half of it down in a single gulp. "Well, I'm not surprised, an intelligent man like you. Why would you have anything to do with them?" The hail-fellow-well-met expression faded from his face and he grew serious. "Then it was not out of, shall we say religious conviction that you joined the church back in London?"

"You seem to know everything, man. Keep talking why don't you?"

Brill didn't seem to be put off by his antagonistic tone.

"The way I hear it, you joined because you were hoping to get your children back." As if that were not enough he went on to say their names: Danny, Elias, Benjamin, Mara and Cherish. Got them all right and all in order, too.

Ezra hated the man, hated him for what he was about to do. And it didn't matter that he had no idea yet what that was.

"You would like to see your children again?" A rhetorical question. Ezra didn't answer. "It can be arranged."

Ezra couldn't contain himself. "They're all safe, they're alive, they're well?"

"Yes, all of them. The church looked after them."

Ezra wanted to hear nothing about the church. "Where are they? When can I see them?"

Brill held up his hand. "Hold on, just listen to me for a minute, Ezra. You can see them in due time. As soon as the weekend you'll be reunited with your wife and children. . . ."

Ezra's face darkened. "I don't want to see my wife, I don't want to see Nassa ever again."

Some surprise crossed Brill's face. So, Ezra thought, he wasn't up on everything.

But he recovered fast enough. "If that's how you want it, we'll make certain your wife stays behind."

He was going mad, he couldn't believe that this might happen, that he might actually lay eyes on his children again. Dear Lord, let it be so. "The end of this week you say? This Friday?"

"Possibly. But you must agree to help us out in return."

Ah, of course. Ezra dreaded what would come next. His heart was racing. All he could think about were his children, his children. He would do whatever the son of a bitch asked for if there was only a chance to be back with his children.

"You are a friend of Diana Cleary's."

It was not a question.

"I was assigned to watch over her by Ken Snape."

"But in the last few weeks you have become quite friendly, as I understand it."

"We've talked, we get along." Ezra was reluctant to volunteer any information, having only a vague sense as to what Brill might already have learned.

Brill was smiling his smile. "You've met John Lightman."

"Yes, briefly."

Brill leaned back, nursing what remained in his glass of dark rum. "We have reason to believe—"

"'We?' Who do you mean when you say 'we?'"

"It is not so important."

"The church? Do you speak for the church, man?"

"I speak for who I speak for. I speak for the people who can reunite you with your children. Isn't that enough?"

Ezra said nothing, descending into a sullen, anxious silence.

"Let me continue. We believe that Diana and Dr. Lightman are planning on leaving Mauritius sometime soon. We would like you to tell us when. We would also like you to guarantee their presence where we direct you to bring them."

"What will happen to them?"

Brill looked irritated. "I don't think that that's anything you should have to concern yourself with, Ezra. You just do as we ask and by Saturday at the latest, you'll see your children again."

"If I refuse?"

"If you refuse, Ezra, it would be a terrible mistake." Brill raised the glass to his lips though there was nothing remaining in it to drink. Then he said, "You will never see your children again. I could tell you that your life might be at risk but, frankly, why would I do that? You'll be perfectly safe so long as you remain healthy. Nothing will happen to you." His smile was fixed on his lips and wouldn't go away. "But to be honest with you, Ezra, I wouldn't want to be in your shoes if you don't go along with us. Because you'll have to spend the rest of your life with the knowledge that you sent your children to their graves—"

Ezra sprang out of his chair and nearly knocked the table over in his attempt to get at Brill, but Brill, without much trouble, avoided his blow. His voice hardened. "Sit down and listen to me, Ezra, and don't make a scene. Your children's lives depend on what you do."

"You wouldn't kill them?" Ezra glared at Brill, saw in his eyes such indifference that he knew he had lost. "So you would," he said quietly, "you would do that."

"I wouldn't like to give the order, Ezra, I wouldn't want to see anything happen to your loved ones. It doesn't have to." The smile was terrifying and relentless. He was waving to the waiter. More rum. It was as though he considered this some sort of celebration. He again looked at Ezra. "So what'll it be? Remember, it's your choice."

FOURTEEN

Whether he was alive or dead, on videotape Jonas Beck still lived. In fact, he'd never been more alive than when the camera was on him. Truly, he gave every appearance of being one whom God had blessed.

That was the way Martindale preferred him. Imprisoned forever on tape. In his enfeebled condition he would hardly dare show himself in person. Martindale preferred being able to turn him on and off at will.

But now he was on, his voice booming, his eyes intense and piercing, his limbs mobilized by passion. Martindale never tired of hearing his message of destruction, his prophesy of doom. Curiously, it lessened his own fear.

He barely heard the intercom buzz. "What is it?" he snapped.

"Miss Colville is here to see you," Drina said. "She's insistent, she says it's a matter of the utmost urgency."

"Tell her that I'm in conference, tell her anything you'd like, but send her away."

"There are those who say that God is a merciful God. There are those who say that when an innocent child dies it is because God is working in

mysterious ways—ways that we poor mortals cannot comprehend. But I say to you that there are no
innocent children! There are no innocents at all!"

"I'm afraid, Doctor, that she won't leave unless you see
her."

Martindale capitulated. "All right then, send her in."

The screen was full of faces, faces rapt in concentration.
Faces of men and women and children, blacks and whites
and Asiatics, all dressed in their Sunday best. What woman
among them would think of wearing a blouse with a low
neckline or a dress with a slit up its seam? Not one of
them. What man would so much as contemplate sporting
an earring or decorating a half bared chest with a gold
chain? Not one of them. All solid, caring folks, all wanting
something, someone, to believe in.

> "Listen, my friends, to the Word of God, as it
> is revealed in the Book of Joshua. Now Joshua was
> commanded by God to conquer the land of Canaan
> for his people. Now how did he do this? Did he
> negotiate? Oh no, my friends, he did not negotiate.
> The powers arrayed against him would not negoti-
> ate. Now did he put to the sword only the soldiers
> who came out to fight against him? Oh no, my
> friends, he took the counsel of the Lord and slew all
> those who were of the blood of his enemies, permit-
> ting not one of them to survive. And why did he do
> this, why would God want this?"

She was wearing a print dress, slung low over her
shoulders and dropping to her ankles. It was what the
Creole women wore. She'd gone native, he thought.

When she advanced across the room, keeping her eyes
locked on his, her step was tentative, like it was ice and not
a parquet floor that she was treading on. She seemed not to
notice Jonas Beck on the screen behind her.

"Listen, my friends, to the Word of the Lord:
'Now Joshua captured Makkedah on that day, and
struck it and its king with the edge of the sword;
he utterly destroyed it and every person who was
in it. He left no survivors.'"

She no longer looked so beautiful to him. She was drained
and tired, her eyes peered out at him from the dark hollows of
her face. Too many nights without sleep. Too many nights in
desperate longing. For him? For Julian? For some man
glimpsed in the street? He did not know. Nor care.

"Why?"

"Why what? You'll have to speak louder."

"Why haven't you wanted to see me?"

Any moment she would cry. Her whole body was taut,
ready to convulse and fall apart.

"I have been busy, Nancy, I have been terribly busy."

"I called you. You never took my calls."

He wanted to repeat what he'd just said. He had been
busy, terribly busy, not a second to spare. He could think
of nothing else to say.

"I'm late," she said.

Reflexively he glanced at his watch. Late? Late for what?

"I'm trying to tell you I'm pregnant." She paused, waiting. She could have waited forever. "With your child."

"Did you hear what I just read to you? 'He left
no survivors.' Not even an infant was spared. Listen. When Joshua waged war against the people of
Libnah, what happened? 'He left no survivors.'
And when he waged war against Lachish, what
happened? 'He destroyed every person who was in
it.' No exceptions, mind you. No pity for the
women or the children. In Hebron, what happened?
'He utterly destroyed everyone who was in it.' In
Debir, what happened? 'He utterly destroyed everyone who was in it.' In all the hill country and in the

desert of the Negev, what happened? 'He left no survivors.' And, again when he went to war against the people of Hazor, what happened? 'There was no one left who breathed.'"

"Are you certain?"

"That it's yours? Yes."

"That you're even pregnant was what I meant. Two months, it's not long. With the severity of your illness there's every possibility that your menstrual cycle was thrown off kilter."

"I know," she said determinedly.

It might be that she was pregnant, he decided, thinking that perhaps her breasts were fuller now against the loose fabric than he remembered.

"And you have ruled out Julian as the father?"

"Julian," she said, her eyes closing for a second. "Julian was drunk the whole time I was with him. It could not be his."

"I see."

"And that is how Joshua won the land for his people. That is how God expects the whole world to be won for Him now. As His servants, you must be prepared to make the choice. Those who join us, join the Church of the Redeemed, will need to fear nothing. But those of you who resist us, who go your separate ways, those of you who fail to heed the message of Joshua can expect, like the Canaanites, to be utterly destroyed. Not just you but your wives and children, all your loved ones. Because this is a war, make no mistake about it, friends! And in this war there are only two sides. Those who hold with God and those who are against Him. In this war there are no innocents! Please, before it is too late, renounce your wickedness, come to us and let us embrace you—and live!"

The tape fluttered, the screen went blank, and all that was left of that resonant, uplifting voice was an irritating electronic whine. Martindale killed it.

Nancy continued to stare at him, still waiting for him to provide a solution. It occurred to him that it no longer mattered, that he could say anything, give her whatever hope she wanted. And why not? Since it was in his power to grant the illusion, if not the actuality of happiness, why then he would do so.

He stood up and embraced her. Her skin felt hot against him. She was kissing him everywhere in gratitude for this display of affection.

"Tomorrow night we will celebrate this wonderful event."

His voice didn't sound like his own, it might have been dubbed. He couldn't understand why she didn't pick up the falseness in it. But of course, he knew why; it was what she was so desperate to hear him say.

"Tomorrow night?"

"Tonight I'm bone tired."

"Oh yes, I understand. Tell me everything will be all right."

Nothing else touched her. Riots, plague, the death of her drunken husband. Only whatever love she could get from him.

"Everything will be just fine. Now you must go, Nancy. I have more work to do."

More kisses on his neck, his cheeks.

"And Nancy."

"Yes?" She turned, halfway to the door.

"Take good care of yourself. Don't drink any alcohol. You have two lives to look out for, after all."

"You don't have to worry, Patrick, I shall let nothing happen to our child."

Her words made him wince. But she was too intoxicated by her hormones and emotions to notice.

After she left he went into the bathroom to inspect himself. It was worse. Hourly it was getting worse. There was no longer any sense in waiting.

He proceeded to a lab one level down to which only he had access. It was a small lab, far less impressive than those elsewhere in the building. But then he didn't do much research of his own here. All he did was build on what others had done, gathering the fruits of their labor until he had everything he required.

It was here, in plates of agar solution and in harvests of cells, centrifuged into pellets, fixed in glutaraldehyde, postfixed in osmium tetroxide, dehydrated, and embedded in Epon-Araldite. It was here, in plaque bottles, each brimming with juices of viral essences and combined with a toxin to accelerate its action. One more element needed to be added. He got on with it.

Plunging a syringe into his arm, he drew out his blood until it rose to the top of the cylinder. It was infected blood, populated by organisms that were eating him alive.

Hours later, when he'd finished separating the various components of the blood, distilling the virus from it, and then mixing it in with the solution he'd already prepared, he picked up the phone and dialed the number that would connect him with Pilar.

"I knew it would be you," she said.

"It's time," he told her and hung up.

FIFTEEN

There was one place left in Port Louis where foreigners and locals of whatever nationality (so long as they were well-heeled) could mingle without fear of violence. That was in the newly opened casino called La Mouche, situated close to the harbor.

The casino was run by a wizened Chinese gentleman with shrewd eyes and immense wealth who'd made—and lost—several fortunes operating gaming establishments on the island. His name was Ah Wong Su and he never failed to be present from the hour his casino opened, punctually at eight, until it closed, which sometimes it did not.

In the last few days, as the virus and the rioting took an ever greater toll, business flourished in the casino as never before. People drank more, gambled more, lost more. Desperation fueled their gaiety. Each night there was a feeling among the patrons that it could not fail to be their last, that in the morning the sun would come up and shine only on hundreds of thousands of corpses.

So that his patrons could more easily forget about the calamity at their doorstep Ah Wong had seen to it that the walls of La Mouche, inside and out, were splashed with vivid colors, shocking pinks and tropical greens and brothel reds. Mirrors were everywhere, on the walls and ceilings. On even the quietest nights, with the gamblers and the tables reflected into infinity, the casino still conveyed the impression of frantic activity. Music drifted from room to room, never ceasing. While Ah Wong personally favored the music and rhythms peculiar to the Mauritius called the sega, he appreciated the international bent of his customers and kept up a constant bombardment of rock and danceable reggae through the night.

No one entering La Mouche could ignore the young women who paraded back and forth between the rooms, sometimes stopping at the gaming tables where certain patrons welcomed their presence and the promise of their bodies. Nor was it easy to overlook the elegant young men who could go anywhere in the world without a cent to their name and do just fine for themselves. Ah Wong did not encourage prostitution on the premises of his establishment; on the other hand, he was of the opinion that human nature being what it was, accommodations could always be made.

That night, Jack Brill was raking it in. Never could he remember having better luck in his life. Blackjack, baccarat, roulette. His pockets were crammed full of chips and cash, dollars, pounds, francs, and Mauritian rupees. There was no room to put it all.

His entire concentration trained on the rotation of the roulette wheel, the dance of the tiny silver ball along its edge, he gave no thought to Omaru or Cleary or Lightman. He'd executed his instructions. Tonight was his night off. Tonight he was allowing himself the luxury of imagining that, having now acquired such a fortune, he could do something with it. It was a delusion he was happy to maintain, one fostered by an abundance of unblended scotch that held his mind in thrall. Tomorrow he would find that there was nothing more to spend his money on than there was today. At best he could return and gamble it away.

In another room, reached by a set of stairs and a succession of mirrored hallways where couples pawed one another on cushioned banquettes and whispered endearments that they would want to take back the following day, Nancy Colville was standing alone, drinking. She was one of five customers clustered by a small bar, but they knew better than to disturb her. She made it obvious she didn't want to talk to anyone. She was incensed. As she drank more, her fury mounted. It didn't matter that she knew, for the sake of the fetus, she should not be drinking. Martindale had promised her he would see her and that they would celebrate, but the whole day had passed and there'd not been a word from him. Her calls were never taken. Drina shut her out of the office and warned her that the security guards would haul her off if she returned.

She couldn't believe that Martindale would mistreat her so. For the first time in a long while she wanted Julian back. She could almost remember how it was when they met; she could almost bring back the memory of their courtship. But still, it was difficult regaining hold of their faded passion. Yet Julian did love her; she was sure of that much. And Patrick did not; she was sure of that, too. She'd traded drunken certainty for what? For abuse and deception.

If only there were a way home. But there was none. She was stuck there, trapped, doubly trapped with the baby growing inside her. She thought she might hate the baby.

She ordered another drink. It was big and stuffed with slices of tropical fruit and tasted like it hardly had any alcohol in it at all, though it packed quite a wallop. How many of them, she wondered, had she had? It was so easy in life to lose count. Of everything.

It resembled a cartridge for a fountain pen and the mechanism to fire it was simple; so long as the distance for the pellet to travel was under six feet accuracy was practically guaranteed.

As a servant girl accustomed to being ignored and overlooked, Pilar had every reason to believe that she could move among the crowd of patrons at La Mouche without arousing anyone's suspicions, even after she'd done what Dr. Martindale wished her to.

He'd said that the victims wouldn't feel much of anything on impact, a prickling sensation, a sudden itch easily mistaken for the bite of a mosquito.

What he'd purposely neglected to tell her was what would happen to the victims.

Wearing no makeup, outfitted in a simple black cocktail dress that Diana had designed and which Dr. Martindale had selected for her, Pilar entered La Mouche. She took in the scene, absorbing the glittering spectacle, her sharp eyes searching out for those people Dr. Martindale had chosen to receive the gift hidden in her handbag.

Diana knew better than to reflect on what was happening. If she allowed herself to she'd falter, decide not to go through with it. She had to keep reminding herself that she was stronger than she realized. Hadn't she run her own business? Hadn't she fought the virus and won? Surely she could break free of Patrick. This time somebody was sharing the risk with her. She must not think about what would happen should John ever discover the truth. He loved her now, she was positive of that. But once he knew, then she could expect nothing.

Ezra's voice snapped her back to the business at hand. "We must be on our way, Miss Cleary, there's no time left."

Quarter to eight. She had agreed to pick up Lightman at the lab by quarter after. From there they would head to the airport. Though nothing had gone wrong until now she didn't believe that they'd actually make it to Plaisance. Or even if they somehow managed to get that far they would never be permitted to board the plane.

Giving one last look to all that she was leaving behind, she handed the heavier of her two suitcases to Ezra and they set off.

The Porsche was parked around to the side of the apartment complex in an inconspicuous spot.

Ezra reached it first, unlocked the door on the passenger side and held it open for her.

"Wouldn't you prefer it if I drive?" Diana asked, remembering their previous excursion out of the city.

"No, it's only a short distance, I don't mind."

It wasn't so short as all that. There were roadblocks. Often the way was impeded by junked cars, their windows blown out, their chassis scorched with fire. A smell of burning flesh and incendiary devices was in the air.

"I wish you were coming with us at least as far as Nairobi," Diana said. "I'm sure if you change your mind John can get a ticket for you."

Ezra stared straight ahead at the road, shaking his head.

"I will stay on here for awhile," he said slowly.

"You'll let me know how you're getting along if I give you an address to write to?"

"Yes, of course." He offered her a half smile.

She looked out. The mosque ahead of them she was certain must be the Mosque of the Martyrs. They turned a corner and headed down a darkened street which, as it drew closer to the harbor, turned pink and gold from myriad fluorescent lights. That would have to be the casino, she thought, La Mouche.

To Ezra she said, "Are you sure we're going in the right direction?"

"Yes, of course I am. We have had to take a detour because of the roadblocks."

Still, Diana felt that they should be closer to the lab than they were. Casting a sidelong glance at Ezra she couldn't help but observe how anxious he was. "Are you certain you're all right, Ezra?"

"Oh yes, Miss Cleary, I've never been better. We are safe now."

SIXTEEN

It wasn't uncommon for Lightman to turn up at the lab at odd hours. Often he'd wake up in the middle of the night, inspired by an idea that might lead to a solution of a problem he'd long been wrestling with, and he'd go back to work rather than wait in suspense until morning.

Only with the riots security was a good deal tighter. The scrutinizing stares he elicited from the guards at the door only fueled his paranoia although he had a feeling that their interest in him wasn't personal. Lately everybody was a suspect, a potential saboteur. It was for that reason that he'd thought it better to leave his gun in his desk instead of carrying it with him despite the danger.

Although he had every right to be in the lab he kept expecting a security officer to accost him and grill him. But the only people he saw were two technicians completing some hemagglutinination tests. They nodded curtly, barely bidding him hello.

He appreciated their lack of curiosity. Opening the door to the refrigeration unit he scanned the specimen bottles and test tubes, afraid that the vaccine wouldn't be there. But it was in the spot he had left it. He dropped it into his pocket. The technicians were out of sight; they wouldn't have been able to see it.

Five past eight. The only thing that remained to do was pay a call on the experimental monkeys to see how they were faring. If the vaccinated three had come down with the flu then he'd have to accept the fact that this had all been for nothing. He would go ahead with the plan and leave the island with Diana, but there was no escaping the failure that it would mean.

As anxious as he was to see what had happened to the animals he was also frightened. More frightened than the possibility of being found out. Too much was riding on this.

Finally it was the press of time that forced him to leave his desk and make his way to the primate room. He steeled himself for the worst.

The door to the primate room was locked, but that was routine. In any case, he had a key.

His entrance for some reason caused a fearsome outburst from the animals. The sudden light must have disturbed their slumber and caused considerable annoyance, he suspected.

Stepping over to cage twelve he saw the final act in the drama that had begun for the animals when he'd inoculated them with the virus. The two controls he'd seen the previous day were gone. A note taped over the cage indicated that they had been transferred to pathology for a postmortem. The third was listless, all wet and shivering; it threw

Lightman a look he interpreted as accusatory. And well he should be accused; it was he who was responsible for its plight.

Then to cage thirteen.

All three of the monkeys were alive. One didn't appear to be as responsive as its mates. It was possible that it was suffering from a milder form of the virus or equally possible that it was experiencing a reaction to the vaccine alone. But the outlook for them was obviously brighter than for the controls. Maybe the vaccine wasn't a hundred percent effective—few vaccines were—but it was a damn sight better than nothing at all. And nothing at all was what they had at the moment.

So, he thought, it had been worth it. Because it seemed to him that his greatest challenge had been met, he didn't give too much thought to what came next: getting the virus safely out of the country.

As he went toward the door it was swept open. Lightman expected to see another researcher, or perhaps the portly Chinese man who fed the animals, but it was neither. The man who faced him now was Patrick Martindale.

SEVENTEEN

More and more people were crowding into the casino all the time. Guards, dressed in the comic opera style that Ah Wong insisted upon, were posted at the door. Their hulking size for the most part served as deterrent enough although they carried small arms as a precaution.

Anyone who wanted to could get into La Mouche; it was getting out that was a trick. The guards, politely but firmly, prevented people from leaving, explaining that conditions were too dangerous on the streets and that Ah Wong didn't want to see his patrons coming to harm.

Yet because it wasn't even nine o'clock there was scarcely anyone to be found who had any desire to leave. Things were just getting started, after all; many hours more would have to pass before these people's urge for gambling and intoxication had been sated.

Excitement and sexual electricity were almost palpable in the ostentatiously decorated rooms. The gamblers, charged up by the possibility of cheating fate one more time, clustered about the tables, feverishly willing the ball to drop into the right slot, the die to show the desired face, the next card to be an ace. The women, all jewels and exposed flesh, looked even more rapturous than the men who were ready to part with their entire fortunes in one fell swoop.

The music changed from room to room, but so ingenious were the acoustics that there was never any overlapping or collision of rhythms. In the front they were playing something tinged with an Arab inflection that at the same time sounded like a Chicago blues number, filled with horn flourishes and choked guitar riffs. Where the blackjack and poker tables were there was juju booming out; a room further in and it was ska; in the room adjacent to that one soca from Trinidad; beyond those there was salsa and samba and calypso and high life and tropicalia out of Brazil which segued into a propulsive jazz piece driven home by a fiery tenor. And, in every room, repeated endlessly, was the latest hit from the Blue Angel Boys. It was the kind of music that inflamed gamblers, who cherished both suspense and resolution.

"Trent-et-un, monsieurs et mesdames," the croupier announced, raking in the lost chips.

Jack Brill stood by, an indifferent expression on his face. That particular loss appeared not to faze him, not with so many chips still piled up in front of him.

He placed another sizable bet, putting his chips on several numbers in no particular pattern that Pilar could see. Then, almost as an afterthought, he placed several additional chips on red.

"Pas de parier, s'il vous plaît. No more bets, please."

The wheel began to spin. Pilar slipped up behind Brill. It didn't seem strange to her at all that she should feel nothing for this man she'd taken into her bed more times than she could remember. He'd been like other men, no better, no worse. Spectators pressed in around her, intent on observing which number would come up. No one was more interested than Jack Brill.

Unobserved, Pilar took the cartridge-like device from her purse and aimed it at the fleshy part of Brill's neck, directly above his collar.

It made no sound at all, or if it did, she couldn't hear it with the crowd. Brill's hand slapped the back of his neck. That was all. He never once looked around. Pilar, burying the device in her purse, stepped back, out of his line of sight.

"Double zero." The croupier's announcement produced an audible groan among those clustered around the table.

Then Jack turned and began to push his way out of the crowd. "Excuse me, please, pardon me, I've got to get through," he was saying.

He was tottering, his face had gone white. He gasped and clutched his stomach. There was a sound of something cracking inside of his head. Then blood shot out of his nostrils. By opening his mouth he disgorged only more blood. People were screaming, trying to get out of his path. Beautiful women shrieked at the sight of his blood all over their Georges Armani and Saint Laurent dresses. Thousands of dollars of haut couture ruined.

Brill collapsed, his body overcome with spasms. Pilar had never expected anything quite that dramatic, quite that instantaneous to happen.

People were fighting to get out of the room, out of the

casino itself, but their way was blocked. No one was moving at all.

Except for Pilar. She wasn't making any attempt to leave. She began to look for Nancy Colville.

She wasn't difficult to locate. Further back in the casino the panicked screams couldn't be identified as such; it did not sound like an emergency as much as an outburst of happy surprise at an especially lucky wager. No one surrounding the small bar in that part of the casino bothered to get up to discover the cause of the commotion; it wasn't worth the effort.

When Pilar approached, Nancy paid no attention, never having seen her before. Pilar had seen her, though, many times, but almost always on videotape. What was it about her that had Dr. Martindale so enamored? Pilar wondered, not without a certain twinge of jealousy.

Pilar took a seat next to Nancy and ordered a drink, mineral water and lime. She couldn't risk anything alcoholic, her aim must be steady.

"Aren't they all such bastards?"

Pilar looked up and realized that Nancy was addressing her. Her face was red from the drinking she'd been doing and twisted with anger.

"Who do you mean?" Pilar asked.

"Men. All of them. I married a boozer and then look what happened. I deserted him for a man who said he was in love with me. What is it, do you think, about thinking you're in love and wanting to be in love that tears you up inside? Am I making any sense?"

Of course she wasn't, Pilar thought, but she told her that yes, she was making perfect sense. What worried her was that Nancy might ramble on interminably. There was no way she was going to get her job done if Nancy insisted on carrying on a conversation.

"Because really, I wanted things to be beautiful. I thought that Julian was the best thing that ever happened to my life. He was so funny, so . . . I don't know. I thought I could deal with the drinking, I thought I could cure him of it, but look what happened. God, I'm such a mess." She turned and stared at Pilar as if trying to see her through a tinted lens. "Do you think I'm pretty? Lots of men say they think I'm pretty, but I don't know really. I look at those women I see in the magazines and they're pretty. And I look in the mirror, I look at pictures of me, and I don't know. Julian thought I was pretty. Patrick did, too, once, the bastard." She paused, waiting.

"Yes, you're very pretty," Pilar said. "Many men will want you."

"You have a peculiar accent. Where do you come from?" But she didn't have the patience to wait for a response. "You'll excuse me? I have to go pee."

Pilar watched her until she'd gone inside the red door with the female silhouette on it, then followed her in.

Everything inside was pink tile and highly polished mirrors framed by gold leaf. It smelled of lavender.

Only Nancy was using the facilities. Pilar decided to wait. When Nancy emerged she looked over and saw her and for a moment appeared to have difficulty recognizing her. Then it came to her. "Oh, hello," she said.

She wasn't quick enough to understand what had happened. Her eyes traveled from Pilar to her bare shoulders where the skin was rapidly turning a blazing red. Incomprehension was in her eyes.

This time when the blood flowed it came not only from her mouth and nose but also from between her legs.

The panic had somehow been subdued. The roulette tables were as mobbed as before. There was no sign of Jack Brill. The management must have seen to it that he was swiftly removed.

Pilar spotted the venerable Ah Wong himself and stepped up to him. "How is it going this evening?" she asked.

"Oh, very well, thank you. Everyone seems to be enjoying themselves, don't you think?"

"Yes, it certainly looks that way. Tell me, Ah Wong, do you know Diana Cleary?"

"Of course, I have seen her in here from time to time."

"I'm trying to find her."

"Oh yes?" For the first time Ah Wong allowed himself to tear his eyes away from his gaming tables and regard her. "Well then, you are in luck. You shall find her in the bar closest to the entrance."

Thanking him, Pilar began in the direction he'd indicated, pausing only once to insert another pellet into the projectile she carried.

EIGHTEEN

He didn't look well. The fatigue was evident in his eyes but it was more than that. Lightman had acquired enough experience to know by now; it was the virus, making itself known in the flesh. How long had he been sick?

Martindale shut the door behind him. "You never did understand," he began.

"Understand what?"

"That it would all have to end, that there is nothing left for any of us."

Lightman realized he'd been set up. He'd allowed himself to be set up. What stupidity on his part to believe that Martindale would have let them leave the island.

"Where's Diana?"

"Diana is in the air, Diana is in the dirt, Diana is no

more." He made it sound like an incantation. His voice was toneless, the voice of a man who had renounced the world and all things in it.

When Lightman made a threatening move in his direction Martindale brought his hand up. In his hand was a gun pointed at Lightman. Lightman saw that it was his gun.

Lightman cursed himself for his carelessness. Always losing things, always overlooking things, always missing the point.

"If she is still among the breathing, Diana is at La Mouche. Her last night's gamble. Perhaps in her final moments she will remember the one principle that gamblers inevitably seem to forget." His eyes were feverish and alive, though his voice was dead. "Which is that the house always wins."

"Why are you doing this?"

"You just don't understand, do you? It is the job of scientists like us to understand. To preserve, to dissect, to know. I have suffered from a grievous loss. My family. Dead, you know?"

Lightman nodded, aware that any precipitous motion, even the wrong word, might set him off. His madness, for madness it was, was just barely, fitfully under control.

"My fault. An accident but my fault. The strange, the curious thing was that the virus didn't want me, it neglected me in favor of my wife and children. That was what perplexed me most about the virus, how it would touch some and leave others unscathed, how capricious it was, like God laughing at us, like God mocking us. And I thought, you see, that I could go God one better." His tormented eyes found Lightman, a wan smile playing briefly on his cracked lips. "I decided to distill a strain of the virus that would never fail to deliver on its promise. A virus so pure, so essential, that its effect could always be calculated in advance. A virus to which I could contribute my talent and my blood, my contaminated blood. A virus which, once administered, would spread through the body instantly, with the aid of a special toxin, recapitulating its entire repertoire of symptoms in a few minutes what it would otherwise take weeks to accomplish. A virus which would waste no time. And you, my dear friend, helped me do this. That is why I wanted you here, that is why I let you live, why I let you have Diana."

Listen, Lightman told himself, listen but do not believe him. To believe him was to be coopted, to be joined to his madness.

"All of your research was devoted to creating this virus, so pure and so lethal that it will spare no one. What a paradox was forced upon you—to create the most potent vaccine you were obliged to create the most potent virus."

He broke off, he had to cough, his chest quaked, something yellow and gumlike appeared on his lips. He quickly wiped it away.

Around him the faces of the animals pressed at their cages; there was a strange silence, almost as if they were straining to hear his words.

His hand went out, the gesture mimicking a bum demanding change. "You have something else I need. Please give me the vaccine."

He brought the gun up menacingly. Lightman felt that he had no alternative but to give it to him. He was devastated. Martindale barely glanced at it and then deposited it in his own pocket. "You should have remained in your lab," he said. "The outside world isn't for you. People such as myself and Diana are too much for you. You may understand a pathogen but you will never understand us.

"Shall I tell you what Diana never did? Now that she is no longer with us, it could hardly matter, could it?" He was swaying on his feet, wobbly like a drunk. Somehow, though, he managed to maintain his balance. There was a stench of corruption about him that Lightman only then picked up on, a smell of something inside him festering.

Lightman willed himself not to believe what Martindale was telling him. He refused to accept that Diana was dead.

"Just as I made you my accomplice so you see I made Diana my accomplice too. Would you like to know who George Marsh was? Of course you would. All this time looking for George Marsh and George Marsh is dead. He was and is no more, lost and dead like our dear Diana." He attempted a laugh but it came out sounding like something else, like a whimper. "George Marsh was Nicholas Cleary, member in good standing of the Ariadne Society, vice president of Obelisk Medical Supplies, millionaire, husband of Diana, friend of the Apostle Beck, food for maggots."

It was his smell more than the gun that caused Lightman to recoil from him. But Martindale seemed not to notice. "One thing more: dear dead Nicky was also the deliverer, and I mean that in both senses of the word. For it was he who brought me the virus. But do you know that without Diana it would never have been his? What, my dear collaborationist, do you think induced that unsavory wretch in Samothrace, that fool Jim Jillian to open up late at night and hand over all that remained of Joe Taylor to Mr. Cleary/Mr. Marsh? You must know, you must have guessed, it was our dear dead Diana, who seduced Jim Jillian just as she seduced you, my friend. And if she knew only that she was helping me and doing the bidding of Jonas Beck is she to blame? She understood the mutual destiny to which we all are joined. We are all guilty, all murderers. You, too, my dear sir. You came all this way to find the truth. Now look! Look at what the truth is!"

Before Lightman's astonished eyes Martindale unzipped his trousers and produced what no longer resembled a penis or any kind of human organ at all, but rather the blackened and shrunken remains of something that had burned completely to a crisp.

Gangrene: the virus' final humiliation.

NINETEEN

Ezra couldn't face her. She continued to ask him, "Why, Ezra, why have you brought me here? What are we doing here?" But she knew. He knew that she knew.

They made him, he wanted to say, they left him with no choice. In the whole world all that mattered to him were his children. To find them again was the only thing that was important. But he could say none of it.

They were standing in a vast room with rows and rows of one-armed bandits. Almost every one of them was in use. There was so much noise: silver coins jangling and bells ringing and buzzers going off and people crying out in excitement or happiness or disgust. They were the noises of people thinking they were going to get suddenly lucky.

"Nothing will happen to you," Ezra said. "I promise nothing will happen to you, I won't let anything happen to you."

His words of assurance failed to convince her. "You're with them, aren't you? This whole time you've been spying on me." She didn't sound angry, only resigned. He wished to God that she was angry. That would have somehow made it better.

"No, never, I never spied," he said, his voice nearly breaking with frustration. "I could never do that to anybody."

She threw him a dubious look. "It's all right, Ezra, you do what you have to." She stole a glance at her watch. Past ten. There was no possibility of making the flight now.

Ezra suspected that, from the start, she'd never believed that she would be leaving, that she would be free of Martindale. She must have been expecting something like this.

If Ezra hadn't detained her then someone else would have.

But knowing that did not in any way diminish his unhappiness, his loathing for himself.

And then he began to think that it was all a ruse, a cheap trick, that regardless of what Brill promised him he would never see his children. He had not only been led to betray, he'd been made a fool of as well.

"We should go," he said. He had decided that there was no point in staying at the casino. The obscenity of the place, the greed and the extravagance disgusted him.

He wouldn't allow her to protest although he wasn't sure that she meant to. He took her hand and began to guide her through the crowded floor, little caring that he was upsetting the concentration of the people standing at the one-armed bandits as they pulled the levers again and again, hoping for apples to come up in all the windows.

But when they reached the door the guard wouldn't let them through.

"Man, we have to get out," Ezra demanded.

"Ezra, don't," Diana said.

But the guard, who was a bigger man than Ezra, remained adamant. "No one leaves until the situation outside is clarified."

"What the hell does that mean, clarified?"

Diana was trying to pull him back. The confrontation was drawing a great deal of interest from those in the vicinity. Pilar kept pressing closer but she couldn't quite get close enough. Just when she thought she had a clear sight at Diana, Ezra got in her way. She waited, then as soon as she had Diana in view again, she took aim.

Ezra refused to move his ground.

"Please, sir, you're blocking the doorway. I don't want to have to use force."

A couple, a man and woman wearing everything white, were trying to make their way in around him.

But Ezra was so infuriated, so filled with anguish and rage, that he refused to comply. He was ready to kill someone. It was a pity that those he most wanted to lay his hands on, those people who'd done most to destroy his life, were nowhere present. Nassa, Jonas Beck, Ken Snape, Jack Brill—where were they? There was only this guard who in Ezra's mind embodied the spirit, the foul, corrupted spirit, of all of them. His anger burned so hard in him that he could scarcely see anything clearly. The guard's face blurred, then filled with blood.

Ezra was astounded, amazed that he'd actually struck the man who crumbled to the floor. Behind him people were shouting. He heard Diana but couldn't make out what she was saying.

And then something happened. It was impossible to know what exactly, but he felt a sting in the back of his neck. Then the world began to spin and go black. His body seemed to be exploding from the inside. Inside out.

He could see only darkness. No, that wasn't quite true. Faces had begun to appear. The faces of his children: Danny, Benjamin, Elias, Mara and Cherish. They were all smiling at him, their hands reaching out to him.

He smiled back and went toward them, his hands reaching out to them in turn, almost touching, almost touching, almost. . . .

TWENTY

Lightman knew that if he didn't act soon—at that moment —everything would be lost. But he was borne down by a terrible paralysis, incapable, it seemed, of moving even his hand. It was shock, it was numbness, it was the falsely seductive idea that Martindale would put down the gun and allow him to leave.

Zipping himself back up, Martindale stared at him with a curious look of satisfaction, as if his decaying organ was a stigmata, elevating him to sainthood. I am dying, he was saying, and I am dying in this wretched, humiliating, yet so very appropriate way that it gives me the right to do whatever I wish. No punishment is possible, no retribution can mean anything; I cannot be punished more.

"Now you know what no one else does."

He lowered his eyes and it was in that moment, that instant of distraction, that Lightman lunged at him—lunged at him almost before his brain registered what he was doing.

Almost at once all the animals—the spider monkeys and the Mauritian monkeys and the orangutans and the baboons—began to cry out, joining together in an incredible uproar of screeching and howling, made worse by the clawing against the bars of the cages that they were doing.

Martindale lurched back, resisting Lightman's effort to wrest the gun from him. The two were gasping from the exertion, Martindale more than Lightman. They became locked in a clumsy embrace, like inexperienced lovers.

Lightman's glasses flew off. Martindale's face blurred. The faces of the animals took on a nightmarish aspect, like the faces of gargoyles, hideous eyes and gaping pink mouths filled with deadly teeth. It was the strangest audience that Lightman could have imagined.

And then the gun exploded, no telling how. A chunk of the ceiling dropped down. The protest from the animals was so horrendous that it was a wonder it hadn't roused an alarm.

Suddenly Lightman managed to get ahold of the gun, but then it slipped away. Martindale's breath gave off the same stink as his dying flesh. Maybe the disease had weakened him but his resolve apparently gave him back his strength. It was amazing how powerful he was. He got Lightman's arm twisted behind him. The pain was searing. Something fell away from him—his watch, Stephanie's gift.

Martindale was trying to throw him down and pin him. There was a sound of the watch being demolished underfoot —his or Martindale's, he couldn't tell. But it was gone.

The only thing that mattered to Lightman was extricating himself from Martindale's implacable hold. He reared up, wrenching his arm free simultaneously, grabbed again for the gun. It slipped to the floor, Lightman heard it drop, looked blindly, desperately for it, saw not the gun itself, but its glint and reached for it just as Martindale did. He felt the steel, felt Martindale's flesh.

It went off.

Martindale rose from the floor, his head all bloody. His right ear looked shot away although there was too much blood for Lightman to tell.

"My God, my God, it hurts, it hurts like hell," he was muttering.

The gun dropped from his hand but he didn't seem to notice. He was acting like a man about to nod out on heroin who somehow clung enough to consciousness to remain upright. He was staggering about in ever smaller circles as if he couldn't figure out where else to go.

"Oh damn, does it hurt, my black hen."

Lightman didn't think he heard right. Not that it mattered. He retrieved his glasses. They, unlike his watch, were still in one piece. Astonishing.

And then the gun. Keeping a wary eye on Martindale, he approached the weapon and stooped to recover it. Martindale didn't appear to be paying attention. "My black hen," he repeated, "hickety, pickety, she lay eggs with quill and pen."

"What, what are you trying to say, Patrick?"

The blood was pouring thicker, covering half of his face, his neck, his chest. He was having a terrible time standing up. "Gentlemen come every day to see what my black hen's eggs say."

Black hen's eggs? What was this?

There was one thing more Lightman had to get. The animals, perhaps crazed by the sight of the blood, leapt up and down, hurling themselves against the walls and bars, cackling and howling like mad, their eyes red and gaping with some sort of violent lust and apprehension.

"Some say ask, some say—hickety pickety—given, some say, black hen's eggs, my black hen's eggs. Some say given. Some say come and be not driven. . . ."

It was a nursery rhyme, Lightman realized. A goddamn nursery rhyme. The bullet must have reached some part of his brain where his childhood lived on.

Martindale sank to his knees but continued his recitation, apparently mindless of the bedlam going on around him. "Some say seek and some say find, some say—hickety pickety, my black, my black . . . Some say find, some say leave things behind."

He raised his eyes toward Lightman but it wasn't at all clear that he knew what he was seeing.

Lightman reached into his coat pocket and extracted the vaccine.

"And some say come back again."

His eyes fluttered; he was having great difficulty keeping them open.

His voice lowered and it was nearly impossible to make out with the pandemonium from the cages. "Some say ask, some say given, some say ask, some say given, some say, hickety pickety, my black hen, my black, my black, my black . . . Some say, some say, my black, my black . . ."

What of his face Lightman could see was waxen, his head wobbled back and forth; death seemed to have had him cornered.

There was nothing more for him there. Lightman started toward the door. Looking back, he saw Martindale in the same position, his mouth moving frantically without any sound emerging. His eyes gleamed with some secret, hidden knowledge.

It was only after Lightman got out on the street that it struck him that there was one thing he would never learn the answer to: Which one of them had pulled the trigger?

TWENTY-ONE

Lightman ran. He had no car and he knew enough not to seek public transportation. A taxi would have been welcome but none was in sight.

He was scared, he was more scared than he'd been in the room with Martindale. Lag time maybe. His nerves were bad, a hot, nasty taste was in his mouth. It hurt to exert himself in the humid, dense atmosphere. The whole city was shrouded in smoke and rain. It was a fine rain that seemed to be suspended between heaven and earth, not quite making it to the ground.

He wouldn't even contemplate the possibility that Diana was lost, dead.

If there were rioters loose on the streets they had gone elsewhere in the city; by the harbor it was deserted. Deserted by the living anyway. The dead were anywhere he cared to look for them, only partially hidden by the darkness and smoke.

There was blood on him, Martindale's blood, and he could only hope that his appearance wouldn't cause the doorman to refuse him entrance.

The pall of smoke and rain had the effect of distorting

the letters of the blazing sign that identified the casino, blurring them in a cloud of color.

No doorman tonight, he saw. There were two armed guards instead with bright red jackets. One of the guards opened the brass door for him. His face had only recently sustained an injury of some kind, probably a blow from a dissatisfied patron; there was a big bruise on his cheek and one eye was closed.

Since no one said anything, Lightman assumed that a blood stain on a jacket was not the sort of thing to keep a person barred from La Mouche.

It was noisy and frantic and mobbed. How was he ever going to find Diana if she was there?

He had no choice but to plunge into the crowd, so he did just that.

Diana was drinking. She was drinking with a determination to become drunk. Any awareness she had of what was going on was inadvertent. Her difficulty was that the alcohol wasn't doing the trick; she remained frustratingly, maddeningly sober. It was the fear that was preventing the mimosas from having their desired effect. It was the fear that what she'd seen happen to Ezra would happen to herself. One moment he was healthy, the next he was writhing on the floor, hemorrhaging, dying. She was convinced that before the casino shut its doors for the night she would suffer the same fate. That was why Ezra had been ordered to bring her there. There was no escape, no out.

She'd gone from room to room, making her way through the multitude of gamblers, bypassing the games of chance, the roulette, the baccarat, the poker, the blackjack and the one-armed bandits, and ended up in the last room, sitting at the small bar in the company of people she'd never seen before. While she'd been in the casino many times previously, she'd never penetrated so far into its recesses.

One thing she was intent on doing was making certain that she spent all her money. She would throw it away at the tables if it came to that, so that when death found her it wouldn't be with a lot of extra cash that she'd be forever denied the pleasure of spending. Or squandering.

The couple in white that had come into the casino while Ezra was trying to get out had taken the seats next to hers. The man looked older close up, with a tan that had turned his face to the consistency of leather. The woman was younger, but not so young that she hadn't gone through the mill. Diana could always tell, mainly by the haunted look in the eyes. It wasn't invariably the eyes; sometimes she could tell in other ways, too.

The man introduced himself as Michael and said that he and his friend, referring to the woman next to him, had just arrived in Port Louis—that very day as a matter of fact— and that he'd heard that La Mouche was the place to go at night.

"It's the only place," Diana said. "They won't let you in anywhere else."

Michael and the woman, whose name turned out to be Ada, were surprised.

"Why is that?"

"The flu, the rioting. It's not good out there at nights."

It was difficult keeping her mind on the conversation. She was too occupied by the need to try to determine how exactly she felt. The idea was to separate out the sensations accompanying the introduction of a large quantity of alcohol into her system from any other symptoms that might indicate the virus had gotten in as well. She remembered how it felt from the last time she'd been stricken, the onset of dizziness, the clogging in the sinuses, the intense dryness at the back of the throat, the heaviness in the chest. Nothing like that was happening to her now. But as she began to dwell on the possibility she became aware of how very dry her throat was feeling. If she didn't stop it she'd start to imagine all the other symptoms besides.

"We're sure it'll boil over," the woman said. "It has in the other places we've been to."

"I'm sorry, what did you say? I'm afraid I wasn't paying attention."

"I said that in the other places we've been to, once the epidemic's over, things pretty much settle back to normal. We were in Athens, why, they couldn't make coffins fast enough. Then one day they had a surplus. Not enough dead to fill them up."

"That was in Tangiers," Michael corrected her. "In Athens it was cemetery space they lacked, not coffins."

God, she didn't want to hear it, Diana thought, wishing they would go away. She supposed she could excuse herself but she couldn't seem to muster enough energy to go anywhere.

"We've been lucky. Never got sick once," Michael said.

Although she wasn't really interested, to be polite, she asked, "Why have you been traveling so much? I mean, do you do this for business, go around the world?"

The two exchanged a secretive look. Knowing smiles broke out on both their faces.

"Should we tell her?" the woman asked.

"I don't see why not. She doesn't look like an Interpol agent to me."

What was this? A joke they were playing?

"We're on the run, if you must know," Michael said. "Ada's husband . . ."

He paused for so long that Diana said, "Ada's husband what?"

"Well, Ada's husband was . . ."

"In our way. And we . . ."

Michael gave Diana a sheepish grin. "We really didn't have much of a choice. Certain circumstances intervened."

"It was painless," Ada said, "relatively. Really, better than he deserved."

"And now we're, well, frittering away his money."

"And enjoying ourselves immensely. It's quite amazing when you come to a time like this."

Maybe it *was* a joke, designed to titillate the unwary, but

Diana had the uneasy feeling that they were serious. "What do you mean, when you come to a time like this?"

"I mean when everything goes to hell, people dying all over the place, civil insurrection, that kind of thing," Michael said. "There are certain advantages, if you get my drift, if you know how to exploit them. There are those of us who thrive on chaos, who are just waiting for an opportunity like this, you see."

Diana thought that maybe, if she tried, she could get herself to move.

"I think, honestly, that I'll be sorry when it's gone," Ada said. "The epidemic, I mean. I really think I'll actually miss it. It's been so . . ." She wanted to make sure she had the exact word. "Exciting. Don't you think so, Michael?"

He smiled, he nodded.

"Tell her about that fence we saw in Nigeria," Ada urged.

"The one with all the skulls?"

Just then Diana heard her name being called. She looked around. Grateful to see somebody she knew who could relieve her of these people, she said, "I hope you'll pardon me. A friend of mine has just arrived."

"Nice meeting you," the couple said in unison.

"I hope you enjoy your stay in Mauritius," Diana said.

They didn't appear to catch the sarcasm in her voice which, she supposed, was just as well.

Then she turned from them to greet Pilar.

There was smoke in the casino just as there was in the streets; here it wasn't coming from fires burning out of control but from too many people lighting up. The rooms he passed through held a combustible mixture of perfume and Turkish and Virginia tobacco.

He was operating on adrenaline, feeling as if he'd been seized by some force which he'd never experienced before; it was like being swept along by a tide, driven toward shore. He was in the thrall of a madness that might not have been so very different from the kind that Martindale had displayed.

No time to think things through, time enough only to find Diana. He didn't care about the dark looks he drew from women into whose faces he stared, mistaking them, from the back, from the side, for Diana.

The mirrors confused him so that he began to lose track of whether he'd been in a particular room before or not. His eyes wearied from looking too hard at too many women.

Growing more desperate, he stopped people to ask them if they knew Diana and if they had seen her.

Behind him, over the blaring music, Lightman could hear what sounded like a disturbance. The crowd was so thick that Lightman could not see much of anything, but there was no mistaking the detonation of glass breaking and the screams of people thrown into panic.

"They're breaking in," he heard someone say.

Suddenly the bastion that was supposed to guarantee immunity from disease and violence was no longer secure.

The smoke that trailed through the rooms now was different, bearing with it a stench of things burning which were never intended to be set afire.

But Lightman was concentrating all his energies on finding Diana. He refused to be diverted from his purpose; after what he'd been through already that night, the threat posed by a mob of looters seemed almost beside the point.

And then he had Diana in sight.

She was standing at a bar obviously distraught, looking for a way out. Pilar was standing behind her. There was a man in a tux next to them with the sullen, dyspeptic expression of someone who had just watched a fortune go down the drain. And next to him there was a couple, dressed in white, clinging to each other, oblivious of the uproar, furiously kissing while the man's hands wandered all over the woman's bare back.

But the problem was determining where exactly this bar

was. For the view Lightman had of it was in a mirror. And looking to where he assumed the reality should be, he discovered a second mirror set at an angle to capture the reflection of yet a third mirror.

Stymied, Lightman went first in one direction, then another, knocking into some people, buffeted by others who demanded that he watch where he was going. Every so often he lost sight of Diana altogether and could see only the embracing couple or Pilar.

He stopped for a few seconds, confused by what Pilar was doing. She seemed to be removing an object from her purse, but in a furtive manner, apparently anxious that Diana not be aware of her action. But Diana was so distracted by the noise and the smoke trailing through the casino that her eyes were everywhere but on Pilar.

Lightman moved. He had a passageway in view; more mirrors were hung on the walls, dark, distorting mirrors that played with perspective like those in a funhouse. They turned Pilar into a monstrously large figure and made Diana appear so diminutive she could have been a porcelain doll.

The smoke was becoming denser, the pandemonium growing worse than all the primates combined could have produced in their wildest rage. People were scattering, unsure of how to escape. Bits and pieces of the casino—progressively bigger bits and pieces—were giving way and falling as the flames reached them.

Lightman kept going. Then he found a mirror in which the rightful proportions were restored. Diana looked like Diana and Pilar like Pilar. What was she doing? A device that looked like a straw or a pipe of some kind was held in her hand, trained on Diana.

Suddenly it occurred to Lightman how Martindale was transmitting his pure strain of virus.

Diana turned back toward Pilar. Her eyes gaped as she tried to comprehend what the girl was doing.

Lightman slid the gun from underneath his coat, at the

same time hoping that, with all the mirrors and smoke, what he believed to be real would turn out to be just that.

He fired.

In response, glass clattered to the floor, half of a mirror blown away.

For some seconds Lightman lost all sight of Diana. He was ready to shoot again but he feared it wouldn't do any good. He'd wasted the one opportunity he'd had.

Then Lightman saw Pilar. Her face was in shreds, blood trickling from scores of lacerations, and fragments of glass were glinting in her hair.

Lightman was too anxious to reach Diana to make any attempt to confront Pilar. He saw that she was being swallowed up in the smoke. Her hair had caught fire and flames began to leap from the crown of her head, forming a weirdly brilliant nimbus.

Gagging and sputtering, his eyes stinging, he struggled to move forward against the crowd.

He saw her through the whorls of smoke.

"Diana!" His voice died in a spasm of coughing.

As he raced toward her he saw, out of the corner of his eye, the couple in white.

Lightman thought it was strange that they were so slow to react to the chaos sweeping around them, but then he saw why. The woman was making an attempt to move but she was immobilized by the man whose passionate embrace had pinned her to the spot. He was kissing her still, but his kisses were leaving her lips red with his blood which was draining into her mouth.

It occurred to Lightman that the pain and shock of being struck by the flying glass had caused Pilar to lose control of her aim. It was the man she had hit, not Diana.

Diana saw Lightman and slowly began toward him as if she couldn't quite believe he was there. Her eyes went to the gun, then back to his face.

He reached out to take her hand. The fire was closing in

on them, racing along the ceilings, causing the walls to cave in and blackening the mirrors.

Cinders dropped on them, smudging and blackening them.

They held each other, not long; there was no time. "Love..." she said. "Too long...We're never going to get out. We'll die here together."

"There's got to be another way out," Lightman said. "We'll find it."

TWENTY-TWO

It took all the strength he could summon, but he got himself off the floor and into motion. He walked with difficulty, one step at a time. His breath rattled. Last breath, death breath. Something in him wouldn't allow him to die, wouldn't give up without a fight. Some say, some say, some say...Nothing more of the verse would come to him. Some say, some say, some say....

He could hardly see. And the pain was unbearable. He wanted so much to sink into unconsciousness, into death, but whatever wanted him alive wanted him to be aware of what was happening. There was one more thing to do, but how could he do it with this pain?

Along the corridor, blinking into its fluorescent light, he kept walking, somehow finding his way to his private elevator. He stared blankly at the numerical keypad, struggling to remember the code. His fingers knew which keys to press though his mind resisted coming up with them.

He descended in the elevator as far down as it would go.

Stepping off it he proceeded through a storage area that was impregnated with a cold dampness that might have been there for centuries. What he needed to do was get outside, breathe in cleaner air. Maybe somehow it would help.

When he stepped out of the building, using a fire door, his ears picked up on a strange and unnerving sound, like the wheezing of a dozen old men. He staggered forward. The air wasn't what he'd wanted, it was hot and fetid and enervating. He had it in mind to stop, maybe turn around, but he didn't. Something wanted him to keep moving.

Then he did come to a stop. The wheezing was louder. He looked up to see ten, maybe more, scrawny, starving dogs. Gathered in a semicircle, they were the source of the strange sound. It was more like whistling, he decided, than it was like wheezing. Their faces lifted toward him, their eyes were already devouring him. It occurred to him what they must be waiting for.

TWENTY-THREE

The Chinese had a saying: After war comes the plague. But what, Lightman often thought, came after the plague? Millions were dead, but so soon after the flu had rampaged through the population it was impossible to estimate how many millions. WHO statisticians hadn't been able to keep up with it, not because of incompetence, not because of subversive bugs in their computers, but because they simply hadn't been able to collect all the data. Some governments refused to disclose the number of fatalities or underestimated them. Others were unable to compile them, thwarted by lack of resources. Then there was the problem of knowing which deaths to include. It was impossible to determine whether the flu had hastened the deaths of people afflicted with cancer or weakened by heart or muscular disease, or whether they would have died when they did in any event.

What was certain was that without Lightman's vaccine the virus would have spread through the population with so much virulence that, in the best estimates of WHO experts, twice the recorded fatalities would have occurred.

Q. Dr. Lightman, there are reports that you are in line to receive the Nobel Prize for Medicine for the flu vaccine. Do you have any comment?

A. It's a great honor to even be mentioned in that context, but no, I don't have any comment.

Q. Are you familiar with a discredited cult leader named Jonas Beck?

A. I know the name.

Q. Then are you aware that he claims to have foreseen the rediscovery of the virus in a vision?

A. I've heard something of that nature.

Q. So perhaps you know that he believes that just as Dr. Martindale was destined to find it, you were destined to ultimately develop a cure for it.

A. As a scientist, I naturally don't give much credibility to a cult leader who purports to have visions. From what I know, all his followers have left him—some for another world.

Money could behave like a virus, obeying its own bizarre and unfathomable rules. Why was it that one minute it was in hiding, while the next it was everywhere, inescapable, ready to drown a person in its abundance? One minute a person didn't know what to do with it, the next he'd kill for a dime. Whatever the explanation, Lightman now had an extraordinary amount of it available to him. Foundations and government agencies were falling all over themselves to give him and his lab money. Applying for grants was like ordering Chinese food; no sooner had he placed his order than it was set in front of him.

Q. Dr. Lightman, in developing the vaccine you worked closely with Dr. Martindale. Since he's not able to speak for himself, how much credit would you give him?

A. There is a misconception here. We never worked together.

Q. But you did know each other?

A. We met.

Q. There are rumors that Dr. Martindale might have faced criminal charges had he lived. Would you care to speculate on what those charges might have been?

A. No.

There were gratifyingly fewer and fewer cases of the flu, and most that did occur were not as serious as those that characterized the outbreak in the late spring and summer of 1998. It was as if the virus had run out of targets or had burned itself out and gone underground.

Q. In the last several months there have been rumors that the virus might have leaked from a laboratory in London.

A. If that's true, I don't know anything about it.

Q. Prior to the outbreak of the pandemic you were on special assignment from the National Institutes of Health investigating several strange deaths in Alaska. Is that correct?

A. I prefer not to comment on any assignments I might have undertaken for the National Institutes. But as regards the case you're referring to, just for the record, there were only three deaths involved, not several.

It was uncanny how he sometimes missed those days when he was in the greatest danger, when he lived in despair and longing. Practically a year had passed, and he couldn't get used to his newfound prosperity or happiness. He wondered if he would ever be able to recapture the excitement of that time. More than that, he wondered why he missed Martindale. He didn't like to have to acknowledge it, but it was the truth. He hated the man, yet he missed him.

Q. Are you acquainted with someone named George Marsh—Dr. George Marsh?

A. No. Should I know who that is?

Q. *L'Aurore*, a Paris newspaper, ran a report recently saying that in your capacity as NIH investigator you were searching for Dr. Marsh in connection with missing specimens.

A. I know nothing about that report, I have no idea where *L'Aurore* got its information.

It was in his mind to confront Diana, to ask her whether what Martindale had said was true, that she'd collaborated with Nicholas and seduced Jim Jillian, all for the purpose of smuggling the virus back to Mayfair House, but he never could bring himself to do so. It wasn't a question he wanted to put to the woman he'd married, the mother of his unborn child. No, it was something more than that; he didn't want to know the answer because he'd never have any way of identifying the truth. And the truth, once known, might only hurt him.

Q. Is there any chance we'll see a virus this devastating again in our lifetime?

A. I'd like to say we're safe but there's no guarantee.

Q. The same virus could recur then?

A. Either that or another strain of it, one we have no protection against.

Q. Where does the virus hide in between epidemics?

A. If you could figure out the answer to that, you could win the Nobel Prize for Medicine yourself.

Sometimes, in and around Boston, Lightman would spy a green cross painted on the sidewalk, but enough time had elapsed and enough rain had lashed at it that it was fast fading away. Soon it would not be there at all.

> Some say seek,
> Some say find,
> Some say leave things behind.
> Some say come back again.

AUTHOR'S NOTE

Although the symptoms described in this novel sound grotesque and even bizarre enough to owe their origin to the author's overstimulated imagination, the fact is that they are all documented by studies of the 1918 influenza pandemic. Readers interested in a detailed account of the Spanish Lady are advised to hunt out a copy of *The Plague of the Spanish Lady* by Richard Collier (Atheneum, 1974). For a discussion of just how baffling the whole phenomenon of flu outbreaks actually is, readers might turn to chapter 18 ("Searching for the Flu") of Pascal James Imperato's true-life story, *Medical Detective* (Marek, 1979). Those readers who wish to explore the history of diseases may wish to browse through *Invisible Armies: The Impact of Disease on American History* by Howard N. Simpson, M.D. (Bobbs-Merrill, 1980), *The Black Death* by Philip Ziegler (Pelican, 1970), and the first volume of Ferdnand Braudel's *Civilization and Capitalism 15th–18th Centuries*, entitled *The Structures of Everyday Life* (Harper & Row, 1981) which describes the devastating effect and historical implications of the Black Death. For those readers curious about religious movements and millennial cults spawned by apocalyptic fears there's probably no better book to read than Norman Cohn's seminal study, *The Pursuit of the Millennium* (Oxford University Press, 1970).